NETHER STATION

BOOKS BY KEVIN J. ANDERSON

STANDALONE NOVELS

Nether Station

Stake

Mr. Wells & the Martians

Enemies & Allies

The Last Days of Krypton

Sky Captain and the World of Tomorrow

The League of Extraordinary Gentlemen

Hopscotch

Captain Nemo

Fantastic Voyage: Microcosm

Supernova

Blindfold

Climbing Olympus

Resurrection, Inc.

Persephone (with Jeffrey Morris)

WITH DOUG BEASON

Lifeline

The Trinity Paradox

Assemblers of Infinity

Ill Wind

Ignition

Virtual Destruction

Lethal Exposure

DUNE SERIES (WITH BRIAN HERBERT)

Dune: House Atreides

Dune: House Harkonnen

Dune: House Corrino

Dune: The Butlerian Jihad

Dune: The Machine Crusade

Dune: The Battle of Corrin

Hunters of Dune

Sandworms of Dune

Paul of Dune

The Winds of Dune

Sisterhood of Dune

Mentats of Dune

Navigators of Dune

Tales of Dune

The Duke of Caladan

The Lady of Caladan

The Heir of Caladan

Sands of Dune

Princess of Dune

HEXWORLD

Roll

Play

End

WAKE THE DRAGON

Spine of the Dragon

Vengewar

Gods and Dragons

THE SAGA OF SEVEN SUNS

Veiled Alliances

Hidden Empire

A Forest of Stars

Horizon Storms

Scattered Suns

Of Fire and Night

Metal Swarm

The Ashes of Worlds

SAGA OF SHADOWS

Whistling Past the Graveyard

The Dark Between the Stars

Blood of the Cosmos

Eternity's Mind

DRAGON BUSINESS ADVENTURES

The Dragon Business

Skeleton in the Closet

DAN SHAMBLE, ZOMBIE P.I.

Death Warmed Over

Unnatural Acts

Hair Raising

Slimy Underbelly

Working Stiff

Tastes like Chicken

Services Rendered

Double-Booked

Bats in the Belfry

TERRA INCOGNITA

The Edge of the World

The Map of All Things

The Key to Creation

CRYSTAL DOORS (WITH REBECCA MOESTA)

Island Realm

Ocean Realm

Sky Realm

STAR WARS

Darksaber

Jedi Search

Dark Apprentice

Champions of the Force

Tales from the Mos Eisley Cantina

Tales from Jabba's Palace

Tales of the Bounty Hunters

X-FILES

Ground Zero

Ruins

Antibodies

NONFICTION

Million Dollar Productivity

Million Dollar Professionalism for the Writer

Worldbuilding: From Small Towns to Entire Universes

Writing as a Team Sport (with Rebecca Moesta)

Slushpile Memories

NETHER STATION

KEVIN J. ANDERSON

BLACK STONE PUBLISHING

WTales

Published in 2025 by *Weird Tales*® Presents and Blackstone Publishing
Cover illustration and design by Jeff Wong
Book design by Blackstone Publishing with Jeff Wong

Printed in the United States of America
Originally published in hardcover by *Weird Tales*® Presents and
Blackstone Publishing in 2024

First paperback edition: 2025
ISBN 979-8-228-39627-2
Fiction / Science Fiction / General

Version 1

Blackstone Publishing
31 Mistletoe Rd.
Ashland, OR 97520

www.WeirdTales.com
www.BlackstonePublishing.com

PROLOGUE

Four years later, the probe signal returned.

By then, the Earth-based Nether research team had been disbanded—budget cuts—and public interest in the mysterious, distant wormhole had waned. One of the greatest astronomical headlines in human history was relegated to a tiny note far down on the search feeds.

Though the anomaly was her life's obsession, Cammie Skoura didn't even notice the story until a day later.

It changed her life.

It changed everything.

A decade earlier, back when she'd just started high school as an awkward kid fascinated with astrophysics, the quiet and mysterious object was discovered at the far edge of the solar system—a gravitational distortion in the fabric of spacetime.

The Kuiper Belt was an enormous, diffuse disk of cosmic debris beyond the orbit of Pluto, too far away to hold anything of interest—until the wormhole. The anomaly was no cosmic show-off like a blazing nova or flare star, but it was definitely there, lurking on the threshold of the solar system.

Fascinated, young Cammie had followed the slow-moving train of discoveries. In school, she jabbered about the wormhole and the cometary cloud with her so-called friends, who shared none of her excitement. They teased her about it, but they weren't really her friends anyway.

She was a college undergrad by the time the International Space Agency got around to launching a sequence of probes from the lunar base under high acceleration, like bullets streaking out to the nether regions of space. Thus, the wormhole got its name.

While the probes flew onward, year after year, Cammie buried herself in university studies: astrophysics, cosmology, wormholes. Her parents sighed with disappointment that she didn't turn her energies toward something practical, like business administration, but she thrived under her mentor, Dr. Zachary Tendari—a tall and quiet man thirty-five years her senior. She admired his knowledge and expertise in her favorite obscure subject, and he paid a lot of attention to her, singling her out as a prodigy.

Through Tendari's patronage, Cammie joined the International Space Agency Nether analysis team. As soon as the probes arrived, she and Dr. Tendari would be among the first to study one of the greatest mysteries of the universe.

As the first, fast probe flashed past, it sent grainy images of a black opening on black space. In the ISA Nether ops center, Cammie marveled at those images. Standing close beside her, Dr. Tendari wore a wide grin, and he swept her up in a congratulatory hug. He held on to her for a long time, and two of the other techs gave them strange looks, but Cammie was hyperfocused on the exciting science. She had never understood the nuances of human interactions anyway.

The Nether team members studied the telemetry; some of them acted as if it were just another day at work. Each image, each signal, took two weeks to travel down into the inner solar system, but for Cammie everything was fresh and new. She and Dr. Tendari pored over the data, ran simulations, and compared wormhole models, several of which had been developed by Tendari himself. She could talk very fast when she was intent on something, which often annoyed "normal" people, but he listened to everything. They worked together for hours to modify the theories while waiting for the next stream of data.

Cammie learned much from her mentor, and she admired his knowledge. "We're in good hands. You're the world's foremost expert on wormhole theory."

Tendari had chuckled, letting his hand linger on her shoulder. "That's only because you haven't caught up with me yet. I've never seen someone with so much potential. And please, call me Zach."

His words made her swell with pride, but she had a hard time ever thinking of him as anything other than Dr. Tendari.

A week later, the second Nether probe shot past, giving a more detailed mapping of the wormhole neighborhood with a smattering of misshapen asteroids and a possible comet, and more details of the hole in space.

A month later, when the third and most important probe arrived at the wormhole, Cammie could see the intensity in Dr. Tendari's expression. "Time for the main event," he whispered, as if it were a secret between the two of them. Her own pulse was racing.

The final probe sent out a clear pulse beacon when it reached the wormhole, a joyous shout-out from humanity: "We are here!"

The Nether analysis team—Cammie had never gotten to know any of them personally, even after months in the ISA center—gathered around their stations, probe techs counting down the moments. Cammie stared at the screens until her eyes burned, not wanting to miss an instant.

In theory, a wormhole was a shortcut through the structure of spacetime, like a highway bypass. The other end of the passage could be on the opposite side of the solar system, or the opposite side of the Galaxy. Or maybe it just went nowhere.

The staccato signal bleep played over the speakers, a distinctive sequence of notes as the probe plunged over the event horizon.

And vanished.

The beacon was cut off like a head beneath a guillotine. The probe cameras went blank. Nothing.

A day later, nothing.

And a week later.

And that was the end of the international Nether research project.

Young and naïve, Cammie had assumed that a second wave of probes would be launched to gather more data, even if it took years to get back up to the Kuiper Belt. That was all she thought about. To her—and why not to everybody?—wormholes were profoundly fundamental to understanding the universe, and Nether was the only one that had ever been discovered.

But public fascination faded—been there, done that, nothing else to see—and Cammie didn't understand why. The world showed brief interest in the original probe pictures, but a grainy blur in space could not compete with political scandals, celebrity marriages, and a brushfire war over iridium supplies in northwest Africa. Getting another glimpse of the astronomical anomaly was too much trouble—and too much cost—and what practical benefit was there to a wormhole, really?

When the ISA Nether research project was disbanded, it felt like a funeral to Cammie. She didn't know what to do with herself. She had never planned for anything else. Her parents always said she had her head in the clouds, or in the vacuum of space, and didn't think about how she would get a job and pay the bills. So she went to graduate school.

Clinging to her fascination with the subject, Cammie

pursued her Master's degree at MIT and completed it in less than two years. That had caused the final break with her parents, and now it was too late to ever make it right. But because of her obvious academic brilliance, as well as unflagging support from Dr. Tendari, and also partially because of her neurodiverse condition, she received scholarships to fund what she needed.

After the probe work faded, Tendari went back to an admin position at Stanford, and Cammie went straight through to pursue her PhD in wormhole dynamics. Cammie could never be a teacher, could never be around so many people and certainly not in front of even a small class. Other space research positions were available, but with a pragmatic focus. Wealthy industrialists, like Benedict Noor's corporation, built orbiting hotels and expanded their operations on the lunar base. NOOR also built outposts on Mars, even extended industrial work into the asteroid belt.

But pure wormhole science gained no traction. Nether was far away—out of sight, out of mind.

Cammie eventually resigned herself to a lackluster job in a quantum-circuitry company. She tolerated it, did excellent work, received good pay, and felt no passion whatsoever.

Then, more than four years later, the probe signal came back.

Living alone in her austere apartment, which was all she wanted or needed, Cammie rarely looked at the news, but her personal AI scout flagged subject alerts for her in a weekly digest. The lost Nether probe's hail was distinctive among the hiss of cosmic background noise, its "We are here!" pattern easily recognizable. But it was so out of context, and in an entirely different part of the sky, that it took radio astronomers a few days to realize what they were hearing.

The ISA probe that had vanished into the wormhole now reappeared in the Alpha Centauri system, 4.3 light-years away from Earth. The probe had traveled through the cosmic passageway and exited intact, still sending out its signal. But due to the great distance, the radio waves took four years and three and a half months to arrive back here . . . the exact signal time from Alpha Centauri to Earth.

The wormhole worked!

When the news story appeared in her weekly digest, Cammie read it with disbelief and amazement. With her pulse racing, engaged in something real for the first time in years, she pored over dispersed media reports, and in astronomy circles, she finally found the enthusiasm she longed to hear. The International Space Agency announced it would put together an exploratory committee to discuss other possible probes to the Kuiper Belt. Someone even suggested an actual crewed mission with scientists and explorers—but that wouldn't be for a decade or two, and such an expedition would take years to reach its destination.

Dismayed by the glacial pace of bureaucratic research programs, Cammie still made up her mind to submit her application to any wormhole committee, engineering project, or analysis team she could find. She needed to be involved, one way or another.

She had no one to share her excitement with—the same as always. She had not stayed in contact with any of the ISA probe techs, who had often snickered at her in the analysis center. When she was younger, her parents and brother had never shown any scientific curiosity, and now they were all gone after the house fire. Her current coworkers at the quantum-circuitry company were electronics engineers and theoreticians, but they weren't her friends, and they didn't dream of esoteric astrophysical problems.

But Dr. Tendari would understand what this news meant.

They'd drifted apart once she finished her Master's degree, after an awkward moment when he'd told her his wife had insisted he break off communications with her. Cammie didn't know why that would matter, since Tendari's wife had never shown any interest in their wormhole theories. He had moved to Stanford and had not contacted her since.

Now, though, this revelation changed everything. She and her mentor had always shared a true interest in the astronomical wonders, and she needed to talk with him right away.

Before she could even track down his current contact information at Stanford University, however, Tendari called her. It was as if he had been waiting for an excuse.

When his face appeared on her vid screen, she saw how the time had softened his features like a comfortable leather glove. He looked much older than she remembered, but it made him seem distinguished. Cammie was older, too, but she never really looked at herself the way others did.

The excitement on Tendari's face was just like when he had hugged her upon seeing the initial probe images. Cammie smiled when she saw him after so much time, felt glad to hear his voice, and it seemed as if they had never stopped their daily brainstorming sessions. Now the work was real again.

Why had it been so long since they'd talked? She should have paid more attention, but she had never been good at maintaining friendships.

Zach Tendari had a long face, tan skin, and crow's-feet around his eyes that gave him character. His dark hair was cut very short in tight curls, like moss, and now it had a smoky tinge of gray throughout. He was lean and fit, but in his midsixties, she realized, a lot older than her father had been. But Dr. Tendari *understood* her.

Cammie didn't waste time on pleasantries and blurted out, "I know why you're calling! I saw the press releases. I can't believe it! Now we know where the wormhole goes—the Einstein-Rosen bridge works! Four point three years means Alpha Centauri."

"Proxima Centauri, actually," Tendari said, his voice rich and wise. "The third star in the system, a red dwarf, which is actually closest to Earth."

She leaned closer to the screen, imagining that he was right there as they talked about fascinating esoteric things. Just like old times.

His eyes sparkled. "And it's just a start, Cammie. We could explore the next star system decades faster than we would normally get there."

She groaned as she remembered the ponderous pace proposed by the bureaucratic programs. "The international space agencies will take years to get their act together, but I'm going to apply for some part of the work." Her expression fell as she thought about all the requirements she would face, all the paperwork she didn't comprehend. "Could you write me a reference, Dr. Tendari? I really want to be involved."

He gave her a warm smile. "How many times have I told you to call me Zach?" His eyes seemed very intense.

"Sorry." The name just didn't feel right to her. Sometimes it was hard for her to understand the expectations of conversation.

His face grew larger on the vid as he pressed closer to the screen. "Don't give up hope, my dear. It won't take that long. I've arranged everything." He paused, tantalizing her. He seemed to have a secret.

She looked for cues, tried to determine if he was teasing her. "What do you mean?"

"Not everyone stopped working on the problem just because the ISA shut their mission down. Benedict Noor has something up his sleeve—and that man gets what he wants."

Her face went blank as she pulled together information. Noor was an ambitious, abrasive, but determined space industrialist who had pushed his interplanetary operations beyond the reach of Earthbound laws or treaties. He put his money where his dreams were—and he had a lot of money. "Is he sending his own probe? Can I be on the team?"

"Better than that. Mr. Noor has been planning all along, and he has a mission ready to go to the wormhole." Tendari's words came out in a rush. "He's had it in development ever since the Nether probe vanished, but he kept it quiet. He never lost interest when everyone else did."

"I never lost interest," Cammie said, a little defensively.

"Of course not, dear." Tendari chuckled. "You'll be happy to know that Noor quietly dispatched five probes over the years and already has a wealth of data and high-resolution images. He knows more about the Nether wormhole than anyone."

Cammie gasped. "I haven't heard anything about other probes! There's been nothing in the scientific press."

Her mentor's expression darkened. "Nothing has been released. Since Noor paid for it all himself, he says the information is a trade secret, industrial data to be used for his company's benefit, and he has no obligation to share it."

Her throat tightened, feeling frustration. All these years she had felt empty, with her passion gone, working at her dull quantum-circuitry job. She could have been reading about these new discoveries. "He can't do that!"

"Well, he did—and now he's given me access to the full suite of data. He's been following my work at Stanford." He paused to let that sink in, and Cammie's heart started racing. She couldn't think of the right thing to say.

He continued, "Now that the signal came back, Benedict

Noor is wasting no time. He plans to mount a crewed mission up to the Nether wormhole as soon as possible. A screw-you to everyone else who took their eye off the ball." On the vid screen, his face glowed with a satisfied smile. "I'm going along as his primary wormhole expert."

Cammie caught her breath. "I'm so excited for you, Dr. Tendari! You're the best person. And you'll be right there—*right there*!"

"Call me Zach," he gently insisted, then held for a long, teasing pause. "And I want you to go up there with me."

SIX YEARS LATER

CHAPTER 1

When the *Lethe* closed in on the Nether wormhole, Cammie was part of the "last shift" awake before the other ten crewmembers would be revived from hibernation. She herself had been out of the cryopod for six months, preparing, taking telescopic measurements, growing anxious . . . and a little bored.

Ever since the mission had departed from the NOOR asteroid hub five years earlier, she'd been filled with anticipation, never doubting that this was her life's work. The scientific breakthroughs they would gain from the mysterious wormhole made her heart and mind glow, and she could barely focus on anything else. None of the other six awake crewmembers understood her passion, but she counted down the days until Zachary Tendari emerged from hibernation.

Alone and self-absorbed, she walked down the big ship's corridors toward the observation bridge. Her real work wouldn't begin until they arrived at the wormhole in a few weeks, but she liked to gaze out at the starry blackness, even if the bridge wasn't a place to find solitude.

When she wanted to be alone, she'd seal herself in her quarters, as some of the other crew did. During her alternating shifts out of the cryopod, Cammie had made her best effort to forge friendly relationships on the *Lethe*, though it was out of her comfort zone. Soon enough the ship would be much more crowded with all seventeen members awake, and they had to get along with one another.

The voyage up to the Kuiper Belt took five years, and the team was scheduled to remain at the wormhole for six months of extensive study, and then it would be another five years back down to the inner solar system. Cammie didn't regret such a major investment of time; she couldn't think of anything she would rather do with her life.

When the mission crew had gone through their briefings and exercises back at the NOOR asteroid hub, they were warned that they'd be away from family, friends, and most other people for more than a decade. Cammie wasn't intimidated by the idea. She didn't like crowds, her family was gone, and she liked being by herself, so long as she had real research to do.

This mission was what she had been born to do. She wanted more than just theories and models, more than wire-frame diagrams in simulations, but an actual wormhole.

Nether.

Reaching the bridge, she braced herself before she entered. The extensive viewing windows showed the black velvet panorama—so vast, so mysterious. But Benedict Noor and his acting commander, Karla Arkourian, were both on duty. She would not have the bridge to herself.

In the center of the room, Noor lounged in the captain's chair as if it were a throne. He was a lanky man with a bald head that gleamed in the artificial lights. Years ago, when his hair had begun to fall out from experimental life-extension treatments, Noor had simply shaved his head.

His face was as well known as any world leader's. He'd been the subject of excoriating media coverage, countless profiles, scandals, and technological triumphs. He did not care what other people said about him. When forming his company, he used just his own name in all caps, NOOR—with the two *O*'s linked, like an infinity symbol. Initially, Cammie thought he was arrogant, but over the *Lethe*'s long voyage, she realized he was more complicated than that.

Though she entered the bridge quietly, Noor turned to give her a disarming yet wily smile. "Ah, Dr. Skoura—come to build anticipation for the wormhole? Or just in search of two other cardplayers?" He turned to the other officer on the bridge, who was busy studying readings at her command station. "What do you say, Karla?"

Karla Arkourian had been a Space Force captain and fighter pilot in the wars before she'd joined the private sector and worked her way up at NOOR. She was in her sixties, presumably at the tail end of an aerospace career. She was lean to the point of being gaunt, with steel-gray hair in a short, serviceable cut. Cammie liked her.

Arkourian barely looked up from her screens in response to Noor's comment. "No time for games. I have a vital mission-systems profile to run this afternoon."

The older woman was effectively in command of the mission, making any necessary snap decisions, but Benedict Noor insisted on being the "captain," since he had paid for the whole expedition. Arkourian didn't care a whit for administrative titles, because everyone knew who was in charge.

Bored, Noor tapped his fingers on the arm of the captain's chair. "Come now, Karla. *Lethe* is decelerating on schedule. Everything is on autopilot and constantly monitored, and it'll be two weeks before we're close enough to the wormhole to worry about course corrections." He raised his eyebrows. "What duties do you have that could possibly be more urgent than a card game?"

Arkourian gave him a hard expression. "All of them."

Cammie hoped the trillionaire wasn't serious about playing cards. Noor didn't try to intimidate her on purpose, but he wasn't overly warm either. Now she flushed with embarrassment. "I just came up to think. I get good ideas when I stare out at the stars. Sorry to interrupt. Sometimes it . . . doesn't seem real to me."

During the *Lethe*'s long voyage, only a small crew of five remained awake at any one time to do maintenance and research work, while the other ten slept in cryopods until they were revived for their own shifts—six months awake, one year down—plus an alternating two-person command crew that was out of phase with the other sleepers.

Four other crew were awake now during the final approach. Glinda Roybal was a loud and exuberant lead engineer, without personal boundaries. Pedro Ashe was the young secondary engineer; Warren Drake would be the pilot for the probes and recon ships; and quiet Kem Stelland served as the ship's doctor, medical researcher, and greenhouse monitor.

For Cammie, though, the schedule meant that Zach Tendari was in hibernation most of the time she was awake, and vice versa. She wished they could brainstorm and fine-tune their theories as they grew closer to the destination. Soon enough, during final approach, the entire crew would be revived, ready to get to work.

Making no further conversation, Cammie stood by the wide observation window. Looking out at the emptiness, she felt dizzy, tipped down into an infinite hole with stars in every direction. Out there, she could fall up, or down, or in any direction forever.

The Kuiper Belt was a diffuse veil of rocks and ice left over from the formation of the solar system, untouched and unseen, and the Sun was no more than a bright star. The *Lethe* was farther from home than any humans had ever ventured.

"You won't be able to see the wormhole yet, no matter how

hard you look," Noor said. "You do have telescopes and the quantum-imaging chips in the observatory chamber."

With his clout and wealth, Noor could lecture whenever he liked, and people would politely listen. She didn't let the boss-splaining annoy her. "I know, sir. I've been using them, but there's nothing to see yet."

"Not yet, but soon. On the *Lethe*, we'll be among the greatest scientific explorers in history," Noor continued, starting to sound grandiose. "Like Darwin on the *Beagle*. And I am its captain."

"Nobody remembers the captain of the *Beagle*, Benedict," Arkourian said.

"Robert FitzRoy. He was also the second governor of New Zealand—one of my explorer heroes," Noor quipped, and then kept talking. "I'm convinced the Nether wormhole is a direct conduit to the Alpha Centauri system, and that means I'll be able to set up an outpost here and another one at the other end. Think about the possibilities, Dr. Skoura—or Cammie? Can I call you Cammie?"

He had asked her the question several times already, and she'd given him noncommittal responses, which he either forgot or didn't consider satisfactory.

"I . . . I don't have a preference," she said.

During the pre-mission briefings, Dr. Tendari had tried to coach her through her difficulties with personal interactions, and Cammie had taught herself to get along with her fellow crewmembers. While she understood complex astrophysical models, she wasn't comfortable with friendships. Back on Earth, she could function on the surface of society but wasn't very good at it, mystified by how people just *knew* what others were thinking, what they were implying. They understood when to tease and when to be serious. Though she tested as a true genius, that was all a mystery to her.

Noor didn't even notice she wasn't paying attention. "What I envision, Cammie"—apparently, he decided to use her first name—"is that this isn't just a wormhole tunnel to one star. What if there's an entire network, like a subway system underneath the universe? Passages to countless star systems across the Galaxy?"

Cammie turned from the windowport to look at him, though he was saying things she already knew. "Theoretical models allow for that, sir, but we simply won't have enough data until we reach the Nether wormhole." Cammie hesitated, out of her depth. "Dr. Tendari would be a better person to ask. Once he's revived from the cryopod, the two of us will start testing our theories."

Noor nodded. "I understand. We start waking the rest of the crew in three days, and I'll make sure Dr. Tendari is the first one out of the cryopods." He shifted in the captain's chair. "Oh well, if nobody wants to play cards, I'll go see Warren in the hangar bay. He's probably caressing his ships."

Arkourian had never shifted her attention from her station. When Noor departed, Cammie gladly went back to staring out at the stars.

CHAPTER 2

All gassed up and no place to go.

Warren Drake ran his fingers along the smooth anodized hull of the first recon ship. It was a beauty, he had to admit, and he was eager to put it to use.

The *Lethe* carried two identical craft for operations around the wormhole, both equipped with a full array of scientific instrumentation, survey apparatus, and even heavy machinery for excavation and sampling. Warren thought of them as flying Swiss Army knives.

Originally, the ships had been unimaginatively dubbed Recon One and Recon Two, but Mr. Noor had rechristened them after two explorers he admired—*Lewis* and *Clark*. Warren approved.

But he didn't have anywhere to *go*—not yet. Once they reached the destination, he would have something fun to do. During the long voyage, during the shifts he was out of hibernation, he spent his time flying simulation after simulation, but that didn't cut it. As a test pilot, he needed to be prepared for anything, and he didn't dare let Mr. Noor think he was the slightest bit nervous.

"Getting ready for the main event, Warren?" The entrepreneur walked jauntily into the hangar bay.

"We'll have lots of main events, boss—scoping out the Nether neighborhood, piloting the test probes, maybe even flying into the wormhole—but that'll be a while yet." He walked between the two recon ships. "I'm ready for something to happen! When you picked me for this mission, I thought it would be a little more action packed. Man, if I'd been awake for the whole five years, I'd be stir-crazy by now."

"I have utter confidence in your demonstrated abilities. You saved my butt from burning up in the atmosphere."

"One time," Warren said, feigning modesty but secretly pleased. "And it was just a shuttle flight."

"That one time was all I needed," Noor said. "And I've never used another pilot since." He left the *Lewis* and *Clark* and walked up to the largest, most innovative vessel in the hangar bay, the star of the show. The expedition ship could hold a crew of eight, with all the equipment and supplies needed for an extended mission in the Alpha Centauri system. Noor smiled. "The *Neil Armstrong*, a perfect name. One small step . . . to another star system. We'll just call it the *Neil*, for short."

The pilot grinned. "I like being on a first-name basis with my ships, considering what we go through together."

Noor reveled in just being here. He spread his arms wide. "You'll be the first, Warren—and I don't give up that role easily. You'll fly the *Neil* through the wormhole and be the first human to see another star system."

"If the wormhole actually works." Warren maintained his confident demeanor, because he didn't want to admit he was uneasy about the prospect. "It'll be a while before all the tests are completed though. Test probes first." He glanced at the three automated vessels locked in their own cradles in the hangar bay. The first was a strictly automated probe that would fly through the Nether wormhole and back—if it could. Once that worked, the second would carry lab rats, one group sedated and one group wide awake.

In the *Lethe*'s medical lab, three rhesus monkeys slept in their own cryopod, the primate test subjects that would experience the wormhole journey next. Only after everything passed with flying colors would Warren become the first human test subject.

"I can handle the flying, boss. It's the wormhole itself that psychs me out."

"We do know it's possible," Noor said brightly. "Otherwise, I wouldn't have devoted so much time and NOOR resources to this expedition. The old ISA probe went through intact. We all heard the signal across four light-years."

Warren leaned his elbow on the front of the expedition ship. The large craft was indeed a marvel of design, carrying everything a true, brave explorer might need. "Yeah, but that old probe stopped transmitting after only a week."

Noor clucked his tongue against his teeth. "Very likely that its batteries were drained, or that it suffered mechanical failure."

Warren said, "Or it might've been damaged during the interdimensional passage." He forced a joke. "Could be it was even destroyed by an alien civilization."

The entrepreneur snorted. "I don't put much stock in those theories. And neither do you."

"Neither do I, boss." He went back to the *Clark*, which was much more familiar to him. "First, I'm excited to explore around the wormhole neighborhood. The initial probes showed some asteroids, familiar stuff. We're going to need to do a survey run, for sure."

Noor saw the gleam in his eyes. "Captain Arkourian is worried you'll fly too close to the event horizon."

"Define *too close.* Besides, I'm going to fly right into it sooner or later, like the first man going over Niagara Falls in a barrel."

"Actually, the first to do that was a woman, Annie Edson Taylor, in 1901. And the *Neil Armstrong* is far better than a barrel. Still, I would rather think of you as an explorer, Warren, than a reckless daredevil."

Warren grinned. "It takes a little of both to make this work."

Noor seemed amused and satisfied. "You'll get your chance. Soon."

CHAPTER 3

Mr. Noor called the *Lethe*'s cryopod bay the "bed-and-breakfast deck," but Cammie didn't relate to the humor.

Seventeen oblong insulated chambers filled the deck in alternating positions, like the teeth of a zipper, one cryopod for each crewmember. Even with the frozen people inside, Cammie forced herself not to imagine the pods as coffins, though the dim deck always had an eerie chill. And the silence, except for the hum of life-support monitors and the faint hiss of venting vapors, reminded her of a morgue.

She had hibernated three times during the voyage, tucked inside the protected bed with coolant-laced sidewalls. Before going to sleep, she remembered the enriched oxygen flow like cold breath in her face, the IV lines filled with nutrients and soporifics that flowed into her bloodstream.

Cammie had been nervous enough her first time. Noor's company had developed the proprietary hibernation technology and used it on their employees for transport out to the asteroid belt operations. The success of cryopod tech had given NOOR yet another leg up against the competition.

Despite having read numerous research papers—several of them authored by Kem Stelland, one of the *Lethe*'s doctors—Cammie felt a moment of claustrophobia and terror just after the pod lid sealed shut that first time. She felt the stick of the IV needles, then the cold fluids traveling through her veins.

She breathed hard into her oxygen mask and blinked, trying not to show her irrational fear as she looked up through the small viewing pane.

Dr. Tendari was above, watching her, and his smile seemed more intense than usual, more possessive. He would be there with her, every step of the way. The cold IV drugs felt like creeping death closing in on her heart, her mind—and then total oblivion.

No nightmares, no dreams.

When she woke up after her first shift, she'd felt achy and nauseated, her thoughts muddled—a typical cryo-hangover that went away after enough coffee, real food, and regular drug-free naps. Now she no longer worried about the cryopods. They were a means to an end, and hibernation was the only way they could reach the distant Nether wormhole. That was the only thing that really mattered to her.

Once, during the brief overlapping period when they were awake between hibernation shifts, Tendari had gone out of his way to tell her, like some kind of confession, "My wife and I separated several years ago. Mena and I had an arranged marriage, as I think you suspect—no romance and barely any sex."

Cammie had wondered why he would tell her that. She responded with, "I left some notes for you to look at—a new way of considering the Schwartzschild horizon. We have to focus on the wormhole study from now on."

"Yes, we do. You and I."

But she hadn't seen Dr. Tendari for most of the five-year voyage, and now she was anxious to have him awake again so they could do their real work.

With growing anticipation, Cammie arrived early for the revival process. Dr. Stelland was already in the chilly cryopod deck, checking readings on the ten inhabited pods. He had brought electrolytes and anti-nausea medication in case any of the reawakened crewmembers needed a jolt.

Seven of the cryopods were empty and open, on standby for the crewmembers currently awake. Noor could have cut corners, alternated the occupants in the pods rather than providing one for each person, but he insisted on "private beds for everybody."

Now as she walked down the line of sleek pods, she noted the NOOR logo, the life-support panels, the humming generators. Each pod had a name tag, though the faces themselves were visible beneath the viewing panes.

At each unit, she tried to call the individuals to mind, as a mental exercise. She had met the full crew during the months of mission prep at the asteroid hub, and she would get to know them during the six months working together at the wormhole. Still, she made a point of memorizing them: Peter Hamada, Noor's personal assistant; Eli Hankins, the mission psychologist; Amibi, the other medical doctor; Chao and Waller-Onn, two more engineers; Krondike, Ensari, and Gomez, general technicians; secondary pilot Intecca; and Skah, maintenance worker and mission poet.

When she looked at the waxy, mannequin-like faces, they seemed at peace, with smooth expressions, gently closed eyes. Their skin looked grayish from the hibernation chemicals and the cold.

At Tendari's cryopod, she rested her hand on the viewing pane. He would be awake soon enough.

"Preparations aren't yet complete." Dr. Stelland's voice was crisp and businesslike. He didn't look up at her from the base of the pod as he checked the flow of diagnostics, reviewing the long-term record of the hibernation cycle. "I won't start the process without Mr. Noor and Captain Arkourian."

She flushed. "I'm anxious to have my colleague back. Can I help?"

"Nothing that I can think of."

Stelland was thin and androgynous, with a wide, smooth face that carried a mix of Asian and Pacific Islander features. He had brown eyes, short dark hair, and a star tattoo above his left eye. The quiet doctor wasn't unfriendly, nor was he outgoing, just not interested in anyone else's duties. Cammie got along well with him.

The doctor went from cryopod to cryopod, making notes as he spoke in a low voice, not really to her. "All systems check out so far. These people have been down and up multiple times, and the life-support machinery has been used repeatedly. This should all be routine."

Since he'd been in the first cryopod shift, Dr. Tendari had slept through the heavy acceleration as the massive *Lethe* climbed up from the asteroid belt. But Cammie had been awake when the force pushed her back into the recliner seat, like an oppressive hand pressing down. She struggled to do her basic duties for the first week or two, but she'd grown accustomed to it.

Her mentor had been blissfully unaware, feeling no bruises or sore muscles while in the protected pod. Six months later, when it was Cammie's turn to go down into hibernation, she and Tendari had made the most of their few hours of overlap, but it wasn't enough to catch up. Now, he would finally be awake for the rest of the mission.

She stepped closer to Stelland. "You're waking Dr. Tendari first?"

"They'll all be revived by the end of the day. The order doesn't matter."

"It matters to me," she said, then waited. "So, Dr. Tendari first?"

The doctor shrugged. "So long as Mr. Noor doesn't object."

As if he'd been summoned, Benedict Noor emerged from

the lift at the far end of the deck, accompanied by Arkourian. "Rise and shine! Soon we'll have a full house—all seventeen crewmembers ready to make history." He strolled ahead of his exec, looking at the sealed cryopods as if they were birthday presents to unwrap.

"I'm glad this is a large ship, and we will deploy the second hab module once we're in position," Arkourian said. "Nothing causes friction more than eccentric personalities in cramped quarters for long periods of time."

Noor gave her a quirky smile. "You're talking about Glinda. I think she's amusing. Sometimes."

Arkourian frowned. "Engineer Roybal is not the only strange one in the crew."

"We're all family." Noor sounded magnanimous as he joined Cammie beside Tendari's pod. "And you must be eager, Cammie—may I call you Cammie?"

"Yes." She kept looking through the misty viewing pane at Dr. Tendari's intellectual features, prominent jaw, thin nose. He did look a lot older than she remembered.

Her reflection on the pane was fainter, but she saw her warm tan skin, high cheekbones, full lips. Tendari had once called her green eyes otherworldly, a hint of what was really going on inside her mind. Cammie had never considered herself pretty, because her social awkwardness had driven away anyone with a romantic interest. She never really knew what she saw in the mirror, because her thoughts went inward.

In the last few weeks, she had felt more alone than ever aboard the empty *Lethe*, and now she couldn't wait to talk with someone she could relate to, someone who understood astrophysics and theoretical wormhole mechanics. Tendari had told her stories—as if he wanted to impress her—that he had once met Kip Thorne, one of the original wormhole theoreticians. He and Cammie had discussed cosmic string theory, the potentiality of wormhole boundaries, Einstein-Rosen bridges. Over the past few months, she had worked out several variations on Tendari's core theory of two-way wormholes, and she wanted to show him. No one else here understood what she was talking about.

Noor paced among the cryopods now. "We'll have a welcome reception tonight, a family reunion once everybody's awake."

Stelland checked the cryopod diagnostics with his AI pad. "Ms. Skoura requests reviving Dr. Tendari first. Is that acceptable, sir?"

Noor smiled. "She likes to be called Cammie." He gave a dismissive wave. "And yes, of course. Whatever order you like, left to right, alphabetical order. Time to wake them all up." He sniffed. "I'll be glad to have my assistant, Hamada, back to take over some of my workload. I forgot how much I depend on him—wake him up second. I can have him help with tonight's reception."

Stelland ran through a sequence of commands on Tendari's pod, using his thumbprint so he could enter the reactivation sequence. "Beginning the initial phases. Temperature rising to nominal levels."

He studied the frost patterns on the viewing pane like an ancient soothsayer handling bloody entrails. Cammie's heart raced. Arkourian watched the wall chronometer. Noor joked about playing a card game while they waited.

The doctor rattled off a list of vital readings. "Increasing oxygen levels in the chamber, adding adrenaline solution."

The pod's medical monitor showed the slow, steady drumbeat of Tendari's heart, and the AI scanners mapped his brain activity. Though Noor acted bored by the slow process, the doctor remained completely professional, though the star tattoo twitched at the corner of his eye.

Cammie spotted the amber warning light first. "What's that?"

"The readings are subpar. Let me reset." Stelland entered more command strings but was rewarded with more amber lights.

Then two red ones.

"What's happening?" Cammie felt a prickle of cold perspiration.

Stelland's words were clipped. "The subject is not responding well." He hurried to the life-support panel, added a jolt of adrenaline into the IVs, pumped in more saline and electrolytes. As Tendari's body warmed up through the revival cycle, his heartbeat became erratic, then slowed.

Stelland wore a stony expression. "I'm losing him."

"No!" Cammie cried.

Arkourian pressed forward, taking command in the emergency. "Don't you have a jump-start protocol? You've done this dozens of times!"

"Hundreds," the doctor replied, as if announcing a score in a sporting event. "I've seen this once or twice, possible hibernation sickness."

Cammie was frantic to do something, but this was not her background. The unexpected sheen of sweat on the doctor's forehead made her genuinely afraid.

An emergency alarm tone rose from the monitoring panel.

"Shouldn't we break him out of there? Do CPR or something?" Noor asked. "Karla, get a crowbar!"

The doctor muttered under his breath. "Smashing the pod open would certainly kill him, sir. Sophisticated life-support and biomaintenance systems are connected to him now. Pulling his body out and pounding him on the back won't do any good."

"Can we stop the revival sequence?" Arkourian asked. "Put him back under until we figure out what's wrong?"

"No."

Cammie pressed close to the viewing pane, saw Tendari's face flinch and twitch. He winced as if in deep pain. She called out, knowing he couldn't hear her. "Dr. Tendari!" *Call me Zach.* "Zach!"

Inside the pod, his eyes flickered open, and he stared up at her, but the eyes were gray and milky, showing nothing. Then the eyelids fell slack. Something changed in his waxy face, turning into a haunted grimace.

Cammie yanked herself away, shocked by what she saw.

The shrill alarm grew louder. Every monitor light on the panel turned red. The readings of brain activity and heart function flatlined.

Stelland reset the revival procedures two more times, without success. "All systems have failed. He's not coming out of it."

Cammie groaned, felt the sound build to a sob as she looked down at his slack, deceptively peaceful face inside the cryopod.

"I'm sorry, sir." Stelland looked up to Noor. "He is dead."

CHAPTER 4

Karla Arkourian was no stranger to unexpected loss, and she understood all too well what Cammie was feeling.

The young woman rested her forehead against the pod's viewing pane, quietly weeping. When she lifted her head, tears streamed down her cheeks. Arkourian had witnessed sudden shocking deaths and slow, lingering deaths, and she let Cammie have her grief. But the situation right now went beyond consoling her for the loss of her mentor.

The implications of the failed cryopod were staggering. Was it a fluke or a widespread problem?

Dr. Stelland stared at the readings in confusion, then reran the diagnostic report from the life-support systems, as if he might have simply misread the results. "This should not have happened." The doctor looked deeply shaken, and it was unusual for him to show real emotions. "There was no error in the process. Preparatory diagnostics on the cryopod equipment and Dr. Tendari's biological readings were completely optimal."

Stelland was fully qualified to handle the crew's basic medical needs, but Noor had chosen the man for his research abilities, not his bedside manner. He was one of the foremost experts in hibernation science and cryopod engineering. Now he continued as if he were presenting a paper at a medical conference. "I don't know if there was a breakdown in the cryopod supervisory loop, or a contaminant in the revival chemicals—or some undiagnosed condition in the patient himself."

Noor bent down to look at Tendari's gray face behind the frosty pane. "The patient himself? Tendari went into that pod five times previously. Did he just have an . . . expiration date?"

"It does happen, sir. Some subjects have a lower tolerance for repeated cryogenic suspension."

Arkourian spoke sharply, making them recognize the bigger problem. "Doctor, we have nine more crewmembers in hibernation. Was this a onetime failure, or is there a systemic problem with all the pods? Run a full diagnostic on each unit. We must be absolutely sure before we attempt to revive anyone else."

Noor rubbed his temples. "That's half of the *Lethe* crew!" Arkourian had worked with the man long enough to know he hated to have his complex plans thrown off track. "How are we going to finish our mission if they're all just dead Popsicles? We needed—"

Cammie groaned, and her face flushed with sudden anger. "Popsicles?"

"Benedict." Arkourian said it in a low voice, but everyone else heard. She knew the precise tone of voice and the attitude to take with him. "Shut. Up." The words were so startling that Noor fell silent.

Arkourian had a long and distinguished career as an astronaut, pilot, and commander, but at sixty-one, she was generally considered too old for an edgy exploration mission. But Benedict Noor had said he wanted her, and she had agreed.

Now, as the *Lethe*'s operational captain, she needed to demonstrate why she was here. "Could it have anything to do with proximity to the wormhole? Subliminal distortions in the fabric of space having an effect?"

Preoccupied, the doctor moved from one unit to another, loading his AI pad and running streams of comparisons, winnowing out any troublesome readings. "We've never been to a wormhole before—anything is possible. I'm not an astrophysicist."

He looked at Cammie, who remained in shock by Tendari's malfunctioning pod. The young woman got to her feet and stumbled off to her quarters, as if fleeing. Arkourian thought that was a good idea for her.

"So, how are we going to wake up my other nine people?" Noor asked. "We need them. They're our research crew—and one of them is my personal assistant."

Stelland considered. "We need more data about the malfunction. We should try to wake up another subject—this might have been a onetime failure."

Arkourian cut him off. "You're not experimenting with any more of our crew, Doctor. Not until you know what's wrong."

"That's not what I meant." He frowned. "The cryopod in the medical bay contains three rhesus monkeys for our wormhole experiments. I can try to revive them, which will be indicative."

"Great idea," said Noor. "Let's go to the monkey house."

Preoccupied, as if he didn't have an audience, the doctor inspected the monkey cryopod, checked readings, made adjustments. He linked his datapad and let the AI run deep diagnostics before he started the revival process.

Arkourian was tense. If it was a systemic problem, did that mean ten of the seventeen crewmembers were lost? And without functioning cryopods, how would any of them get back home? They couldn't survive a five-year voyage on the *Lethe* while awake. The ship didn't have nearly enough supplies.

She parked her concerns in the back of her mind, as she had learned in the military. She would wait for answers first. Dr. Stelland went about his work.

For the Nether mission, experimental lab rats were stored

as embryos in the frozen cabinet, easily brought to term when needed. But the grown monkeys had to travel in hibernation, three of them together. Their cryopod was the same unit as the rest of the crew used.

"This isn't the type of experiment the monkeys expected to participate in," Noor said as Stelland began the revival cycle.

"I'm sure they don't have a preference, Benedict," Arkourian said.

"This will be a useful test." Stelland frowned at his diagnostic pad. "Perhaps it was just a false alarm."

"A false alarm wouldn't have killed Tendari," Arkourian pointed out.

The doctor shrugged. "He could have died from hibernation sickness—we can hope. I'll have to do an autopsy at some point."

"Let's just see if the monkeys wake up," Noor said, sounding edgy. "Maybe we can solve this, quick and easy."

"Nothing about this is quick and easy," she said.

Stelland activated the revival sequence and watched through the transparent viewing pane. Beneath the thin tracery of frost, three cinnamon-furred monkeys were curled up together like brothers in an orphanage. They had slept in cold storage through the five years of the journey.

As the chamber temperature rose, the frost on their fur sparkled and evaporated. Stimulants and nutrients were pumped into their bloodstreams. The cryopod's panel displayed three sets of readouts. Not knowing how to interpret the screens, Arkourian watched the doctor instead, reading his expressions.

Noor was antsy, but Arkourian remained outwardly calm. After preparing for numerous combat missions, she'd learned how to turn off her mind and wait.

When the revival cycle was complete, the doctor raised the pod's canopy. The three monkeys lay together in a ball of unruly fur, as if they had clutched one another in fear, trapped in the coffin-sized tank as the cold settled in.

Stelland held his breath, watching.

One of the rhesus monkeys twitched and muttered, blinked its large, intelligent eyes, and lifted a brown-furred arm. It extricated itself from its two companions and stretched, shook its head. It sat up, saw them, and whimpered.

When the doctor reached down to check the animal's vitals, it raised its arms, obviously wanting to be held. Awkwardly, Stelland pulled the monkey against his chest, and it seemed groggy, confused. "You're awake now. We just need to run some tests."

The other two monkeys remained motionless though. The cryopod monitors flatlined, and the alert lights burned a steady red. They were dead.

"Two out of three?" Noor grumbled. "Does this mean that if we try to revive the other nine crew, maybe three will wake up? We could play the odds."

"We're not going to do that," Arkourian snapped. "*We* don't get to roll the dice with our crew."

"Well, otherwise all nine of them are dead." Noor gestured in the vague direction of the bed-and-breakfast deck.

"In hibernation. Not dead—unless and until we try to revive them and screw it up."

The monkey pressed against the doctor's chest, and he frowned at the distraction. "We have a cage for you. That'll be your new home."

The animal looked forlorn when Stelland locked him in the med lab's large cage. Then the doctor considered the two motionless creatures still in the pod. "I can dissect them, maybe discover where the fault was."

"But what about my other nine crewmembers?" Noor asked.

"Let them remain in deep hibernation," he said. "They are

just as safe now as they were a week ago. We can't risk reviving them until we have a better understanding of what happened to the pod systems."

"Run a full check," Arkourian said. "You're the expert on hibernation tech and medical effects. I won't authorize reviving another one until we can be sure. Worst case, we might need to bring them back to the full NOOR facility at the asteroid hub."

"That'll be years!" said Noor. "What about our wormhole mission?"

"Yes, it'll be years," said Arkourian. "Right now each one of them is like Schrödinger's cat. They're dead or they're alive, and the only way to know for sure is if we open the pods, which might kill them. We're not going to do that."

He let out a petulant huff. "We're a week and a half away from the wormhole. You're saying that nine of my crew are just going to sleep through the greatest discovery in the history of humanity?"

Dr. Stelland shrugged. "They will either sleep through it, or they will be dead."

CHAPTER 5

Cammie wasn't prepared for this. She felt helpless, because she didn't know how to grieve. She'd had a sheltered life, not even a pet growing up. Her parents and brother had never been close, and their loss in the house fire still seemed so distant, so unreal.

But she had watched Dr. Tendari die, personally—from a stupid glitch, a technical error.

On her best days, Cammie did not know how to handle emotions, and now they swept her away like a kidnapped passenger. Now she squeezed her eyes shut. This made no logical sense. Hibernation was simply a way to fast-forward the long voyage up to the Nether wormhole. Dr. Tendari had been sealed in his cryopod, deep asleep, and then, with no visible change, he was dead.

Not knowing what she was supposed to do or how she should react, she sealed herself in her quarters, alternating between disbelief and anger. "No . . ." she whispered, then pressed her face into her pillow so she could shout louder. "No!" It was as if spacetime had bent around her and cut her off from the universe, and there wasn't even anywhere to fall.

Later, on her personal screen, Cammie called up images and reread casual correspondence from her mentor that had not felt significant at the time, but now had much greater import. She revisited ideas they had bounced back and forth, brainstorming theories and mathematical nuances, and now she tried to hide in the science.

There were three types of possible wormholes—traversable wormholes, non-traversable wormholes, and one-way wormholes. Since the original ISA probe signal had come through from Alpha Centauri, that meant the Nether wormhole was traversable—but was it only a one-way trip? She and Dr. Tendari had debated both possibilities in a vibrant and exciting intellectual interaction. She thought of how much she had depended on him—how he had guided her, shaped her, told her what to do.

On the original Nether probe project, they had waited together, day after day, for telemetry from the first primitive probes. Cammie had been so absorbed in each new bit of data to share, but she remembered the raised eyebrows and snickering comments of other techs, in particular a dark-haired woman named Leila. "And what kind of research is he doing on *you*, girl?" The others had laughed, and Leila added in an undertone, "Creepy old man."

Cammie shook her head, wishing she could erase their hurtful comments. It was nothing like that.

But when she read the correspondence more closely now, Tendari's warmth came through clearly, expressing his feelings, but she had shared very little in return. He said compassionate words to her, but her responses were direct and to the point, focused only on the topic under discussion. She had never known how to make light conversation, didn't understand the purpose of it.

What had he really wanted from her?

Growing up, Cammie had always felt like a changeling in her household. How had she ended up in *this* family—parents and a brother who had nothing in common with her? Early on, she had been given the label of "neurodiverse," or "on the spectrum," but that hadn't changed anything. Even her father blamed her for being socially inept.

He was a factory manager, and her mother was a real estate agent. Her older brother, Jason, got his high school diploma and managed a chain restaurant, which was something her parents could understand.

But Cammie always had her head in the clouds, a straight-A student who couldn't seem to keep any friends. When she was teased and ostracized in junior high, her father had blamed her. "Can't you even *try*, Cammie? Those kids don't understand you, but you're making no effort to understand them either. Try to be normal."

She got on the honor roll without a second thought, won academic awards, and her parents were proud of her, but they were just as proud of Jason. When she got accepted into MIT, her mother insisted that she turn it down because their family couldn't afford the extravagant tuition. But Cammie was determined to go, so she found scholarships and the highest-level honors. She took care of herself.

Cammie remembered that awkward last meal before she left home for MIT. Her mother had made her usual chicken marsala, and her father asked Cammie what a wormhole was all about anyway. She did her best to explain. Her mother insisted that Cammie wasn't prepared to live alone.

After dinner, the conversation turned to Jason's announcement that he would be opening another chain restaurant, and Cammie said her goodbyes, gave quick, cordial hugs, and ended the night early, because her mother had a real estate showing the next day.

She drove off to her new life, excited to immerse herself in the mysteries of the universe, free to follow her dreams at last.

That night, her old home had caught fire. Her parents,

and even Jason, who had decided to stay over, died of smoke inhalation.

Since then, she had built her life and her scientific career with Dr. Tendari. He had shown her name to Benedict Noor, giving her a glowing reference, putting himself on the line for her. She had followed him out to the very edge of the solar system, where they would do their greatest work.

And now she was entirely alone, out in the middle of nowhere and looking down a hole into eternity.

CHAPTER 6

That evening Noor had planned to host a welcome-back pep rally after the whole crew was revived, but now it was a different sort of strategy session. Time to make lemons out of lemonade, make an omelet out of a few broken eggs.

He grimaced at his parade of thoughts. Time to get a few new clichés.

They gathered in the mess hall because he insisted, but Noor quickly got the sense that no one wanted to be there. Cammie Skoura stood with her back to the wall, as if trying to withdraw into a singularity; she was wan and wrung out, her eyes red. But if she wasn't here, he knew she would just be sulking in her quarters, so it was good to get her out among people.

Arkourian stood in professional problem-solving mode, but she let Noor take the lead. He had tasked her with rerunning their mission plan to map out how best to complete the Nether objectives with a drastically reduced crew. She was good at that. Warren Drake talked with her, but she didn't seem to be in the mood for conversation.

Glinda Roybal, the loud lead engineer, was teasing her companion, Pedro Ashe, but the young man paid little attention to her. His ear implants played immersive music unless his AI alerted him to something more important around him, and Glinda's comments were not considered important.

Ashe had thin arms and legs, and his spine showed a

pronounced curvature. Under Earth's gravity, he would have been confined to a wheelchair, but he had excelled at the NOOR lunar base and then out in the asteroid hub. Aboard the *Lethe*, he was in his element.

Dr. Stelland was the last to enter, carrying a bowl of fresh produce he had harvested from the greenhouse dome—strawberries, tomatoes, even a sliced zucchini. The garden served as a counterpoint to the ship's packaged meals, which were dense in nutrients but lacking in flavor. Tonight no one seemed interested in the treats.

Noor decided to get this over with, to encourage the troops. He clapped his hands for their attention. "Thank you all for coming, even on this difficult day. Now, I've studied the greatest explorers throughout history, and I can tell you that no human triumph is achieved without setbacks. For this mission, I picked the very best team with the most knowledgeable experts, and you're among them. So, even though half my team is gone, we'll get this done."

"Fucking A!" said Glinda, as if she expected everyone else to cheer with her.

Noor paced, now that he had their attention. "I think of the first people to venture into hazardous, unknown environments, leading to great triumphs—and you're among good company." Noor closed his eyes in reverence. "Marco Polo, Ferdinand Magellan, James Cook, Zheng He, Christopher Columbus—I don't care that he's fallen out of favor; he still *did* it. Or in the modern era, Neil Armstrong, Chuck Yeager, Yuri Gagarin, Ernesto Bosco on Mars—"

Arkourian muttered, "All men."

"Valentina Tereshkova," Noor added.

Warren quipped, "And the first person to go over Niagara Falls in a barrel was a woman."

Noor was on a roll. "We could name many more. Personally, I'm fascinated by the early Antarctic explorers. Such fortitude! Everyone has heard of the South Pole expedition of Robert Falcon Scott, which ended in disaster. I'm more intrigued by the lesser-known Miskatonic expedition in 1930, led by William Dyer. And the bravest man among them, Archibald Benton." He smiled, lost in his own reverie. "Such incredible stories."

"I've never heard of him," Cammie said in a quiet voice, still leaning against the wall.

Noor was pleased that she had at least said something. "That's because Benton never returned. Only a fragment of a manuscript—"

"Benedict, you are not inspiring us with reminders of epic failures," Arkourian scolded. "This mission has already suffered significant setbacks, and we haven't even reached the wormhole yet."

Noor took a moment to reorient himself. "Yes, Karla—of course, you're correct. To the matter at hand. Dr. Stelland, you spent the afternoon running a deep AI analysis of the cryopods. Any report on the malfunctions? How soon can you have them fixed?"

"Fixed?" The doctor seemed surprised by the question. "Taking all ten of the cryopod monitors as a system, including Tendari's pod and the monkey pod, I created a large data set. The AI deep dive finds faint anomalies in our quantum circuits, an odd undertone in the monitoring systems, like a malignant carrier wave. The glitch is prevalent in all nine remaining units, an altered subroutine in the cerebral monitoring and tandem life-support circuitry."

Glinda furrowed her brow, thinking like an engineer. "Like a virus? So how do we wake them up?"

"In order to fix the problem, we'd have to clear the systems, purge the pod subroutines, and reboot each unit from scratch."

Paying full attention now, Ashe asked, "But won't that kill the nine people left in hibernation?"

The doctor nodded slowly. "Yes, that is likely. We don't have secondary facilities here to support the pod occupants through the reboot process. We might be successful if we do it down at the NOOR asteroid hub though."

Glinda looked around in disbelief. "Whoa! You mean they just have to stay frozen for five and a half more years?"

The side of Stelland's face twitched, making the star tattoo flicker. "If we attempt to revive them here, most will die."

Noor decided to focus on a more positive comment. "In the meantime, you're saying we can reboot and reset the seven empty cryopods—the ones that we use. It's a start."

"And how will that help?" Arkourian asked.

He frowned at her as if the answer were obvious. "We'll need cryopods for our own journey home after six months. Just thinking ahead."

The other crewmembers shifted uneasily, absorbing the news. Before the gloom could get heavier, Noor continued his planned speech. "Fortunately, with the hibernation scheduling, I kept one primary specialist awake each shift. Yes, we lost Dr. Tendari, but Dr. Skoura—Cammie, I mean—is capable of doing wormhole research and theory. Congratulations, young lady. You're our lead astrophysicist now."

Cammie looked as if he had twisted a knife in her chest, and Arkourian scowled at him, exasperated. Noor sensed the awkward silence, but he didn't understand what he had said wrong.

Eventually, Cammie muttered, "I'll do my best. If I need help, I can always transmit a message back to other astrophysicists on Earth and get their advice. Dr. Tendari had many respected colleagues in the field."

"That'll take four weeks," Ashe said. "Two weeks for a signal to get to Earth, two weeks for an answer to come back."

"Won't be much of a snappy conversation," Glinda said with a snort.

"I will send regular briefing reports, but we have to keep in mind that we are effectively on our own up here," Noor said. He meant for them to pull together, to meet the great challenge, but they didn't seem to take the comment that way.

CHAPTER 7

After another day of hiding and grieving, Cammie rubbed her face with a damp cloth, then changed into a fresh ship uniform so she didn't look like a rumpled rag. She didn't really want company, but she forced herself to go to the greenhouse module, which she always found peaceful.

Once through the hatch into the segmented dome, she could smell the mist in the air, the heady loam of fertilized soil. The Sun was much too far away to help the plants, but banks of artificial solar lights shone down like a bright summer day.

The garden thrived in the controlled environment—compact rows of tomatoes, peppers, legumes, potatoes, carrots, even an unruly squash vine, all fertilized with recycled human waste and mulched vegetation, supplemented by chemicals. Back home, Cammie had always looked to the stars, not down in the soil; no one in her family had ever planted a garden, not even a bed of petunias.

She closed her eyes and inhaled the verdant aroma.

"I'm very sorry for your loss." The voice was more assertive than warm. "There was truly nothing I could have done." Kem Stelland bent over a line of bean plants and continued picking, dropping the beans into a woven polymer sack. "Apologies and explanations don't change anything, but it needs to be said."

Though words caught in her throat, she managed to say, "It's not your fault." She knew that if she had not insisted that Dr. Tendari be revived first, then someone else's cryopod would have malfunctioned, and Tendari would still be frozen in a half-alive, half-dead state. Schrödinger's cat. But now she *knew* her mentor was dead, and that was far worse.

Stelland handed her another mesh sack, like a peace offering. "You can pick the tomatoes. We'll eat them in the mess hall tonight." He paused with a sudden realization. "Oh—do you want to be alone here?"

"Yes, I want to be alone," Cammie admitted even as she took the sack from him. "But I'll help you anyway."

The healthy tomato plants held green globes, as well as some that had turned scarlet under the solar lamps. She plucked them, while Stelland harvested five bell peppers. He had planted the zucchini as an experiment from the *Lethe*'s seed bank, and now the broad-leaved vines took up an inordinate amount of space.

The doctor didn't talk as he worked beside her, and she appreciated that. His presence gave her human comfort, and staying busy kept her from the gravitational well of memories. She and Dr. Stelland often ate together in the mess hall, but separate, because he preferred his own thoughts and didn't ask about hers. Now, his quiet, undemanding company was what she needed.

When they had filled their sacks with the day's harvest, Stelland set some aside to give to the monkey, and gave her a selection of berries and vegetables to eat in her quarters so she wouldn't have to endure a group meal, not yet.

Just outside her stateroom, she saw that Pedro Ashe had left his door open, and she heard humming and intermittent singing inside. The young engineer sat in a gyroscopic chair that simulated a weightless environment, preoccupied with simulations projected in his augmented-reality goggles.

The travel sims were Ashe's passion, since his bone disease and atrophied muscles prevented him from partaking in adventure expeditions on Earth. Now, rocking back and forth in his chair, he simulated a rigorous mountain ascent while singing along to the music from his implants. Some of the spectacular scenery was projected on his wall as well.

Cammie backed away, not wanting to intrude, but Ashe's active AI monitor must have detected her presence. He stopped humming and tapped his temple to deactivate the virtual lenses. He looked at her, embarrassed. "I apologize if the music was bothering you. Sometimes I don't notice when I'm singing along."

"That's all right. I was thinking my own thoughts."

After an awkward pause, he added, "Sorry about your friend."

"Thanks." Ashe was a quiet and self-absorbed young man, though she didn't think he was also neurodivergent, or even borderline. But he was an excellent engineer—Benedict Noor did not hire mediocre employees.

He swiveled in the gyro chair to let her see more of the rugged ridge and blue sky he was experiencing. "Real work starts in a week, when we reach the wormhole." He glanced at the paused mountain-climbing simulation. "I wanted to get some exercise in the meantime."

Holding her sack of fresh produce from the greenhouse, she wanted to get back into her own quiet silence and leave Ashe to his, but the young engineer gave her an unexpected smile of invitation. "I've got an extra set of goggles. Do you want to join me? I usually hike alone, but this is the ascent of Capitol Peak in Colorado, over fourteen thousand feet high. I'm just about to go across the Knife Edge."

Cammie didn't know what to say. "I've . . . never climbed a mountain before. I've never done a lot of things."

"I *can't* do a lot of things, but this is a decent alternative." He reached under his sim deck, pulled out a second pair of AR goggles. "Even without a full haptic suit, it'll still be an experience. Have a look at some fresh air."

Though a part of her wanted to flee, she wrapped the goggles around her eyes, and Ashe did the same. As soon as the system connected and she blinked to clear the view, Cammie gasped at what she saw.

The whole sky was around her, and she saw herself on a steep, rugged pile of gray-white boulders. In the near distance rose a prominent majestic summit—Capitol Peak?—but right in front of her was a terrifying razor line of rock with sheer drop-offs on either side. She glanced down, dizzy, to see green meadows and beautiful mountain lakes far, far below.

"It's a thousand feet down to the basin," Ashe said. "But don't worry—you can't really fall."

His avatar stood next to her. She recognized his face, but instead of his thin and oddly bent arms and legs, Ashe wore climbing shorts, sturdy boots, and a short-sleeved shirt beneath a climber's backpack. Her own avatar was similarly clad. She flexed her fingers, saw climber's gloves.

"Now, you're just a participant, and you'll follow along with me while I head across." Ashe set off, moving up onto the Knife Edge. "I've done this four times already."

"Why would anyone want to do this more than once?"

The young man scrambled across the razor ridge, beckoning her to follow. Cammie's instinct was to straddle the sharp line and hold on to the granite for balance as she scooted along, but Ashe gripped the top edge with his hands and found footholds on the rough rock below. Swiftly, but carefully, he scuttled across the entire length, and Cammie's participatory avatar did the same.

Though terrifying, it was also breathtaking—and very vivid. She looked all around her, saw the open sky and numerous other peaks in the distance. She had never seen a landscape so breathtaking. It was Earth, the Rocky Mountains in Colorado—and it really existed—but even back home she had rarely left her apartment or office. She would get groceries, go to necessary appointments, but she never did any sightseeing. Cammie began to realize what she had missed.

When the two of them reached the far end of the Knife Edge, her heart was pounding. Ashe reached out a virtual hand to help her up. "Wasn't that fun?"

"I'm not sure how to answer that."

"The sims are the only way I can do things like this." He was clearly excited. "In my personal library, I've got whitewater kayaking simulations, and the Amazon jungle, even an Antarctic journey. You can see the glaciers and the famous mountains, and you don't even have to feel cold."

Cammie peeled off her goggles, flushed. "I've got a lot of prep work to do and observations to make. We're almost at the wormhole and . . . and it's only me now."

CHAPTER 8

A week later, when the *Lethe* finally arrived at the wormhole, Benedict Noor was overwhelmed with awe and wonder. He had already conquered many things, broken many records, but this was truly a *first* for the entire human race. Every cell in his body was smiling. It might even be enough to impress his sister, Margo, who had remained behind to manage all NOOR corporate operations.

The bridge internal imagers captured the moment, which he would later edit for appropriate historical footage—"one small step" and all that. The seven crewmembers had gathered on the observation bridge, and he could feel their excitement as well.

The wormhole was just a suggestion against the universe, an *absence* that was frightening in its indefinability—a smudge on the emptiness, as if a thumbprint had erased the background universe. In the vortex of oily, transcendent colors, the pinpricks of stars were bent into curves and whorls of light.

"Looks like a big sphincter," Glinda said.

Noor flinched in annoyance. He was tolerant of the engineer's loud humor, which often broke the ice like a sledgehammer, but she had no boundaries. "There are times when I'd prefer respectful silence, Glinda. This is one of them."

"So I should save my joke about the Nether orifice?"

Warren Drake propped his hands on his hips and studied the view. "I'm ready to pilot a flyby, boss—scout the vicinity."

"All in good time. We must do our due diligence and proceed with caution. After we have the station set up, you'll pilot the first automated probe."

Noor was also burning to explore the possibilities, right now, but his team had come this far, and he wanted every step done right, all the ribbons and bows tied up. He wasn't just planting NOOR's flag here. He would establish a significant outpost for six months, converting the big ship into a full research station by extending the modules they had carried with them.

And it was just a start.

While Pedro Ashe and Cammie Skoura absorbed the view, Arkourian remained at her station, preoccupied with long-range scans. "We can park right here, Benedict. It's a gravitationally neutral spot close enough to the wormhole for research purposes. Nether Station has position-keeping thrusters, but we won't need much right here."

"Didn't the old probes find a few asteroids in the vicinity? Cammie can use the telescopes and imagers to map them, in case we need the raw materials," Noor said, hoping to engage the quiet astrophysicist.

She looked startled for a moment, then nodded. "I have my standard telescopes down below, but once I have the full astronomy module, I can do a rough mapping from electromagnetic reflections and occultations of background stars. That will give us a reasonable picture."

"And we need some test flights," Warren suggested again. "Bring on the recon."

Noor crossed his arms over his chest. "The wormhole is our first priority, as soon as we deploy the station modules."

"Benedict the First," Arkourian said, with just a hint of sarcasm.

He smiled. That was why he'd kept her around for so many years. "Yes, Benedict the First."

Noor reveled in the moment, thinking of himself as an explorer. Not the richest, not the most powerful—he already had all that. Other achievement records could be broken, but if you were the first, you would forever be the *first.*

He intended to hold on to this high ground too. Other Earth space agencies would take forever to get their act together, and by then it would be too late. While the *Lethe* was en route, he had already initiated more construction at his asteroid hub, gambling that the wormhole would work as he envisioned. NOOR engineers were building additional modules to launch as soon as he sent initial reports from the wormhole. Eventually, he might even have outposts on those nearby asteroids in the Kuiper Belt, using local comets for water ice, air, and fuel.

Even better, once Warren successfully took the *Neil Armstrong* through the wormhole, later NOOR explorers could set up a beachhead on the other side and establish the first human settlement in the Alpha Centauri system.

First. First. First. No one could take that from him.

Warren said, "It's not much of a race if nobody else even has their shoes tied yet."

Noor smiled to himself. "The Earth politicians whined that I was going out of bounds—as they always do—but they'll be eager to exploit my discoveries. They can squawk all they want. No one has any legitimate claim out here."

"Safety regs exist for a reason," Arkourian said. She fancied herself as his conscience.

"Ambition and caution are in a constant tug-of-war. I'm not reckless, but I trust my engineers. I wouldn't have come along myself if I didn't believe in the mission. I put my money where my mouth is."

Glinda laughed. "And sometimes he puts his foot in his mouth."

Cammie stood by herself, obviously still wallowing in sadness about Tendari, even though this should have been her greatest career triumph.

Now that he thought of it, Noor wasn't quite sure what to do with Tendari's body. For now, the malfunctioning cryopod served as a morgue freezer, but he wasn't sure of the protocol for a crewmember who died during the mission. On the bed-and-breakfast deck, the other nine cryopods remained sealed, with life-support monitors still active and the inhabitants in deep hibernation. Or dead.

Peter Hamada, Noor's quiet and competent personal assistant, was sealed in one of the nine pods, possibly never to wake up. Now, if Noor had asked his PA, Hamada would surely have volunteered to test the hibernation revival systems. But if Hamada died as well from the strange programming glitch, then the rest of the waking crew might turn on him. A mutiny at the edge of the solar system! He couldn't risk that with so much potential in front of them.

He watched Cammie Skoura as she stared out at the intriguing enigma, transfixed. The Nether wormhole was hers to understand, and now he had to count on her.

Noor placed a hand on her shoulder in an awkward supportive gesture, but Cammie flinched, so he quickly withdrew. He'd had close calls with hypersensitive employees and their personal-space issues. "Sorry, Cammie. Do you have what you need? Tomorrow, Glinda and Pedro will deploy your astronomy module, and we'll start gathering data by the boatload."

Her brow furrowed, distracted. She was entirely clueless about how attractive she was, and that gave her an innocent charm. "I've been monitoring the data during our approach.

Some of it matches our existing theories, while other readings are outliers. I'll cross-reference competing models to see if I can align them." She looked away. "Dr. Tendari should be here as my sounding board."

"You'll do fine on your own." He tried to sound reassuring. "You've got the skills and the brainpower to solve this yourself. Once Warren flies the first probe through the wormhole, you can help me map a direct passage to Alpha Centauri." He hoped she would light up with the exciting possibilities, see what was really important. "And that's only a start. Once I set up a whole Galaxy-spanning transportation grid, we can go anywhere."

"We don't even know yet if it's a traversable wormhole," Cammie said. "A one-way Einstein-Rosen bridge is also theoretically possible. The probe could go through but never come back."

Leaning close to the windowport, Glinda breathed hard until her breath fogged the glass. She drew a squiggle in the mist. "If this is Grand Central Station in an intergalactic subway system, why would they put the Nether orifice out here in the middle of nowhere?"

CHAPTER 9

With the *Lethe* in a stable position, it was time to set up the base camp and command center. The first automated probe would be launched in two days, but Karla Arkourian kept a tight focus on her own duties. During her years in the military, she knew how to prioritize and perform her specific tasks.

Now, her job was to convert the *Lethe* into Nether Station, which would remain in position for six months.

The original ship, constructed out in the asteroid belt, was enormous, a luxury liner compared to the stripped-down, budget-crunched probes the International Space Agency had dispatched a decade earlier. During the five-year voyage, the *Lethe*'s awake crew had appreciated the elbow room, and now the station would be expanded even more. To his credit, Noor did not scrimp on things that mattered.

Arkourian met Glinda and Ashe in the engineering bay so they could suit up for their external work. "Are you both ready for EVAs? Do your exosuits still fit after the long trip out?"

"Hey, I exercise with resistance weights!" Glinda patted her abdomen, which was as solid as a tree trunk. "No winter fat here."

Ashe tapped his temple to switch off the implant music. He indicated his skinny frame. "Haven't gained an ounce. I'm ready to go outside and play."

"Outside to *work*," Arkourian said. "We have to deploy and

sync up the external modules, the astronomy module, and the expanded living quarters."

"Work, play. Tomato, to-*mah*-to," Glinda said. "I've been looking forward to a good outside run."

"I'll be at my station in the hangar bay and begin extending the external modules." Arkourian turned to leave as they pulled their exosuits from the lockers. "Contact me when you cycle through the airlock. We can get this done in a few hours."

"We know what to do," Glinda said with a snort. "Right, Jack?"

Ashe tapped his temple and immersed himself in music without responding to her comment.

Arkourian controlled her annoyance. "His name is Pedro. Don't be unprofessional."

"But what if I need to call him a Jack Ashe?"

"As I said, unprofessional."

"Okay, Mom, I'll behave. The two of us have twice as much work to do without the rest of our engineering crew, so we have to be efficient."

On her way out of the bay, Arkourian paused at the wall intercom. She had left Noor by himself to babysit the bridge, only because she knew this was a routine operation. "Benedict, is everything under control before these two go out the airlock?"

He just chuckled. "I am the captain of the ship, Karla. Of course everything is under control."

She imagined him lounging in his solo chair.

He added, knowing that the two engineers were with her, "I'll keep myself occupied. I found Mr. Ashe's wonderful library of hiking and exploration simulations. I have my own set of AR goggles, and I plan to build up my experience as an explorer."

Arkourian didn't know how to respond to that. Noor had pried into Ashe's private library?

She glanced over at the young engineer, who had paled. "My . . . simulations, sir?"

"I hope you don't mind," Noor said. "They look wonderful. Antarctica particularly calls to me."

"But they were my sims," Ashe said, holding his helmet in the crook of his arm.

"I have access to everyone's personal folders, you know. The *Lethe* is my ship."

Arkourian felt indignant on the young man's behalf, but Glinda snickered. "Looks like the boss found your porn stash, Jack."

"It's not—" Ashe snapped, then stopped himself. "It's all right, Mr. Noor. I hope you enjoy them." He placed his helmet on, cutting off further discussion, and went to wait for Glinda by the airlock.

Leaving the two engineers, Arkourian went to the hangar bay control room, which she had all to herself. She activated the monitor screens to get a full view of the *Lethe*. Beneath the vessel's core hung the large water reservoir, like a metal-hulled balloon that held enough water not only for their drinking and life-support needs but also to be converted into hydrogen, oxygen, and fuel for the recon ships. Another screen showed the exterior modules tucked against the *Lethe*'s hull like bullets in a bandolier.

She powered up the deployment systems one at a time. The great pistons and hydraulics began to extend, pushing out the first cylindrical module, the new astronomy complex. By the time the cylinder had locked in place, ready for the two engineers to connect the external systems, Glinda and Ashe had emerged from the airlock. They made their way over the hull to the first module.

Truly in his element, scrawny Ashe clambered along with

grace and ease, while the bulkier Glinda favored momentum over agility. Despite their banter over the helmet comms, the two worked well together. Over the next hour, they hooked up the astronomy lab's power couplings, while Arkourian deployed the new habitation module on the opposite side of the *Lethe.*

Over the comm, Glinda quipped, "Since half our crew is permanently stuck in cryopods, why bother with the next habitation module?"

"Lebensraum," Arkourian said.

Glinda absorbed that, then responded with, "*Bullscheisse.*"

"Take it up with Mr. Noor. I'm not writing off those nine cryopods just yet. There's a chance they could still be revived."

No sense looking for sorrow until it was necessary, she thought. Arkourian had led a dangerous life, yet she had outlived three husbands with relatively bland lives.

In her younger years as a fighter pilot, she had flown dozens of successful combat missions. In the Belarusian Incursion, she'd even crashed her ship and walked away—or actually, run away, hiding and ducking behind enemy lines. She had holed up in an abandoned barn, under fire. Though she had only a service pistol, she'd taken out all three members of the enemy search-and-kill team. She'd gotten medals for that.

Arkourian had married her first husband, Alan, when she was young, naïve, idealistic, and completely in love. They'd met while she was stationed at Ramstein Air Force Base, where almost daily she flew death-defying missions in Belarus. And then Alan was struck and killed by a passing car as he crossed the street.

She'd married her second husband, Wen, when she was more mature and less horny. She and Wen had much in common. Physically fit, they would run miles together . . . and then one day Wen dropped dead of a heart attack trying to keep up with her. Running in the zone, she'd kept going for more than a block before she realized he was no longer behind her . . .

Her third husband, Afo, was a midlevel manager at NOOR, and by then Arkourian had left military service for the private sector. She and Afo were a power couple, and she used her no-nonsense military leadership skills to work her way up in the company. As an executive, Afo opened many doors for her. And then he was diagnosed with pancreatic cancer, and he wasted away before her eyes. Never giving up, trying every treatment, he insisted he was going to beat the disease—up to his dying breath.

Even after those tragedies, Karla Arkourian never stopped mountain climbing, skydiving, or solo flying in low orbit. She took so many risks, and yet she survived while her husbands died. That gave her a "who gives a fuck" perspective regarding fate, and she decided to live her life however she wanted. Fate would take her, or ignore her, and there wasn't a damn thing she could do about it.

Benedict Noor had appointed her to manage the NOOR asteroid yards. He respected Arkourian because she had no aspirations to climb higher. She did an excellent job, and most importantly, she wasn't cowed by Noor. She spoke her mind, even occasionally talked him out of unwise decisions. He admired that, so long as she understood that he had the final say.

At Nether Station, her goal was to achieve the mission objectives. Period. And now she watched the next module as it was deployed. Mission accomplished.

CHAPTER 10

Lounging in his captain's chair on the bridge, Noor swiveled from side to side as he took in Arkourian's empty station, the communications deck, the observation wall. He was eager for the first automated probe to be dispatched the following day, which would prove everything he had banked on.

But setting up the station came first, even if it did take a tediously long time.

He watched Glinda and Ashe emerge from the engineering bay to perform their routine operational spacewalk. Meanwhile, Noor decided to occupy himself with something more interesting. He pulled out the interactive goggles and connected them.

He had been surprised to find Pedro Ashe's library of simulations, at first assuming they were just games, like Warren Drake's space-combat exercises, but as he scrolled through the delightful possibilities of adventure expeditions, Noor learned a new dimension to his junior engineer. Free-climbing El Capitan, racing dune buggies in the Sahara, scuba diving in the last remnants of the Great Barrier Reef.

The Antarctica simulation drew his attention most. He had always been fascinated by the white, cold emptiness, a raw landscape that had seen very few footprints, ever. Yes, that was the one he'd try first.

He wrapped the goggles around his face and secured them to the back of his smooth head, then scrolled through the available polar simulations until he activated one marked *Mount Erebus*. Antarctica landforms had the most spectacular names—not just Erebus but the Vinson Massif, Mount Terror, the Mountains of Madness. As the details loaded, he smiled with anticipation.

He knew of the great explorers of that cold final frontier, which was untouched until as recently as the twentieth century. The race to the South Pole! When Scott's Terra expedition in 1910 had fought its way to the bottom of the Earth, only to find that Amundsen had gotten there first. Scott and his defeated team had frozen and starved to death on the way back—and frankly, that was the only reason they were still remembered, for their failure.

Noor intended to do better than that.

As the simulation unfolded in front of his goggled eyes, he saw the endless white ice broken by black crags draped with ancient snow. Ahead rose the titanic peak of Mount Erebus, like a giant frozen in ice.

He set off at a swift pace. He glanced down to see that his avatar wore fur-lined boots with ice spikes. His gloves were inside thick mittens, and his parka was warm against the whipping wind. Noor didn't feel the cold in the sim, so his experience was not the same as what those other heroic explorers had endured, but he could use his imagination.

After the poignant tragedy of Robert Falcon Scott, Noor preferred the obscure Antarctic expedition funded by Miskatonic University to the Mountains of Madness. In that forgotten venture, most of the team had also been lost, but the fragmented and much discredited journal of William Dyer told of horrific and unbelievable experiences. Dyer's account was considered the ravings of a delusional man, and he had spent his last years in a lunatic asylum babbling about mind-bending horrors.

But Noor had dug for more information and bought access to the rarest, most confidential documents. He discovered letters from another member of the Miskatonic expedition, Archibald Benton, who seemed to be the bravest explorer among them. But Benton had vanished in the glacier-clad slopes of the Mountains of Madness, never to be seen again.

Despite his fascination, Noor had not traveled to the south polar regions himself, though he could have arranged a posh tour if he'd wanted to. To him, Antarctica's virginity had been lost. Too many others had been *first*. He did suggest to his sister, however, that NOOR might sponsor an exploration team to search the polar ice caps on Mars. It was just another dream on Noor's list of things to do . . .

Thinking of Benton, whose body was no doubt frozen forever somewhere in the southern ice cap, he asked aloud, "What would you think, Archie? Would you explore a place like the Martian poles?"

His lost imaginary hero didn't answer, of course. Nevertheless, Benedict Noor was smiling as he trudged off into the simulated ice field, engrossed in the artificial reality around him.

He glanced behind himself, thrilled to see his footprints in the snow. The only footprints. He turned and headed into the cold mountains.

Inside the *Lethe*'s observatory in the lower deck, Cammie used the basic telescopes and high-resolution imagers for a thorough initial survey of the area. Soon, after the astronomy module was deployed, she would have a far more extensive setup, but she could make a good start.

Here, so far from the Sun, all objects would be dark, so Cammie had to find them by indirect means, surfaces reflecting a glint of starlight like a tiny signal flare, or occultations when an object passed in front of a background star.

After days of close observations, she had confirmed the

vague results from the very first ISA probe cameras. She flagged at least twenty significant asteroids not far from the wormhole, but she would need more time and data before she could project accurate orbital paths.

She liked being alone in the *Lethe*'s lower observatory room, looking at the stars through various parts of the spectrum. The universe comforted her, because she knew it followed the rules of mathematics and physics.

In preparation for the following day's probe launch, she had taken countless static measurements of the wormhole, mapping out the gravitational and magnetic distortions as well as faint wisps of gas. The actual anomaly left very little mark on the surrounding fabric of spacetime.

Now she glimpsed two silvery figures moving outside the station, Glinda and Ashe doing their work to extend the additional modules. After today, Cammie would have all the capabilities she needed for their six-month stay. When the mission departed again, they would leave the modules behind in anticipation of a second NOOR expedition to establish a bigger base. Cammie didn't think she'd ever come back here though.

One of her monitors blinked with an alert, sounding a warning. Leaving the windowport, she hurried over to see what it was. Her automated deep scans from multiple instruments had tracked a new object—very close! She zoomed in and triangulated, drawing upon the different telescopes and radar imagers.

It was a space rock, only about three meters in diameter—but it was extremely close and tumbling directly toward the station. Her fingers skittered across the touchscreens, and she enlarged the detail. The meteoroid was so small that it hadn't been spotted until now. It drifted along, but at a significant enough velocity that it would cause severe damage if it struck.

Her projected orbital path showed a direct intersection with the *Lethe*, well within the error bars. The target was the *Lethe*'s large water reservoir beneath the station.

Her heart lurched. She needed to tell someone, but the observatory chamber was empty. Cammie drew one breath, centered herself, and hit the wall intercom. "Calling the bridge! Captain Arkourian, Mr. Noor, are you there? There's a meteoroid heading for the station. I think it's going to impact, but it'll be very close. We might be able to dodge. The rock is only the size of a . . ." She scrambled to think of an appropriate metaphor. "Of a car, but it'll cause real damage."

She waited. No one responded.

"Hello? This is an emergency!"

She ran through every possible scenario, every calculation, every engineering twist she could remember. There had to be something they could do.

Of course! It would be a near thing, but they didn't need a drastic fix. "Bridge! You have the station-keeping jets. Use the controls to nudge the *Lethe* to . . . to starboard. It only needs to be ten meters or so. We can do that."

She waited. The intercom remained silent.

"Please, it has to be now!"

But no one from the bridge answered.

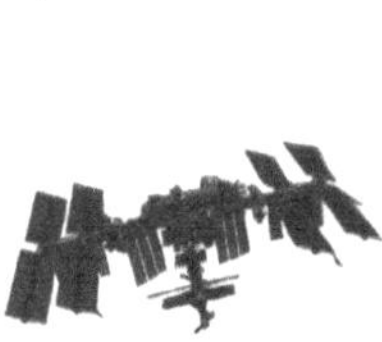

CHAPTER 11

As she watched the last of the two new hab modules lock into place, Arkourian checked in with the two engineers outside. "You've got about an hour of oxygen left. Pack up and come back in through the airlock."

"Can't we stay out and play a little longer, Mom?" Glinda said. "Pleeease?"

Warren Drake sauntered into the hangar bay control room, looking bored. "Hmmm, I'd like to go out and play, Captain. Let me take the *Lewis* out for a spin around the neighborhood—a recon before we dispatch the probe tomorrow."

"Not necessary," Arkourian said. He had asked her five times previously.

The pilot gave her a lopsided smile. "But *advisable.* I've been itching to fly something for five years."

"You were in hibernation most of that time. Content yourself with flying the probe vessel."

"Remote guiding, not flying. Not the same . . ."

Then Cammie's urgent warning came over the intercom, and Warren immediately went on high alert. He turned to Arkourian. "Those little rocks can be real bastards—I had enough close calls in the asteroid belt."

But Noor wasn't responding from the bridge.

"Dammit!" Arkourian said under her breath and sprinted out of the hangar bay. She didn't doubt Cammie's calculations, and if the intersection point was indeed that close, the station-keeping jets might be sufficient to nudge them out of the way. But every second of delay would make it harder and harder.

Thankfully, the lift was still open from when Warren had just arrived. Leaving him behind in the hangar bay, she shot up to the bridge deck. During the trip, she communicated with Glinda and Ashe over their suit comms. "Look out! There's a meteoroid coming for the station."

"Great," Glinda said.

"Keeping an eye out," Ashe replied.

When Arkourian reached the bridge deck, she saw Noor sitting oblivious in his captain's chair. He wore his AR goggles, deep in one of Ashe's simulations. He hadn't even heard Cammie's shouts over the intercom.

Ignoring him, she bounded to her station and accessed the full suite of *Lethe* controls, found the station-keeping jets. Cammie had also sent the projection of the tumbling rock and its anticipated impact point, which she kept refining as more and more accurate measurements came from the observatory chamber below. "Smart girl."

Arkourian activated the jets, but the *Lethe* had an enormous amount of inert mass. Even as the station started to move, she saw with sick certainty that it would never be enough and not in time. The rock kept closing in.

Noor peeled off his goggles and blinked. "What's happening?"

Placing her gloved hand above her faceplate, as if that would help her see better, Glinda squinted into the starry distance. "There's not enough light." She worked her way down the *Lethe*'s axis toward the large water reservoir. The expansive tank made one freaking big target.

Ashe had anchored himself on a strut tower and continued to scan the vicinity. "I still can't spot it. Is it getting close?"

Then the station-keeping jets fired up with a gush of vaporized exhaust. With a yelp, Glinda held on as the jolt rippled through the structure. "Whoa! Two meters different and that would have burned my ass!" She climbed farther down.

"I see the meteoroid now!" Ashe said. "It's coming alongside the *Lethe* like a slow-motion cannonball."

Glinda saw him pointing outward. Breathing hard, she tried to find a black rock against black space. The lights from the station itself illuminated the vicinity like a lighthouse in emptiness. Finally, she caught a glimpse of the uneven boulder slowly rolling right toward them.

The station jets kept thrusting, but it was like moving an oil tanker, and they had only a few minutes. The meteoroid approached at an angle, and Glinda caught her breath. It was going to be close. Maybe it would skim past.

She scrambled hand over hand down toward the water reservoir. The jets kept thrusting, and Glinda could see the *Lethe*'s angle changing, the big body moving. The meteoroid's projected angle of impact grew more oblique.

"Get ready for whatever happens, Jack," she called into the comm. She kept pushing herself. The rock was approaching until she could almost reach out and catch it—and as an engineer, she knew that wasn't an entirely stupid idea. Its velocity wasn't great, and Glinda was all muscle. Maybe with just the right nudge against the rock, she had enough mass to shift its trajectory. Momentum versus momentum.

It was close . . . so close.

She pushed off hard, hoping she could hit the car-sized rock like a billiard ball.

But she didn't close in time and missed it by less than a meter, and the rock cruised past. She drifted in free space, knowing she would have to use her suit jets to get back to the *Lethe.*

The rolling meteoroid struck and slid along the side of the water reservoir, a grazing blow that sliced open the hull like a surgeon's scalpel, cutting an enormous gash.

The rock caromed off, and as soon as the breach opened, the contained water spilled out like arterial blood—and Glinda was right in its path. Jets geysered around her as if she had just been hit with a sideways waterfall. The curtain of liquid bowled her farther from the station, and froze instantly around her like an armored fist.

"Dammit," she yelled into the comm. She couldn't see through her faceplate, which was covered with ice. She struggled to move, but she was in a thick cocoon. Her left arm was entirely frozen against her, but the right moved just enough that she could activate her suit controls.

The maneuvering jets didn't work—completely icelocked. Like a big snowball, she tumbled in the vacuum, completely helpless. "Whoa, I have no controls. My suit jets are not operational, and I can't see where the fuck I'm going."

"We're losing huge amounts of water!" Ashe yelled.

Cold fear twisted her guts. "Not my biggest concern right now, Jack." She had seen enough freak orbital accidents, sometimes caused by poor planning, other times by dumb bad luck. This sure as hell was bad luck.

She struggled, flicked the suit thrusters on and off, but nothing happened. She was in an icy straitjacket.

She checked her suit oxygen levels, saw that the tanks were reaching the red lines. "Great, now only twenty-five minutes left." Then she grew even more afraid. Out in space, nothing could be accomplished in only twenty-five minutes.

She heard overlapping shouts in her helmet comm: Arkourian trying to move internal containerized baffles in the reservoir to stop the water loss. Ashe kept calling to Glinda, making inane promises, but none of them sounded like solutions. She hoped she didn't drift along until she fell down into the wormhole. That would suck.

But she would run out of air long before that.

"Easy there. Just don't move," came a voice in the comm—Warren Drake's?

"Don't move?" She was breathing hard, on the verge of hyperventilating. She couldn't see anything through the ice covering her helmet. "How the hell can I move even if I wanted to?"

Her suit jerked as something grabbed her.

"Got you." Yes, it was Warren's voice. "This is like herding kittens."

Glinda felt herself being pulled along. "Somebody tell me what's happening," she demanded, although she wanted to giggle with relief.

"Thanks for the excuse to try out the *Lewis* recon craft, Glinda. Who else was going to fly an emergency rescue run?"

"I could kiss you," she said.

"Keep talking like that, and I'll drop you off right here," Warren teased.

"Just get me back inside the station. I, uh, don't have much air."

"I'll take you straight in through the hangar bay—with all those blobs of ice on your suit, you won't fit through the airlock. We'll get you defrosted and give you a warm cup of hot chocolate."

Glinda glanced at her tank levels. Eleven minutes remaining. She tried to calm herself and breathe slow, shallow breaths. "Don't take too long, okay?"

CHAPTER 12

While Glinda was brought back into the hangar bay and Warren locked the *Lewis* down, Noor was able to find humor in the situation as he observed from the screen on the bridge deck. After all, the engineer looked ridiculous with her exosuit and helmet encrusted with blocks of ice. She reminded him of a novelty cocktail ice cube.

But his humor was just to deflect his embarrassment that he'd been so involved in the Antarctica sim that he hadn't heard Cammie's urgent call to action. Now the station was damaged, and Karla Arkourian had barely begun to assess the extent of the water loss.

But after a lifetime of complex operations, Noor knew that shit just happened. His crew could fix it.

Pedro Ashe, still exosuited, had followed the recon craft into the hangar bay. Even before the pressurization finished, the young engineer was pounding with his gloved fists to break the ice loose from the suit connectors. Warren jumped out of the *Lewis* to assist Ashe, and moments later, Arkourian ran through the bulkhead door. They all worked together to hammer the ice away.

Glinda struggled in place, barely able to move.

Noor didn't know why they were so frantic, because the suit would have protected her. Still, he decided to go down to the hangar bay, for leadership and moral support, if nothing else.

By the time he arrived, Ashe had removed his own helmet

and tossed it aside. He and Warren wrestled with a thrashing and convulsing Glinda, struggling to unlock her helmet from the collar. Finally, they cracked the seal and wrenched it free.

"Hurry!" Arkourian yelled. "She's been out of air for four minutes!"

They pulled the helmet off, and Glinda heaved in huge, loud gulps of air. She rolled over, even though her suit was still cluttered with clumps of ice. She got to her hands and knees and just kept breathing like a bellows, and then she vomited on the deck. For once, she had no sarcastic comment.

"Looks like we got to you just in time," Noor said. "Good work, Warren. Another hotshot rescue for your résumé."

The pilot looked pale and shaken. "Thanks, boss."

Arkourian turned to Noor, and he could see the effort it took for her to control her temper. He began to realize just how grave an error he had made.

Arkourian took several long, slow breaths before she spoke. "Preliminary estimate is that we've lost two-thirds of our water supply. I containerized some of the chambers, but the breach in the hull extends across multiple blocks."

"Bad news," he said.

Arkourian looked stricken. "Benedict, I don't think this is sinking in. We needed that water for hydrogen, oxygen, and propulsion fuel. Nether Station is supposed to stay here for six months. We need to drink and breathe. We need to fuel our spacecraft, or we can't perform any of our mission. This changes our situation significantly."

Ashe laboriously stripped his scrawny body out of his exosuit, while Warren and Arkourian helped Glinda with hers.

"Then we'll have to find a source," he said, still not letting this feel like a disaster. "Down in the asteroid belt, we ransacked every rock in order to find inclusions of water ice, and for the most part we were able to sustain our corporate operations without shipping in water from Earth. Let's not panic until we've searched around for resources. We know there are at least a few dark bodies floating around here."

Arkourian looked skeptical, but Noor raised his chin and announced, "In the meantime, we have work to do, and we'd better stay on schedule. Every great exploration team suffers adversity. We just have to get through it."

He didn't want to think of the Robert Scott expedition . . .

"We came to investigate the Nether wormhole. We'll send out the first test probe tomorrow, on schedule, while we work to fix this other crisis."

CHAPTER 13

"Probe's on its way," Warren said with undisguised joy in his voice.

Benedict Noor had been waiting to hear those words for years, but now he remained uncharacteristically quiet in his captain's chair, rather than making a grand pronouncement. So many questions to be answered, so many incredible possibilities—and the loss of two-thirds of their water reservoir certainly put a damper on his exploration plans . . . and even the team's survival.

Right now, though, this was most important. All problems could be solved.

"Off to the Nether regions." Glinda laughed at her own joke.

Oh, what the hell—he would make a speech. "We're at a turning point, and this could go many different ways. We have to be open, imaginative, and flexible with whatever the probe finds. This is our simplest, but most consequential, test mission. Nether could be a portal to another star system, or it could just be a dead end."

"A traversable wormhole," Cammie said. "If the probe returns, then that shifts all the theoretical models and opens a lot more possibilities."

"A one-way wormhole would be very disappointing to me," Noor said. He imagined, in the long run, he would be able to find pioneers desperate enough to take even a one-way trip, with supplies and colony modules, who would hope to establish a human foothold in another star system, even if it might take decades or centuries before anyone discovered another way to get home. But that would not be his preferred outcome for the Nether mission.

At the piloting station, Warren concentrated on his virtual joysticks as well as his analog and manual controls. "I've got this."

Everyone was hushed, excited. Glinda, the doctor, and Cammie stood at the observation wall, staring out into the emptiness. Arkourian and Ashe both monitored systems at their bridge stations. The probe's carefully plotted course was projected on the main screen.

"The old ISA probe made it through," Noor said, trying to quell the butterflies in his stomach. "The flaw in the original mission was that the probe couldn't turn around and return."

"Nobody knew where it was going, so they couldn't plan for anything," Cammie said, sounding defensive. "And the signal died after a few days."

Why would she sound like that? Noor frowned, then recalled that she and Zachary Tendari had been part of that original international project. "No disrespect for your work back then, Cammie, but NOOR builds better tech. Our probe will last longer."

The experimental craft was a shielded pod two meters in length, studded with sensors and cameras, guided by automated propulsion systems and an AI pilot that would react and carry out the mission. The next two probes were larger, with life support to carry living specimens—first lab rats, then the lone rhesus monkey. Then Warren would go on the *Neil Armstrong*.

If this first one returned. Noor held his breath as the probe accelerated away from the station.

"Easy, Mr. Drake," Arkourian said, as if expecting him to show off.

"It's very easy. Kindergarten level in any simulator. I can make the probe do some barrel rolls or loops if you want, boss."

Noor frowned. "Just send it into the wormhole, and let's hope it comes back safely."

Warren noted the change in his voice. "Yes, sir."

As the probe arrowed toward the blank, swirling hole in space, Noor thought of that first primitive probe—mostly a waste of time and tech. So many additional diagnostics could have been added, and so much data could have been gathered once it arrived at Alpha Centauri. Instead, the International Space Agency had minimal ambitions and lackluster funding.

They watched on the imagers as Warren guided the probe to the event horizon. "Ready to go in, boss?"

"I've been ready for years, Warren. Go."

"Just like a barrel over Niagara Falls," the pilot muttered.

The probe crossed the wormhole's threshold.

And winked out.

Everyone held their breath. Warren looked down at his virtual joysticks. "My controls are dead. All contact with the probe lost."

Cammie spoke up, trying to sound reassuring. "That makes perfect sense. The probe is in a different kind of space now. Our signals wouldn't penetrate. And if it does pass through successfully, it'll be four light-years away. We won't hear anything."

Arkourian said, "Unless it comes back."

"A non-traversable wormhole would fit with two of Dr. Tendari's models," Cammie said. "We might not receive a response for four years."

"Let us hope your mentor was wrong," Noor said.

"The automated return systems won't let us down," Glinda

said. "I designed them myself, and Jack Ashe checked my work. Once it gets to the other end, the probe will start blasting out its 'We Are Here!' locator beacon, like those Whos from Dr. Seuss. It'll take quick images of the star system, then do a one-eighty and duck back into the wormhole."

"It's a hobbit probe," Ashe said quietly.

Noor smiled as he understood what the young engineer meant. "Ah. There and back again."

"Manage your expectations," Arkourian said. "We have no idea how long the passage both ways will take, from our perspective."

Glinda chuckled. "Worst case, in four and a half years, we'll get a bleep from Alpha Centauri. I'll make the popcorn while we wait."

"Wormhole dynamics are complex," Cammie explained, sounding shy but serious. "It's a shortcut underneath spacetime, and what we understand about *time* might be completely different. Even if the wormhole directly connects point A and point B, and even if it can penetrate the wormhole from the other side, the trip might take a million years from the probe's internal frame of reference."

"We can ask the rats when they go through," Noor said.

"I am growing sixteen specimens from the stored embryos right now," said Dr. Stelland. "They will be ready when it comes time for the second probe." His voice was flat and emotionless, as usual.

The first five minutes were interminable. Noor got up from his captain's chair and paced around the bridge, anxious, although even the most optimistic scenario required more time than this. "We could play cards," he mumbled.

Glinda said, "Jack Ashe always cheats."

The young engineer sat in his support chair, immersed in

music from his implants, intentionally deaf to his partner's comments. Noor didn't blame him.

"We're not waiting four years," Warren said.

As more minutes passed, Noor felt the burden of everything he had strived for, the billions of dollars he had spent to get them to this point, the time and sacrifices. If the probe didn't come back, if the Nether wormhole was just a one-way shaft, then his dreams and plans would go up in smoke. He despised wasting time.

"Any idea how long this is supposed to take, Cammie?" he asked, though she had made her answer clear. She just shook her head.

Noor set his jaw and prepared to reset his priorities and parameters. Defeat depended on how victory was defined, and Benedict Noor could always write victory in his own way. He had been the first to lead an expedition up here, where no human being had ever gone. He and his team were the first to see the Nether wormhole, the first to watch a real probe go into the dimensional passage.

That gave him some satisfaction at least. Yes, even if the probe didn't return, the Nether mission was not a failure. Not a defeat. In fact, it was a boatload of victories, each one of them attributed directly to him. He would still be a heroic explorer.

Then, with a small flash of light, the probe reappeared.

Having anticipated a power drain or damage to the probe transmitter, Arkourian had increased the signal gain, and now the obnoxious bleeping signal blared out like a scream. But the rising cheers from the crew overwhelmed the rhythmic pattern of bleeps as Ashe reduced the volume on the comm station speakers. Tension and disappointment vanished like a wisp of vapor sucked out of the airlock.

Warren laughed out loud. "We made it! In and out, in and

out!" His virtual joysticks were active again. "Come on home, baby. Give me half an hour, boss, and I'll have it in the hangar bay."

Cammie looked both starry-eyed and intimidated, breathing so hard Noor worried she might hyperventilate. "A traversable wormhole! Now the probe data can help me prove or rewrite all the theories Dr. Tendari and I developed." Cammie's shoulders sagged. "It's not fair that Dr. Tendari isn't here."

"Neither are Einstein or Sir Isaac Newton," Noor said. "This is your time, and you'll shine." For some reason, he didn't think his comment had helped.

CHAPTER 14

With the success of the probe mission, Cammie wanted to hole up in the new astronomy module and bury herself in the data. The round-trip passageway through spacetime was no longer theoretical. Nether was a traversable wormhole.

But Benedict Noor insisted that every crewmember attend a celebration dinner, even with the brooding anxiety from the loss of their water reservoir. Social activity was the last thing Cammie wanted to do, but she had skipped the previous meal.

In the communal dining area, she heard Glinda laughing too loud, already on her second glass of champagne. Pedro Ashe sat alone against the wall, casually hanging on one of the support bars. His head bobbed to the rhythm of a bright tune playing inside his skull.

Noor acted like the victorious general in a scientific campaign. Cammie was the last one to arrive, and he poured her a glass of champagne and forced it on her. Rather than arguing, she accepted it and took a polite sip. This was likely the most expensive brand from Earth, but she couldn't tell the difference.

Karla Arkourian distributed heated food packs around the table so that everyone could feast on spiced noodles with mushroom balls. Dr. Stelland had brought sliced zucchinis and a large bowl of strawberries from the greenhouse.

Cammie was surprised to see that Glinda was holding the leash for the rhesus monkey, which had been let out of its cage.

The animal was calm, possibly sedated, and Glinda fed it scraps of vegetables.

Seemingly friendly, the monkey approached Cammie, though she had heard that such animals could be problematic. It extended its furry hand to her, and she hesitated but reached out to take it. Apparently satisfied with her response, the monkey went back to Glinda and accepted a piece of zucchini.

Stelland frowned. "Those vegetables are supposed to be for us, Ms. Roybal."

"Fluffers deserves fresh food too," Glinda said with a sniff. "Might as well keep him happy before you start doing your experiments."

Noor said dismissively, "The greenhouse produces more than enough to meet our needs, now that we only have seven crewmembers on duty."

That put a cloud over the conversation.

"We're going to need to limit water to the greenhouse dome," Arkourian cautioned. "And we'll have to start rationing until we can find a solution to the water reservoir."

Noor did not seem concerned. "Cammie can use her new telescopes to find us an iceberg or a comet." He raised his glass. "Tonight we celebrate the proof that the Nether wormhole can be an interstellar transportation system."

The others raised their glasses and dutifully cheered.

"And to our hotshot pilot, Warren Drake! He served so well as my personal pilot back home, but now he has more important challenges ahead of him. His greatest trip lies ahead."

Cammie was surprised. She had imagined Warren Drake to be some decorated military aviator. "You became our mission pilot because you're Mr. Noor's . . . chauffeur?"

Groans rippled around the mess hall. Warren let out a laugh full of false humility. "Yes, just the limo driver. That's all I am."

Glinda blurted out, "Go on, tell the kid about your asteroid rescue. I can't believe she hasn't heard about it—a nail-biter on all the newsfeeds. Don't you watch the newsfeeds?"

Cammie flushed. "My interest filters select for astronomical discoveries. That's about all I read. I don't care for politics or pop-culture stories."

Warren shrugged, not able to hide his smile. "Well, I was a pop-culture hero for a while. A heartthrob."

Noor clapped a hand on the pilot's shoulder. "I give you permission to brag, Warren. Impress our astrophysicist."

"But make it short." Glinda sat down and peeled the film off her meal pack. "So we can eat."

As Dr. Stelland arranged the salad and doled out the strawberries, Warren leaned back against the bulkhead, champagne in hand. "I was doing asteroid runs for NOOR mining stations around the belt. They're not much more than rocks with domes and life-support systems, very isolated outposts. Asteroids really aren't very close to each other, even in the heart of the belt."

Noor sniffed. "Apparently, they're closer than we'd like. With a million asteroids, and a one-in-a-million chance . . ."

Warren looked at Cammie, raised his eyebrows. "One station suffered a catastrophic collision. Wrong place, wrong time. Four people killed instantly, six more trapped in a secondary habitation bubble that was designed for two. They had only forty-eight hours of air, and they were out in the hind end of space."

Glinda interjected, "*We're* out in the hind end of space. That was more like the armpit of the asteroid belt."

"It was much too far away for an easy rescue. The bubble had a pair of cryopods, and the six survivors drew straws. Two people went into hibernation to leave more air for the remaining four, and that extended survival time to maybe seventy-two hours.

The last four each took sedatives from the module's pharma synthesizer to lower their metabolism. Experts at the NOOR asteroid hub privately said there was no chance they could last long enough for a ship to get there."

Warren flashed her a bright grin. He seemed to be trying to impress her. "Not with a formal rescue mission, for sure, but I was the best and fastest pilot. I gave Mr. Noor my pitch to take a swift scout ship with two spare seats. If I flew with no safety margin, trusted my skills and reactions, I could make it there barely in time to pick up two of the stranded miners."

Cammie was growing interested in the tale. "Only two? What about the others?"

The pilot's smile widened. "On the way out, I brought an extra supply of air for the last two. I ripped through the asteroid belt at top speed with my high-resolution sensor net deployed, my reactions on high alert. I dodged every obstacle—just like the simulation games I practiced."

He looked over at Arkourian, who gave him a grudging nod.

"I got to the mining station, off-loaded the cargo of air, took aboard two of the survivors, and raced to the nearest NOOR primary transfer station. They disembarked while I refueled the scout ship, and I turned around and raced right back. By the time I got there, the last two survivors had less than an hour of air left." He spread his hands, as if expecting applause. "Plenty of safety margin. From that point, we could retrieve the cryopods at our leisure. Everyone was saved." The pilot's expression grew more serious. "Afterward, I reviewed the probability mapping on the course I flew. My chances of success really weren't very high." He brightened again. "But I trust more in *me* than in calculations."

Cammie sat at the table as they all began to scoop up their noodles. "So, you're more than just a chauffeur."

"Maybe he can find a miracle solution to our water crisis," Arkourian said.

"As soon as you let me go out and look, Captain."

"I am running full scans of all the nearby objects," Cammie said, "now that the astronomy module is up and running." She looked at Warren, realizing she shouldn't pigeonhole him just because she'd had other bad experiences with people like him. She remembered her foolish first crush on a track star at her school, and she winced to think of how badly that had turned out . . .

"These mushroom balls are nasty," Glinda said. The monkey sat on the chair next to her, looking meaningfully at her food container. She tossed the mushroom ball, and Fluffers caught it in its mouth; then she let it lick the sauce from the bottom of the tray. The monkey turned its attention to the strawberries, and Glinda gave it one.

Noor seemed aloof and amused. "We are all explorers, even the monkey. Before Annie Taylor became the first person to go over Niagara Falls in a barrel, she sent a cat in a barrel first. It survived."

Glinda chuckled. "Fluffers is your version of a cat, Warren."

The pilot picked up the last strawberry from his plate and gave it to the monkey. "Then I guess I owe it another berry."

Noor popped a mushroom ball into his mouth, chewing loudly. "First, though, we'll send lab rats through and see how they respond."

"Sixteen rodent specimens will be ready in five days," Dr. Stelland said. "We have plenty more embryos in the med lab freezer. But only one monkey subject remaining." He took the leash from Glinda and gave a gentle tug. "This is not a pet. Time to go back to its cage."

The monkey hopped down from its chair and joined him. The doctor continued, "This primate is the closest analog to how humans will react to wormhole conditions. It will make great sacrifices for science and for NOOR. We may have to dissect the specimen once it returns from the trip."

Cammie felt queasy to hear the idea. "Is that really necessary?"

"Jerk," Glinda muttered. "We're all part of a big experiment around here."

"I'd object if you intend to dissect me after my run," Warren said.

On its way out, the monkey snatched another handful of strawberries from the bowl, and no one stopped it.

CHAPTER 15

Cammie had already used the *Lethe*'s external telescopes and high-resolution sensors to study the wormhole, but that had only whetted her appetite. Now, with the new observatory module and the results of the first probe, she could get serious.

She sorted through her astronomical instruments like a chef inspecting a pantry full of ingredients: optical imagers, infrared and ultraviolet detectors, energetic-particle scoops, and a range of spectrographs—every conceivable way to measure the distortion in space. The best part, though, was the large windowports that let her see outside with her own eyes. This place made the setup from the old ISA probe project look like a child's playset.

But the big module felt empty, with too much space to think. It had been designed for her and Dr. Tendari to work together alongside two technicians, both of whom remained frozen in the cryopods.

Still, Cammie had always insisted she did her best work alone.

Wearing warm friction slippers on the metal deck, she stared out at the obsidian-iridescent blur of the wormhole. From a purely scientific perspective, the module wall space might have been better used to hold more sensors, since the human eye was a woefully unreliable instrument. But Cammie felt the wormhole calling to her, throbbing, hinting. It made her *want* to understand it.

No theory ever survived actual engagement with the data. What if they were wrong, down to first principles?

A deep voice from the module hatch startled her. "If you want a closer look at the wormhole, all you have to do is ask. I'll fly you out there."

She spun so quickly that her momentum made her lose her balance in the low gravity. She grabbed a handhold, embarrassed, wondering how long Warren had been watching her stare out the window. "I . . . you took me by surprise."

"Quiet and subtle, that's me." The pilot showed his bright smile, and she thought he was trying too hard to impress her. His dark hair was cut to regulation length, though he still managed to look rakish. "Just came to see if you had luck finding any nearby asteroids with water ice. The wormhole might be sexy, but Captain Arkourian is a lot more uptight about our water supply."

Dr. Tendari had instructed her to make friends among the crew, but the pilot rubbed her the wrong way, making her remember too many past experiences with brash young men with fast cars and inappropriate humor. People like Warren always made her feel ashamed for excelling in school. Her clumsiness in social situations made her a prime target for teasing.

She quickly turned away to the much larger display screens, calling up diagrams of her scanning efforts. "I'm focused on the wormhole calculations, but I did use the instruments to do a detailed astronomical mapping." Talking was much easier than awkward silence.

The pilot leaned closer to look at the blips. "Are those our nearby asteroids? A lot more than I expected out here in empty space."

"Random distribution. This section of the Kuiper Belt could have had a dense knot of leftover material when the solar system formed." Cammie tapped the screen and called up the data set for one of the larger nearby objects. "This one—look at the spectra and the density."

"I'm looking, but you need to explain it."

She realized that all the information wasn't as obvious to everyone. "It's not a stony or a metal asteroid—definitely a comet, composed primarily of water ice. This dark line in the spectrum—that's the water molecule."

He brightened. "Now you're talking! Nobody's ever set foot on a comet before. We could fly an extraction mission, bring back enough to refill our water supply—once Glinda and Ashe fix the tank. Towing an iceberg from a comet should be easy-peasy." In his enthusiasm, he clapped her on the back. When she instinctively flinched, he backed away, embarrassed. "Sorry, I was just excited. You solved a crucial problem. Good work, Cammie!"

She wasn't sure how to respond to him. "It's what Mr. Noor told me to do."

Oddly, Warren's voice grew quieter, more serious. "I think you and I got off on the wrong foot. I really just meant to—"

Then something smashed into the windowport right in front of Cammie's face, and she let out a startled scream. She caught a glimpse of a dark, irregular object, a shape with a central core and angular extensions. Then the object slid down the window and drifted away into space.

She pressed her face against the glass, trying to see. Arms? Legs? It was gone too fast.

Warren grabbed her, which made her scream again. Entirely unafraid, he shouldered up to the window, peering down the length of the observatory module. "What the hell was that?" The station lights glowed into the empty darkness, but didn't illuminate enough. He shook his head. "Can't see it now, whatever it was."

"A piece of debris maybe?" Cammie forced herself to look through the observation window. "Another meteoroid?"

Warren gave her a skeptical look. "It was only for a second, but you know that was no damn rock."

She remembered the rough shape, the disjointed limbs, a rounded lump that might have been a . . . head? Cammie's voice was shaking. "We better report this to Mr. Noor."

Before she could turn to the wall comm, another of the bizarre *things* smashed into the windowport. And this time it stuck.

Warren yelped. "Holy shit!"

Cammie couldn't tear her gaze away. It was not possible.

Splayed against the window, as if someone had casually tossed a rag doll at the station, was a creature that looked utterly wrong. Its oval body reminded her of a maggot or a grub, from which extended bent crablike legs. Its back had a carapace, like from a giant beetle, and a round head with polished black eyes. It looked like a mutant cricket, or a cockroach.

An . . . alien.

Its external shell had cracked in the deep cold of space, and fluids had leaked out and flash frozen in the vacuum. One of the black insectile eyes had jagged, crazed lines, as if the brain inside the head shell had burst. The mouth was a collection of mandibles, or chewing mechanisms.

Cammie absorbed every detail in a horrified second as the cricket-like thing slid down the window, then dislodged and drifted away.

Warren scrambled around. "Damn, we didn't get any images! You're the scientist—what on Earth was that? An alien? A real honest-to-god alien?"

She didn't know how to answer, couldn't find words at first. "How would I know what an alien looks like? That's nothing I've ever . . ." She felt nauseated. The thing was put together *wrong*, evolved from nonterrestrial biology. "There's no such thing as aliens . . . but it certainly didn't look like anything from Earth to me." She turned around, disoriented. "And what was it doing out here?"

The station alarm rang, a red alert. Karla Arkourian's voice rattled through the wall comm. "All personnel! Report to the bridge immediately."

"Come on." Warren dashed through the connecting tube, with Cammie following him. "Maybe they know what it was."

On the observation bridge, Arkourian and Noor stood at the wide viewing wall. Glinda Roybal and Pedro Ashe had just arrived, and Glinda blurted out, "Holy balls!"

Two more insect-like figures were plastered against the broad window. As Cammie rushed onto the deck, one more of the creatures slammed against the transparent barrier. Its sticklike, jointed legs jittered with the impact, as if the thing still lived.

"Like bugs against a windshield," Warren said. Cammie realized that was exactly what she'd been thinking.

"Alien bugs," Ashe said.

"In all our mission meetings, we didn't plan for aliens," Noor said, as if it were a failure of management.

Within seconds, the creatures drifted away into space, leaving no mark on the wide windows. They waited ten minutes, but no more impacts occurred.

They all stood in awed and terrified silence. "Did we just fly through a cloud of space locusts?" Ashe asked.

Arkourian said, "We've never seen any direct evidence of aliens in all our exploration of the solar system. The Moon, Mars, the asteroid belt . . ."

Noor narrowed his eyes. "I would never suggest that we've seen or found everything out here. We came looking for mysteries."

"Better make sure there's no damage to the station," Glinda said. "No telling what harm those impacts might have caused."

"We can look when we go out to patch the water reservoir," Ashe pointed out.

Cammie couldn't get her head around what they had all just witnessed. At this point, when she gave her big news about finding a nearby comet and potential water source, it seemed anticlimactic.

Even though the creatures were gone, Noor stood laser focused. "More importantly, how are we going to retrieve one of those things to study?"

CHAPTER 16

After hundreds of EVAs in her career, the novelty had worn off for Glinda, but she never took the space environment for granted—that was how you ended up dead.

Before stepping into the main engineering airlock, she checked her glove seals, life-support pack, heater units, water bladder, and feeding tube with snack gel. She wore a snug high-capacity absorbent undergarment (a fancy term for diaper). Considering how long it took to suit up and strip down, she didn't want to be distracted by a call of nature.

Behind her, Ashe slithered into his exosuit. Somehow, with his bent spine and atrophied arms and legs, he managed to don the entire ensemble faster than she did. He secured his helmet. "Comm check, Glinda."

She locked her unit into place, toggled her helmet comm. "Don't be an Ashe, Jack."

"Comm systems functioning," Ashe replied.

She never managed to get a rise out of the kid, no matter how often she teased him. Damned annoying. They were both equally qualified in the *Lethe* systems, life support, recycling, structural repair, power systems, even plumbing, but Glinda was proudest of her acerbic sense of humor. Her parents had named her *Glinda*, after all.

Karla Arkourian's voice came in their headsets. "Do a

damage assessment to see if those bug things harmed any part of the station. You're our eyes on the scene."

Glinda and Ashe entered the airlock together and sealed the inner door. "We'll look for scratches and dents."

"More important, inspect and determine how to patch the water reservoir. I will schedule an extraction mission to the comet that Cammie just discovered. I won't sleep easy again until Nether Station is stable."

"Yes, Mom," Glinda said as the outer airlock cycled open to space.

Ashe tethered himself, then sprang out, moving like a spider. Glinda wasn't terribly graceful, but in microgravity in her exo-suit, she could almost be a ballerina. She just didn't want to turn into a snowball this time; that was an experience she hoped never to have again.

They separated, working their way along the external habitation module they had recently installed. "I'm going to be pissed off if some bug-eyed Martian cockroach wrecked something."

"All cockroaches are bug-eyed, by definition," Ashe pointed out. "And I highly doubt those aliens came from Mars."

"Jack Ashe," she muttered.

In addition to her sense of humor, Glinda was also proud of her tattooed engineering equations. Once, in college, she had written a thermodynamics equation on her wrist to cheat during an exam. After being caught and punished, she defiantly *tattooed* the equations on her arms, just to spite the tight-assed professor. She'd thought it was funny at the time, but the joke faded over the years, even though the tattoos didn't. So she'd gotten other tattoos as a diversion, and she liked to show them all off.

Now, tethered, she pulled her way along the hab module,

relieved to see no flaws, dents, or chips. "I guess the bugs bounced. Maybe they were just rubber toy aliens."

A minute later Ashe reported, "No apparent damage to the astronomy module either. I ran an external integrity test on the windowport where the impacts occurred, but the reinforced polymer held. Not even a scratch."

They joined forces again to inspect the observation bridge. From outside, Glinda felt like a window washer peering in on some business meeting. Benedict Noor stared out at her and cocked an eyebrow. Arkourian spared Glinda only a glance, then went back to work at her station. With a gloved hand, Glinda gave a dopey wave to the people inside.

After finishing the inspection of the *Lethe* and its satellite modules, she announced, "Nether Station is bugproof." Checking her reserve, she saw that the exosuit still had more than ninety minutes of air remaining. Plenty of time. "Now to the water reservoir, Jack. Let's see how bad it is—I brought my duct tape."

In their element, the two engineers easily worked their way down the length of the station to the bulky tank beneath the main core. The breach was open and ominous, and Glinda felt a shudder, remembering the ordeal she had gone through . . . blind, covered in ice, running out of air.

Ashe pulled himself down to poke around in the ragged, open wound. "It's bad. Be careful—don't cut your gloves. That's sharp metal."

"I'm not always a klutz," she muttered, forcing her breathing to slow. "This'll take more than duct tape to fix."

"*Lethe* has a stockpile of patch plates," Ashe said as he moved down the length of the gash. "And we both know how to apply them. We can make a serviceable patch in an afternoon."

She toggled the helmet comm. "Captain Arkourian, we

can have the tank fixed soon enough. How is Cammie's comet looking?"

"Even the best scopes in the observatory module can't give us a high-resolution image, but we know it contains water ice. And that's all I need to know. We will go prospecting soon."

Glinda looked at the wide breach on the reservoir tank, mentally mapping out where they would apply the repair plates. Ashe moved on to check the girders that connected the reservoir tank to the main station structure, climbing out of view. She measured and counted, mapping out the next stage. It sure would be nice if they had a whole engineering crew to help with the work, as expected.

Her partner suddenly called out in a voice strangled with surprise. "Glinda! I need your help."

Though she teased him, Glinda knew a serious situation when she heard it. She set herself in motion, pulling herself along the reservoir tank to the reinforced girders below. She looked through her faceplate, trying to find him.

Ashe had lowered himself into a junction of struts and support bars and now bent over something that was caught in the angles.

"It's one of them," he said.

Glinda was panting hard from the exertion as she pulled herself up to him. "One of what?"

Then she saw it.

An alien cockroach had been snagged in the girders, a frozen body that had drifted among the other insectile bodies. Now it hung there like a prize.

"Whoa, that's even uglier up close," she muttered, then spoke louder. "Mr. Noor, we found one of those bug-eyed aliens for you."

He sounded delighted in the comm. "What a serendipitous occurrence!"

"Being splattered by a swarm of space locusts—serendipity all right," Glinda replied.

Ashe gave a crisp report. "Captain Arkourian, establish containment protocols and inform Dr. Stelland that we have a specimen for him to study."

CHAPTER 17

Like every afternoon, Arkourian knew exactly where to find Warren Drake. He practically lived in the flight simulation chamber.

With sophisticated augmented reality and projection screens, the room didn't need to be large. The wall panel outside indicated that Warren was engaged in an intense simulation, but Arkourian used her override to enter. If she waited for him to take a break, it could be hours.

Warren sat strapped in his gyroscopic chair wearing a haptic suit and an unnecessary pilot's helmet—to get in the mood, she supposed. Filmgoggles over his eyes gave him full immersion into his space daredevil course, which was projected on the wall, 360 degrees.

The simulator images froze when she interrupted the routine. He had been racing at top speed through an astronomically improbable asteroid belt, where rocks flew at him like snowflakes in a blizzard. Though he continued to grip the cockpit controls, his shoulders sagged. He took a moment to pull himself out of his mental state, then peeled off his gloves and removed the filmgoggles to look at her. "Jealous of my high score, Captain?"

"I can beat your high score any day." She gestured to the frozen images on the wall. "You'll never fly through a target-rich asteroid field like that."

The drifting chair wobbled in response to his slightest

movements. "If I only prepare for realistic situations, I'll miss out on all the fun."

"It's not always about the fun. We've got a job to do." Her voice wasn't scolding, just stating a fact. She got along well with the pilot, saw much of herself in his brazen confidence. "But don't expect anything like that sim in real life—space battles and alien attacks and asteroid storms."

He called up a new program to project on the walls. "Never hurts to be overprepared." He cracked his knuckles. "That automated probe was like flying a model aircraft, and I want to be inside a real cockpit! When am I flying the comet recovery mission?"

She avoided the answer. "Glinda and Pedro are patching the damaged reservoir tank tomorrow. They had enough excitement just bringing in the dead alien."

He snorted as he rose from his chair, making it wobble in place. "Ha, and you made fun of my space-combat simulation. Alien ships don't seem so unlikely anymore, do they?"

"We'll launch the comet mission very shortly. As an added complication, Mr. Noor has insisted on joining the flight. He wants to be the first person to set foot on a comet." Her disapproval was plain in her voice. Furthermore, Arkourian had considered the situation and made up her mind, and she knew Warren wouldn't like what she was going to say next. "Therefore, I've decided that I will fly the first trip over. For safety reasons."

His expression darkened. "But I'm the best pilot."

"You're *one of* our best pilots," she said.

"Okay, I'm the youngest best pilot."

"And I'm the oldest, wisest, and most experienced pilot. You know this mission should be a piece of cake for either of us. You flew the automated probe, and now I'll fly over to the comet." She cut him off before he could show more frustration. "It's not a negotiation, Warren. I promise I'll let you scout the asteroids around the wormhole next. You'll have more than enough prospecting to do, and it's in your wheelhouse."

"Damn right." He enhanced the projected asteroid field on the walls and gave her a wry look. "All right, Captain, prove to me that *you* know what you're doing."

"I flew actual combat missions. You want me to fly through that silly rock storm?"

"No." He gave her a cocky smile. The simulator suddenly displayed even more rocks, then explosions of dust from multiple impacts, sparkles as the shards caught distant sunlight. "Let's make it even more interesting."

Now the field was filled with a dozen wedge-shaped armored vessels—fast alien fighter ships that fired blue lasers at the asteroids.

"This is ridiculous," Arkourian said.

"If you want to just concede defeat, then let me fly the comet mission."

She took his place in the gyroscopic seat. "Space battles and alien attacks . . ."

Warren leaned over her shoulder and whispered, "You never know what you might encounter on the edge of the solar system. We already know there are alien bugs out here. At Alpha Centauri, we could find an interstellar fleet of little green men out to steal Earth women."

"Or Earth studs," she said.

"Or cats, for all I know. It's not about the realism of the story. It's about reaction speed, flexible responses, and knowing the capabilities of your craft."

She donned a spare pair of filmgoggles, mentally preparing herself as she strapped in, gripped the controls, and sank down into the game.

Before long, her mind was back in some of her fastest, most difficult firefights over the Balkans. Yes, she was older now, but her reflexes had not slowed. That muscle memory was what she needed now . . .

At the end of the simulation, she peeled off the goggles. "I hope that proves my point."

Warren was laughing to himself. "You gave me a new score to beat, Captain. Not bad for an old lady."

She rose from the chair. "I prefer the term *skilled veteran*."

CHAPTER 18

Kem Stelland had never imagined an opportunity, or an obligation, like this. The surreal alien specimen waited for him inside the med lab's surgical chamber. The cockroach-like creature lay on the table—fascinating, horrifying, and so incredibly different from any terrestrial specimen that he didn't know where to start.

Before Glinda and Ashe had brought the thing aboard, Stelland insisted that they wrap the body in a protective envelope while it was still frozen. From the engineering bay, Arkourian had cycled a tarpaulin of clinging polymer through the airlock, and the two engineers had sealed it around the specimen before bringing it into the med lab's isolation room.

The cadaver had spent twelve hours slowly coming to room temperature. In the meantime, Stelland made his initial observations from outside the surgical chamber, using the room's measurement apparatus. He weighed the specimen and gathered basic parameters with penetrating imagery.

The creature's oval body was four feet, two inches long, with wing carapaces on its back, like a beetle or a grasshopper. It had four upper limbs, each of which had four digits and a thumb-like claw. Two muscular lower legs made the creature look more like a cricket than a cockroach, in his opinion.

While preparing for the physical inspection, Stelland input his measurements and sketched out notes, while mentally preparing for the actual procedure. Benedict Noor had asked for hourly updates, then pestered the doctor every ten minutes.

On the opposite side of the med lab, the rhesus monkey was in its cage, but intensely agitated. The animal scuttled from side to side, baring its teeth and grasping the bars, but it could not figure out the enclosure's complex lock. He went over to the cage, not sure how to console it, but he could not be distracted right now. "Calm down." He knew his bedside manner was no better with animals than it was with people. "Let me give you a treat."

Though it seemed a crime to give the prized strawberries to a lab specimen, Glinda Roybal had already spoiled the creature. Stelland offered it a fresh berry he had set aside as an incentive to behave.

Normally docile, the monkey snatched the strawberry out of his hand and lunged forward, striking its face against the cage bars. Stelland recoiled. "Enough of that!"

From now on, he decided to add sedatives to the food. Since this was their only primate specimen, he had to prevent it from harming itself.

Making pathetic whimpering sounds, the monkey grasped the cage bars, rattled the complicated latch, and glowered at the operating chamber that held the alien body.

Benedict Noor sauntered into the medical center, a mass of restless energy. "When are you going to start? Surely it's thawed by now."

Stelland checked the temperature inside the chamber and the thermocouple readings on the specimen itself. "It should be warm enough for basic pliability, sir." He sighed. "But . . . I'm not prepared to do an alien autopsy."

"Isn't science exciting, Doc? Be a biological explorer—be the first."

The doctor wrestled with his reservations. "You're certainly correct that nobody has had this experience before. I'll do my best, sir, and draw general conclusions."

Noor sniffed the air. "What's that smell? It's like someone farted into a rotten cabbage." He glanced over at the monkey cage, then looked elsewhere for the source.

The doctor realized that the lingering scent had been in the background as he worked. "I'm not certain what it is. The decontamination field is functioning inside the surgical chamber, and no vapors from the alien cadaver should be able to escape."

"I'll have Captain Arkourian bring in pine-scented air fresheners." Noor walked up to the transparent wall of the surgical chamber, where he would observe the autopsy. "Now let's have a look at that thing."

The doctor pulled on gloves, donned a protective suit and hood, and secured an air mask and goggles, then cycled into the operating chamber. Inside, he paused to stare at the wrapped alien on the table.

For the first step, he undid the polymer edges and rolled the tarpaulin back to expose the specimen. Looking at the strange, inhuman face, Stelland fought down a wave of revulsion, reminding himself he must be clinical.

The large black eyes were impenetrable hemispheres, like a locust's. The oddly fleshy lips covering its mandibles and mouth looked biologically *wrong*.

He pulled the tarp farther back, saw the thin jointed forearms, claws that looked like skeletal fingers, a segmented abdominal plate.

The doctor spoke his observations into the voice pickup, like a coroner dictating an autopsy report on an old crime program, but Noor interrupted him. "Let's call the specimen Jiminy—for the historical record."

Jarred by the humor, Stelland paused to gather his thoughts before he turned back to the cadaver. A chill rushed down his spine as he made a sudden, obvious observation. "This specimen is wearing some sort of garment."

Covering the abdominal plate was a conforming film that sealed against the segmented limbs, like gaskets. A ring surrounded the thorax, some kind of coupling. Had this creature been wearing a helmet?

Stelland remained silent for so long that Noor prodded him for further details, but the doctor wasn't sure how to put his thoughts into words. He poked with his gloved fingers.

Just above the joints of the thick lower legs, a band wrapped around the body, tucked under the outer wing carapaces. The band, or strap, had small pouches and pockets, thin rods, and a burned-out device of some kind.

A toolbelt!

Stelland froze, not sure what to do.

"Now that's an interesting turn of events," Noor said. "Space crickets wearing clothes and toolbelts. Where did it come from?"

"Maybe these creatures originated from the other side of the wormhole?" Stelland suggested. "Alpha Centauri?"

The words sounded absurd as soon as he uttered them. The very idea of aliens—much less a group of them floating around in empty space—seemed impossible. And yet he had one right here on his examining table.

Stelland manually inspected the specimen, poking and prodding. He detached the toolbelt and set it aside, then bent the jointed limbs to check their flexibility. When he rolled the cadaver over, he noted that "Jiminy" was lightweight, as if porous inside.

He studied the chitinous wing coverings, gingerly lifting them to expose softer greenish tissue underneath. He looked up at Noor, who stared at him from the other side of the transparent barrier. "I'm reluctant to crack open the exoskeleton, sir. This specimen is extraordinarily valuable, and I dare not damage it."

"We need to find out what we can, Doc. Besides, a whole cloud of those things drifted past the station, so maybe they're not so rare out here."

Stelland tensed. "If we had multiple specimens, I would be more willing to run destructive tests, to cut and probe and fumble my way. At the moment, we can learn a great deal from direct observation. Let's take this in stages."

Knowing Noor was impatient, he played a sonogram imager over the alien body, seeing blurred masses of organs, gray shadows and dark tissues. "I can speculate on the creature's circulatory system, lungs, digestive tract, a heart . . . perhaps two hearts." After the sonogram, he used various cellular probes, x-ray, and magnetic-resonance imagers.

"Can you tell if Jiminy was intelligent?" Noor asked.

"It wore a partial environment suit and carried a toolbelt," Stelland pointed out. "Given the size of its eyes and the network of optic nerves, this specimen could see farther into both ends of the spectrum than human eyes. It has significant cranial capacity—not necessarily an indicator of intelligence, but it implies that this was a thinking creature."

"If it was a sophisticated thinking creature, then what was it doing out here?" Noor asked.

"Well, *we're* out here, sir."

"Good point."

After long consideration, the doctor finally decided to use a small laser scalpel. He cut into one of the thorax joints, breaking the membrane in order to get a fluid sample. As soon as the body integrity was breached, the air visibly rippled, as if strong fumes wafted up. Even behind his faceplate and breathing mask, Stelland was sure he smelled a nauseating stench.

Outside the chamber, Noor commented, "Ugh! Turn up the air recirculators."

Working swiftly and professionally, the doctor drew three sample vials of the alien bodily fluid, but he felt uneasy. "I'm not certain our filtration systems are adequate to handle this." He pulled the tarpaulin back up, wrapping the polymer around the corpse and sealing it as best he could. "I'm going to store the specimen in the morgue locker as a precaution."

He knew the insect-like cadaver had much more to offer science, but he was not ready to do a complete dissection and cellular analysis. "Maybe we should keep it preserved in storage until we return to Earth. NOOR facilities in the asteroid hub will have far better experts." Stelland swallowed and said again, "I have no training in this."

"That's a long time, Doc. But yes, I agree we should keep the body in storage until you feel ambitious enough to do a follow-up autopsy. Write up a report, and I'll transmit it in my next briefing to my personnel."

Relieved to be done, Stelland began gathering his surgical instruments, making up his mind to sterilize everything multiple times.

"I have to prepare for my field trip to the comet." Smelling the powerful stench where there should have been no smell at all, Noor retreated from the med center. "Keep it locked up tight. Who knows? After we send more probes through, we might find a whole civilization of cricket aliens—and they'll want their Jiminy back."

CHAPTER 19

In the hangar bay, Karla Arkourian prepared for the ice-extraction mission. Together she and Warren double-checked the *Lewis*'s systems; ran engine diagnostics; and verified the fuel reservoirs, oxygen tanks, the heavy equipment, and cutting lasers.

Warren rolled his shoulders, still not happy about being left behind, but he wasn't a sore loser. "Once you bring the water back from the comet, we'll be able to manufacture enough fuel so I can explore wherever I want to fly. No more excuses!"

"Yes, with our reservoir restored, we can proceed with the original mission plan," Arkourian said. "I know how much is riding on this." She also knew that the existence of the comet ice allowed Noor to expand his ambitious vision of a large transport station—or a fortress—here at the wormhole.

The lab rats would be ready for the next probe in a few days.

Glinda Roybal and Benedict Noor arrived early, wearing their exosuits with helmets tucked under their arms. Both looked eager.

Arkourian still didn't approve of him coming along. "We just finished the inspection, sir. *Lewis* is ready to go. Departure in half an hour."

"Then we can head out right now," Noor said, cocking his eyebrow. "We're not punching a time clock here. Why wait?"

"I'd rather keep to the plan, sir," Arkourian said.

Glinda wore a mock-serious expression. "I could use a few minutes to check Benedict's suit fastenings anyway. We wouldn't want an important man to go out into hard vacuum with his zipper down."

Noor gave her an impatient look. "I have been on twenty-seven exterior walks, Glinda. I'm not a rank amateur."

"Good to know." Nevertheless, the engineer busied herself like a master tailor, checking his cuff seals, his life-support pack, and his comm unit before handing him his helmet. "You passed the test."

Arkourian decided to try one more time to get through to him. "Considering our mission, sir, it makes more sense to bring Mr. Ashe instead of yourself. A second engineer to help extract blocks of ice would be more useful than—"

Noor cut her off. "Are you saying that I'm useless, Karla?"

"Not saying it out loud," she replied. "I would never suggest that you're useless. In fact, you've been extraordinarily useful with your money and your ambition, and you single-handedly created this mission. Without you, we wouldn't have reached the Nether wormhole at all." She opened the side hatch of the recon ship, ready to board. "But right now what I really need is another engineer to extract water from a comet."

"That's not happening, Karla." Noor was adamant. "As acting captain, I'm pulling rank. I am personally going to the comet."

"As I knew you would." She was already sure that when they landed on the frozen surface, Noor would emerge first and make some pompous speech: "One small step for a trillionaire, one giant leap for my company."

Arkourian boarded the *Lewis* with the other two behind her. The craft had a pilot seat, copilot seat, and rear jump seat for one passenger. She gestured inside. "Glinda, you're in the back."

The engineer's expression soured. "Have you seen how petite and delicate I am?"

"I've got the copilot seat," Noor said, as if stating the obvious. "Hence, by process of elimination . . ."

With a huff, Glinda worked her way into the cramped back.

Warren gave them a farewell wave. "Good luck. Call me to come rescue if anybody sprains an ankle."

"Given the comet's low gravity, I doubt anyone is going to sprain an ankle," Arkourian said.

From the back seat, Glinda spoke up. "I've been known to trip and fall even on a flat, smooth surface."

"Warren's already rescued you once," Noor said. "That's enough."

Arkourian sealed the hatches and powered up the engines. After the hangar bay doors opened, she used maneuvering thrusters to guide them out.

The *Lewis* dropped away from Nether Station and moved at steady speed. Warren would have launched out of the bay like a rock from a slingshot, but there was no emergency. In Arkourian's experience, most disasters were caused by stupid mistakes—and she wasn't stupid.

The wormhole loomed like a stain in space, iridescent and tantalizing, but Arkourian set course for a faint nearby glint, an object dimmer than most of the stars—the comet Cammie had identified.

The journey took more than an hour, and Glinda made wry comments, mainly to keep herself company. Benedict Noor offered only brief conversation as he peered through the windowports. He clasped his gloved hands on the knees of his exosuit, antsy.

The comet took shape ahead of them as an irregular spheroid, like a wave-smoothed rock washed up on a shore. Its pale surface scattered faint light from the stars. As the *Lewis* approached, Arkourian played the scanners across the rough primeval ice. Optical telescopes enlarged the terrain enough for her to discern bowls and canyons and cliffs. Strangely, the dark comet was brighter than expected in both the infrared and visible portions of the spectrum.

"It looks like a ghost," Noor said.

"The comet gives off more energy than it should." Arkourian double-checked the readings. "It's possible that a recent impact created additional thermal energy that hasn't entirely dissipated. Or it might be internal radioactive-isotope decay."

She pinpointed the most concentrated source of the glow, a bowl-shaped crater with a sheer cliff wall that remained in deep shadows. "That crater floor is a good landing area, and we can excavate blocks of ice from the walls and tow them back to the station."

"I leave the landing site to your discretion," Noor said.

Ahead, the irregular frozen surface was cloaked in dimness. Arkourian whispered, "This world has never seen daylight."

"It's pristine," Noor said. "All that ice reminds me of Antarctica before the first human set foot there. I suppose I get to name the new landforms? Maybe I'll name this crater in honor of Archibald Benton and his Miskatonic expedition."

"Do I get to have a Glinda crater?" the engineer asked from the back.

The comet had low enough gravity that landing would be a snap. Arkourian activated the recon ship's front beams to play bright light across the dusty, pockmarked surface.

As the *Lewis* swung around for a soft landing, the spotlights spilled across the sheer cliff walls to reveal immense pillars hewn out of the ice, an overhang, and a platform. She saw only a flicker as the beam passed, but it instantly caught her attention. The unexpected columns had to be sloughed-off sections of water ice, natural crystalline monoliths.

A sudden alert drew her attention back to the controls, warning of a large boulder beneath the ship. With quick reflexes, she jerked the craft sideways by a few meters to land on a safe, solid field.

But the others had not stopped staring out the windowports. Noor's mouth was open behind his faceplate. "What the hell is that?"

Glinda leaned forward. "That's not supposed to be here."

Arkourian finally settled the ship down, felt the landing pads get a good grip on the ice. She returned her attention to the front windowports, where the forward beams illuminated the blue-white cliffs of the comet.

What

The

Hell?

Her mouth went dry with dread and awe.

This was impossible.

Carved into the wall of the comet crater was a mammoth artificial structure—immense columns as tall as skyscrapers, weathered by countless years of exposure to cosmic rays. They were imposing and yet *ornate*. For what purpose? A sequence of broad frozen stairs rose from the crater floor, designed for giants, to reach a great open dais.

Arkourian could not tear her eyes away from the central figure there—the towering, *impossible* thing seated on a cyclopean throne made of primordial ice. The huge seat held a hideous, indescribable being, like an alien god gazing across the solar system. Ten meters tall and radiating an overwhelming dominance and majesty, the ice statue had a humanoid body, an immense torso, treelike arms and legs, and angular folded wings.

Its carved head and face were so abominable that Arkourian winced away in disgust—a smooth-headed horror with evil eyes and a lower face full of ropy tentacles, as if someone had grafted a mutant cuttlefish beneath the eyes. The statue emanated malevolence, colder than the heart of the frozen comet.

Noor was breathing hard inside his helmet, which echoed across the comm. "We aren't the first ones here." He turned to her, and through the faceplate, she could see his stricken yet intense expression. "Another race used the wormhole before us!"

CHAPTER 20

Alone in the station's observatory module, Cammie immersed herself in the wormhole data. Until now, she had devoted her time to straightforward astronomical mapping in search of a water source, but now that the *Lewis* had gone to the comet, she could work on the results from the probe flight.

The probe's external cameras had recorded confusing images of the actual journey through the dimensional tunnel, flares and swirls of colors, and then the imagers had gone briefly offline, as if stunned.

Once the craft passed through the wormhole, the next array of photos showed the new star field: a couplet of bright but far-off stars—Alpha Centauri A and B—and the much closer red dwarf, Proxima, a roiling crimson sphere. The probe's imagers weren't good enough to gather high-resolution pictures of the star system, and certainly not any planets, but that wasn't the goal of this test.

The probe had proved that Nether was truly a traversable wormhole. It could travel more than four light-years in seconds and return home safely, there and back again.

Later missions could map the destination system in greater detail, and Benedict Noor was a very methodical person. The next probe would carry lab rats, and if that went well, then the monkey. Then Warren Drake. And then, presumably, all of them.

She never forgot that Dr. Tendari should have been here, hovering, always close, pushing Cammie to do her best work . . .

She noticed another detail. Since the red dwarf was so close, it meant that Nether's terminus was much closer to the inner star system than the Earth end, which was far up in the Kuiper Belt. Benedict Noor would consider that a good thing for his plans. If interstellar travelers needed to undergo *another* yearslong journey to get to new planets on the other side of the wormhole, then it would not be a very efficient transportation system.

But Cammie was most interested in the physics of the wormhole itself, not the faraway stars and planets. When she was young, before she even met Dr. Tendari, she'd read about Einstein-Rosen bridges, Stephen Hawking, Kip Thorne, the possibility of mysterious conduits through spacetime. And now she was here.

She called up the probe records in the astronomy module, trying to visualize the journey itself. According to the internal chronometer, the round-trip journey had lasted nine minutes of subjective time—a straightforward answer, she thought, but that was a mechanical measurement. In distorted space, spinning through a gap in the fabric of the universe, how would a human *perceive* those nine minutes? Might it stretch into an infinity of dementia, or pass in a stunned flicker of an instant?

The sensors had measured gravitational stresses and electromagnetic radiation bathing the outer hull. She found the numbers interesting, but she couldn't draw any extensive conclusions with so many outlying data points. The probe had encountered numerous flares and gaps that did not correspond with the rest of the readings.

Maybe the sensors simply couldn't take adequate measurements inside altered spacetime. She compared the probe results to predictions from competing models of wormhole dynamics.

It was the first actual test of so many foundational mathematical theories, from Einstein to Wheeler, Schwarzschild to Thorne.

Cammie realized that this—now—was what she had strived for all her life. She imagined Tendari's voice in her head. "You are the best student I ever had, Cammie, the best and most beautiful astrophysicist—and you will far surpass me. Find the answers and unlock the universe. You can do it."

The thought brought a smile to her face, and she turned to the probe data with greater vigor. She compared the results with Tendari's initial models, as well as three alternative theories, and then her own modifications. Cammie's model turned out to be closest to the actual data.

She would take the models together and refine her mathematics until she had the right answer based on empirical evidence. At last, wormholes would be *understood.* She wanted to get it right before Noor sent a report back down to Earth for other astrophysicists to study.

It intimidated her to realize that she was shaping scientific history here.

Wanting to get everything right, she decided to get a hands-on look at the probe in the hangar bay. Normally, the data itself was all she needed, but now she felt a strange need to actually *look* at the craft, even touch it—not for any scientific reason, since she was not an engineer, but she wanted to be in contact with something that had made the incredible journey.

In the bay, Pedro Ashe was bent over the probe, running materials tests. He flitted from one panel to another, applying stress-test pads, connecting leads to the information grids as he hummed along to the music from his implants.

Startled, he snapped his head around to look at her, but she held up her hands. "Sorry! I've been running wormhole calculations, and I . . . I just wanted to see the probe."

He gestured to the vessel. "Be my guest."

Cammie stepped closer, musing, "I wonder what it was like. Did you find any damage or stress in the probe materials?"

"Exactly what I was looking for right now." Ashe removed another panel. "I see no crystallization of the metal or polymer components, no stress fractures, no damage to the circuits."

That was interesting, and heartening. "So no physical effects from the wormhole passage?"

Ashe disconnected the leads, logged the readings he had taken. "Just like new. We could use the same probe again, if we need to."

Cammie walked around the long, polished assembly. "When we return home, will we bring the original probe back so other scientists can study it?"

The young man blinked at her. "That's a long time from now. Who knows what Mr. Noor will decide?"

"When you get your results, we should transmit them so other astrophysicists can assess what we know. They must be eager to start work." Due to the two-week signal lag, though, nobody on Earth even knew that the *Lethe* had arrived at the wormhole . . . or that Dr. Tendari was dead.

Ashe was surprised by her comment. "You think he'll just hand all the data to outside scientists? Mr. Noor considers all our work to be a company trade secret. He's spent billions on this mission."

"But . . . this is pure science. These are major discoveries. The scientific community will build upon them and make more discoveries, expand our knowledge of the universe. For the benefit of everyone."

From the odd look he gave her, Cammie realized she was missing something vital again. She tried to process the cues, but she still didn't understand.

Ashe sounded pragmatic. "How would that profit Mr. Noor? Half of Earth already hates him, thinks he's a loose cannon." He shrugged again, which looked like a nervous tic. "But he usually succeeds while everyone else dithers. That's why I joined his team. He's betting that Nether Station will be a major anchor. His sister is running the company while he's gone, and the asteroid operations are already building follow-up ships for the follow-up mission. I'm sure he's itching to send the go signal."

Cammie blinked. "But we haven't even started our work here yet."

Ashe's eyebrows hooded over his dark eyes. "Doesn't mean he isn't thinking ahead. Glinda and I deployed a second habitation cylinder with more room than we could ever need, and you have your large laboratory module. Does this look like a quick-and-dirty base camp to you? Noor will leave large parts of the station behind and in place when the *Lethe* detaches to go back home."

"Oh . . . I thought those quarters were for the other ten crewmembers who were supposed to wake up from hibernation."

Ashe shook his head on his thin neck. "Count the cabins. That's a lot more space than even a full crew would need." With a slap of his palm, he sealed the access plate on the bottom of the probe and sprang off with his skinny legs toward the hangar bay's exit.

Cammie followed, confused and embarrassed, again sure she had missed something obvious.

"Mr. Noor is thinking long term." Ashe looked over his shoulder, and she followed him out into the corridor and then up a level. "Eventually, this will be a permanent base."

He cut through the bed-and-breakfast deck, and Cammie paused to see all the cryopods lined up in front of her. Seven empty ones, whose base programming had been reset now. Nine pods sealed and still technically functioning, holding frozen crewmembers neither alive nor dead. One pod was nothing more than a morgue freezer to hold her mentor's body.

Ashe passed through without any hesitation or concerns. "If the wormhole really is an expressway to Alpha Centauri, Mr. Noor intends to send those spare modules through so they can be reassembled on the other side and set up as a receiving station in the next star system. It's all pretty spectacular."

From the beginning, she had understood that the Nether mission was not purely for scientific research. Dr. Tendari had explained to her that science needed to accept strange bedfellows for the sake of acquiring knowledge.

"But . . . we're going home," she said, sounding uncertain.

"Eventually. A lot can happen in half a year." Ashe moved past the quiet cryopods, paying no attention to the suspended crewmembers. "But we were the first ones here. Nether Station is like a flag planted by an explorer. It's a citadel, holding the high ground for the first interstellar transportation system."

Cammie felt disappointed. "In other words, he'll be like a medieval robber baron controlling access to a riverway." She should have known this, should have asked more questions, but she'd been so enamored by the possibilities when Dr. Tendari invited her.

The young engineer gave her a wry smile. "It's Noor's wormhole." Seeing her obvious disappointment, he rapped his knuckles on the curved surface of the nearest cryopod as he walked by. "Besides, are you in a big hurry to spend years going back home in one of these? No thanks. I might just stay here."

CHAPTER 21

The three exosuited figures stood on the comet's surface, facing the impossible.

Benedict Noor could not tear his gaze away from the fantastic temple. The frozen structure was so huge he had to turn his helmet just to see the entirety of the architecture—the massive steps, the throne, the pillars, and the statue of the hideous titan. Behind the throne, the cliff of ice had been carved into twenty-meter-tall doors, blocked now, but suggesting an even greater structure inside the cometary ice. The barrier looked as if it had been frozen shut for millennia.

The helmet comms were oddly silent because all three of them remained speechless, their questions stifled by profound awe. Noor heard only a ringing in his ears and his own heavy breathing.

On the crater floor where they stood, the high cliff wall made the shadows deeper. The enormous ice columns towered against the cliff like frozen redwoods, where they supported an immense overhang with a façade designed to evoke majesty and fear. The frozen stairs that ascended to the throne platform were grimy with eons of cosmic dust and pitted with tiny impacts. Each riser was almost two meters high, built for massive beings.

The Olympian figure on its giant throne dominated the tableau. When Noor looked directly at it, his eyes kept slipping away, as if the horrific giant were coated with an eldritch substance that repelled his gaze, and the frozen eyes evoked a feeling of disgust. Its hands were enormous, its garments spiked with jagged edges.

When Noor shifted his attention away, his pulse began to slow, and his breathing felt less desperate.

"Are we getting all this on the cams?" His voice came startlingly loud over the comms. "Images preserved for history? I want everyone to know what we saw . . . that I was the first."

"I think I was the first to shit my exosuit," Glinda said.

"Our helmet cams record everything we see," Arkourian said.

Noor tried to control his instinctive reactions, feeding his curiosity and pushing down his horror and disbelief. "We're here—let's have a closer look." Taking the first steps forward, he walked across the ice toward the looming temple.

Glinda took long strides behind him. "Here's a question: On a low-gravity comet, why would they need giant stairs?"

No one suggested an answer. Arkourian made another chilling observation. "What if that thing on the throne is life sized?"

The first cornerstone step rose in front of them, taller than any human. Noor thought they might need ropes to climb, but Arkourian simply crouched and leaped. She easily cleared the top of the step and landed, knees bent. She caught her balance and turned to them. "I can pull you up if you like."

Glinda jumped, and Arkourian snagged her hand, pulling her onto the broad tread. Noor made the leap himself, then used his momentum to keep going up to the next step. The others followed, all of them finally ascending to the throne platform.

On the great dais, they stood together, dwarfed by the appallingly ugly figure. Some alien king or god? Noor's skin crawled with lizard-brain revulsion, and he turned the opposite direction to look across the comet. He realized that the throne faced the wormhole. The god-statue could stare at it from this perch.

Glinda's voice on the comm startled him. "Benedict, why don't you jump up and sit on his lap—like Santa in a shopping mall?"

He snapped back, "I'm losing patience with your sense of humor."

"Whoa! If there was ever a time we needed to lighten up a little . . ."

Noor turned to the towering doors behind the throne, intrigued by what might be inside the cliff. "Open sesame," he said.

Nothing happened.

"Try, 'Speak, friend, and enter,'" Glinda suggested.

Noor regarded the repugnant statue. "Friend? Could we ever be friends with *that*?" He moved to the frozen barricade. "These doors must be meters thick. If there's more to this temple, we aren't getting inside without thermal explosives or laser cutting tools."

Arkourian pointed out, "The *Lewis* has heavy excavation equipment for harvesting ice blocks. We could blast our way in—if necessary."

Glinda walked behind the throne and crossed to the far edge of the dais, where the enormous door was embedded in the cliffs. "Nah, that won't be necessary. A meteor already did it for us."

He and Arkourian joined her on the far side of the throne, where a small meteor had struck the cliff wall—maybe centuries in the past—cracking and melting a meter-wide hole at the bottom of the door.

Arkourian bent to shine her suit light into the gap. "We can fit inside. I see passages and chambers in there, a much larger complex." When Noor hesitated at the ominous opening,

Arkourian turned her faceplate toward him. "You're the one who always wants to go first."

The inky blackness gave him pause. "I've been known to make exceptions."

Arkourian ducked into the passage, playing her suit light in front of her. When she encountered no deadly booby traps, Noor followed her, with Glinda right behind him. Once they were away from the faint starlight, the interior shadows were even deeper and more suffocating, but their exosuit lamps provided enough illumination.

"Did anybody bring breadcrumbs so we can find our way back out?" Glinda asked.

"I'm dropping EM markers," Arkourian said as she forged ahead.

The tunnels were surprisingly ornate, with arches etched into the ice and support pillars like stakes rising to the low ceiling. Deeper inside the complex, they passed alcoves adorned with bulbous stalactites, niches with basins designed to hold offerings, or perhaps blood. *Like a tub in a slaughterhouse?* he wondered. The thought gave him a chill.

Corridors branched off at strange angles, as if the builders didn't understand perpendicular and parallel. In the low gravity, he felt a strange sense of disorientation.

Arkourian entered an expanded grotto and stopped so abruptly that Noor almost ran into her. "It's more of those cockroach things—a lot of them."

Inside the temple chamber, at least twenty insectile bodies lay scattered about. Faded, frozen fabric covered the hard carapaces like thick robes.

"Doc Stelland will have plenty to dissect now," Noor said.

Arkourian knelt to inspect the closest alien corpse. "These ones aren't wearing protective suits, like the other specimen was."

Glinda whistled in her helmet mic. "Does that mean this temple was pressurized? Maybe they all died when the impact breached the seal."

Arkourian said, "I won't extrapolate. Come closer, Glinda, and we'll take images of everything."

While his two companions rummaged among the alien bodies, Noor continued exploring, expecting to find a treasure vault or a breathtaking alien laboratory. He was more intrigued than frightened—this place had been dead and frozen for a very long time—and he wanted to see everything and know all the answers *now*. He was glad he hadn't let Arkourian convince him to stay behind on Nether Station.

On the near wall of the grotto, he found the entrance to an adjacent chamber, like a side chapel or contemplation room. The doorway was rectangular but skewed, as if it came from a plane of existence beyond normal.

While Glinda and Arkourian inventoried the cockroach bodies, he poked his head into the alcove, shining his suit light around. Instead of a basin to hold holy water or sacrificial blood, this mysterious niche held some kind of distorted window or mirror, not oval or rectangular but an irregular rhomboid. The frame held no reflective glass but rather a substance darker than obsidian, like a bottomless pit.

Curious, Noor turned his suit light directly on the blank surface, but no reflection returned. Instead, the dark plane drank the beam, as if mocking him. He peered at it from different angles, but nothing changed. Then as he watched, the mirror distorted and twisted, sending a sickly glimmer back at him. *For* him.

Unlike the giant tentacle-faced figure on its icy throne, which he couldn't bear to look at for more than a second, this strange black emptiness refused to let him tear his gaze away. Though it gave off no light, Noor felt a strange sensation *inside* his eyes. Not colors or hues . . . it was like singing or chanting.

Unable to stop himself, he leaned closer to the strange mirror. The singing turned into distant screams that crawled into his subconscious mind. He was the first to gaze into this tarry window of nothingness, but he felt no triumph in it. He was seeing what no other human had ever glimpsed.

But *should* any person see this?

The empty surface evoked unsettling thoughts and memories in him. It seemed to suck away his ambitions, his hopes, his confidence. Noor considered his own myriad accomplishments as a captain of industry, an innovative entrepreneur who had changed commerce in fundamental ways. And once he tamed the Nether wormhole, he would change space travel for all time. He had made fortunes, created and destroyed countless careers, altered the course of human history.

And yet . . .

The irregular obsidian mirror was like a twisted kaleidoscope filled with shattered nightmares. The surface sparkled and swirled and drank all hope from the air. It made his thoughts go in a stifling, dark direction, leaving only despair.

What if he—Benedict Noor, Benedict the First—was ultimately nothing? The builders of this temple, the worshippers of that fantastic god on the cold throne, had once been part of a great alien civilization, but now they were lost and completely forgotten. They didn't matter at all to the current universe.

What if that future awaited him?

Noor felt the dark tendrils of doubt work their way into his eyes. He heard and saw the chanting within his vision, and he felt a clear connection with the undead presence inside this frozen temple . . .

Noor thought of the Scott expedition to the South Pole, which was remembered now only for its spectacular failure and tragedy . . . or the Miskatonic mission and the curious observations from Archibald Benton's fragmented journal—now also forgotten, despite the explorers' tremendous achievements.

The black void in the mirror drew him in, showed him his own future, his utter lack of impact as an insignificant speck in the universe. In years, or centuries, he would be lost, forgotten, less than cosmic dust . . . Whatever the time frame, it *would* happen.

Noor lurched back out of the votive alcove. "I'm not nothing," he muttered, trying to sound defiant, and then realized that the comm channel was still open.

Glinda grabbed his arm, and he bit back a startled scream. "Hey, Benedict—are you all right? What happened?"

He shook his head inside the helmet and pulled himself away from her. "Nothing. I'm fine."

He tried to fill the fear with anger. He refused to be forgotten! He was Benedict the First—and he was *here*, even if these extinct aliens had disappeared into the cold of space.

Arkourian joined them, saw the dark alcove. "What was in there?"

"Nothing you need to see," he snapped, guiding them away. "Dangerous."

Trying not to appear to be fleeing, he strode out of the temple grotto and its alien corpses, away from the strange side chamber and the nightmare mirror. "We've done enough here."

He hurried down the long frozen passage, back the way they had come, desperate for the starry opening that led outside. "We'll send a team later when we have time. Today we need to get the comet ice for our reservoir. Priority one."

He was breathing fast and hard inside his helmet. Even

though his suit heaters were working, a deep chill penetrated his bones.

"I'm up for that," Glinda said.

As they exited the temple, hurrying to the enormous stairs, Noor felt no desire to look back. Even so, he felt the monstrous frozen god-figure staring at him.

CHAPTER 22

Extracting a mountain of cometary ice was a challenge, but at least it was a straightforward engineering problem. A *sane* problem—that was how Arkourian viewed it.

After the eerie alien temple, she embraced the task with fervor and relief to finish their primary mission. She wanted to be away from that monstrous statue and back at Nether Station as soon as possible. She could tell her companions felt the same, although Noor seemed even more shaken by something he had encountered, which made him giddy and almost manic. Arkourian didn't press him for details; there would be enough time for that later, if she decided she really wanted to know.

They boarded the *Lewis*, and Arkourian engaged the thrusters, blasting cold fog and ice chips from the jets. Glinda was too unsettled to make any wisecracks as they rose up from the frozen floor and away from the shadowed cliff.

Arkourian set course for the opposite side of the wide crater. Ice was ice, and from those steep walls they could extract the resources Nether Station needed. She eyeballed the rugged uplift ahead, where wide vertical fissures zigzagged through the cliff. Huge blue-white slabs hung in the low gravity like icebergs poised to calve off a glacier. One of those would do perfectly.

"The *Lewis* has industrial lasers that can slice cometary ice like butter," she said.

"Break it and take it," Glinda said.

"NOOR mining machinery is the best in the solar system, developed for our asteroid operations." Noor said it by rote, but with a ragged edge in his voice. "Cracking ice will be easier than extracting iron ore."

Arkourian hovered the recon vessel in front of the blue-white cliff and activated her sensor suite. Resonance scans played into the ancient ice, tracing cracks and identifying the weak points.

There, that one.

She highlighted the image on her main screen, where fissures and voids delineated a block of ice the size of a tall building. "See the fracture lines all around it? It's hanging on by a thread—and more than enough water for our purposes."

"Then let's knock it loose and grab it," Glinda said from the rear seat. "What's the plan? Laser cutting? Explosive charges?"

Using the new scan data, Arkourian ran different models, letting the AI assist with the best option. "I'll cut into the connecting ice with the laser; then, Glinda, you'll climb the wall and implant three charges." She touched the projection with her gloved finger. "Here, here, and here."

Glinda leaned forward from the back. "No offense, but we should have brought Jack Ashe. The scrawny kid could clamber into any of those fissures."

In the copilot seat, Noor stared at the rugged ice wall before them but offered no advice. Arkourian was glad for that. He had insisted on joining the mission, even if he served no purpose, but at least he wasn't getting in the way.

"Will our tow cables hold?" Arkourian asked. "We'll be pulling a mountain."

Glinda spoke up. "Yeah, but in low gravity and in open space. Trust the engineers."

Arkourian powered up the heavy mining laser and selected where to burn through the thickest ice. Once she had cleared the solid bridge, Glinda would exit the craft and work her way through a wide fissure into the ice wall. The resonance scan had already identified the three sweet spots to plant the explosive charges.

Glinda pretended to crack her knuckles, though the exosuit gloves were too thick. "I'm your demolitions expert . . . but part of me wants to lob charges inside that nasty temple instead."

"You will not damage it," Noor said. "That artifact needs further study."

"The temple shouldn't be here in the first place, and I'm still having trouble grasping the very idea of ancient aliens out here at Nether."

"Or anywhere," Glinda said.

"Nevertheless, they were here—and they may have done much of our work for us," Noor said. "Though I don't understand why they would have a religious *temple* out on a dark comet, if that's what it was."

Arkourian drove back her atavistic fears, then focused on the real mission. "Let's just get the ice, sir. Glinda, careful with the explosives so we don't fragment that ice slab. We need it in one easy, portable unit."

Glinda unstrapped from her seat and got ready to move to the hatch. "I've got this. I used to work at an ice cream parlor."

When the excavation laser had reached full charge, Arkourian deployed the beam, and vapors erupted where the intense light sparkled on the ice. Fresh steam filled the area like fog, obscuring her view, but the resonance scanners showed the laser's progress. The infrared mapping was also muddy, but Arkourian could still see the structure of the cliff.

"Integrity of the target chunk is still solid, and the main ice bridge has been weakened. One more section to cut. Get ready to go. Our excavation explosives are in the back cargo locker."

"You want me to climb through that fog with bombs strapped to my pack?" Glinda asked. "It's like pea soup out there."

In the low gravity, the mist would take a long time to dissipate. Arkourian said, "You've got this, remember?"

As the laser burned deeper into the connecting ice wall, her resonance scans suddenly revealed an area of lower density, an unexpected void in the cliff. She enhanced the view, then realized it was a gaseous inclusion—just as the hot beams sliced into the bubble.

Heated by the laser, the trapped gases expanded outward like a geyser, cracking the remaining material and blasting frozen shrapnel at them like a meteor storm.

The shock wave knocked the hovering *Lewis* aside, and Arkourian fought with the attitude jets to stabilize them. The bombardment of ice fragments was like a loud hailstorm against the hull. In a secondary explosion, another gaseous inclusion deeper in the cliff erupted like a chain of firecrackers.

Arkourian struggled with the reverse thrusters to withdraw from the rubble. The obscuring fog smeared her view, but in the bright beams of the spotlights, she saw part of the rugged ice wall calve off toward them like a giant swatting hand.

With a burst from the starboard jets, she shoved them out of the way as the iceberg fell forward like a slow-motion dancer. The *Lewis* retreated to a safe distance from the parent cliff, and she, Glinda, and Noor watched as the frozen slab slid to the crater floor. Even in the low gravity, the impact sent up showers of ice fragments.

"Whoa, guess I won't need to plant those charges after all." Glinda sounded shaken but relieved. "Any day without needing explosives is a good day."

Noor said, "Good work, Captain."

Arkourian felt embarrassed, surprised by her mistake. "We almost got smacked." Engineering was supposed to be an exact science. Normally, a full team would have spent days doing a thorough analysis of the comet, finding exactly the right chunk of ice, mapping out all contingencies. But normally, Nether Station wouldn't have been so desperate for water.

Also, the incredible alien presence had made her jumpy, impatient. She had been in too much of a hurry.

The ice fog continued to dissipate into the vacuum. "I just hope that didn't break it," she said. "We need a big piece to take back with us."

Tense, she scanned the fallen block of ice, then let out a sigh of relief. "It's intact, not fragmented. Our very own iceberg. We're good to haul it."

Applying constant thrust, slow and steady, the *Lewis* towed the frozen mountain back to Nether Station. Arkourian felt shaky, not wanting any more drama for the day.

Like a welcoming beacon, she could see the bright station ahead, the *Lethe* with its extended modules. The bright lights and exterior markers made the station look out of place—much like the impossible alien temple on the comet. Centuries hence, if some other mysterious race found an abandoned Nether Station drifting near the wormhole, what would they think?

"Special delivery," Glinda said in the comm.

Ashe had already suited up to help guide the ice block to where it could be used. "I completed repairs in the damaged reservoir and did a full integrity check while you were gone. Patches are in place."

"And boy, do we have some sightseeing pictures to show everybody!"

As the *Lewis* pulled up, Glinda emerged to help her

engineering partner corral and stabilize the iceberg. Arkourian watched, nodding in satisfaction. "Our power generators can convert the ice to liquid for our use. Our mission is stable again, and we can proceed as planned."

Now that they were away from the ancient alien ruins, Noor's mood had changed. He transmitted in a triumphant voice, "Mission accomplished! And we can always go back to get more water as we build Nether Station into a larger and larger outpost."

CHAPTER 23

The discovery of the alien ice temple, as well as the dead cockroach creatures, changed Benedict Noor's conception of the universe—and made him even more determined to conquer the wormhole.

The images they had recorded from the comet—the titanic and hideous ice statue, the temple complex—astonished the remaining members of the mission. From the *Lewis*'s transmissions and their suitcams, the four people on the station had already learned of the amazing discoveries, but Noor, Arkourian, and Glinda had given them a full report. They grappled with the very idea of the ancient extraterrestrial outpost.

None of NOOR's previous operations on the Moon, on Mars, or in the asteroid belt had shown even a hint of the existence of aliens, and now it was clear that they had also used the Nether wormhole. What else had they left behind? And why had they been here at all?

The mind-bending sensations he'd experienced from that eerie obsidian mirror added a new frame of reference and gave him a more urgent context to their presence. Maybe it was more than just exploration, more than an outpost. From that horrific thing on the ice throne and the psychic shout of the bottomless-pit mirror, perhaps the answer was more malevolent . . .

Nevertheless, Noor defiantly shoved aside the doubts and

fears. His mission still needed to move ahead on schedule. Dr. Stelland had reported that the group of rodent specimens had matured, and it was time to launch the second probe.

Whistling with anticipation, Noor went to the medical center, where the doctor busied himself over two wire-mesh cages that each held eight white lab rats grown from stored embryos. The specimens scurried about, sniffed at the kibble in their food dish, and licked water from the hanging bottle—oblivious to their real purpose in life.

He cleared his throat to get Stelland's attention. "Are the critters ready, Doc?"

The doctor did not even look up. "They are mature." He tapped his finger against the side of one of the wire-mesh cages. Intrigued by the sound, the rats sniffed the air, raised their tiny paws. Two of them came close to the wire bars, staring at the doctor. "I grew a nice variety, with different genetic markers and susceptibilities, as well as varying levels of intelligence as determined by maze tests. We'll get a good set of data."

"I don't care if they can sing in a barbershop quartet. I just want to send them through the wormhole and back."

"They are ready for that, Mr. Noor. And I can always grow more."

In its own much larger cage, the rhesus monkey squatted down and rolled a bright red ball from one paw to the other, muttering to itself. Seeing Noor, the monkey hurled the ball against the bars, rattling them.

Startled, he took a step back. "That creature tried to hit me!"

The doctor glanced at the animal. "It's just bored."

Noor frowned in annoyance. "It isn't our job to keep the lab animals amused. They're here for an important purpose."

"Agreed, though Glinda Roybal spoils the monkey more than I would like." Stelland opened a cabinet and removed a pair of soft-sided fabric carriers for the rats. He reached in through the top of the wire cage and plucked the squirming rodents out, one by one, and dropped them into the two carriers.

Noor stood by the bulkhead door, anxious. His stomach had been in knots ever since he'd seen that twisted mirror in the temple. That throbbing, infinite echo had gotten inside his head somehow! "I'm anxious for results. We will be better prepared once we have more answers."

Stelland dropped the last rat into the carrier. "After what you found on the comet, sir, I strongly suggest you send briefings back to Earth. Full briefings, for the general public. No competitor is within years, or even decades, of getting here. The human race needs to know about what we found. You would be a hero—think of the discovery you made, the first person with real proof of an alien civilization."

"I'm already a hero by investing the money and taking the risk." Noor sniffed. "I've sent regular reports to my asteroid hub."

"But your people will keep the details to themselves," Stelland said with a hint of disapproval. "I understand the need for industrial trade secrets, but you have little to worry about from other researchers, sir. Nether Station gives you command of the wormhole."

"I doubt anyone's even paying attention," Noor said. "I intend to use that to my advantage before everyone else decides to rush up here and grab something for themselves."

He knew that the short human attention span had wandered elsewhere during the five years of the *Lethe*'s voyage. His sister, Margo, had run NOOR operations in his absence, and she would have been the face of the company for years—a hard and competent woman, a battle-axe, but he was happy to let her take all the media and political bombardment, and the occasional praise. By now most people would have stopped thinking about when his team would reach the wormhole. Out of sight, out of mind. What sound bites have you given me lately? Any reporters would likely assume the ship had been lost en route—especially if Noor kept his reports confidential, for his own people.

Still, he wanted everyone to know that he had reached this vital place, high up in the Kuiper Belt—like Amundsen planting a flag at the South Pole, before Scott's team had gotten there. He wanted credit, a prominent place in the history books, a grand statue somewhere . . . bigger than that giant tentacle-faced thing on the comet throne.

But poisonous doubts still infested him after what he had encountered inside the temple alcove. He, Benedict Noor, Benedict the First, didn't want to be forgotten, didn't want to be insignificant.

He felt a chill. True, Amundsen had been the first man to reach the South Pole, but today Robert Falcon Scott was the most famous Antarctic explorer, because of his disastrous failure. Noor didn't want to be remembered like that . . .

Feeling uncharacteristically unsettled, he turned to leave the med center. "Let's get on with it. Bring the rats so we can tuck them into the probe."

The doctor nodded. "I need to prepare them first, anesthetize the control sample with sleeping gas. I will follow shortly."

As Noor left, the monkey hurled the red ball against the bars of its cage.

Now, with building anticipation, all seven mission members had gathered in the hangar bay for the launch of the second probe, and Noor was anxious to get back on track after the recent setbacks.

Arkourian looked at the open and empty probe vessel. "We

already know a physical object can survive the trip, but we have no idea how a living creature will react."

Noor lifted his chin. "That, my dear Karla, is what these little pioneers are about to show us. And this probe is a two-fer—combined experiments to give us even more bang for the effort, and to save time." He straightened, squared his shoulders, and cracked his spine with a sigh. "Since these are the first living creatures to go through the wormhole—"

"Except for the entire race of the cricket aliens," Ashe pointed out.

Noor frowned. "The first living creatures that we send. We will use the test probe to measure biological effects and also mental effects. Half the rats will be awake, and the other half will be unconscious, so we can get some idea how brain activity is affected by the dimensional passage . . . although rats have very small brains."

Stelland entered with the two containers of rodent specimens, eight of them active, sniffing, curious, while the others were huddled together at the bottom of their cage, sound asleep.

Noor glanced at Cammie Skoura, who stood at the entrance to the hangar bay. "According to the theoretical models, there's nothing about the wormhole that would harm any biological organism. Right, Cammie?"

"I didn't say that," she said. "The suite of available wormhole theories can't say anything at all on the subject. We don't have any basis yet."

"We will send two groups through in the same probe, same conditions." Stelland tapped the side of one mesh carrier, and the rats sniffed his fingers through the screen. "The control group is sedated."

"We have rats to spare," Noor said.

Ashe accepted the carriers from Dr. Stelland and bent to

install them in the padded inner compartment. Unlike the first reconnaissance probe, this one had an airtight interior chamber and a full life-support system, heater, air, and medical monitors. Imagers would monitor the rats during the nine-minute passage through the wormhole to Alpha Centauri and back. Based on the results of the first probe, Noor was confident they would survive the journey; too bad half of them would sleep through it.

Stelland continued to explain. "The monkey's brain-wave pattern will be more indicative of how a human will respond, but these rats will provide our first set of biological data."

Warren Drake was fidgety. "Do we need speeches, boss, or can I just fly the thing? Quickest way to get results."

"I share your impatience, Warren," Noor said, nodding to Ashe.

After the young engineer sealed the rats inside the vessel, then double-checked the monitors and external sensors, the group withdrew from the hangar bay into the adjacent control chamber. Warren once again took the joysticks and virtual controls to ease the torpedolike craft away from the station, then accelerated it toward the darkly swirling trapdoor in space.

Noor watched Cammie go to the chamber's windowport and look outside, apparently tense, as if worried another one of the frozen bug aliens would splatter in front of her. He wondered if she was worried that her theoretical work would not hold up to the practical tests.

Dr. Stelland observed the vital signs on the monitors, announced that both groups of rats were doing just fine.

Noor watched the screen, fascinated as the small probe's forward cameras showed the wormhole growing larger and larger. He imagined the twirls and tendrils of spacetime, bending downward. "It looks like the lair of a tunnel spider," he said.

Glinda groaned. "Now I won't get *that* image out of my head."

"Here we go," Warren said.

The probe crossed the event horizon and disappeared—as before. Warren lifted his hands from the joysticks and leaned back in his gyroscopic chair. "Nine minutes, if it's like last time."

Arkourian set a timer. They waited inside the control chamber, restless. Nobody was going anywhere.

"Oh, to be a rat right now," Warren said. "I wonder what they're experiencing."

Arkourian was deep in thought. "I wonder how many times those aliens traveled back and forth to build that comet temple."

"And what were they doing out here?" Cammie asked. "Why would they come to our solar system? There must be more than just the comet facility."

"Maybe it was an interstellar tour bus," Noor said with a smile. "The possibilities are endless." He could also think of ominous possibilities . . .

Exactly on schedule, the probe popped back out, transmitting its "We are here!" signal. Taking the joysticks again, Warren reestablished the command link and guided the probe back home. "So far, so good. Easy-peasy."

Dr. Stelland watched the medical readouts from the monitors inside the vessel. "Vital signs look stable, Mr. Noor. The rats are still alive—both sets." He sounded surprised.

"Well, that's something." Noor locked his hands behind his back and waited for the probe to arrive. It seemed longer than the tense silence during the wormhole passage.

"I am pulling up the vital-sign histories now for a first assessment." Stelland concentrated on the displays. "Heartbeat, respiration, blood pressure . . . Hmmm, a flurry of erratic activity occurred during the interdimensional travel. Some of the conscious specimens reached extreme limits of tolerance, but nothing noticeable in the sedated ones." His voice trailed off.

Noor said, "Of course the creatures would be terrified going through a wormhole. No surprise at all. The important part is that they survived."

"I'll run direct tests as soon as we get the specimens back in hand, sir."

"Working on that. Give me ten more minutes," Warren said, then lowered his voice. "Captain Arkourian doesn't like me to go fast."

When the pilot finally brought the probe back to the hangar bay, Ashe opened the casing to retrieve the rats.

Not letting the other engineer have all the fun, Glinda pulled out the soft-sided containers and handed them to the doctor like prize envelopes.

Stelland lifted the carriers one at a time, peering through the mesh. The control group remained asleep, while the eight active rodents moved about but seemed dazed and disoriented. "They're quieter than I expected them to be."

Noor quipped, "Maybe they're just pleased with the service they did for humanity. One small step for a rodent, one giant leap—" He looked inside as the doctor opened the top of the soft carrier.

He realized that all eight of the small animals were shivering. They huddled together and looked up at him. All the rats had distant, flinty gazes. Their normally stupid eyes held a weird glint, as if they had seen something beyond anything their little minds could comprehend.

CHAPTER 24

Though Nether Station hung motionless in space, Cammie still imagined she was tumbling out of control. She had no frame of reference in the emptiness, no up or down, no guiding star on the horizon.

Unable to sleep, she gazed out the windowport in her quarters, drawn to the hypnotic wormhole. She had given up everything else to come out here—for this, bubbling with ideas and tests to refine humanity's understanding of physics. She had never imagined she would face the remnants of an extraterrestrial civilization, which also seemed to understand the wormhole. How else would they be out here?

Dr. Tendari—*Zach*—should have been there with a shoulder for her to lean on, a sounding board to give her confidence. What would he have thought about the discovery of the strange aliens? He always watched her so closely.

One time, when she was a grad student, Cammie had attempted to be sociable, awkwardly accepting an invitation to a party on campus. It was loud and uncomfortable, with music she didn't like and lots of alcohol. Probably even drugs exchanged and consumed, but she'd been oblivious to that, and no one offered her any.

Cammie hadn't worn provocative clothing or put on makeup, but apparently people found her attractive, with her green eyes and soft features. When young men attempted to make small talk, she just didn't know what to say. The topics weren't interesting. Why did people consider this activity enjoyable? A party was, by definition, supposed to be fun.

She accepted drinks that people gave her, more than she should have. Cammie had never consumed so much alcohol before, and she was losing her ability to think straight and make articulate answers. One young man asked what her parents did, and she blurted out that they had died in a house fire. He quickly found someone else to talk to.

Before she knew what was happening, she'd been swept up in a small group that wanted to play spin the bottle, but she didn't know what that was, didn't know what she was expected to do. And they laughed at her. When they told her what the game entailed, she couldn't respond, couldn't react. So she fled outside, running away from the party house. She just hid in the hedges of the house next door, shivering and crying.

Not knowing what else to do, she'd called Dr. Tendari. He came right away, swooping in like some comic-book hero. He found her outside and rescued her, wrapped his arms around her, and told her she should come with him. *Call me Zach.*

She wasn't articulate enough to explain exactly what had happened, but he took her back to her dorm, kissed her on the cheek, and stayed there, sitting on the bed next to her while she slept. She didn't think anything else of it.

Who was going to comfort her now, on the edge of the solar system in the darkest part of space? And how could understanding aliens be any more of a challenge?

She chastised herself for wallowing in sad memories. Tendari was always there with a hand on her back when she felt downcast. He was a father figure, when her own father had never known how to support or understand her.

The more she thought about him, though—and why did he

keep insisting that she call him Zach?—Cammie felt a nagging hint of doubt. Some of his close attentions could be interpreted differently, and she was just oblivious. He often teased her for not picking up on subtleties. What had he meant by that? What had she missed?

She remembered the ISA probe tech looking at Cammie oddly, muttering "Creepy old man!" with a glance at Dr. Tendari.

She shook the memories from her head and stared out the windowport, letting her gaze slide away from the wormhole to the broader sea of stars. One of those dim lights was the comet, with the astonishing temple the expedition had recently found. It had been there all along, and now they knew it was a bastion for a long-lost alien race.

Or were they entirely lost? The dead cricket creatures had drifted through space until they struck the station's hull. Many more of them were dead inside the frozen temple. Perhaps their species had just abandoned this outpost? What if more of the creatures traveled through the wormhole now and were surprised to encounter Nether Station? Even just the recorded images of that monstrous ice statue on its throne made her shudder. If they came back, how would the aliens react to trespassers?

Cammie felt uneasy as she considered Mr. Noor's plans to build a transportation hub here. Down at the asteroid hub, numerous supplementary ships and modules would be preparing to launch—or maybe they were already on their way.

Impatient to stop her spinning thoughts—to keep the questions, doubts, and fears out of her mind—she finally took a sleep tab, so that at least she could have some peace.

Cammie didn't want dreams, but apparently the dreams wanted her. She had not visited the gigantic comet temple herself, but the team's images haunted her, fascinated her. A feeling of infinite vastness settled in the pit of her stomach.

She saw herself standing at the base of the immense frozen steps below where the tentacle-faced behemoth loomed on its throne. The monster had been carved with such perfect detail that she imagined she could see it twitch and move, its baleful eyes shifting to stare at her. The dangling appendages of some dying cuttlefish writhed on its frozen face. She flinched away, raising her hands to ward it off.

When her dream-self let out a scream, Cammie saw the steam of her breath curl out like flash-frozen fog. The logical part of her mind scoffed at the idea, because she was standing in open vacuum on the surface of a comet—she couldn't possibly be breathing! She could never survive out here.

But a nightmare was bound not by logic but rather by fear and horrific possibilities. Behind the carved throne, the immense door opened, and a host of the cricket aliens marched out like terrified supplicants. The creatures chittered in a language no human had ever heard, and she couldn't understand their twitching gestures. They chanted a name that meant nothing to her yet still made her skin crawl. "Agoc! Agoc!"

When they had gathered in front of the frozen figure, the insect things suddenly turned on one of their own, choosing a random sacrifice. They seized it with their claws, yanking the victim's segmented limbs. The creature struggled as it tried to fight back. Mandibles clicked open and closed as it let out a shrill, inhuman squeal. The helpless sacrifice spread its wing carapaces, but the other insects tugged them back until they broke off with a wet, ripping sound.

The creature whistled and warbled in pain.

The other crickets solemnly bowed their heads. Their black hemispherical eyes held no emotions as they kept attacking their chosen one, uprooting its angled forelimbs from the sockets of its body core. Next, they pried open its abdominal plates, pulled out moist interior organs, and splashed greenish ichor onto the dais before the monstrous statue.

Cammie couldn't close her eyes, couldn't turn away, but she was desperately thankful that the other aliens didn't see her in the dream, didn't close in on her as another sacrifice.

At last they wrenched off the victim's head and raised it up before the squid-faced god. Dripping nerve fibers and tendons dangled down, leaving a stain on the icy base of the throne. "Agoc! Agoc!"

The dream sky brightened, and the landscape changed from a frozen cometary wasteland to a field of black grass surrounded by a forest of jagged thorn trees. She saw another temple, this one carved from sandstone.

Thousands and thousands of the cricket creatures fought among themselves. It was a slaughter, partly a bloody sacrifice, partly a rebellion. As if she were watching a whirling documentary, she witnessed fires spreading on other worlds, cities constructed with insane geometry, explosions in the air—a great war.

Across her dream were fields covered with millions upon millions of murdered insect aliens. The dead smoke-stained buildings rumbled as something huge approached—

Cammie tore herself out of the nightmare just as a mammoth figure appeared with bloodred eyes, sharp dragon-like wings, and poisonous tentacles on its face.

She woke in her dim cabin with only the light of the stars and the stain of the wormhole leaking in through the windowport. Her sheets were sweaty, and her pulse raced. She might have cried out. Her thoughts were still thick and clumsy, hampered by the sleep tab.

The nightmare details had been as vivid and dangerous as a scalpel, but now they blurred into dream forgetfulness. She knew it was just a silly nightmare conjured by the eerie images brought back by the comet team, mixed with her unsettled emotions. She closed her eyes and took deep breaths, tried to center herself to restore calm.

Then Nether Station lurched violently. The deck tilted, and she tumbled off her bed. A strong vibration rang through the deck, and the station wrenched again, turning as if shaken by some invisible hand. Alarm lights winked on, and she braced herself, ready to respond to the emergency, wondering if another meteoroid had struck one of the modules.

Soon, though, the station became stable again, and the alarms stopped. Pedro Ashe's voice came over the comms. "Sorry about that. We were adjusting the station's position to anchor the new ice block into a safe lockdown. I didn't expect the jolt to be so severe. We're good now."

Cammie slumped onto her bunk, glad for the innocuous explanation, but it took her a long time to relax. She gazed out at the wormhole, wondering if the cricket aliens originated from Alpha Centauri, or if that was just another outpost of their civilization, one of many . . . like the ones she had seen in her nightmare.

Benedict Noor had been thrilled to discover the shortcut through space, but Cammie wasn't so sure. Maybe there was more to it than just the simple physics and wormhole mathematics, the convenience of an instant passage across the light-years.

What if it was a shortcut through the bad part of town?

CHAPTER 25

After her long career at NOOR, Karla Arkourian was used to her boss's pushy impatience. Already he wanted to send the third probe and the rhesus monkey into the wormhole, before Dr. Stelland had time to assess and analyze the lab rat groups.

Arkourian was one of the few who could stand firm and force Benedict Noor to slow down and reconsider. When he was convinced of something, he became a juggernaut, but now she used her influence to stop him from pushing recklessly hard. When the two of them were alone on the observation bridge, she stood behind his pretentious captain's chair and said it again. "Benedict, give Dr. Stelland time to finish his tests. We've got six months here. Let's do it right."

Noor's face pinched into a sour expression. "We can see that the rats are fine. We'll have a lot more data for the doctor to compare once we send the chimp through, and it'll be applicable to human physiology."

"It's not a chimp; it's a rhesus monkey—as you known damn well. The doctor needs time to run comparative tests on the rat specimens. He has to take cell samples, blood samples. It's only been a day. We can't predict long-term effects." She narrowed her eyes. "Step-by-step, sir. There's too much at stake to be sloppy. We have only one surviving monkey, and that test is crucial. Without solid primate results, we don't dare send Warren through. That's why we're here, isn't it?"

Noor's shoulders drooped in a sulk, but she could see he knew she was right. "Yes, of course that's why we're here. I'll bet Warren would go right now, if I asked him. Hell, if you want to be more cautious, we could even send one of the cryopod bodies and test for physiological effects on human anatomy."

Arkourian did not budge. "Don't harass the doctor, sir. Let him finish his analysis."

Obviously not happy, Noor swiveled in his captain's chair, looking out the broad window walls. "I can't just sit and wait, now that we've come all this way. Besides, it's clear the aliens came through the wormhole."

She stepped closer to the captain's chair. "We have a lifetime of research opportunities here, including that comet temple. We could send a team back there for a full exploration."

Noor slowly shook his head. "But who's really qualified in alien archaeology?" She could see a glint of fear cross his expression. "Maybe we should leave that place alone. It has been there for a long time—it can wait. When I have Margo launch the next wave of NOOR ships from the asteroid hub, I'll have them bring a qualified archaeological team to study that site. Yes, that's better than us bumbling around."

Arkourian remained silent for a long moment. "Instead of returning to the comet, I was thinking of something a little more straightforward. Warren is anxious to take a recon ship out and explore the neighborhood." She called up the chart Cammie had developed over the past week in the astronomy module, then projected the holo image to fill the observation bridge. "We've identified twenty significant asteroids in the vicinity."

Nether Station was the center of the map, and bright green dots showed the nearby asteroids like bees circling a hive, with the wormhole a prominent empty circle on the display.

Arkourian touched the controls, and a glowing red tag appeared, apart from the asteroids. "This one is the comet, which obviously comes from a different parent body."

Noor craned his neck around as he studied the projection, taking a silent tally. "Yes, we know how to deal with asteroids, and Warren has experience around them. Sure, let's send him on survey flights." He decisively activated the comm from his captain's chair. "Warren, please come to the bridge. Are you ready to take a recon ship and have some fun?"

Not wanting to give the cocky pilot free rein, Arkourian mapped out possible flight paths among the twenty asteroids, creating the most efficient flyby course, the greatest number of asteroids before Warren needed to refuel. "Looks like he could skim past eight asteroids by the end of the day for an initial survey. That'll give us a good glimpse of what resources we have available."

Noor smiled. "Good, we can mine and process the metals, and that'll allow us to build a much larger Nether complex here. Better than shipping components up from the asteroid hub."

Arkourian was glad to have distracted him. She studied the bright green points scattered around the projection. "Yes, those asteroids could serve as staging points, substations for transport operations here."

Noor chuckled, and he wore a wistful look as he stared out at the starscape. "Or they could be . . . hotels."

CHAPTER 26

In the hangar bay, Warren paced around the *Clark*, running his fingers along the hull's metal-ceramic composite. This craft was just as beautiful as the *Lewis*, which he had flown to rescue the Glinda snowball. Though he was still a little nervous about taking the expedition ship through the wormhole, he had been aching to do a real recon flight for months now. The walls of the *Lethe* had been giving him cabin fever.

Leaning into the *Clark*'s cockpit, he went through the checklist with swift familiarity. In the pilot's seat, he checked the fuel levels and battery output, cycled through the thrusters, maneuvering jets, and main rockets. All indicators were green. He toggled on the comm. "Time for me to leave the nest, Captain Arkourian. You don't get to have all the fun." The hangar began its decompression cycle.

She responded over the comm. "Finding a giant alien temple was not exactly *fun* for me."

As soon as the bay doors opened, he patted the piloting controls. He was eager to punch the main thrusters and feel the acceleration press him back against the seat, but he restrained himself.

Arkourian transmitted, "Follow the course we plotted in, and you'll be able to take first-cut images of eight asteroids with the fuel you have."

Warren studied the projected flight path that connected

the dots. "I could hit nine on this run, if you don't mind me coming back on fumes."

"I mind. Now that we have the reservoir filled again, we have enough fuel and enough time. Save the cocky stuff for when it's necessary."

He grinned inside his helmet. "And when exactly is cockiness necessary? I'd like to know."

"Never."

"Tell that to those asteroid miners I saved. Knowing my limitations and my ship's capabilities comes in handy in case of an emergency."

"Yes, it does," Arkourian agreed. "But this is no emergency. Just a routine mission. Behave yourself."

"Yes, Captain."

He guided the ship away from the station like a good boy, then punched the main thrusters. When he felt the *Clark* rumble and roar, he let out a whoop, leaving the comm channel open, just to make sure Arkourian heard him.

Off to starboard, Warren kept an eye on the undeniable presence of the wormhole, though his course did not take him anywhere close. He headed for the nearest asteroid, sure that NOOR would eventually strip-mine it for materials to expand the hub here. No great loss.

In a decade or two, the wormhole zone would be a bustling interstellar truck stop. Warren imagined planting a sign on one of the asteroids, pointing toward the inner solar system: *Wall Drug—4.5 billion kilometers.*

Soon he spotted the first drifting lump ahead. He took infrared and laser-reflective images, measured the size and density, mapped the irregular peanut shape that was marred by craters. It looked like a floating turd.

With Arkourian's rigid flight path, he could make one loop,

taking images and readings all the way. He felt like a tourist visiting a famous landmark and stopping only long enough to take a few photos. After his quick survey, he sent the results back to Nether Station. "Just a rock. A lot of dust, stony materials, and some metals. It'll make a good depot for whatever NOOR needs."

The asteroid was too small to give much of a gravity assist, and he used the *Clark*'s maneuvering thrusters to align him toward the next destination. The recon ship flew like a charm. This felt so much better than sitting in the simulator chair or even remote-operating the two probes.

An hour later, he reached the second target, another stony-metal asteroid, no surprises. Feeling complacent, Warren made his way to the third asteroid, checking items off a list.

The initial infrared readings showed hot spots not found on the other two rocks. When the new asteroid became better defined in his forward sensors, he saw glints of light that were brighter than what should have been there.

"Uh, laser-reflective readings are screwy on this one. The structure is irregular but . . . the wrong kind of irregular."

"What does that mean?" Arkourian asked.

He cruised closer. "Hold on. Fresh images coming right up."

The asteroid was oblong and slightly tapered at both ends, like a celestial seedpod. On the surface, long *trenches* had been scraped from end to end in a perfect line—clearly excavations!

"Holy shit, it's a construction site!" he said. "Looks like somebody built a base camp."

Benedict Noor's voice surprised him on the comm. "Get good images, Warren. We want to see."

Flying closer, he followed the excavation lines and saw rectangular and rhomboid patches that had been mined from the surface. As the *Clark* looped over the abbreviated horizon to the side that faced the wormhole, Warren saw the alien complex. "It's a . . . a factory town!"

Tucked into craters and against rocky protrusions were tilted cubical structures, metal enclosures covered with centuries of dust. He saw curved constructions like crucible bowls or dishes impaled with thorny artificial spines. Signal antennae?

He heard a chatter of disbelief and excitement over the comm, but Warren didn't know what to say. He checked the thermal imagery. "It's warmer than it should be. Maybe somebody left a night-light on." As the recon vessel orbited the asteroid, he burned more fuel at his discretion. "Getting a better look."

He found partially buried opaque spheres and armored domes, lines of cylinders connected with looping, serpentine pipelines. To him, the architecture looked much more industrial than the images he'd seen of the comet temple's fantastic opulence. In fact, much of this place reminded Warren of the NOOR asteroid mining bases.

"So, boss, should I land and have a look around?"

Arkourian's voice came back instantly. "No—Recon Two is not equipped for a landing mission at this time."

"Bullshit," Warren muttered under his breath. He knew the *Clark*'s capabilities as well as anyone.

Noor's voice sounded uneasy. "After our experience on the comet, I'd rather be cautious. Let's think about our next step. For safety, you will need at least one partner before you venture onto an alien base."

"If you fall down a hole, you'd need somebody to pull you back up," Arkourian said.

Warren was sorely tempted to land anyway. Maybe this was one of those "emergency" times to be cocky. Nether Station would send a team anyway in a few days, and why shouldn't he get the first look? Maybe some historical footnote would call him Warren the First.

Arkourian's response was stern, as if she knew exactly what he was thinking. "This is strictly a survey mission—swift initial reconnaissance of the asteroids. Take your images, and we'll review them. Go to the remaining five destinations. What if there are more outposts?"

Staring down at the mysterious alien ghost town, he sighed. "If that's what you really want me to do, boss, but the other ones are probably just boring rocks like the first two."

After one more flyover of the alien base, he set course for the next target, not surprised when it indeed turned out to be nothing more than a metal-rich lump. The composition would have excited an asteroid miner, but now it seemed mundane.

But each of the remaining four asteroids held another abandoned alien base, even larger than the first.

CHAPTER 27

After conducting a battery of tests, Dr. Stelland could find nothing wrong with the experimental rats. Not specifically.

But that couldn't be right.

He tested the two groups in separated cages. He monitored their body temperature, blood pressure, heartbeat—all readings remained within normal parameters. He drew blood samples, ran full panels on each specimen, and found very little variation from the detailed panels he'd run prior to the excursion through the wormhole. Nothing had changed.

As he watched them in their cage, the eight rats that had been sedated during the journey did not seem unusual at all. He studied them and kept a log of his observations, but he was not concerned. Typical rodent behavior.

Not so with the group that had remained awake during the passage.

Wearing gloves, Stelland picked up each rat from the second cage, inspected its fur, felt for cancerous lumps. All eight seemed fine.

Yet they weren't.

These rats now had distant eyes, as if they held some echo of the void, but he couldn't measure that. He noticed it only in quick glimpses. Their behavior was sluggish and meek, as if they were stunned. Before the probe mission, they had exhibited the usual random scurrying, sniffing, and interacting—as the other test group still did. They had climbed over one another, touched noses, twitched pink tails.

After the wormhole, though, they were more alert but less active. Several times he caught the animals just staring at him, in a group, and that was greatly unsettling. But he couldn't demonstrate that anything was wrong with medical data, and Mr. Noor would accept nothing less.

Even stranger, these eight rats horrified the rhesus monkey. The animal had paid little attention to the rats before, but now it pressed against the back bars of its cage and whimpered, flicking wide eyes back and forth.

Curious, Stelland carried the first rat cage closer to the monkey, and the animal went wild, shrieking, clawing at the bars, baring its long, dangerous fangs.

When the doctor looked into the sturdy wire cage, all eight rats stood erect on their back legs, turning their empty gazes in unison at the monkey.

He felt such a wash of nauseating dread that he moved the rat cage to the counter and draped the light-blocking cover over it, so that neither he nor the frightened monkey needed to look at them.

The other group of rats just rustled about in their cage, oblivious.

That afternoon, when Stelland attempted to take follow-up blood samples from the rats, they turned on him.

He wore gloves due to good practice, but also unease. He reached into the container and wrapped his hand around the nearest rat, grabbing it just behind the shoulders. The rodent writhed and thrashed its pink tail, as if it had transformed into a scorpion. Its little claws slashed at the air, and it turned its head farther around than its neck muscles and tendons should have allowed. The rat gnashed at his hand and managed to sink its teeth into his forefinger, biting down on his glove.

Startled, Stelland flung the rat back into the mesh cage and looked in astonishment at his hand. Thanks to the glove, the sharp teeth had not broken the skin or drawn blood, but he could feel the bruise, knew the strength of the rat's powerful jaws.

The other seven rodents leaped, squeaked, and scratched, as if the floor of the cage had been electrified. They lunged up, trying to attack him.

Stelland slammed the mesh cover back on top just before the first rat struck. The chittering noises became a loud, restless clamor. Breathing heavily, he covered the cage with the shroud again so he didn't have to see them.

The rhesus monkey cradled its head in its paws, moaning.

Stelland knew he needed to brief Mr. Noor and express his concerns. Though the blood work and vital signs checked out for all the specimens, something had clearly changed in the awake group, profound neurological alterations.

Needing time to find calm again, the doctor left the medical center and went to the greenhouse dome, where he could enjoy the silence and solitude, collect his thoughts. Walking amid the greenery, he poked into the sprawling squash vines and harvested two perfect green zucchini. He picked beans and pulled a few fresh scallions for garnish, even snipped some mint leaves, deciding to boil water and make himself sweet tea. Yes, that would relax him.

He almost managed to convince himself that the situation was normal again . . .

But when he returned to the medical lab, the monkey was shrieking so loudly that flecks of blood came from its throat.

Stelland rushed in to see what had driven the animal into

such a frenzy. The second rat cage was still covered with its dark shroud, and he heard no sound from the rodents inside. He hoped they had just gone to sleep, but he doubted that would be the case. The monkey plucked at the bars of its cage, tried to defeat the complicated latch.

He pulled the covering off the cage and saw lines and smears of blood on the walls. Red pawprints marked where the animals had tried to rip their way through the tough wire mesh.

Seven of the rats rose on their haunches to peer up at him. Their white fur was spattered with blood, their tiny paws and snouts caked with gore.

On the floor of the cage, one rat had been torn apart, its eyes gouged out, its fur ripped to shreds. The chest had been split open, and small, curved ribs stuck up out of the cavity. Entrails lay strewn about, as if in celebration.

Bile rose in Stelland's throat, but he pushed it back down. Somehow he was sure that the victim was the rat he'd picked up, the one that had tried to bite him.

He backed away from the mesh cage, shaking. The monkey kept whimpering as it huddled in the corner, and Stelland realized he was making a similar sound deep in his throat.

The surviving rats faced him and locked their flinty, aligned gaze with his. They stared at him with nothing inside their eyes.

CHAPTER 28

As Noor watched the images from Warren's asteroid flyby, he wanted to know more, and he was not accustomed to delayed gratification. As soon as something piqued his interest, he would acquire it. Right now he imagined himself as a boy staring at unattainable toys in a store window and counting down the days to his birthday.

The Nether wormhole and the exotic alien artifacts were his toy store. The asteroid bases and the comet temple were vast mysteries, and they excited him, justifying his grand vision. They proved this was a base of operations, and it was possible to travel to other star systems and extraterrestrial cultures. He could build his own Nether complex here. It would be the NOOR gateway to a galactic empire.

He had invested much of his fortune in these grandiose plans, and he had also spent his *time*, which was more important than wealth. He remembered Margo's skepticism and their heated arguments, but he was certain it would pay off in spades, especially now. Every astonishing new discovery proved it.

As Warren flew the *Clark* back to the station complex, he transmitted his congratulations. "I knew you wouldn't let me down."

"Of course I wouldn't." The pilot sounded puzzled. "Get ready to refuel this ship so I can scout the rest of the asteroids. Who knows what else is out there?"

Karla Arkourian sat at her control station, taking charge while Noor relaxed in his captain's chair. He had started to think of the seat as a throne, like the one in the comet temple.

Arkourian said, "I'll schedule you to fly out again in four hours, Warren. That gives you some downtime."

Warren guided the *Clark* into the main hangar bay. "Downtime? This is my first actual flight in years."

"We need to process Recon Two and run a safety check. Because of the extra time you spent at the first alien base, you're well past the consumption projections. You passed the safety line ten minutes ago."

"I wanted to be thorough." Warren sounded sheepish. "And we both know how extensive the margins are."

"He did gather highly useful data," Noor said. "It's a good enough trade."

"See, the boss wants me to head out again," Warren said.

"We still have to wait until your ship is refueled," Arkourian said.

"But the *Lewis* is fueled and ready—I can just switch ships, like an old Pony Express rider jumping from one horse to another."

Noor gave Arkourian a satisfied smile. "The young man does have a point."

She looked resigned. "It'll still take an hour, minimum."

Noor nodded. "You can have an hour, Captain Arkourian. Warren, make the most of your coffee break. Or potty break."

The pilot let out a loud whoop.

Glinda Roybal was already in the hangar bay when Noor and Arkourian arrived to meet the returning ship. As soon as Warren swung out of the *Clark*, he dropped to the deck and made his way over to the other recon vessel. "Toss me the keys to the car, Glinda."

The engineer snorted. "After that long flight, you need to

refurbish your exosuit." She tossed him a wrapped package. "Slip on a new comfort pack. You must have filled your diapers when you saw the first alien outpost."

He grabbed the pack. "I've got a sphincter of steel and a very large bladder . . . but no good pilot ever misses an opportunity to pee." He grinned at her. "Want to help me put these absorbent pads on? Check that the seals are tight, no leaks?"

Glinda's wide face reddened. "Gross."

As the pilot went to clean up and relieve himself, Arkourian loaded the *Lewis* with the next flight path for Warren to survey the remaining asteroids. Meanwhile, Noor couldn't keep the wonder out of his voice. "We've already found enough to keep us busy for a long time—but there's nothing wrong with having more. Of everything."

Twenty minutes later, Warren returned, breathless and eager. "If you top me off with a little extra fuel, I could set down at one of those stations, knock on some doors. You *know* you want me to."

"No," Arkourian said firmly. "I do not want you to. We'll set up a well-equipped expedition."

Warren seemed antsy, but he relented. "Just put me at the front of the line for the real trip."

Back to the observation bridge as the *Lewis* started the second mapping run, Arkourian projected the holographic map of all twenty asteroids again, with Nether Station at the center. She flagged the five sites that the aliens had occupied.

Noor stared at the image. "This wormhole complex must have been a bustling transportation complex in its heyday, maybe back before the first human civilizations rose."

After reaching the first spot on his run, Warren checked in, reporting that the target was disappointing, just a stony asteroid with few metals of interest, so he wasted no time poking around. At the second asteroid, though, he hit the jackpot.

"This is a completely different level! If those other bases were outposts or supply depots, this one must have been command central." He transmitted a flurry of images.

A wide, shallow crater at the asteroid's equator looked like a giant navel. A dark dome poked up like a giant blister next to rows of connected cylinders. Large parabolic reflectors or signal amplifiers filled hollows in the crater floor, and rhomboid structures protruded from the cliff walls.

Viewing the images, Noor was amazed at the extent of the base. This was where he would direct the first expedition team. At one time, it must have been crowded, busy, thriving . . . but it was all dead now.

Warren pleaded, "You sure I can't just drop down, plant a flag or something?"

"Finish scoping out the remaining asteroids so we have a complete survey," Arkourian said.

"You will fly the first mission there, I promise," Noor said.

"Yes, boss."

By the end of the day, Warren had identified three more alien ghost towns. Because he had done a little "discretionary exploring" on the way, the *Lewis*'s fuel levels truly were in the red zone, and Arkourian scolded him to come back immediately. "Don't make me fly out there to rescue you."

"That would be embarrassing. On my way."

Noor kept reviewing the asteroid images with a rising sense of amazement, although he still shuddered from the primal doubts the temple's obsidian mirror had given him. Benedict Noor had no time for doubts. He was a visionary who saw the larger picture—the expansion of human civilization.

By the end of Warren's survey, they knew that nine of the

twenty large asteroids around the Nether wormhole had been inhabited by the ancient race, and Noor was sure that he could reuse those outposts in some fashion.

Glinda and Ashe came onto the bridge, followed by Cammie, who still seemed like a wisp of a girl, but at least she was showing curiosity instead of moping around. They looked up at the holographic display of all the asteroids.

Noor leaned forward in his captain's chair. "Karla, highlight just the ones with alien bases."

Nine of the green blips switched to neon yellow, randomly arranged. As he connected the dots in his mind, he envisioned where he could put NOOR settlements, research stations, cargo outposts—and yes, even hotels.

"It's gratifying to know that another civilization saw the same benefits that I did. Nether is a strategic point where all the train tracks come together, just as I imagined."

Ashe spoke up. "But what happened to them? The bugs, or Tentacle Face—are they all dead? Everything is a ghost town."

Cammie studied the asteroid projections overhead, rearranging, recalibrating. "When I compiled this map, I used Nether Station's frame of reference, because it's our own starting point. But our position has no particular significance." She pointed into the air. "Karla, can you recalibrate with the wormhole as the center point? That makes more sense."

"Let's see what it looks like," Noor said.

Arkourian rearranged the asteroid images: eleven plain rocky bodies scattered around in the emptiness, highlighted in green, and the nine occupied asteroids in bright yellow.

The ancient alien bases lined up in a startling perfect circle, equidistant around the wormhole.

"Those are substations," Cammie said. "Or watchtowers."

Noor felt a jolt of excitement. "Somebody installed the asteroids there on purpose!" He clapped his hands together and rose from the captain's chair. "And the aliens have already done most of the work for us!"

CHAPTER 29

Cammie sat by herself in the chilly bed-and-breakfast deck, leaning against the cryopod that held Dr. Tendari's body.

The team's original psychologist, Eli Hankins, might have expressed concerns about her inability to move on, but Hankins was frozen in one of the sealed cryopods, and he wouldn't be dispensing any personal advice. She had to deal with her feelings as best she could, sitting vigil with her back against the pod.

As she watched her breath in the cold air, she listened to the other humming cryopods. Seven empty pods stood ready, their covers raised like dangerous jaws, waiting for an unsuspecting victim to climb inside. Dr. Stelland and Captain Arkourian had overwritten the base subroutines to deal with the fatal glitch, but that fix would not save those other occupants. Or her mentor.

Closing her eyes, she leaned her head back against Tendari's pod. She felt no humming or throbbing, no reassuring signs of life support. It was no more than a morgue refrigerator, like the one in the med lab.

Dr. Tendari had always been there to guide her, to tell her what to do when she didn't know how to react. He had spotted her exceptional intelligence and admired her potential.

Cammie knew why she didn't fit in with other people, fully aware of the neurodivergent diagnosis she had received when she was only twelve, even if her family made little effort to accept how she was. She had never had the social graces that let her be comfortable in normal company, and she'd been teased for being a "brain," made to feel awkward by the rowdy jocks and cocky young men with too much testosterone.

One time on campus, just after she had started work under Tendari, he had angrily scolded a pair of uncouth university football players after they muttered rude comments within earshot. "Why is being intelligent a handicap? You should beg to have this young woman's skills."

Tendari had put his arm around her and led her away. That night he took her out to a nice dinner, where they continued to discuss her thesis project. With him, she'd felt free to talk about things that fascinated her. He listened warmly, smiling at her with a bright gleam in his eyes. He had paid for the meal, even though it was an expensive restaurant.

Call me Zach.

But uneasy thoughts nagged at her again. She had never paid attention, never thought about it, but she'd heard whispers among the faculty and didn't understand what they were implying. Something about the way Dr. Tendari—Zach—had looked at her, treated her, how he was always there to care for her like a superhero, a protector . . . and that look in his eyes.

She knew she was always slow to see the obvious. What if he had thought of Cammie as something more than a colleague or a protégée? He had always comforted her, pampered her. Was he grooming her?

She felt confused as she finally, *finally* started to notice the signs. Had Dr. Tendari wanted something more from her, a different type of relationship? There was such a substantial difference in their ages, thirty-five years at least.

She'd never thought of him in that way, never considered it—but not because she rejected the idea. It just hadn't occurred to her. What had she missed?

She remembered Leila in the probe team snickering, "Creepy old man."

Feeling like a fool, she remembered Tendari's intense eyes, how he had kissed her on the cheek after rescuing her from the drunken college party. Had he wanted her romantically? Sexually? Before the Nether mission, he had gone out of his way to tell her he was separated from his wife. The idea confused Cammie, and she felt a flush on her face. She had never . . .

Alone in the cryopod deck, she touched her chest, her chin, felt her neck pulse. She ran gentle fingers along her cheeks, remembering what she looked like in a mirror and trying to imagine what Zach Tendari saw in her. What had he fantasized?

She began to shake. What else had she missed by being so oblivious? Had she missed her whole life?

Cammie stood up from the cold deck and braced herself against the cryopod. She bent over the cover and looked through the frosty viewing pane, where she could still see Tendari's slack, peaceful face.

The first time she had gone to sleep in a cryopod, nervous, he had been there to close the lid, wishing her pleasant dreams. She'd thought of it as a reassuring action, but what if he saw it as more like a lover saying good night?

The idea made her feel strangely uneasy. That wasn't what she had wanted from him at all. Tendari had come out to the wormhole—his dream and his passion, just like hers. But he had never seen it with his own eyes. Now he was gone, yet still here.

She supposed his body would be brought back to Earth when the *Lethe* departed in six months. But Zach Tendari had no family, no close associates back home, separated from his wife in a loveless marriage. He had come on the mission to be with her, for whatever emotional reasons he had in his mind.

It made her uncomfortable now to have him on the station,

a constant reminder, always here. She would rather not keep thinking about these questions and doubts.

Cammie knew it was time to break free, time to move on—number five in the stages of grief, acceptance—and escape this limbo in a clear and direct way. She stared down at his lifeless face, remembered their intense conversations. But as colleagues, not as lovers. And every time she saw him, she would be plagued by those same questions.

Now, he could no longer help her with the science. They couldn't talk about Lorentzian traversable wormholes or the solution manifold of Einstein's field equations for a vacuum spacetime. No, Tendari would be kept in a freezer for years before they returned home, and he would be buried somewhere on Earth with a memorial headstone.

No, Zachary Tendari wanted to be out here at the wormhole, and this was where he truly belonged. A small part in the back of her mind remained uneasy to think of him here, still with her, for five more years.

A grim smile came to her lips as she considered an alternative and convinced herself it was what he would really have wanted, as a scientist—a traditional burial in space. The crew of Nether Station could hold a ceremony, and she would write a nice eulogy for him, make sure he was remembered *as a researcher.* They could eject his body out the airlock, and he would drift in the uncharted vicinity of Nether. Maybe with the vagaries of momentum and gravity, he might even fall down the wormhole.

Yes, Dr. Tendari—*Zach*—would like that.

And then he would be gone. Cammie could move on and not think about those disturbing ideas anymore.

She left the bed-and-breakfast deck and headed for the observation bridge. She needed to talk to Mr. Noor.

Benedict Noor swiveled in the captain's chair, recently

arrived after his sleep shift, dressed in comfortable, dark garments. Still bleary-eyed, he sipped on a fresh coffee bulb, and he brightened when he saw her enter. "Ah, Cammie! What world-shaking discoveries today?"

She braced herself. "There's something I'd like to do for Dr. Tendari. It would help me move on, and the whole crew could participate. A kind of funeral."

"You mean like an Irish wake?" Noor smiled and nodded. "We can all tell stories and celebrate."

"Not exactly that." She felt her cheeks flush but pressed on. "Instead of taking his body all the way back to Earth, I think Dr. Tendari would like to be buried in space near the wormhole." She explained in greater detail what she had in mind.

Arkourian turned from her station. "It makes sense, Benedict. Better than keeping his body preserved for years and hauling it all the way back down."

Noor seemed pleased. "A burial in space would be dramatic and poignant, and it's fitting for an explorer. I see why it appeals to you, young lady." He pursed his lips as he pondered. "And we do have the Jiminy alien in the regular morgue freezer, so we don't have the spare room."

Arkourian said, "We'd have to put a pinger on the body so that he doesn't become a hazard in space—like those drifting bugs."

Cammie shuddered as she thought of the cricket aliens floating in space. For how many centuries? Had those bodies been from some sort of mass funeral, a group of dead aliens scattered like ashes on the solar winds?

Noor glanced out at the blur of the Nether wormhole, and thoughts were obviously churning in his head. "That idea would definitely appeal to Dr. Tendari. I knew him rather well, after all." He rose from his seat, growing more animated. "But there's something else. He has another chance to make a scientific contribution. Something no one else has done! He could be the first human through the wormhole—I'm sure Warren won't mind."

Cammie's stomach clenched. "What do you mean?"

"He was physically fit and biologically sound, and he only died because of a silly cryopod malfunction." Noor raised a finger like a teacher lecturing. "His body could serve as an excellent laboratory, a perfect specimen. Tomorrow we'll send out the next probe with the monkey, but there's room in the inner compartment. Instead of just ejecting him out the airlock, we could use him as a test subject. Dr. Stelland would be happy to have another round of data before we send a living human subject."

Arkourian was also looking at Noor, her eyebrows raised. "What is a dead subject going to show us?"

"Who knows? Cellular effects? Brain-tissue response? The frozen bodies of Robert Scott's expedition members were still used for science." He rubbed his hands together and looked at Cammie. "Indulge me. Don't you think he'd like that?"

Cammie balked at the idea of using him as a lab experiment, but how was that different from simply dumping his body out in space? This way he could participate in the actual science, contribute other data for the Nether mission.

Seeing the intensity on Noor's face, Cammie didn't have the strength to debate him, knowing she would never win that argument anyway. She had no logical, scientific basis to object. Fundamentally, Mr. Noor was right. Even if the data only confirmed the data from the other test subjects.

She often heard Tendari's whispering conscience in her mind, still acting as mentor and advisor. She was sure he would agree to this.

Cammie found herself nodding. "All right. When the next probe goes out tomorrow, he should be inside it."

CHAPTER 30

In the greenhouse dome, Dr. Stelland tended his plants under the full-spectrum artificial lights. He monitored and recorded the growth, kept logs of the different species for scientific purposes, but in truth he simply enjoyed the gardening activities. It was a respite from the med lab, away from the eerie rats.

He had to mentally prepare himself for the next major probe test the following day. The rhesus monkey would be sent through twice, first sedated and then again while fully awake to check both biological and neurological responses. The awake group of rodent specimens still acted oddly, but he couldn't give Mr. Noor any specific test result that showed biological alterations. Even rats killing one of their own in a crowded cage environment, especially under stress, was not unknown behavior.

Mr. Noor refused to change the probe schedule. And now the human corpse was also going to accompany the sleeping monkey on the first test.

Stelland needed time alone in the greenhouse.

Each day he harvested fruits and vegetables in the neatly organized plantings. The station crew would always have carrots, beans, onions, green peas, parsley, spinach, tomatoes, potatoes, and dwarf corn to eat. The strawberry bed was a reliable source of fresh fruit.

Lately, he had an embarrassment of zucchini, since the

unruly vine threatened to take over the greenhouse. It was a dark, velvety thicket, and he heard the vines and leaves stirring gently in the draft from the ventilation system.

He slung the mesh bag over his shoulder and went to the strawberry bed first, sure he would find a few handfuls to pick. The rhesus monkey had a fondness for the berries, thanks to Glinda Roybal's pampering, and Stelland decided he would give the animal a last meal, in light of the scientific ordeals it would soon endure.

He brushed the dark strawberry leaves from side to side to reveal fresh blossoms and more berries to come. But when he looked closer, the white petals were dingy and brown, like coffee-stained teeth. They didn't look right.

He rummaged through the vines until he found a dozen or so large red strawberries, which he plucked and dropped into his fabric sack. They were bright and shiny, intensely scarlet, slippery in a way, and he glanced at his fingertips. The juice had left a dark red smear, uncomfortably like blood, and it was sticky. That was odd.

He popped the last berry in his mouth as a treat.

He gagged and spat out the crushed red pulp, then spat three more times to get rid of all the juice. It tasted like acid and raw sewage, a sour chemical flavor that made his eyes burn. He worked up saliva and spat again, not sure he would ever get the taste out of his mouth.

The mangled berry on the deck was thick and red, but with a brownish undertone like imminent rot.

Opening the fabric sack, he inspected the other strawberries he had picked. They all seemed soft and moist, even a bit slimy.

Behind him, the squash vines rustled again, and the thick, hairy leaves drifted gently, as if in a mocking wave. A large zucchini protruded, and it looked *wrong.*

He turned to the squash and pushed the leaves aside for a better view. The fine hairs stung his skin like nettles, and he snatched his hand away. The elongated green squash lay exposed, the familiar phallic shape, but crooked and warty. Several more squashes lurked in the thicket, and all of them had lumps, as if they were knotted tumors instead of vegetables.

Stelland donned a pair of sturdy gardening gloves and reached in to collect the cancerous zucchinis. Underneath the thick leaves, he saw hairy brown masses, drooping squash blossoms.

What kind of blight could have occurred in their sterile planting zone? And how could it have spread so quickly? He wondered if some contaminant or chemical leak had gotten into the irrigation systems or the soil matrix. Where could it have come from? Glinda and Ashe would have to fix it, and soon.

He moved down the row of green beans and found all the plants blotched with a leprous blight. He pulled one of the carrots and found it soft and moldy, split open and leaking a brown ooze.

The sheer unnaturalness filled him with horror, followed by more analytical, pragmatic thoughts. This greenhouse dome was Nether Station's secondary food source. Their stockpile of supplies would last for a significant amount of time, especially with the reduced crew, but the garden supplemented the pre-packaged food.

The doctor walked up and down the rows he had planted, the shoots and bushes he had tended. He had monitored each variety, understood the growth patterns, the harvest rates. But now something had poisoned them all.

He winced at the lingering foul taste in his mouth. Even if the plants were not actually toxic, they were inedible. He carried the harvest bag, determined to analyze the berries in the medical lab, but he was already sure they were laced with contaminants.

He spat again, but the taste wouldn't go away.

The crew might have to uproot all the plants, then mulch and incinerate them. He didn't dare risk using the remains as a replacement soil matrix.

As he walked past the squash vine, it inexplicably stirred again. The warty, tumescent zucchini poked out between the leaves, slumping under its own twisted weight.

Stelland backed away, passing the tomato plants, and a ripe, red globe split like a suppurating wound that oozed foaming slime. The white seeds looked like maggots.

He pulled off the gardening gloves and fled the greenhouse module.

CHAPTER 31

Though it was all part of understanding the wormhole, Cammie felt uneasy about the next probe mission. Even if Dr. Tendari wasn't alive, his physical body would go where no human being had ever gone.

Even though she understood the scientific reasons, she didn't want to watch his body extracted from the cryopod and taken to the hangar bay. She didn't want to see his cold and lifeless body, his limbs thawed enough to be supple. Dr. Stelland would hook monitors to his skin, insert needles and probes into his flesh, and prepare him like a crash test dummy.

So, Cammie stayed in her quarters and distracted herself by reviewing data from the first two probes—measurements of the wormhole environment, dynamics of interdimensional physics, gravitational stresses. All in preparation for when Warren did the main test flight in the *Neil Armstrong.*

Dr. Stelland hoped to get more conclusive results with the rhesus monkey, since the primate was closer to a human subject than the rats, and Tendari's body would also give invaluable data. Still, she wasn't eager for it to happen.

After an interminable time, Stelland's voice came over the wall comm. "The human subject is installed in the probe compartment, all sensors and monitors hooked up. I am bringing the anesthetized primate subject to the hangar bay. We'll be ready to launch soon."

Cammie imagined Dr. Tendari's voice in her head, encouraging her, and she emerged from her room and went to join the others.

The rest of the crew had gathered near the next probe vessel, watching the final preparations. Pedro Ashe moved around to the front, testing the external sensors. The compartment lid remained open, and Cammie hesitated as she saw her mentor laid out like a body in a coffin.

Dr. Stelland came into the hangar bay carrying the rhesus monkey in his arms like a small child. The brown-furred animal draped an arm around Stelland's neck, but it seemed lethargic.

Glinda lit up. "Fluffers!" The monkey sluggishly turned at the sound of her voice, and then its heavy-lidded eyes drooped.

"I gave it a fast-acting sedative," Stelland said. "It will be asleep for the trip."

Noor paced with nervous energy. "We don't have any extra monkeys, so this one will have to do double duty."

The original plan for the primate test missions had been to use the three specimens: one awake and one sedated for the first trip, with the third monkey in reserve for another probe. But with only one primate available, the same one would have to go through twice to see how the wormhole affected its brain activity.

Stelland carried the now-sleeping animal to the open probe. "There's enough room inside next to the cadaver specimen." Once he had settled the creature beside Tendari, he applied electrodes on the head, arms, and chest, then connected the leads to the probe's main systems.

As Ashe sealed the lid, Cammie caught a last glimpse of Tendari, wondering if she would ever see him again. Would the interdimensional tunnel somehow swallow him up? She knew she shouldn't be worried, since the other probes had successfully passed through the wormhole and back.

At least he would be gone. Buried in space somewhere. She blinked at the thought, then shook her head.

In the adjacent control room, Warren took up the piloting joysticks to guide the probe out. Dr. Stelland monitored the sedated monkey's readings as the capsule moved across open space to the threshold of the wormhole. "The specimen is ready. Vital signs show he is in deep sleep."

The probe hovered on the event horizon, and Warren glanced up as he held the joystick controls. "Should I go ahead, boss?"

Noor crossed his arms over his chest. "Down the hatch, Warren."

Cammie watched the screens, tense, but said nothing.

The probe plunged into the blurry emptiness and vanished from real space.

Later, when Pedro Ashe released the canopy, they all gathered around the returned vessel. Cammie's heart was pounding hard as she pushed closer to see. She didn't know what she expected.

Zachary Tendari's body lay stretched out like a wax figure, unchanged. Maybe she had imagined some foolish miracle, as if the wormhole passage might be some kind of rejuvenation experience. Did she really expect him to sit up and smile, stretch his arms, and ask about his bad dream?

But his face remained cold and gray. Dead.

The monkey also lay perfectly still, as motionless as the corpse, but just sleeping. Glinda shouldered her way forward. "Fluffers?"

Dr. Stelland clucked his tongue. "All readings are stable, perfectly normal." He pulled electrode monitors from the primate's fur. "It will wake up momentarily."

Warren fidgeted, but he seemed encouraged. "Don't expect me to sleep like a baby on my first trip through the wormhole. It's eyes wide open for me."

Glinda reached in and lifted the sleeping monkey out. "Good job, Fluffers."

Stelland stood pondering. "I'll run tests on both subjects and perform a preliminary autopsy on the cadaver."

Cammie turned away, controlling her breathing with great effort. It was as if she could hear Tendari's critical voice in her mind.

Noor seemed satisfied for now. "First, we need to send the monkey through for one more test. Conscious this time."

The following day, the rhesus monkey was restrained but wide awake when they brought it back to the hangar bay. The doctor's workup had shown no changes at all from the initial passage, not even in behavior or appetite—just like the control group of sedated rats. This time the monkey was clearly uneasy and confused, struggling. Cammie felt distressed to see its wide eyes, its panic.

"Shit . . ." Glinda muttered. She scratched the back of the monkey's head. "You're about to be a great explorer, Fluffers, and when you come back, I'll give you all the fresh strawberries you can eat—" She stopped as she remembered the strange blight Stelland had recently discovered in the greenhouse. "I'll find you some strawberry preserves in the stores."

The animal tried to twitch away from her touch.

Warren regarded it with a serious expression. "Show me the way, buddy."

Noor was anxious. "Let's not take all day."

Glinda flashed him a critical glare. "You've never had a pet, Benedict."

"Other people had them for me."

With businesslike efficiency, the doctor placed the restrained monkey into the probe chamber, as if tucking a doll into bed. The monkey grunted and squirmed as he applied the electrodes to various points on the furry body.

Cammie felt edgy and upset. She was not a biologist, concerned only with mathematics and physical sciences, but she still hated to see this. She knew Tendari's body had been a necessary experiment, but no one had suffered for it. She rationalized why this had to be done to the monkey, but still it affected her.

Warren let out a long sigh. "No one likes to be a lab animal, but I'll be the next one up, and I want to be as prepared as I can."

"But you know what you're getting into," Cammie pointed out.

Glinda said in a soothing voice, "It's just a quick ride, Fluffers. There and back again." She scratched under the monkey's chin, but it cringed.

The doctor was impatient with the distraction. "Let me finish, please, Ms. Roybal." He checked the sensors, then nodded.

Ashe sealed the probe canopy in place.

Stelland monitored the remote medical readings as the probe came back. "Heartbeat, blood pressure, brain activity—all vital signs are elevated, as might be expected under increased stress, but the specimen survived the passage."

"It saw what no one else has seen," Noor said with a hint of awe.

The tense mood lightened somewhat, until Ashe opened the canopy.

The rhesus monkey stirred and looked around, though its furry body was still restrained. The doctor began pulling off the electrodes, but Glinda reached down to wrap her arms around the animal.

Cammie saw that it was trembling.

Glinda lifted the monkey up, holding it close. "You're home now. What an adventure!"

Fluffers whimpered.

CHAPTER 32

Once the monkey probe had returned, Arkourian authorized the first expedition to one of the alien asteroid bases. She realized that if she didn't let Warren fly the mission, he would probably steal a recon ship and go on his own joyride. She intended to be more organized than that.

When she informed him, Warren practically donned his flight suit right in front of her, ready to go. "*Clark* is refueled after my last run, and I gave it a quick once-over. After working for the boss all these years, I learned to be prepared to fly on a moment's notice."

"We leave within the hour. Glinda will take the third seat."

He sniffed. "To provide sarcastic commentary?"

"I want an engineer's perspective, especially if we need to figure out how to get inside." She didn't add that she also wanted to make sure Benedict Noor didn't insist on going along again. This time they knew it was an alien facility, and she couldn't guarantee his safety, depending on what they found.

Next, she went to the greenhouse module, where she found Glinda crawling out of a maintenance alcove near the hatch, covered in dirt and grease. Both engineers had been tinkering with the irrigation and fertilization systems, trying to figure out how a widespread blight or toxin could have entered a closed system.

Climbing to her feet, Glinda wiped a grimy hand on her jumpsuit. "Sure, I'll go to the alien base. Can't be any weirder than that comet temple—and it's better than digging around in recycled sewage."

The odor of sour decay drifted into the main corridor from the open greenhouse. The wilted plants looked like a rotting swamp. "Any answers here?" Arkourian asked. "We depend on those crops for fresh food."

Glinda shrugged. "Jack is crawling into places where I can't fit so he can dissect the systems. He might have it figured out by the time we come back from the asteroid base—he likes to work alone. Says I talk too much." She turned from the rotting vegetation, smeared her palms on her jumpsuit again. "In the meantime, I'll just have to forgo salad, which isn't such a big sacrifice."

As the *Clark* approached the largest of the alien complexes from the survey, Warren enlarged the image on the screen. "Here it is, alien Grand Central Station."

In the copilot seat, Arkourian said, "Or maybe it's their Pentagon. We don't know what they were doing here."

"I just don't want to see any wormy-faced creeps," Glinda said. "The ice statue was enough for me."

With the enhanced cockpit windows, Warren sharpened the view in front of them and activated the intense front beams to illuminate the pockmarked surface. Covered in ancient dust were numerous artificial structures: geometric tanks, supply vaults, conduits, curved dishes, with a central embedded metal dome like a large, festering boil.

Arkourian had seen Warren's preliminary images, but actually being here made the enigma even more profound. She couldn't shake the feeling of awe, although this base seemed less terrifying than the comet temple—a working outpost instead of a looming cosmic tomb.

Glinda let out a snort of surprise. "I've visited a lot of asteroids for NOOR, but nothing like this."

Arkourian studied the sensor screens as they cruised over the surface, scoping out the extent of the base. "Given the density readings, that asteroid must be honeycombed with tunnels and underground chambers."

Warren searched ahead for the best landing area. "I need a flat, stable place that isn't too crumbly . . . Well, look at that." The *Clark*'s lights illuminated a hardened area near the main dome—clearly a landing zone. "That must be visitor parking."

He activated the reverse thrusters as they settled on the paved area. In the asteroid's gravity, the touchdown wasn't difficult, though Warren exerted extra care. Arkourian looked at the cockpit controls and noted two amber lights in the fuel-coolant lines.

Warren spotted them too, but when he tapped the screen, the readings flickered back to green. "Let's go see some aliens," he said.

Glinda said from the back, "We should have brought flowers or a card."

As they emerged from the ship, they stepped gingerly on the hard, dust-covered surface. No other alien craft were present, but this was clearly the landing area. Arkourian looked up at the deep darkness above, the stars, the ill-defined wormhole. She wondered what sort of short-range vessels the cricket creatures would have used around here.

Near the landing area, several cylindrical tanks were connected with conduits and bolted to the rock surface. Storage containers? Water tanks or fuel reservoirs? Armored doors and sealed hatches dotted the sheer cliffs. On the crater floor, curved parabolic dishes were tilted at conflicting angles but generally facing the Nether wormhole.

"This place is intimidating as hell," Glinda muttered.

Arkourian saw nothing that was immediately threatening. "The aliens had a huge operation here. Benedict is probably right—the wormhole could be the entryway to a significant transportation system between here and Alpha Centauri, or farther."

"Let's not forget the headline," Glinda said. "We had *aliens in our solar system*. What if they invaded Earth in prehistoric times?"

"Maybe they were wiped out by the same asteroid that killed the dinosaurs," Warren said. He ventured over to a shielded bank of modules, whose outer metal casings had been pitted by centuries of micrometeoroid strikes. "Looks like all the systems shut down a long, long time ago."

"Glinda, do you think you can get any of this machinery working again?" Arkourian asked.

"We didn't cover alien tech in engineering school." After a brief pause, though, she said in a resigned voice, "Still, engineering is engineering. I can probably figure something out, given enough time. Although . . ." She hesitated, as if reluctant to speak a compliment. "Jack is best at that sort of thing. He's freakishly intuitive."

"I'll assign him to the next team, after we see what's here."

Staying within visual range, the three spread out to explore different areas of the mysterious base. Their visor cams recorded everything they saw.

The nucleus of the complex was the large main dome, a sunken metal blister covered with armored plates and more dust. Arkourian made her way toward the perimeter. If the primary alien base was beneath the armored bubble, then the entrance had to be here somewhere.

She wondered how many of the cricket aliens had inhabited

the base—hundreds? Thousands? Were they the only alien species to come here from the stars? And what was the intimidating tentacle-faced figure on its ice throne? Did that represent a real sentient being, or just a frightening idol of some vengeful deity? She certainly hoped such things did not exist.

From a scientific perspective, Arkourian knew that the base inside the dome would hold a treasure trove of information, possibly even logbooks or records—if they could figure out how to translate them. On-the-job training, she supposed.

Leaving footprints in the ancient dust, Arkourian followed the rim of the dome, trying to peer inside, but the armor plating blocked any view. She felt an eerie sense of being watched. A quarter of the way around the circle, she came to an ellipsoidal structure that looked like a hatch leading inside. She recognized the surprisingly similar form of an airlock.

Her voice cracked as she transmitted, "I think I found a way in."

If they could comprehend some of the nonhuman systems and controls, her team could enter the dome and start exploring the full alien base.

Approaching the airlock, she checked her oxygen-tank levels, her battery readings. Hours still remained before they would need to return to Nether Station.

Arkourian came to an abrupt halt as she saw a figure sprawled outside the sealed hatch—a body, mostly covered in dust. It had fallen to the ground just outside the sanctuary of the base.

She bent down and used her gloves to wipe away the dust. It was another one of the cockroach aliens, wearing no environment suit. Its black hemispherical eyes had cracked. This made no sense. Had it been abandoned outside, caught in some accident? Had all the insect creatures within the dome died from some environmental catastrophe?

Maybe there was no obvious explanation at all.

Before she could report her discovery, Glinda's urgent voice came through the helmet comm. "Whoa—Warren, are the *Clark*'s coolant hoses supposed to be spraying steam into the air like that?"

"There's no air here; it's a vacuum," Warren said.

"Not the point, idiot!"

Arkourian hurried away from the dome so she could see the landed recon ship, and she immediately spotted the faint plume of steam rising up. Leaving the frozen alien body behind, she sprinted back.

The pilot was bounding toward the vessel, taking long strides in the low gravity. Glinda was already there. Warren opened the access port to the *Clark*'s rear engines. "Dammit, I checked that!"

One of the coolant hoses emitted a thin jet of sparkling vapor into the vacuum. Scrambling, Glinda pulled a repair kit from her suit. "I've got puncture seal right here, and it'll hold before we lose too much coolant."

From all her exterior work, the engineer knew how to do repairs on the fly. She and Warren patched the leaking hose and stepped back, shaken but relieved. "Crisis averted," Glinda said.

"We only lost fifteen percent," Warren added. "Good enough for us to get home. Damn, I love those safety margins."

Arkourian stood behind them, arms at her side. "This makes me very uneasy. What happened?"

Warren sounded sheepish. "The cooling line must have been stressed from my last run. I checked it during my inspection, but apparently not well enough." She could see his embarrassed expression behind the faceplate. "Well, even if we were stranded here, Nether Station still has the other recon ship. Someone could rescue us with the *Lewis*."

"You and I are the best pilots—and we're both here," Arkourian pointed out.

He turned away, mumbling, "Well, that's poor planning. We have to go back to the station."

Arkourian had no choice but to agree. "At least we got an initial assessment. We'll come back with a full-fledged expedition." Disappointed, she turned toward the dusty dome, anxious to get inside.

Next time.

CHAPTER 33

Benedict Noor had never let superstitious fears or self-doubt deter progress, or profit. He thought of what he had seen deep inside that comet temple, the kaleidoscopic void that had tried to suck him in, filling him with unknowable dread. That encounter had been like a stake through the heart of his self-confidence.

But he shook himself and drove that atavistic fear away. The unknown was nothing to be afraid of—it was something to be understood. So much to learn, so much to document. If those cockroach aliens could do it, so could he.

In his youth, at a mountain retreat, he had lain on a blanket after dark with his sister, looking up into the night sky. He and Margo had slipped away from their camp caretakers so they could watch the Perseid meteor shower.

Young Benedict had flicked his eyes from side to side, trying to spot the next meteor, but it would always streak across his peripheral vision from a random direction. Margo treated it as a competition, calling out her victories, but by the time he turned his gaze, the tiny flare had ignited in a final flash of glory.

In the two weeks since their arrival at the Nether wormhole, his team's discoveries were like that. One flash, then another from a different direction, then another. There hadn't even been time for a round-trip transmission to Earth, though he had dispatched several encoded message bursts down to the asteroid hub. His NOOR experts would just now be receiving his first report . . . and there was so much more to come.

Noor was very careful with what he wanted the general public to know, although some of his crew assumed he was broadcasting each day's miracles to awed crowds on Earth. These breakthroughs were proprietary information.

Only Karla Arkourian, whom he trusted completely, was aware of how he curated the reports, and his reasons for doing so. She disagreed, even had the backbone to argue with him, but eventually she backed down.

Since it took a month to say, "How are you?" "I am fine," the conversation hadn't even started yet, and there wouldn't be much useful dialogue in the six months of their mission here.

Once his company understood the basic science and made their moves, after Margo dispatched the second wave of facility ships, then he could distribute redacted reports and let the international space agencies and university teams try to play catch-up. By then he would have it sewn up.

Once again, he stood impatient outside the medical bay, watching the doctor begin his work on the cadaver that had returned in the recent probe vessel. Not needing a full decontamination outfit for a cursory autopsy, as he had with the alien dissection, Stelland wore a regular surgeon's gown, gloves, and mask. Tendari's naked body lay arranged on the metal-composite operating table. The man's eyes were open but glassy, staring up at the harsh lights.

Stelland seemed uncomfortable, and he glanced at Noor through the observation window. "Autopsies are not normally a spectator sport, sir."

"Do I make you nervous? I am your employer."

"Indeed. My current ability to send out job applications is

rather limited." He slowly circled the cadaver, poking the cold skin with a finger, lifting the eyelids, pulling back the lips.

Noor leaned against the wall in the medical lab, continuing to make conversation. "I have always viewed science as a spectator sport. I'm anxious to see what effect the wormhole has on a human body."

Stelland bent forward and studied the man laid out in front of him. He spoke as if recording a report, not to Noor. "The specimen appears to be intact and undamaged. From the previous two probes, we have evidence that interdimensional travel causes little direct physical effect." He frowned. "Though the lab rat specimens might have suffered neurological changes, particularly the group that remained conscious. It is too soon to draw full conclusions about the rhesus monkey, though it does show certain behavioral changes after the ordeal."

"The monkey was probably scared out of its mind," Noor said. "Warren will be fully aware of his circumstances. Makes all the difference."

"Possibly."

The doctor had taken scrapings and cellular samples, leaving rough rectangular patches on the cadaver's skin, and he had already drawn blood and cranial fluids for analysis. "From my initial tests, there are no obvious cellular changes—as I expected. No harm to human tissue." He clicked his tongue and looked up at where Noor stood watching him. "Those are the results you want to hear, aren't they?"

Noor chuckled, though laughter sounded grossly inappropriate. "My interest is to see whether humans can travel to Alpha Centauri, and return safely." He added the last part, remembering Kennedy's famous Apollo speech. It had to be said; it had to be thought. But Noor just wanted to *get there*. "I'm being extra cautious for Warren's sake. Tendari's body offered an unexpected opportunity to collect more data before we send a living, conscious human. I didn't want to waste an opportunity."

"All I can do is offer my analysis and my opinion, sir."

"And your opinion is?" Noor pressed.

"Unformed, as of yet." He turned to his surgical tools and continued talking as he made a Y incision down the man's torso. "We can draw a few inferences about wormhole effects on tissue, organs, muscle fibers, the circulatory system. The biggest mystery, however, is the effect on brain activity and thought processes." The doctor seemed hesitant. "To me, the monkey and awake rat specimens do not seem normal, but they of course cannot articulate what they experienced."

Noor glanced at where the specimen cage remained covered with a dark shroud to keep the seven lab rats quiet and calm. The other group of rats bustled about, seemingly normal. "You said the rodents came through all right, no identifiable medical effects. You declared them physically fit."

"But the awake test group killed one of their own."

"Rats do that under pressure." Noor knew he sounded flippant. "Bullying behavior occurs in nature all the time."

"I'm aware of that." Stelland pried open Tendari's chest and began extracting the large organs, weighing them, filling out all the fields in a standard autopsy report.

Noor wandered over to the monkey, which hunched against the back wall of its cage, as if cornered. It seemed hunted, intimidated. "Look at you—shaken up by the experience?"

From the operating chamber, Stelland looked up, holding a bloody scalpel in his glove. "Shaken up? I'd say the behavior reflects abject terror."

Fluffers shifted in its cage, cringing away from Noor.

"Traveling through a spacetime tunnel must be like a

psychedelic experience with bad drugs. It's just a monkey, confused, with no idea what was happening to it. That's where we humans have an edge, Doc. We can understand the inexplicable. Warren's a test pilot—he has faced other death-defying situations. We don't need to fear the mysteries of the universe."

Though he felt and sounded confident, Noor suddenly remembered that soul-sucking black mirror again, the broken fragments of reality inside the ice temple. He shuddered but tried to cover it up.

Noor decided he didn't want to watch any more of the autopsy. He would never admit, at least not out loud, that he was afraid.

CHAPTER 34

Working inside the observatory module, Cammie was not in the mood for conversation. She knew that the autopsy was under way right now.

She understood the reasons for it, and she knew Dr. Tendari's true passion for the science, especially as it related to the effects of the wormhole. Or was *she* secretly his true passion? Maybe she was just imagining it all.

Doggedly, she turned back to the wormhole data. She had pored over their theoretical models, trying to imagine what a person would experience inside that warped dimensional rabbit hole. But mathematics gave no texture, color, or sensation, and the camera images recorded during the previous probe missions had shown little, as if the lenses had also been dizzy and disoriented. Maybe that other inside-out space was something that could not be recorded or understood by real-world measuring devices.

The air inside the module felt cool, and she heard the quiet breath of recirculatory ventilation. The broad windowports showed the wormhole, but she also saw glimmers that she knew were asteroids, the speck of the nearby comet and its profoundly disturbing temple.

The insect creatures must have operated some kind of network based around the wormhole. Why else would they be here? After studying the images, she felt the giant statue on the ice throne seemed to be a figure of religious significance, but the asteroid bases must have been the real operational centers. She waited to see what the first expedition would find. Warren, Glinda, and Captain Arkourian were over there right now.

Eventually, Cammie wanted to go to one of the bases and try to understand. See it with her own eyes. She was an astrophysicist and a mathematician, not an engineer, so she wouldn't be able to suggest any specific purpose to the parabolic antenna structures, the conduits and storage tanks. But she did have a different perspective. Considering the mysteries of the Nether doorway to Alpha Centauri, what if those cricket aliens had been astrophysicists themselves? Wormhole researchers, like her? Cammie might be able to understand what they were doing after all.

Maybe she would volunteer to join the next survey team over to one of the bases. Most of the time she felt like a fifth wheel here on Nether Station.

"Yes, we need to understand everything, no matter the cost," Tendari's voice said inside her mind, so clear that it startled her.

She glanced around. The words sounded so real, so close, but it was just her subconscious. He had always been the voice of reason, the voice of ambition, telling her what to do.

"I'm gone now, Cammie, so it's up to you," he said, as if he were really there. "You have to do your part. No one else can comprehend how the wormhole works. No one else can see the consequences. You're the one who's equipped with the theoretical models and the high-level understanding. You think those engineers know anything? The test pilot? That idiot Noor? Tell the others what they need to do."

"Mr. Noor makes all those decisions," she said aloud, feeling silly for talking to herself. "And Captain Arkourian administers them."

"Then take more of a leadership role. Be assertive!"

He had scolded her for being shy and quiet in the past, encouraged her not to be so passive. He'd been paternal and protective when he was alive, always there to step in as her heroic rescuer. But what if he didn't really want her to be assertive, so she would have to rely on him?

"I always took care of you, beautiful Cammie. I always saved you—not just from predators and bullies but from yourself. You needed me in every possible way."

"I did my best." She felt defensive. "My research and my theories took all my energy and focus. You know that."

"There's no excuse for not taking time to be human." His imaginary voice had a hard edge. "To have feelings."

Through the windowport, the wormhole seemed to pull at her. She whispered, "What was it like when you went through there?"

"You'll never know, unless you step up! I'm not here anymore to stop you from making social blunders, to intercept clods who just want to get into your panties."

With a hiss, Cammie shook her head. Why was she thinking things like that? "I can handle myself."

"You have to, or you'll fail. You are the smartest person on Nether Station. The wormhole is yours, and you're letting everyone else walk over you. That pilot—Warren Drake—wants you. Can't you see it in his eyes? You're always too foolish to understand how sexually attractive you are! You could have used that to your benefit. I saw what you had to offer, but you always brushed me away, never even considered me." He made a disgusted sound. "After all I did for you."

"No!" She squeezed her eyes shut. Her head was pounding. This wasn't her image of him. This wasn't Zachary Tendari. She thought of Leila and the other ISA probe technicians snickering behind her back.

"You were oblivious, and you don't even know how much you hurt me," he said. "You gave me nothing, and then you let me die in the cryopod."

"I had nothing to do with that!" She groaned deep in her throat. "Why are you saying things like this?" Her loud voice in the sealed module startled her. She looked around, discovered that she was shaking.

His voice was even more accusatory. "And then you let them send my body through the wormhole. You should go yourself! See for yourself—only then can you understand the things that I know!"

"I . . . I'm not ready."

"Admit the real reason, Cammie. You're afraid. You're afraid of everything. You're afraid to be a human, afraid to open yourself to love. To me!"

"Not afraid," she snapped. "I just don't understand. I'm not ready." *And I never once thought of you that way.*

"You're afraid to understand, afraid to open yourself. And now you'll never have me."

She strode over to the lab station with the optical telescopes, furiously punched buttons, and called up high-resolution images, trying to concentrate on work. The voice in her head wasn't the real Dr. Tendari. He would never say things like that.

This had to be caused by her stress, her nightmares. For the past several nights, she had slept in contorted positions and awakened in darkness, sure that the nightmares were trying to signal something to her, but right now she was fully alert and awake. She shouldn't be hearing his voice! It was like a ghost, but this couldn't be her mentor, the man she cared for . . . the man who cared for her, perhaps in inappropriate ways.

"This is not you," she said out loud. "Dr. Tendari would never say things like that."

"Call me Zach," he said, and it sounded like a threat.

"Why do you want to hurt me?" She couldn't fathom why he—or her subconscious—was doing this.

"I want you to *understand*, Cammie. And sometimes that hurts."

Then, like an imploding vacuum tube, she heard a sudden silence in her mind, felt no presence, no imaginary lecturer. Zach Tendari's voice was gone.

CHAPTER 35

Cammie got her opportunity sooner than expected when the damaged *Clark* returned to Nether Station, and Captain Arkourian announced she would return to the asteroid base, but she would need one more crewmember. Cammie gathered her courage and volunteered for the follow-up mission.

She went to the observation bridge. She was intimidated by the unknown, but she felt even more unsettled by Tendari's sharp, critical voice in her mind. She faced Noor and Arkourian at their bridge stations and kept her voice strong. "I can offer my perspective, though I'm not sure I'll understand what I'm seeing over there."

Though clearly surprised by her offer, Karla Arkourian supported her. "No one understands what we saw, Cammie, but your point of view is as valid as anyone's—especially if the aliens were doing wormhole science. I'd be happy to have you along."

"And Cammie's smart." Noor laughed. "I think it's a splendid idea. Time for you to get your head out of the theoretical box. You'll be one of the first to explore over there."

After the *Clark* had returned, Warren Drake spent hours in the hangar bay, making repairs to the coolant line and double-checking the other recon ship for the next flight. For the return mission, Arkourian would take the *Lewis* with Cammie and Pedro Ashe to continue exploring the alien base. As a consolation prize, Warren would finish repairs to the *Clark* and then take it out on a thorough mapping mission of all the other asteroid stations. Embarrassed by the coolant-line glitch, he said, "I'm better at flying ships than stomping around in a space suit anyway."

When the second group was ready to depart, Cammie let Arkourian check her suit and systems. Although she had less experience than the others, she had undergone full training at the NOOR asteroid hub. Now, suited up, she felt comfortable enough as she boarded the *Lewis* and climbed into the rear seat, while Ashe swung himself into the copilot's chair. Arkourian sealed the compartment, preparing for launch.

Cammie felt butterflies in her stomach as they flew away from Nether Station. Many things about the entire wormhole mission made her uneasy, but she couldn't help but be intrigued. Yes, she might feel more comfortable working quietly alone in the observatory module, but she could hear Tendari's voice pressuring her. "If that's all you're going to do, Cammie, why did you come all the way out here? You hid in university libraries all your career. Now you're at an actual wormhole. Go get your hands dirty!"

Maybe by leaving the station she could break away from him too.

Finally, when she saw the embedded structures and domes on the barren rock, she was reminded of the NOOR corporate mining facilities she had seen in the asteroid hub. But this was different—this base had been built by aliens.

As they set down near the central armored dome, Cammie could see smears in the dust of the cleared area where the *Clark* had landed the day before. Arkourian powered down the engines. "Ready to go exploring? Let's hope we can get inside this trip."

Ashe spoke for the first time in many minutes. "I saw your images. If it's an airlock, I'll figure it out. Basic engineering."

With the recon ship's hatch open, Arkourian and Ashe dropped down onto the dust, and Cammie emerged last. She paused, astonished to find herself surrounded by extraterrestrial structures—cylindrical pipes connected with a row of supply tanks, massive machinery that looked like generators, and the central dome. She wondered what the mysterious cricket creatures had left behind here.

Taking the lead, Arkourian headed directly toward the main dome, and with light footsteps, Pedro Ashe bounced after her. He asked, "Why would they cover their main dome with metal plates and make it opaque, when they could be looking out at the stars and at the wormhole?"

Cammie suggested, "For shielding? Protection from micro-impacts? If they had exterior imagers, they could see everything anyway."

Ashe considered. "Then why bother building an external dome in the first place? An underground base would be safer, easier to contain."

"Our scans showed that the asteroid has multiple voids," Arkourian said. "This whole rock could be honeycombed with tunnels."

The three walked along the rim of the dome until they reached the recognizable hatch. The vacuum-mummified insect creature lay sprawled outside the airlock door, as if it had died trying to get back in. Cammie assumed those bug aliens were the builders of this complex, or at least the day-to-day workers.

Looking at the creature made Cammie feel sad and unsettled. "Should we bury it? Or maybe take it inside?" She remembered her strange dreams and vivid imagination, seeing swarms of the creatures, either at war or enslaved by the horrific tentacle-faced monsters.

"It's been out here for countless years undisturbed."

Arkourian began using her scrambler probes on the hatch controls. "It can wait a little while longer."

Ashe nudged Arkourian aside. "Let me, Captain." He ran his own handheld scanner along the hatch electronics and diagnostics. "The power system still has sufficient charge. We don't need a battery jump. I think I can decipher these controls." His voice dropped to a whisper. "Remarkable."

Ancient dust billowed around the hatch as the components hummed and shifted. The young engineer stepped back. "That's a good sign."

The seal opened, and the outer door slid aside to reveal a dark closet-sized chamber. Arkourian played her light inside. "There's an inner door. Seems to function like a standard airlock."

Ashe said, "From Doc Stelland's autopsy of the alien specimen, we know these creatures had organs analogous to ours, including lungs. So, similar biological processes."

"We have to go inside that little chamber?" Cammie asked. The alien airlock looked like a crypt.

"We can't get started until we get inside," Ashe added, then turned to her. "Can't be any harder than some of my sims."

"Our exosuits will protect us," Arkourian said.

Cammie drove back her uneasiness, reminding herself that more answers were inside the base, and the potential rewards would justify any risks. "You're right. That's why we're here."

She imagined Tendari's voice speaking inside her head. "Good girl."

Ashe had brought along his full tool kit. "If necessary, we can cut our way back out."

Arkourian entered the airlock chamber, and Ashe followed. "Let's bite the bullet."

There was enough room for Cammie to join them in the

chamber, though she felt claustrophobic. The thick outer door slid shut, making it worse.

Arkourian switched on her suit light in the confined darkness. Now that Ashe was familiar with the basic systems after opening the outer hatch, he studied the inner controls, then managed to activate the inner seal.

A stirring of pressurization wafted around them, and the inner door slid open with a sound like a death rattle. Automated systems flickered on and illuminated the passageway in front of them. Cammie stared into the vast, ancient complex.

No one wanted to be the first to move, until finally Arkourian stepped out into a widening tunnel. Underground, the base seemed to go on and on. Cammie and Ashe followed her to a cavernous central grotto filled with substations, control panels, and dead-gray screens under a huge, curved ceiling. Looking up, Cammie realized that this was the chamber beneath the armored dome.

Though the numerous substations were alien in design, their purpose seemed recognizable, oddly familiar. "This is a control room," she said.

The lights automatically brightened in the main chamber, and several stations blinked and flickered. Arkourian sounded relieved. "The power is restoring itself—even after all these years."

"We must have triggered it out of sleep mode," Ashe said. He moved past Arkourian to the nearest bank of equipment. Each exotic station was a squat monolith with a polished face, which seemed to be some kind of display screen. An angled panel held rows of oddly shaped buttons and levers, meant to be used by insectile forefingers.

Ashe held up a handheld scanner from his engineering kit, turning around in slow circles. "This is unexpected! The interior is pressurized, base integrity still intact after what must be centuries." He waved the scanner in all directions. "The dome and passages are full of air—breathable air."

As Cammie moved to another station, wondering if she could decipher its purpose, she flinched as she saw a slumped figure on the floor. One of the cockroach creatures, petrified in death. Were these creatures scientists like herself, or just drone workers? "Here's another dead alien."

"A lot of them." Arkourian stood by one of the bizarre creatures at a second station, poking it with her gloved finger. Though the insectile body was hollow and decayed, its exoskeleton remained. "Just a husk, less preserved than the ones frozen out in space."

"Did they starve to death?" Ashe asked aloud. "Were they poisoned? Murdered?"

Cammie glanced up as bright, distracting lights appeared on the underside of the dome, a projection of intersecting lines, geometric patterns . . . targeting points. At the apex of the dome, a large black circle stood out like a bull's-eye, with dotted lines and jagged rays like arrows running toward it.

"The central point must be the wormhole. And I think that bright spot"—Cammie pointed down at seven o'clock—"might be the location of this primary asteroid. And that ring of locater points would be the other eight asteroid bases surrounding the wormhole."

Arkourian stared at the patterns, then looked at the stations filling the chamber. "This is an air traffic control center."

Ashe said, "If the Nether wormhole is part of an interstellar transportation network, as Mr. Noor believes, it makes sense there would be traffic control stations around the opening."

"You make it sound very mundane, Mr. Ashe," Arkourian said.

"I'm making it comprehensible."

Cammie crossed the main chamber to where more tunnels led deeper into the base, maybe to living quarters, mess halls, storage units. "It'll take us days just to do a basic survey of this place."

"We've only got two more hours of oxygen before we need to get back to the *Lewis*," Arkourian said, marking the display at her waist. "Doesn't give us much time."

Ashe checked his scanner, testing the air. "The interior temperature is chilly but tolerable. It'll probably warm up as the systems come back online." He reset the filters. "According to this, atmosphere composition is primarily oxygen and nitrogen, some carbon dioxide, a few trace gases. These bugs seem to breathe the same air we do."

"I wouldn't risk it," Cammie said. "There could be—"

But the engineer clicked the latch around his neck collar. "If we rely on our suit air, we'll have to return before we even get started. Too much to see here."

"Don't be brash—" Arkourian warned.

He removed the helmet anyway. "I trust my engineering." He inhaled a deep breath.

Cammie and Arkourian both tensed, half expecting him to collapse in spasms, choking and gasping.

"The air stinks, probably from all those rotting bugs." He took another breath. "But we'll get used to it. And now that we're not on a tight time clock, I can dig into the alien control systems, and we can have a real look around."

"You're an idiot, breaking all the protocols," Arkourian said. "I see why Glinda calls you Jack Ashe."

The young man was not insulted. "You know Mr. Noor will want to occupy these bases for his own uses. Think of the long-term benefit to us if they already hold breathable air."

After a long moment, Arkourian said, "You're absolutely

right." Looking at Ashe standing there, apparently unaffected, she removed her own helmet.

Bracing herself again, forcing herself to look forward, to be brave, Cammie took off her helmet and breathed alien air for the first time.

Ashe was correct. Without the lumbering constraints of the suits and helmets, they made much greater progress. After stripping out of their exosuits, the three split up but stayed in contact as they started to explore the abandoned base.

Filled with a sense of wonder, Cammie moved down well-lit tunnels and found hive-like chambers. Alien sleeping quarters? Next, she came upon smooth-walled, sterile rooms that could have been laboratories or medical centers. Her initial anxiety was replaced with fascination, and her eyes and mind throbbed with everything she was seeing. This was amazing.

Exploring an adjacent section, Arkourian discovered agricultural chambers with long-dormant lighting and irrigation systems. The mulch was dry and ironhard, with scraps of petrified fungus laid out in what must have been crops.

Two levels beneath the main control dome, Ashe found a power center where glowing generators still operated. Pulsing organic machines lit up the shielded room. Power conduits extended throughout the base and into the walls, maybe even to the spiked parabolic dishes in the crater.

Cammie kept following the tunnels, marking her route so she could find her way back to the central chamber. In one odd room, she stood before an intriguing flat wall that held five round portholes, windows filled with a silvery liquid, like a vertical pool of mercury. The metallic fluid shimmered with glowing curves of color that she didn't understand. A strange energetic field pulled at her mind, drawing her closer. She felt no fear, only fascination.

Now that they had reawakened the base's systems, the power inside these quicksilver windows was active. The hypnotic vertical pools throbbed with questions and seemed to promise answers. A shiver of wonder shot down her spine. This was the most intriguing thing she had seen so far inside the base.

Cammie called her two companions to take a look, and when Arkourian and Ashe joined her, they, too, felt the compelling tug of the strange portholes. It seemed to draw them. The young engineer summed it up. "That's really weird."

"We're finding more questions than we're answering," Arkourian said.

"Job security," Ashe quipped. "We still have five and a half months here."

As Cammie continued to stare at the mercury-filled portholes, mesmerized, she pondered the dead cricket aliens and the wormhole transportation hub. It was obviously a once-massive operation center, but it had been shut down and abandoned. What could have happened to it all? She yearned to learn what the aliens understood about wormhole astrophysics—they obviously knew much more than she did. She imagined the conversations they could have had.

Cammie mused aloud, "What are you? Why were you here?" Shaking her head, she stepped closer to the quivering metallic pool in front of her face. "I wish I knew."

"Don't we all." Arkourian leaned closer to another porthole.

With an unexpected thrum, a blob of quicksilver extruded with lightning speed, spilling out like a slimy tentacle. It opened a toothless maw—and engulfed Cammie's head.

CHAPTER 36

Ill at ease after the autopsy, Dr. Stelland slept for four hours before he finally returned to the medical lab. Tendari's tissues had yielded nothing of interest after exposure to the wormhole environment, as expected. All his cells, fluids, and organs seemed normal. The interdimensional transit had caused no additional physical damage to the body. He didn't know what Noor meant to prove with the experiment.

For now, the cadaver remained on the autopsy table, roughly sewn back up. Since the alien specimen remained in the lab's morgue freezer, this body would have to go back into the cryo-pod for cold storage. As he came back to work after his rest, Stelland prepared himself to wrap up the body for preservation.

But when he entered the med lab, he felt an odd tension in the air. Something was not right. In its cage, the rhesus monkey whimpered and moaned—as it had done often since returning with the probe. Stelland swept his gaze around the chamber, alert. He felt the hairs rise on the back of his neck.

Inside their cage, the group of normal lab rats scuttled around. But the shroud covering from the second cage lay shredded on the floor. The fabric had been torn into confetti by tiny teeth.

Suddenly alarmed, he hurried forward. The cage was empty. The steel wire bars should have been sturdy enough against any animal, but now they were bent in all directions . . . *gnawed.*

The rats had not just broken a few wires apart to slither out—they had mangled the container walls in malicious destruction. And all seven of the disturbed rodents were gone.

Stelland froze in place and made a slow inspection of the medical center: the cabinets, the surgery room, the supply closet, the equipment rack in the rear. The rats were loose, but he knew the outer door had been sealed when he entered, so the little monsters must have been somewhere in the medical bay.

He remembered their eerie black eyes—and how they had torn their companion into bloody shreds. Gooseflesh crawled down his arms as he feared the rats might swarm forward, leap onto his legs, and start biting him.

With cautious steps, he went to the supply shelf and pulled out a fresh scalpel, holding it ready to slash and fight, if necessary.

Then he spotted a line of tiny, bloody pawprints on the floor. The rats must have lacerated themselves as they tore apart their cage. They had run in a direct line to the bulkhead wall—where they had peeled off one of the polymer-metal wall plates, bending it back so they could access the gap that held conduits, electronics, ventilation systems, piping.

A sick cold settled into his gut. The rats were in the walls.

Karla Arkourian, Pedro Ashe, and Cammie Skoura were gone, exploring the main alien base, and Warren Drake was already engaged in his survey flight of the other asteroids. Nether Station was nearly empty—and the rats were running loose.

He hit the comm speaker on the wall. "Glinda, come to medical immediately. We have an emergency."

Glinda stood with her hands on her sturdy hips, ready with a wisecrack as Stelland described what had happened. She listened, skeptical. "So, we have a rodent problem, and you want me to be pest control?"

"Their behavior changed significantly after they experienced the wormhole," he said. "They are very different from the sedated batch—angry and destructive. They seem to have a purpose."

She smirked. The doctor had always been an odd duck. "Are you eating some of that tainted fruit from the greenhouse, Doc?"

In the monkey cage, at the back of the room, Fluffers sulked and avoided any contact, even with her. Glinda was disappointed.

"Look what they did!" He indicated the mangled cage and then the intentional—and intelligent—opening of the wall plate. The star tattoo twitched at the side of his eye. "They're inside the station walls now. What kind of damage could they be causing to our systems?"

Glinda scowled as the possibilities occurred to her. "You're right—no time for jokes. There are gobs of sensitive systems in the space between the bulkhead and the hull." She couldn't resist a snarky comment. "It's a rat's nest in there—literally."

"How are you going to find them? Is there a way to pump CO_2 through the walls and suffocate them?" His voice was stressed and raw.

"Oh, I'll figure out a way." The wheels were already turning in her mind. "I'm on it."

Leaving the med center, she headed up a level and passed through the smelly greenhouse on her way to the engineering bay. Standing by herself amid all the equipment, she reviewed the banks of sensitive monitors that displayed the web of Nether Station systems. Seven rats on the loose! If they stuck together like a pack in the maze of the conduits, they might be easier to find. Glinda wasn't going to let a few rodents get the better of her.

The engineering bay held all the tools and equipment she

needed. Wall lockers held their exosuits and spares for the crew. The direct-exit airlock was at the far end of the bay, but she wouldn't need to go outside for this.

After she pulled together motion sensors, her analytical pad, and a rod probe, then clipped a tool pack around her waist, she stood before the main engineering screen. Frowning, she pulled up detailed blueprints of Nether Station, the original central core of the *Lethe* with satellite cylinders and modules around the main body. Throughout, the narrow access gap between the hull and the bulkheads offered miles of narrow passages.

The station's AI ran analyses faster than Glinda could think to ask questions, and she traced hundreds of thousands of wires, circuits, and conduits, looking for any recent gaps, fault clusters, or interruptions in power flow. Glimmers appeared on the high-resolution schematics—some anomalies, some hot spots.

Glinda dismissed most of the alerts as routine glitches caused by wear and tear from systems exposed to the space environment for years. Backup conduits and circuits routinely picked up the slack, so no maintenance intervention was necessary on her part.

But those rats could cause malicious damage, even if they weren't "demon possessed," as Stelland seemed to think.

Staring at the screen, Glinda did notice a pattern like Christmas lights, dots moving in a line that extended from the medical center. She imagined feral lab rats chewing on a particularly juicy-looking wire. So far the creatures had caused no massive damage, as if they were just experimenting, exploring. Scheming.

Taking a motion scanner and thermal reader, she noted the locations of the glitches and hurried down the corridor to the next deck. She emerged in the long, cool deck that held all the cryopods. The nine sealed chambers thrummed as life-support systems tried to keep the inhabitants alive.

Lights flickered on the back wall, and she went to press the motion detector against the bulkhead. Her penetrating scanner showed movement, little figures scurrying behind the passageway.

Setting the detector aside, she pulled a pistol-shaped demagnetizer from her belt to remove the sealed wall plate, but the motion signatures darted off into a different conduit. On the overall station schematics, she saw damage indicators like a series of dots moving away from the bed-and-breakfast deck.

Breathing rapidly, she headed for the observation bridge, where Benedict Noor brooded like a lonely king in his captain's chair. He was watching initial reports from Warren Drake's survey flight. He glanced at her, preoccupied. "You look flushed, Glinda. What did Dr. Stelland want?"

"He wants me to be the Pied Piper, and that's not something engineering school trained me for."

Noor cocked his eyebrows. "Plain answers, please."

She told him about the renegade rats in the station. "Who knows what kind of a mess they'll cause if they start chewing on wires and conduits? Maybe they'll electrocute themselves, but I bet we're not so lucky. I don't suppose we have any rat poison in the *Lethe* supplies?"

He pursed his lips. "Unfortunately, that's not something we thought to include in our initial manifest. Or a ship's cat."

Bending over Arkourian's main station, Glinda pulled up the primary schematics and had the AI highlight the probable location of the moving rats. She grunted in disgust. "I see multiple faults in the secondary habitation module. How did they get out there so fast? They're chewing on wires and ripping wall circuits."

"At least nobody's in the module now," Noor said. "Get over there and find them."

Grabbing her engineering kit, Glinda bounded out of the

bridge and moved along the decks until she reached the airlock connector to the secondary hab module, which held spare quarters for the next wave of Nether Station personnel. Inside the long cylinder, she sprinted past one empty room after another.

The fault-pattern projection led her to one specific stateroom, where she assumed the vicious rodents had congregated. She unsealed the door and entered the cold, empty quarters. She activated the ceiling illumination and stood still, listening. In the silence, she could hear shuffling and skittering behind the bulkhead wall.

"Damn critters." The frenetic scritching of tiny claws was amplified in the oppressive empty room. She pressed her palms against the bulkhead and felt a faint vibration, convinced that all seven rats were here, moving along and wreaking havoc. "Whoa, got you now!"

She ran the demagnetizer along the seams on the wall, popped off the access plate, and shone the bright beam of her light into the gap between the walls.

Furry white forms scuttled along in the tight space. "Come here!" She directed the beam, which reflected a glare from their beady eyes.

Then the rats lunged toward her like bullets. The light glinted off razor-sharp teeth. One sprang out at Glinda, and she swatted it aside by reflex, stunning it and knocking it to the floor.

The rest of the rodents hissed, squeaked, and shrieked. Another slithered out, snapping its sharp teeth as it tried to bite her hand. It caught her tough sleeve and shredded the fabric as she knocked it back into the bulkhead gap. "Holy shit!"

She grabbed the metal plate she had just removed and slammed it like a musician's cymbal against the wall. The rats inside were thrown back, and then they scattered.

On the stateroom floor, the stunned rodent twitched and squirmed. Its spine was broken, but it still crawled toward her, snapping its bloody jaws. Its eyes were blazing red now, as if filled with blood.

Glinda slammed the wall plate down like a guillotine blade, cutting the rat in half. It twitched and bled out on the deck.

She could still hear the remaining six rats rustling between the bulkheads, but they were scattering farther into the station.

Shaking and sweating, she used the magnetizing pistol to seal the plate back into place, then slumped down to sit on the floor of the empty quarters. "Maybe we should have brought a ship's cat."

CHAPTER 37

Lost in a strange and smothering limbo, Cammie swam through an interstellar war. Inside her mind, she witnessed the destruction of worlds, the annihilation of innocent races, and a deadly horror that swept from star system to star system.

Drifting, just a fragment of consciousness, Cammie was attacked, bombarded . . . informed. Data salvos pummeled her with information that was too appalling to absorb, too much incomprehensible history.

She didn't doubt for a second that it was all true.

When the quicksilver tentacle had engulfed her head like some slimy garden slug, Cammie was slammed out of herself. The alien technology pumped information into her mind, force-feeding her, gorging her with the facts.

Because she had requested it.

Because she had spoken aloud and asked to know.

She tried to scream, desperate to make it stop, but the fire hose of knowledge poured into her. Her whole body felt ready to explode, and still the quicksilver appendage kept giving her information.

Now, Cammie knew what the cricket aliens were. She saw their race, knew their culture, their history . . . their torment. They named themselves the *Osskkn*. They were drones, identical in many ways, but each had a glimmer of individuality. And they had been enslaved by . . . something horrible.

Cammie squirmed to get away from the next horrific visage that overwhelmed her: the real manifestation of the malevolent creature carved on the cometary ice throne—gigantic, infinitely powerful, and horrifying.

The thing belonged to a godlike psychic race with a muscular body and baleful eyes. Demonic dragon-like wings sprouted from its back, and its lower face was a mass of disgusting, writhing tentacles—the same thing carved in ice on the comet. Even that dreadful statue did not do justice to the looming power and cosmic horror the actual being evoked.

These powerful enemies were known by many names, words that evoked fear from the deepest atavistic component of an intelligent brain: Cthulhu, Dagon, and other word shapes that her mind could not grasp.

The Osskkn named their malevolent enslavers the *Agoc*—just like what she had heard in her nightmare. The monstrous overlords were few but seemingly omnipotent. They fed on emotions and created manifestations of fear and terror that swept like a scythe through entire races. The cricket aliens were enslaved, along with many other species, and the Agoc demanded countless blood sacrifices to feed their empty psychic well.

While the images continued to flood her mind, Cammie couldn't see or feel her body. She gagged and squirmed, and her thoughts reeled as she tried to absorb a fraction of these revelations. It was as if a vast library of unread books had been crammed into her head, and every brain cell was on the verge of information rupture. She fell into oblivion.

After an interminable time, Cammie felt herself physically slipping and realized she could move her arms and legs again. In the low asteroid gravity, she fell slowly backward. The wet metallic glove of the Osskkn conduit slipped off her head and face, releasing her.

On the floor, Cammie opened her eyes, watched the quivering quicksilver tube withdraw into the porthole like a flaccid intestine. She wiped cold slime away from her eyes. Bile rose in her throat, but she struggled not to vomit. She sucked in deep breaths, gasping for air, weeping for a moment of normalcy.

When she could see again, she was startled to find Karla Arkourian and Pedro Ashe also connected to the horrific quicksilver conduits. Gleaming flexible tubes had lunged out of two other portholes, engulfing their heads and necks like a python swallowing prey.

Arkourian's body jittered. Ashe hung limp.

As Cammie watched, the other two tentacle protrusions pulled free from the victims' heads with a sound like smacking lips, then curled away. They both slumped to the ground.

Cammie crawled over to her companions as they regained consciousness. Arkourian's face was drawn and filled with disgust. "What the hell was that?"

Ashe's voice was raspy. "Is that what those cockroach aliens really are?"

"The Osskkn—slaves, drones," Cammie said. "They built this complex at the Nether wormhole, and other structures on thousands more planets." She shuddered again, but she could not unlearn what she knew. "I . . . I'm more concerned about those overlords, the Agoc."

Arkourian touched her head and hair, wiping away slime. "Now we know what really happened here—why the wormhole was abandoned."

Cammie remained confused. "It's not organized in my head. I don't understand what—"

Ashe said, "It's over now. That's why everything was abandoned. The Agoc were neutralized after the terrible war with the star beings."

"Star beings?" Cammie dug deep into the trove of information. "I'm still processing. What war?" She couldn't imagine any opponents able to stand against the titanic Agoc race.

Arkourian squeezed her eyes shut, then rubbed her temples as she processed the mountain of information. "Other star beings fought them. A race seemingly as powerful as the Agoc, and utterly alien, but maybe not as evil."

Cammie sifted through the yammering knowledge until she found memories of that war, the strange beings with barrel-like bodies, heads like starfish. Huge armies of other exotic creatures, more aliens, more slaves—or conscripted fighters.

Billions of Osskkn and other victim species were slaughtered, but that was the price for the fate of the universe. The star beings had their own unimaginable ways to weaken and finally defeat the Agoc.

Cammie's words came out in a whisper. "How are we going to explain all this? And who would believe us?"

Ashe said, "Everyone else saw the comet temple and the Osskkn bodies. How can they doubt what we're saying?"

"Benedict should come here and stick his head in that quicksilver anus and get the briefing for himself," Arkourian said. "But I doubt he'd do it. He's more of an executive-summary kind of guy."

In the porthole chamber, the lights flickered and brightened. Ashe grasped a protrusion on the wall and pulled himself to his feet. "Another bank of generators just started up, the main power source. This base is awakening."

Cammie said, "Something must have noticed us now."

Arkourian looked at her. "Well, you wanted to understand what's going on. Now we understand."

"Not by a long shot," Ashe said.

Cammie shook her head. "I still have so many questions."

Together, holding different perspectives in their minds, they returned to the main control chamber under the dome. The glowing work modules were fully activated now, and the flat displays throbbed with energy. The roof dome displayed the other asteroids in the ring around the wormhole.

Cammie saw that all the other alien bases were waking up too.

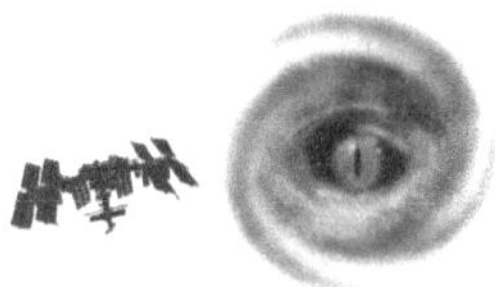

CHAPTER 38

Unwilling to admit she had been spooked by big mice, Glinda backed out of the empty hab module. Those rodents weren't mere vermin—they were malicious saboteurs. Something about the journey through the wormhole had turned them into rat versions of Mr. Hyde. They were fiendishly smart, too, and as violent as a . . . as a cornered rat.

Withdrawing into the main core of Nether Station, she sealed the connecting hatch, but that wouldn't cut off the rats' movement through the inner passages. She had half a mind to simply eject the spare module into space, as it was designed for, although discarding the whole damned cylinder to get rid of six rodents seemed extreme.

But if the rats infested critical systems and gnawed through circuitry, communications, power conduits, life support . . .

She remembered the gleam in their bloodthirsty eyes, how the rats had lunged at her like wild animals. It wasn't normal instinct, fight or flight. They *wanted* to tear her apart, just like they had mangled the mesh cage in the med lab.

Shaking, she checked her hands, her arm, to make sure the little white creep hadn't actually broken her skin. What if it was contagious, like some alien rabies? She saw the equation tattoos on her inner forearm, but not a scratch otherwise.

After catching her breath, she hit the comm panel on the wall. "Benedict, any word from Arkourian's asteroid team yet?

When do they plan on coming back? I could use Jack's help if we're going to block off those rats."

"The team went silent an hour ago, and I'm getting a little annoyed with them," Noor said. "They sent incredible images just as they entered the alien base, but stopped making regular transmissions, and they're not answering my hails either. Too busy, apparently."

Glinda was frustrated by the inconvenience, too, because there was a potential crisis here at Nether Station. "And when is Warren due back from his survey?" She could do the work with the pilot's help. He was proficient enough.

Noor chuckled. "Knowing Warren, not a nanosecond sooner than he needs to."

Glinda used the supervisory controls to move inner baffles and put up as many blockades between the modules as she could. Maybe that would hinder the rodents for now. She went back to the medical lab to see if the doc could help her whip up some deadly gas to use against the rats in the walls.

When she arrived, Stelland was still visibly shaken. He had set the loose wall plate back in place at the floor level and managed to barricade it with a heavy battery pack. Clearly, he was afraid the rodents might return.

At another time she might have snickered at him, but Glinda knew exactly what the doctor was feeling. He looked up at her. "Did you get them?"

"One. Still six more on the loose." She wiped perspiration from her forehead. "They attacked me! Vicious little fuckers."

In their separate cage, the normal rats sniffed the air and looked around. Fluffers crouched and just stared at her through the bars from across the room.

Glinda moved the heavy battery aside and bent down to look at the damaged wall plate. She was astonished to see small teeth marks in the metal-ceramic material, and she knew what the rats could do to the station's circuitry.

She blew a long breath through her lips. "We've got to kill those critters, Doc."

"They are not normal animals," Stelland said. "Whatever they saw in the wormhole must have corrupted their brains." He glanced over at the rhesus monkey sulking in its cage. "The primate subject was also clearly affected."

Glinda said in a soothing voice, "What's the matter, Fluffers?"

The monkey hunched its shoulders, and its fur bristled.

"I wish it could describe what it really saw," the doctor said. "The probe sensors and imagers recorded nothing comprehensible, but the animal obviously experienced something profound and terrifying."

Glinda frowned. "He could use some comforting." From the cabinet above the sink, she pulled out the tray of treats she had stored there during her other visits. Since the greenhouse wasn't producing any edible berries, she had brought packets of strawberry jam. "You need a little TLC. Here, have a treat."

She extended the jam packet through the bars, and the monkey cringed away, as if she had threatened it. Its eyes flared with both anger and inexpressible terror, and then it snatched the packet and held it protectively against its furry chest. After a tense moment, it used fingers and claws to tear open the packet.

"Good boy, Fluffers."

Dr. Stelland turned to look into the surgical chamber, where the naked human body lay stretched out from the autopsy. "Dr. Tendari isn't talking about the experience either. Eventually, I will need your help to place him back in his cryopod for cold storage."

"I'm a little busy with emergencies right now, Doc. Can you come up with rat poison or deadly gas to get rid of them?

We can't let them run amuck in our systems. They could royally screw up the station."

Stelland considered. "Couldn't you just decompress the gap between the walls? Let the vacuum do it?"

"The station interior isn't airtight. Access panels would leak." She turned back to look at the monkey and gasped.

Fluffers had smeared strawberry jam in a line across its throat. The red goo looked like a gash of fresh blood on its neck. She backed away. "That's sick!"

Stelland's face turned gray. "The animal has a twisted darkness inside of it, like the rats—and it is far more intelligent. I believe it should be euthanized."

Glinda reflexively objected, but the matted red line across the monkey's throat was horrifying, even threatening. She remembered the rats' unearthly, empty eyes when they had lunged at her, and she couldn't deny that Fluffers was *wrong*. Like the rats.

"I'll study the database and see what we might use for an effective large-scale lethal gas." Stelland stood at his station, scanning lists of chemicals and pharmaceuticals he could synthesize quickly.

While she waited for him, Glinda bent down to finish repairs on the loose wall plate, using the butt end of her probe rod to bang the damaged corners flat enough to seal the seams with the magnetizing pistol. The repairs weren't pretty, but the rats wouldn't be able to get back in here. She still felt sick with the idea of putting Fluffers down though.

She glanced up just in time to see the monkey's smooth and furtive movement. With nimble fingers, Fluffers reached through the bars and fiddled with the complex latch. Moving like an expert, it pulled out the secondary clips, slid aside the locking bar, raised the hasp, and swung open the cage door—as if it had known how to do so all along.

"Fluffers!"

The monkey bared its fangs at her. The bright red goo on its neck glistened in the med lab's lights.

Then it lunged for Dr. Stelland like a furry cannonball. The animal was the size of a child, packed with muscles. Stelland swung around in alarm, and the monkey's weight and momentum bowled him down.

He flailed to push it away, but Fluffers raised a clawed hand and brought it down like a bludgeon, smashing Stelland in the face. In a flash, the monkey dug its claw in and ripped the doctor's eye out of its socket. Blood spurted. He screamed, and the animal screamed even louder.

Glinda jumped up from the floor, yanking the heavy probe rod out of her toolbelt as she flung herself forward. "Stop!"

The monkey sank its fangs into Stelland's throat, twisting and ripping sideways to pull out a hunk of larynx, windpipe, and blood vessels. The doctor's arms flopped and jittered.

Then Fluffers bit off half his face.

With a fierce, wordless shout, Glinda smashed the monkey in the shoulder with the probe rod, but the creature barely felt the blow. It sprang away from its victim, flashed a face full of gore at her, then bounded past.

Its eyes were black pools, full of stars.

"Stop!" Glinda swung the bar again, but missed.

Fluffers streaked out into the bright corridor, splattering blood as it ran. Glinda howled, "Get back here!" She paused to check the doctor, but there was no question at all that he was dead. And the monkey was still on the rampage.

She slapped the comm panel as she ran out the med lab door. "Mr. Noor, if you're still in the observation bridge, seal all access doors!"

He sounded bored. "What is it now, Glinda? Afraid the rats might get in?"

"The monkey is loose!"

"You seem to have a problem with laboratory animals today."

She shouted, "The damn thing killed Dr. Stelland, and it's running riot!"

Glinda bounded after the murderous primate, barely hearing Noor's response from the speaker. "You might have led with that part."

She put on a burst of speed in the low gravity, following the trail of blood droplets.

With shrieks that sounded like maniacal laughter, the monkey rushed through an intersection and found the rungs that led up to the next deck. Glinda tried to close the distance as it scrambled up a level—heading for the greenhouse module.

Good, she could trap the bastard in there.

When she got to the greenhouse hatch, the monkey spun about and spat a dark red gobbet of Dr. Stelland's throat before bolting into the rotting gardens.

Glinda hesitated at the door before entering, afraid the thing might attack her. She still held the heavy probe rod, and she patted down her toolbelt, blindly inventorying the other items she had. Plenty of potential weapons. She pulled out a long, trusty screwdriver and gripped it in her other hand.

She remembered how sweet Fluffers had been, how she had cuddled it, fed it strawberries. She had felt guilty about using it as a lab specimen.

But Glinda couldn't unsee what it had done to Doc Stelland—or the hollow blackness in its eyes. The real Fluffers had died somewhere inside the wormhole. This was some kind of unholy monster.

All senses alert, she entered the greenhouse. Normally, the

moist smell of growing plants was refreshing, but now the air was rank with a sour, rotten stench. The plant leaves were stained and bruised, as if smeared with drain oil and feces. The bean plants were brown masses of leprous growths. Swollen carrots had popped out of the soil, tumescent and oozing.

The rampaging monkey charged into the tomato plants, where it grabbed overripe red globes and smashed the pulp into its face, covering itself with more dripping goo. Seemingly ravenous, the Fluffers thing devoured some of the tomatoes, as if the poisoned blight would nourish it.

Determined, Glinda sealed the bulkhead door behind her and strode forward. "This is like High Noon in the greenhouse." Unlike the rats, this murderous monkey wasn't going to get away.

Fluffers shrieked at her, and Glinda shrieked right back—then she charged forward, raising both tools.

The animal sprang away from the tomato plants and bounded into the zucchini thicket. The squash plant seemed alive, like tentacles. Fluffers crashed into them and thrashed around, ripping the vines like ropes.

Glinda waded in after the thing, knocking the leaves aside. The monkey whipped the vines at her face, but she slapped them away with the heavy probe rod.

Fluffers launched itself out of the tangled morass and slammed into her. It raked claws across her chest, tearing at the tough jumpsuit fabric as if it meant to rip out her heart. She battered its claws with the long screwdriver.

The wild monkey was a mass of fur and energy, with muscles like steel cables. It snapped its jaws inches from her face, clacking long fangs.

Glinda shoved the animal away, but it was like an industrial spring, hurtling right back, screaming, biting, clawing. Its empty eyes looked as if someone had drilled out the irises and filled them with an empty void.

With a grunt, she used all the strength in her sturdy arms to hurl Fluffers away from her again. As it reeled and shot back toward her, she clipped it hard in the temple with the heavy probe, leaving a bloody gash. The skull blow should have killed the thing, or at least rendered it unconscious, but the creature merely squirmed and snarled.

She struck its head again, and Fluffers staggered back into the tangled squash vines, finally dazed. Glinda pressed her advantage, knowing she would have no other chance. Like Van Helsing driving a stake into Dracula's heart, she plunged the long screwdriver into the center of the beast's chest, impaling it through the heart.

The squash vines seemed to sag around the bloody mess that had been Fluffers.

She dragged herself over to the intercom on the wall. "Benedict, we need to talk."

CHAPTER 39

As the monitors in the alien control room ran through the ominous reactivation routines, the hum in the air grew louder. Cammie could feel a lingering energy, like static electricity around them.

Her mind now had a new framework for everything she saw here, the history of the wormhole, the alien races, the defenses, the war . . . the horrific Agoc.

As the modules shimmered and hummed, she looked at the withered Osskkn corpses scattered on the floor—and one stirred and twitched at the console by her feet. Startled, she skittered back and watched the cricket alien rotate its mummified head. The segmented skeletal arms slowly unfolded, and the claws clicked and swiveled. The dead creature bent its legs, trying to lift itself up.

Cammie took another step back. "Karla . . ." The rest of the Osskkn bodies remained motionless, but this one slowly rolled into a sitting position, moved its stiff limbs, bent its rounded head on its neck. "Karla, this one's waking up!"

Ashe scuttled over, his mouth agape. "Should we bash it? It's a zombie."

The reanimated husk moved so clumsily as it swiveled itself upright that it obviously posed no immediate danger. "Not yet," Arkourian said, waiting as she stood over it.

Cammie said, "After what we all just learned . . . I don't

think anything is impossible." Though a shiver of superstitious fear ran through her, she felt no overt threat.

The Osskkn turned its dull, hemispherical eyes toward them. Then, with a wheezing, dry rattle, it uttered words. "Humans . . . we know humans."

She, Ashe, and Arkourian all gasped. Intellectually, Cammie recognized that this dead Osskkn had not spoken in English, but neural synapses were being triggered in her brain, memories that clicked together. She said, "Those silver tubes made it possible for us to comprehend their language. Maybe this one can fill in some of the blanks."

Ashe let out a whistle. "It's like Yoda—as a bug."

With a clatter and a wheeze of effort, the cricket alien levered itself to its feet and stood swaying and twitching. Its mouth clacked. "We Osskkn knew humans long ago. We are still in your genetic memory—but you don't remember. You don't heed the warning."

"What warning?" Arkourian asked. "Explain yourself."

Cammie wanted to learn so much more, now that she had some of the background. "Tell us about your race, about the ancient war, what really happened."

"I am a mouthpiece, a surrogate . . . The star beings work through me." After a long pause, it continued, "Once, our Osskkn civilization inhabited countless worlds. But we were also weak. Enslaved. Tortured. By the Agoc."

With a wave of fear and revulsion, Cammie thought of those nightmarish beings like the one carved into the comet ice.

The fragile, desiccated creature paused as if gathering energy for more revelations. "Billions of Osskkn were slaughtered, and the rest of us were turned into helpless thralls. Unwilling servants. The Agoc forced us to breed and swarm. We were their builders, explorers, soldiers, drones. Sacrifices. The Agoc demanded constant tributes from the blood of defeated races, so they could feed their empty psychic well."

"How do you know humans?" Arkourian asked. "Did you come to Earth?"

"Eons ago . . . In the raw, early days of your planet, the Agoc left their mark. We watched the rise of reptiles and megafauna. Osskkn were forced to construct gigantic temples, now buried deep under your seas, lost when the oceans rose and the continents sank."

"Little green men," Ashe muttered.

Cammie reeled as she heard the overwhelming information. She knew ancient myths of terrifying elder gods, but they were just stories . . .

The mummified alien continued, "The Agoc conquered swaths of the Galaxy long before the first human looked up at the stars." It gestured, but the brittle body could not withstand even these small stresses, and its left leg cracked, making it fall to one knee.

But the partial collapse didn't interrupt its explanation. "There were many tormented races, not just the Osskkn. The fungoid Yggroths also held a secret strength. Other species were willing to take a terrible risk. We formed a secret alliance, bound together under the guidance of the star beings from afar . . . Over thousands of years, we built a force strong enough to stand against the psychic enemies."

The surrogate alien's other leg cracked, and it dropped to the floor. Cammie rushed forward, trying to help, but the pathetic husk propped itself on one of its segmented arms, desperate to use its last energy to complete the explanation.

"The Osskkn, the Yggroths, and other fighters rose up in star system after star system. That war spanned the Galaxy for millennia . . . but we brought a race of gods to their knees. We overthrew the Agoc temples and destroyed their soul-harvesting machinery. We tore down their psychic batteries and fear-gathering lenses."

With the Osskkn's words, a new flow of implanted memories and information was triggered in Cammie's mind. She saw vast planetary battlefields, with casualties in the billions. So many alien soldiers had fought and died willingly, knowing the stakes.

"But the war is over?" she asked aloud. "You did defeat the Agoc?"

"When the Agoc were at the nadir of their strength," the cricket alien said in a dry whisper, "the star beings turned the dark mirrors and obsidian lenses back on them. They trapped the dark gods."

The withered husk collapsed forward now, sprawled on the floor of the base. It turned its head, stared with rounded black eyes at them. It moved like a puppet. "The star beings rendered them impotent long enough to imprison them between dimensions."

The Osskkn wheezed out one final rattle. "We must keep them there." It raised one long, clawed finger and pointed at them. "Our bases guard the wormhole gate—many wormhole gates. In case the Agoc escape . . ."

Wide-eyed, Cammie turned to her companions. Ashe and Arkourian also reeled with the new information.

"Must keep them there . . ."

With those final words, the Osskkn collapsed back into permanent death. Its exoskeleton cracked, and its limbs fell apart like discarded sticks.

Cammie stared around at all the glowing consoles. "These asteroid bases aren't depots or way stations—they're military *watchtowers*."

Arkourian's expression grew grim. "Guard posts at the opening to make sure the Agoc don't break free."

CHAPTER 40

Now that Cammie understood so much more, she found the Osskkn control center fascinating rather than threatening. She was still intimidated, though, by the power building throughout the long-abandoned asteroid station. She could feel the entire rock vibrating beneath her feet. The ancient systems seemed to be self-activating, and no one knew how to operate them.

"This watchtower is a lot more than just air traffic control." Pedro Ashe moved to one of the monitor consoles, near which another long-dead Osskkn lay slumped. "If this is meant to be a guard station, it must have some kind of weaponry." He moved the alien corpse aside and began to poke at the unfamiliar controls, trying to figure them out.

"We've been out of touch with Nether Station for too long." Arkourian strode over to where they had stashed the exosuits and used her helmet comm to connect to the *Lewis*, landed outside. "I need to give Mr. Noor a full report about what we've discovered. Not sure how to summarize all this, but I'll give it a shot."

"The story sounds crazy, but the three of us can corroborate what we learned," Cammie said. Everything in her head felt like a twisted fever dream, and she wouldn't have believed it herself. But she *knew*.

When Arkourian looked at the suit chronometer, her worn face filled with concern. "This isn't good. We lost two hours trapped in that data dump! Nether Station must be frantic." She tried to get in contact, listening for a response.

Cammie was wrapped up in her thoughts as she looked up at the system diagram projected on the dome interior. The wormhole now had many sinister connotations. The rats, the monkey, and Dr. Tendari's body had traveled through the dimensional passage where the terrible elder gods were imprisoned. Benedict Noor was eager to send Warren through in the expedition ship. What if a living, conscious person went through the wormhole? What would he witness . . . or disturb?

She thought of the obviously troubled group of rats, the terror on the monkey's face.

"We need to rethink our whole mission here," Cammie said. "We've got to stop Mr. Noor before he turns Nether into a big transportation hub."

"You've got a point, and he's not going to like it. But we need to contact him first, and I'm getting no answer." Arkourian toggled the comm again. "I repeat—calling Nether Station. Benedict, I told you not to leave the observation bridge unattended! Somebody needs to be there."

She heard only a crackle of static in response.

Cammie surveyed the control room, visualizing it filled with the insect-like drones, after billions of their race had been slaughtered in the cosmic wars. The Osskkn had worked here not as wormhole astrophysicists, as she'd imagined, but as prison guards to ensure that the horrific Agoc did not escape . . .

Intent on his work, Ashe pulled himself nimbly from one console to another. "I don't understand much about how these control stations work . . . but it is in the back of my mind." He studied the screens, the odd arrangement of buttons and dials designed for insectile hands. "I wish I knew how to read the

Osskkn language. Maybe another alien zombie will wake up and act as translator for us."

Arkourian looked up from where she knelt at the suit comm. "I'm not sure we want that, Mr. Ashe."

As Cammie stared at the panels and control systems, her vision grew blurry with a hint of clarity just beyond the edge of her mind. "You might know more than you expect. We need to process the information those systems poured into our heads, figure out how to access what we need. It's like standing inside a big library, with all that knowledge, but we haven't had time to read the books."

"You're right—these marks and characters look more familiar than before." Ashe hummed to himself as he bent over the alien module, playing his implant music in the background. He touched the side of his head. "Maybe my AI booster can help me sort it out."

Arkourian kept trying to make contact through the *Lewis* but grew frustrated. "Our signal isn't getting through."

Cammie moved to the next console, where all the indicators and screens glowed bright, fully active with numerous subroutines. "The watchtower is activated now. Could it be jamming our communications?"

"Quite possible." The older woman pursed her lips and stood up with a sigh. "Maybe if I go out to the recon ship and transmit directly from the cockpit." She donned her exosuit with swift familiarity and made her way to the airlock.

Cammie followed her to operate the airlock controls for her, but before they reached the inner door, both of them stopped in shock. The systems were already activating! The external door had sealed, and the chamber was pressurizing.

Somebody was trying to get in.

They both backed off. "I don't like this at all," Arkourian said.

Cammie swallowed hard. "Are some of the Osskkn still alive?" She thought of the frozen alien body just outside.

The cycle finished, and the inner door brightened, ready to slide open.

Arkourian steeled herself, standing in front of Cammie as if her exosuit would serve as body armor. "I wish we had weapons. Can you fight?"

"Fight . . . with what?"

A rush of fear hit her. What if the nightmarish Agoc had come to attack them with their deepest inner terrors? Having seen them in her mind, Cammie vowed she wouldn't just quiver and surrender. She would fight the thing tooth and nail.

The inner airlock door slid open, and another exosuited figure entered the base.

Arkourian's voice was amplified by the suit transmitter. "Warren Drake!"

The young pilot looked at them through his faceplate. "Glad to find you alive and kicking. When all communications cut off, I was afraid you'd been eaten by aliens. Your life support should be running out by now."

Cammie was honestly glad to see him. "You can't even imagine what really happened here. We know so much more now about what all these bases are for."

He suddenly realized that Cammie stood there in only her station jumpsuit, wearing no helmet. "Hey, why aren't you in a suit? How are you breathing?"

"The station air is adequate," Arkourian said. "Warren, we've been trying to send a full report to Nether Station, but our comms are jammed. There's a lot Mr. Noor needs to know."

"Same thing happened to the *Clark* when I was flying my scout run," Warren said. "This asteroid lit up, as did several others—like somebody flipped a switch."

"We're the ones who did that," Cammie said. "Accidentally."

Arkourian removed her helmet from the collar lock. "Explain yourself, Warren. Why are you here?"

"I thought you'd be glad to see me!" The pilot reached up to his helmet, hesitated. "You're sure it's okay to breathe?"

"The air stinks like rotted bug corpses, but otherwise it's fine." Arkourian inhaled a dramatic breath to demonstrate.

"Ashe ran tests," Cammie said. "We've been breathing it for hours."

Warren faced her. "You're the smartest person I know, so I'll believe you." He removed his helmet and sucked in a long breath, then grimaced. "That gives a new definition to *putrid*."

"Pedro says the circulators and scrubbers are active now," Arkourian said. "This base seems to be fully functional."

As Warren gawked around the large Osskkn base, Arkourian stepped closer. "I'll ask again: Why are you here, Warren?"

"Because we couldn't get any response from you. I was already out on a recon flight around the asteroids, so I came to do a wellness check." He glanced at Cammie. "I was worried about you." He quickly added, "All of you."

He followed them into the main control room, looking around in amazement. "The *Clark* has a catalog of surveillance images that'll keep scientists busy for years—but it looks like you found even more interesting stuff! Is this the alien train station?"

"More than that," Cammie said in a rush. "There's so much more to the story. The Osskkn have been here in our solar system for millions of years. We've learned so much about the wormhole, these asteroid bases, and that *thing* carved in the ice temple! It's vital information, but we couldn't get through to Nether Station."

Warren turned serious. "Just as I was on approach, Mr.

Noor reported that lab rats had gotten loose on the station and were messing up the circuitry. Now all of Nether's comms are just static too. I couldn't get through."

"Wonderful," Arkourian said. "We need to deliver a full report to Mr. Noor so he can scrap the mission. What we've learned here is profoundly disturbing. It'll change everything—literally everything—about the future of the human race."

The pilot raised his eyebrows. "Well, haven't you been busy?"

Arkourian was stony and serious. "Somebody has to go tell him before he makes further plans. But it's not something we can just summarize. It's got to be a full report—and he's got to believe it!"

Ashe looked around at all the pulsing consoles, the main systems ramping up. "You want us to just pack up and leave? Now?"

Cammie spoke up. "I'll go with Warren. He can fly me back in the *Clark*, and I'll tell everybody."

"This is an active situation, and these watchtowers could go into a full defensive footing," Arkourian said as she followed the logic, nodding. "All right, Ashe and I will keep working. If he really can figure out the Osskkn controls, we need him here."

"Watchtowers?" Warren looked back and forth. "What the hell are you two talking about?"

"Long story," Cammie said.

"And it's a long flight back to Nether Station." He gestured toward her to don her exosuit. "Are these going to be answers that I want to hear?"

"You need to hear them," Arkourian said. "So does Mr. Noor."

"I love it when people tell me what I need." Warren followed them as Cammie retrieved her suit and struggled to pull it on.

Ashe flitted from one console to the next, activating substations and puzzling over others. "This is starting to make sense to me—and that's a little intimidating."

Warren continued looking around at the setup. "This gets weirder and more marvelous with everything I see."

Cammie came up to him, holding her helmet and ready to go. "I'll turn the *weird* up to maximum volume once I tell you everything we've learned." She felt embarrassed as the pilot double-checked her suit systems, but she was glad for the help.

"And we'll try to get the Nether Station comm systems working again so we can communicate," Warren said to Arkourian as he led Cammie to the airlock. "If the damn lab rats haven't chewed through all the wires."

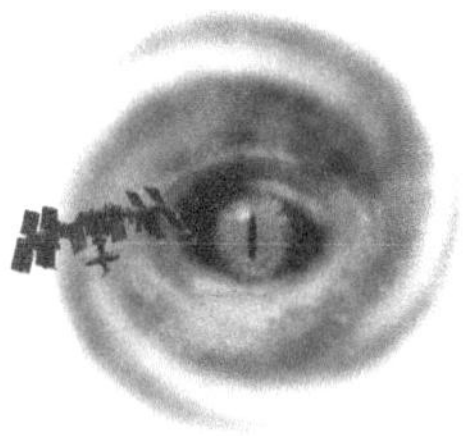

CHAPTER 41

As the *Clark* approached the hangar bay, the radio silence grew more disturbing. Only three people remained on Nether Station—Noor, Glinda, and Dr. Stelland—but someone should have answered the hail.

"Good thing the *Clark* can cycle open the hangar bay doors from outside," Warren said to her. "But I don't like this one bit."

"Could the jamming extend this far?" Cammie tried to sound convincing. "Maybe no signals are getting through at all."

He flicked the comm toggle again. "Anyone home? Is somebody asleep at the switch?" He shook his head. "We're close enough they should be able to see us, even if the comms aren't working."

A burst of static came back, and then the screen image flickered to reveal a blurry form, unmistakably Glinda Roybal. The resolution was poor, the grainy image wavering. "Get the hell back here!" Her voice was distorted. "Help!" The transmission winked out.

Warren bent forward, determined. As he aligned with the hangar bay doors, Cammie took her turn on the comm, trying to reach Glinda again, but couldn't raise her. "Maybe Nether's own communication systems are damaged. Do you really think loose rats could have done that?"

"I hate rats," he said.

He landed the recon ship inside the open bay, leaving room

for Arkourian to return with the *Lewis*. As soon as the chamber repressurized, Warren and Cammie jumped out of the *Clark* and ran to the connecting door to the main station.

Glinda Roybal stood there waiting for them, a mass of anxiety and energy. "It's about time!"

Blood streaked her face and neck, and her torn sleeves showed more red smears. Parallel slashes across the front of her jumpsuit looked as if they had been made by claws.

Cammie was shocked. "What happened?"

Glinda scrubbed fingers through her spiky hair. "Unpleasant run-in with a monkey."

"Fluffers?" Cammie recalled the usually gentle rhesus monkey. "Why would it attack you?"

"Some of those scratches look nasty," Warren said. "You better go see the doc."

Glinda flashed him a hard glare. "Doc Stelland is dead. The monkey went on a rampage and ripped out his throat."

Warren suddenly looked around. "Is it loose?"

"I took care of it." Her expression fell. "Poor thing . . . but it wasn't Fluffers. And we still have six lab rats to worry about. I managed to kill one, but the rest are in the walls chewing on the circuitry, and they've mucked up the comms. It's like they know what they're doing."

"Sneaky bastards," Warren said.

Cammie's head was spinning. "We've got so much to debrief you on! We learned why the aliens built these asteroid stations around the wormhole. There's a threat—"

Glinda interrupted her as she stalked off. "There's always a threat, kid. Follow me to the observation bridge. The remaining rats are in the *Lethe*'s core, concentrated near the communications nexus. I have all the conduits sealed off, but I need a spare hand to rig up some poison gas—and I sure as hell don't want to count on Benedict for the dirty work. We've got to be quick before the critters get into our life-support systems."

"Poison gas and rats?" Warren said, hurrying after her. "I'm in."

Flushed and sweating, the three reached the bridge. Benedict Noor was hunched over Arkourian's station, fumbling with the controls and trying to call up reports, but he wasn't sure what to do. He looked up at them. "None of this was supposed to happen."

"No shit, Sherlock," Glinda said. "Um, I mean sir."

"Where are Captain Arkourian and Mr. Ashe?" Noor demanded.

"Still at the Osskkn asteroid base," Cammie said. "We couldn't contact you over the comm, and there's so much to report—Warren brought me back so I could tell you in person. You had to know right away."

The entrepreneur gave her an impatient glare. She could see his eyes were bloodshot, his expression harried. "I hope you found something useful—more than just an added decimal point in some theory."

Cammie was taken aback by his sudden vitriol. She tried to think of some encouragement that Dr. Tendari would have given—the *real* Tendari—and she responded in a firm voice. "We learned about a war that might end the universe, sir. We know all the details, all the history. We understand the cricket aliens, and why all these bases are around the wormhole."

"And their defensive systems are now fully activated," Warren said. "The alien complexes turned back on."

Noor's expression calmed, as if some of the ragged stress had sloughed away. "Hmmm, that's confusing, but significant enough. Good work."

"Rat bastards first." Glinda led Warren to the life-support substation on the bridge, where she had rigged three large

CO_2 tanks to the wall plates, sealing the nozzles into the input orifices. She tapped a schematic screen that displayed fault indicators, multiple circuit interruptions, and error messages on the complex diagrams. "This leads into our primary comm network. I'm pumping carbon dioxide into the gap between the walls, and it'll eventually suffocate them, but they're tough critters. I'd rather kill 'em dead."

Warren studied the projection while Glinda worked on the tanks. She said, "Doc Stelland was going to figure out some kind of deadly gas, but he didn't get the chance. I improvised with basic chemistry—I've got liquid chlorine, along with chemicals from our stockpile and cleaning solutions from the janitorial lockers. I've improvised a reaction chamber."

"Good old chlorine gas," Warren said. "The bleach will turn those lab rats snowy white." He helped Glinda hook up the reactant tanks, and after removing the CO_2 nozzles, he inserted the chlorine gas output into the wall.

A sheen of perspiration covered the engineer's forehead. "We better wear emergency respirators for a while until the scrubbers clear the air."

Cammie wanted to help. "I know where the face masks are stored."

As they finished rigging their chlorine gas purge, Cammie went to the nearest emergency supply closet and retrieved face mask breathers designed for use in case of smoke or sudden drop in air pressure. When she returned with the masks, a control panel next to Arkourian's station sent up an unexpected shower of sparks. The status lights flickered.

"You'd best move quickly before they do more damage," Noor said.

"Ready for the stink bomb," Glinda said.

Cammie thrust a face mask into her hand, and the engineer

donned it without paying much attention. Warren seated his own mask around his face and crouched next to Glinda. Cammie had to help Noor tighten the bands across the back of his bald head; then she placed her own unit over her eyes, mouth, and nose. The seal was tight; the air filter was working. She gave a thumbs-up.

Warren and Glinda turned the knobs on the reaction canisters to mix the chemicals, and the burbling hiss rolled out as chlorine gas gushed into the gap between the hull and the bulkhead.

"That'll teach you bastards to try to nip my hand," Glinda said, her voice muffled behind the face mask.

Greenish fumes began to leak out of small access gaps and ventilation sockets. Cammie was glad for the face shield, or her eyes would be burning. "How will we know when they're dead?"

"They're getting a supersized dose," Glinda said.

Warren added, "Enough to kill even the most evil rat."

Cammie could see the fumes in the air around the observation bridge. She checked her respirator, saw that it was filtering out the deadly gas.

When the reaction tank was empty, and poisonous mist filled the void between the walls, they finally allowed themselves to relax. "We should let them marinate in that for about an hour," Glinda said.

Noor slumped into his throne-like captain's chair, adjusted his mask. "Since we have time to kill, my dear Cammie, tell us about these discoveries your team made. What were the aliens doing here? Is this indeed Grand Central Station, or McMurdo Sound? Are Karla and Pedro safe over there?"

Cammie struggled with the enormity of all she had to explain, trying to organize it. "The ancient base is still functional, and the power systems are now regenerating. We found hundreds of dead cricket aliens inside—they're called Osskkn. We know what the watchtower asteroids are for, and we know that the wormhole is dangerous!"

Noor gave her a skeptical look through his face mask. "And how did you learn that? Did you interview one of them?"

"Actually, one did come alive and tell us some things." She could see he didn't believe her. "But there's more. The three of us received a complete brain dump, a download of alien information. Karla and Pedro can verify everything I said. We learned about the Nether wormhole and a race of horrific monsters, just like the one carved in ice on the comet."

Cammie watched his expression flinch with instinctive revulsion, but he tried to hide it. "I would like an explanation of those hideous-looking fellows."

"They're called Agoc—that's one of the names. They enslaved the Osskkn, and they came to Earth millions of years ago. They're as malevolent and powerful as you can imagine."

"Whoa, millions of years ago?" Glinda scoffed.

Cammie needed to make them understand. "The asteroid watchtowers are here to guard the wormhole, to protect against the Agoc so they can't get out. We can't just go blundering in there."

Noor frowned. "Guard stations? This is clearly a transportation network. All evidence points to that."

"But we have more evidence now. Yes, there are wormhole passageways to many star systems, but it's also a prison between dimensions. For the Agoc."

Glinda snorted into her respirator. "That's some crazy shit."

Warren looked at her. "Everything we've seen here is some crazy shit."

Cammie struggled to convey all the information in her head, as well as what the reanimated Osskkn surrogate had told them. As best she could, she gave the broad strokes of the story.

She talked in disjointed sentences, showing emotion and fear as she spoke of the great war, the star beings, the Osskkn, the Yggroths, and the appalling elder entities who could tear souls apart and feast upon fear.

"That's quite a remarkable tale, as well as preposterous," Noor said. "And an inconvenient one for us."

"I'm not making it up! You can go there yourself to access the information, if you're willing to do it." Cammie doubted Noor would submit to the quicksilver sleeve around his head. "You saw the comet temple yourself."

The entrepreneur turned away, troubled. He seemed to be dealing with hidden nightmares of his own. "Maybe I don't need to understand it all right now."

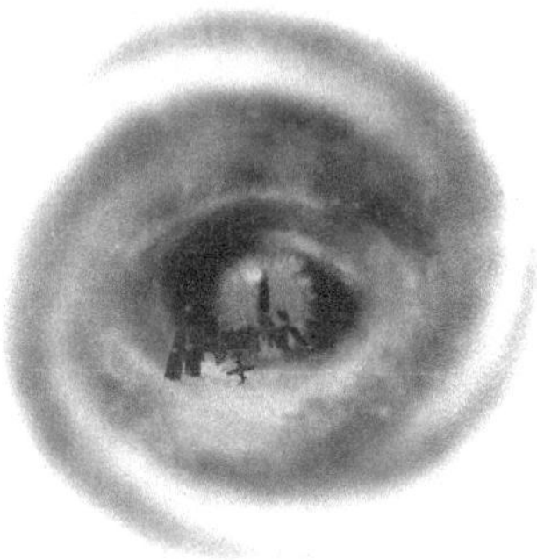

CHAPTER 42

As the organic generators powered up in the lower asteroid chambers, Arkourian could sense an ominous ticking clock that she didn't understand. Her mind still rang like a struck bell from the data downloaded into her brain, and now she felt an urgency to learn what this watchtower intended to do.

The alien base sent out jamming signals that disrupted her weak transmissions, and she had lost all contact with Warren and Cammie in the *Clark*, as well as Nether Station.

Pedro Ashe was trying to understand the Osskkn systems as quickly as he could. They were on their own.

The young engineer moved about, nimble even with his atrophied muscles. He dragged away the mummified corpses that cluttered the floor and piled them up on the side of the chamber. "I need room to move around, unless another one is going to wake up and give me some hints."

None of the dead Osskkn seemed inclined to cooperate.

"Didn't think so." Cracking his knuckles, Ashe tapped the alien control protrusions. "I understand some of these systems now. This one here is a monitoring module, and these screens can be used for communication—but no one on Nether Station would be listening on this frequency."

Arkourian studied the map on the dome overhead. "What about the other asteroid bases? When we triggered this complex, did the rest of them wake up? Or are they still on standby?"

Ashe used his clumsy human fingers to manipulate the Osskkn toggles. The dome overhead shimmered, displaying the Nether wormhole and the array of watchtower asteroids, which throbbed brightly now. "Umm, looks like they're all active now."

Arkourian hunched over as she felt a spike behind her eyes, a pounding inside her skull—the implanted information fighting to the forefront of her consciousness. She studied the positions of the other watchtowers, which came into a different focus, as if she were seeing through extraterrestrial eyes. The purpose of the network became clearer to her—and now the implications were graver.

Benedict Noor's main guess about the interstellar network was correct, but the peripheral consequences were dramatically different. The Nether wormhole was indeed the entrance to a dimensional labyrinth linked to other exits around the Galaxy, including Alpha Centauri. But these Osskkn asteroids would never be made into hotels or rest areas, as Noor had envisioned. They were defensive battlements to stand against the emergence of an ancient enemy.

But they were unmanned, with all the Osskkn monitors dead. If these bases were meant to stop monsters from breaking out of the event horizon, they no longer served that purpose.

What if all the Osskkn were dead on both sides of the wormhole?

Arkourian suddenly lost her footing as a jolt shifted through the asteroid base. Ashe fell away from the console and tumbled to his knees, splaying his palms to catch himself on the hard floor. He pulled himself up again, looked at the module screen. "Something big just fired up down below—more generators or control systems online and powering up."

Arkourian hurried to another console and watched bursts of static on multiple screens, then lines of incomprehensible blips and glyphs. One substation screen showed the scoop-like parabolic transmitters out in the crater. The thorny central rods began to crackle and glow with energy.

Arkourian strained to retrieve more information, something that would tell her what was happening. She'd be able to understand what was going on if she could just find the right information in her mind! She held on to one of the equipment stations as the entire asteroid continued to rumble and vibrate.

She didn't know what had changed, what had triggered this. Noor had already sent four probes through the wormhole, and the defenses had not reacted. Years ago, the original ISA probe had traveled through to the Alpha Centauri system, transmitting its signal for all to hear, which had reached Earth more than four years later.

Then, after only a few days, it suddenly and inexplicably fell silent.

But nothing had interfered with the four quick round-trip probes sent from Nether Station. Not yet.

She felt a chill of dread. "What if we triggered an alarm? Each of our probes sent out a blaring signal. It was like yelling for attention."

Ashe looked troubled by the idea. "Maybe that wasn't such a good idea, if there's somebody on the other side. Who knows what we might have disturbed?"

After moving another alien husk out of the way, he found a comfortable position in an oddly designed seat and began exploring the control subsystems.

Pondering aloud, Arkourian ticked off the ideas on her fingers. "Our first probe had only instrumentation on board. The second one carried lab rats, and the third had a sleeping rhesus monkey and a dead human body. The fourth probe carried a conscious monkey, but it wasn't able to comprehend the interdimensional passage. None of those tests had anything intelligent that would attract the attention of those Agoc god monsters."

Ashe said, "You mean nothing with a soul."

She hadn't known the young engineer to have any religious or philosophical leanings.

Thoughts swirled inside her head. What would have happened if a sentient being—a potential worshipper!—went through and drew the attention of the exiled Agoc? What if the psychic enemy somehow broke the chains of interdimensional imprisonment and surged through the wormhole network? The horrific creatures could emerge not just here but everywhere in the Galaxy.

From what she understood now—and she had barely scratched the surface—that would definitely be a worst-case scenario.

"Maybe we shouldn't let Warren go through in the expedition ship," Ashe said.

"I'm sure Cammie will convince them of that." Then the realization hit her with an even deeper dread. "Wait, what if the data exchange went both ways? We learned so much about them—but what did that conduit learn *from us*? The guardian network now knows that Benedict intends to use the wormhole as a galactic transportation system, with Nether Station as the hub. This asteroid base *knows* why we're here!"

The watchtower asteroids were not just guard stations to prevent the Agoc from escaping—they were also a blockade to keep everyone else away.

Ashe blinked at her as he understood what she was saying. "These watchtowers were designed to stop people . . . like us."

The main base vibrated even more, and the array of parabolic transmitters beamed out a signal that Arkourian did not understand.

Readings scrolled across the screens. The dome overhead shifted in a dizzying rotation, then locked into place again. Arkourian watched one of the bright asteroid bases on the grid throbbing, increasing in intensity.

Ashe pulled himself back to his feet. "I understand now! These asteroids aren't just habitation complexes and watch stations. They are hollowed out and enhanced. Each one has powerful propulsion mechanisms."

"You mean engines?" Arkourian asked.

"Like juggernauts."

On the dome projection, the brightening asteroid base began to move.

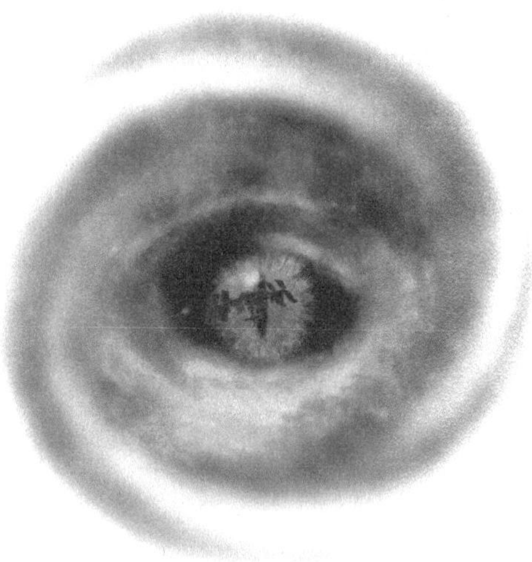

CHAPTER 43

Benedict Noor wasn't a seat-of-the-pants kind of guy, and he hated when things didn't go according to plan. He made use of deep analytics, focus groups, red-team and blue-team role-playing exercises. But no amount of planning could prepare for a mission to an unknown wormhole. And the hits kept coming.

He swiveled in his captain's chair. "Have we connected with Captain Arkourian yet?" He had taken off his full–face mask respirator when the air quality returned to safe levels, and now he rubbed his cheeks and chin. He hated the thing, but his eyes still burned from leftover chlorine fumes.

"The Osskkn tech from the main asteroid is still jamming all signals," Cammie said. "We can't contact her."

"And our own comms aren't in good shape either," Warren said. "Glinda has to patch them up, now that the rats are finally dead."

Muttering, the engineer backed out of the crawl space beneath one of the bridge stations. "First things first—had to get these out of the way." She pulled out the dead lab rats, holding them in two clusters by their pink whiplike tails. Their glassy eyes bulged, and their mouths were covered with blood, as if they had attacked one another when they couldn't find human targets. "Little fuckers chewed through a few more circuits even as they were dying."

She strode over to Noor and extended three of the dead rodents to him. He looked at her, annoyed. "What do you want me to do with them?"

"Keep them as trophies." She dropped them in his lap.

"Sometimes you're not as funny as you think you are, Glinda," he said.

"Funny? I was trying to be efficient. Now, let me go plug in some replacement circuit boards and see if I can get our comms working."

Cammie looked deeply shaken by everything that had happened, but at least she seemed less shy and more confident than before. Noor thought that was an improvement. "What about Dr. Stelland? Has anybody been back to the medical bay? Are we sure he's dead?"

Glinda snorted. "Damn sure."

"So you just . . . left him there?" Cammie asked.

"We've been preoccupied." Noor was irritated that she would bring up the subject, but he realized that someone would have to deal with the mess. "We'll take care of everything once the situation settles back down."

"If it ever does, boss," Warren said.

Feeling a flare of determination, Noor stiffened in his seat. "Take time to consider what we've accomplished! We traveled out to the edge of the solar system and the edge of our understanding. We didn't know what we would find, but we accepted the challenge. We've already sent probes through to Alpha Centauri—and back. We found an extensive alien transportation network, and we found an ancient temple on an isolated comet!" His intestines twisted as he thought of the black prismatic window, hungry for his thoughts and soul. He tried to control his breathing and pushed on. "Not bad for a few days' work. I would say the Nether mission is an unqualified success."

Noor had the determination and the money to do whatever the hell he wanted. The Earth governments and space agencies would take decades to get their act together, and their missions would be cautious and minimal, dipping a toe in, baby steps up to the edge of the greatest discovery in human history.

Not interested in a pep talk, Glinda squirmed back into the crawl space to reach the comm circuitry. "I'll celebrate as soon as I fix the rat damage."

Cammie's face flushed. "When we're able to transmit again, we need to send a message back to Earth. Tell them everything that's been going on, tell them about the guard stations and the ancient war."

Noor frowned. "Let's not be premature. We don't understand it ourselves yet."

"The boss doesn't want to be embarrassed," Warren said.

"The wormhole is dangerous! The Osskkn bases were designed to keep other people away," Cammie said. "We should end our mission now and head back home."

"You sound like you're afraid." Noor lost a lot of respect for her then. With a disgusted sound, he knocked the dead rats off his lap and stood up from the captain's chair. "Remember those old maps used by ancient seafarers? Unknown territories were marked with *Here Be Monsters*—and yet the sailors still explored. That's what made them great. The Nether crew accepted the same risks."

Glinda managed to reroute some circuits under the bridge control deck. Her voice was muffled as she called out, "The larger screens should be working now. They're connected to the high-res optical telescopes in the astronomy module. If Cammie can point them, we should be able to resolve a few of the other asteroid bases now."

The young woman at first was hesitant, then stepped

forward. "Yes, I know how to work the telescopes." Noor sensed that something had changed in her, and she was no longer the awkward and painfully uncertain girl. She seemed to be standing straighter, showing more independence.

Working the controls, Cammie zoomed in on the two large screens at Arkourian's station. "There's the main base. The rest of the watchtower network is powering up—look at the thermal signatures, like they're getting ready for something."

A sudden flare appeared on the screen, and one of the other asteroids grew much brighter. "That's the smallest base, but it has a huge heat trace." Cammie switched the field of view, increased the magnification to the limits of the telescope. "It's . . . *moving*!"

Warren joined her, bending closer to the screen. "I remember that one—just a junior rock, but still a full base with domes and generators. Hey, it's accelerating."

Cammie let out a gasp. "Those are engines!"

Noor turned to the window wall in sudden amazement. "Engines built into an asteroid? That's convenient—it must be how they positioned the rocks evenly around the wormhole." He imagined what his company could do with those bases, especially if Arkourian and Ashe could figure out how to run the control systems. "Where is it going? Are those asteroids actually spaceships?"

"They serve as defensive stations." Cammie rubbed her temples. "They might be giant battleships."

The asteroid moved out of its ancient position, picking up speed. The thermal signature got brighter.

"I don't like this," Warren muttered.

As the smaller alien base crossed space, Cammie was able to track it. She extrapolated its path and displayed the dotted line across the screen. She stepped back, frowning. "It's headed in this direction."

Noor's throat went dry. "Why would an asteroid come toward Nether Station?"

Cammie flashed her intense green eyes at him and spoke so quickly that he heard only a blur of words. "I told you! The watchtowers were established to guard the wormhole, but I think their defenses are programmed to stop intruders. To make sure nobody wakes up the Agoc."

"Don't be ridiculous. That's not why we're here." He could tell she was challenging him to see her point.

"Their defensive systems know why we're here!" Cammie said. "We are intruders, and they'll try to stop us."

Whirls of static crossed the screens, a surge from the astronomy module, and the telescopic images burned out, leaving only empty projections.

"Glinda, can you reach Captain Arkourian yet?" Noor began to feel the edge of desperation. The asteroid kept hurtling toward them. "Maybe she can change some settings from her end and divert that rogue asteroid. Apparently, she and Mr. Ashe understand the alien controls."

"Our comm signal still can't get through to her," Warren said.

Cammie lowered her voice. "And none of us really understands how the base works."

Glinda retreated from the crawl space. "That asteroid better not hit us! I've spent a lot of damned time doing all that repair work."

Cammie stood at the windowport wall, trying to spot the bright asteroid with her eyes. Warren joined her, pressing his finger against the glass. "There's the asteroid! Holy crap, look at the heat coming from the rear! Those are massive propulsion engines—imagine how much energy it would take to accelerate an asteroid."

From the other side of the window wall, Noor watched the

oncoming rock as it grew visibly larger, moment by moment. If NOOR could adapt that propulsion technology down in the asteroid hub, they could move the most useful rocks for convenient processing.

Warren said in an awed voice, "It's coming right for us."

"There's no way to move the whole station," Glinda said. "The station-keeping jets can nudge us a few meters, but that won't be enough. Nobody ever thought we'd have to dance around out here."

The rogue asteroid shot toward them, rotating on its long axis like a spinning bullet. Already Noor could see its craters, the parabolic dishes, and the armored dome. It looked like an oncoming battering ram . . .

Cammie stood weak-kneed, but her expression changed as some realization dawned on her. She whispered, "It's going to miss."

Glinda frowned. "Not complaining, but if the aliens can use propulsion systems and drive a huge asteroid, how could it possibly miss?"

Noor broke into a smile as he watched it grow closer and closer. "Because it wasn't aiming for us."

The asteroid roared inexorably past, driven by incandescent engines. It missed Nether Station by less than a quarter of a kilometer and continued toward its real target.

The wormhole.

The immense rotating rock approached the blurred gateway, exactly on target. It plunged down into the wormhole, and the fiery rear engines winked out as they vanished over the event horizon.

Noor shook his head. "Why would they throw a rock down the hole?" He turned to Cammie, as if she might provide an instant answer from her vast library of information.

She just frowned in disbelief. "I have no idea."

Glinda dropped to her knees and squirmed back into the crawl space. "It didn't hit us—that's the big headline. Now, I've got a few more fixes to make."

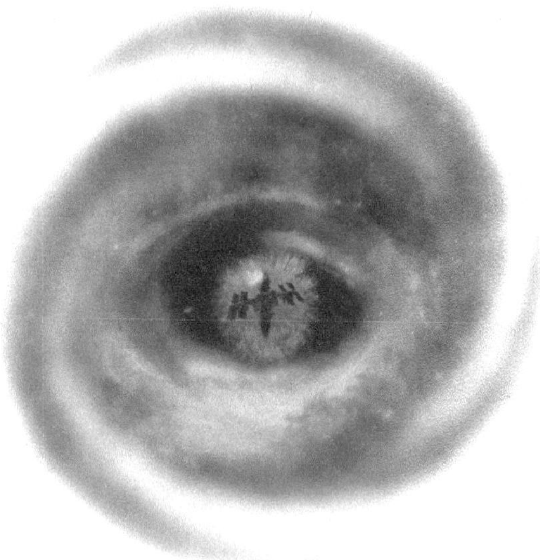

CHAPTER 44

After the runaway asteroid dove into the wormhole, Cammie was sure Mr. Noor and the others couldn't doubt her. The hurtling asteroid might be only the first salvo.

Glinda slumped into the seat at the comm station. "Technically speaking, everything is working, but I still can't raise Captain Arkourian or Jack Ashe. Direct jamming must be coming from the bases."

As Cammie told them more about the swarms of enslaved Osskkn and the horrific Agoc, she kept experiencing bursts of information as more pieces fell into their proper places. "We have to transmit a complete update down to Earth. Tell them everything we've learned, so that the human race knows what the Nether wormhole *is*."

"It'll take weeks before anyone even hears it," Warren said. "And you can't prove most of the story you told us. It'll sound crazy."

Benedict Noor's face was pinched. "Not so fast. Some things need to remain confidential. Proprietary information."

Alarmed, Cammie looked around the bridge. How could she get through to him? "Every human being in the solar system needs to know about the ancient war, the Agoc, the Osskkn race. Think of the implications for all of us! Those things came to our planet millions of years ago."

Noor's brow furrowed. "I have been cautious about what

we tell outsiders. I send regular encrypted summaries to my NOOR specialists, but we have time to decide what to tell the general public." He looked away, stubborn. "As you say, and if it is even remotely true, it's been millions of years. No need to overreact."

Even Glinda blinked at him. "We thought you'd been sending regular updates and press releases—you mean Earth doesn't know all the things we've found up here? The comet temple? The alien asteroid bases?"

"Do they even know we arrived at the wormhole, boss?" Warren asked.

"None of that seemed appropriate," Noor said. His face was stony.

Cammie was upset with him. She had assumed the scientific community was learning about all their amazing discoveries at the Nether wormhole. "But people are dead!"

"Earth can't offer us any help—not for Doc Stelland and not for your dear Tendari," Noor said. "We're on our own. We can take care of ourselves."

Warren looked away, his face flushed. "Seems like a bad call to me, boss."

Cammie stepped away, feeling angry but also useless. She had brought some of the most important news in human history, and Noor refused to take her seriously, even after what he had seen for himself. She could see no point in just standing on the observation bridge, and she needed to go somewhere else.

"I'm going to . . ." She hesitated, swallowed. "I'm going to take care of Dr. Stelland. You said nobody's been back to the med lab, and he deserves it."

Glinda gave her a sorrowful expression. "Be prepared for what you'll see, kid. There's lots of cleanup to do."

After mumbling that she would be fine after the things she'd already seen, Cammie left the bridge, struggling with her emotions. Benedict Noor, for all his billions of dollars, was ineffective in this situation. Why would he keep these enormous discoveries secret? How did it benefit him? Once again she wished Dr. Tendari could be here.

When she approached the medical bay, she could smell the coppery stench of blood. Her steps faltered, and she reconsidered what she intended to do, but she steeled her resolve. Dr. Stelland had just been left there, abandoned, as if nobody cared, and that felt wrong to her. She had liked the quiet, odd doctor, who preferred his personal silence as much as Cammie did. She could at least cover up his body, make him seem a little more at peace, even after what had happened to him.

But as she stepped across the threshold into the med center, she let out a groan deep in her throat. It was like a slaughterhouse inside.

The thin doctor lay sprawled like a rag doll torn apart by a psychopathic child. A pool of drying blood had spread across the polished deck, and more blood splattered the eggshell-white walls, as if the monkey had gone on a finger-painting frenzy.

What remained of Stelland's face was slack, his mouth open from his painful death and half of his cheek torn off. One eye was just a bloody socket, and the other was glassy and bright under the harsh ceiling panels. His larynx had been torn out, leaving a gaping red hole in his throat. His fingers were curled in death, like the legs of an insect sprayed with poison.

Cammie made herself go closer. Now she saw why Glinda hadn't bothered to help the doctor. Nothing would have saved him from this.

In a cage on the counter, the group of normal rats sniffed, scuttled, and squeaked as if they were hungry.

She knew she couldn't just leave Stelland's body like this.

She remembered having comfortable meals with him in the mess hall, helping him in the greenhouse. He was a kindred spirit.

Feeling a heavy obligation in her heart, Cammie crouched down and straightened the body's arms, adjusted his lolling head, closed his one remaining eyelid with a gentle touch. So much blood everywhere!

At the medical sink, Cammie found a sterile towel, which she draped over his mangled face, covering the look of horror. These efforts were useless, she knew, but she felt marginally better for having done them. The doctor's corpse would probably be sent out the airlock for a burial in space, as she had suggested for Zach Tendari.

Would she have to do all of this herself, alone? Move his body, prepare him to go out the engineering bay airlock? She was breathing hard, starting to hyperventilate, as she considered the effort of scrubbing so much blood from the floors and walls. But someone had to do it, even though simply cleaning the marks wouldn't erase what had happened here.

Cammie turned to look into the operating theater, where Stelland had recently performed his cursory autopsy on Dr. Tendari. She sucked in a quick breath when she saw the body lying there on the table.

Her mentor was still there, stretched out on the metal-composite table. He was naked except for a cloth draped over his waist, and his chest showed the ugly marks of the Y incision, the black sutures Dr. Stelland had used. She wondered why the body hadn't been placed in the med center's morgue freezer, but then she remembered it still held the preserved Osskkn corpse.

Stepping away from the slain doctor in his pool of blood, Cammie stood at the door of the operating room. Her heart ached with grief as she saw Tendari as just a husk of what he had been. He had been so much to her, even if she couldn't imagine being what he'd wanted from her. She heard the probe tech's mocking words again. *Creepy old man.* Cammie still couldn't believe that, couldn't think that of him. She knew he had done good things for her.

"I'm sorry," she whispered, meaning so many things by it. "You never got to see what you came to observe." That was all she'd wanted to do together with him. "And I can't finish this all alone."

His face was waxy, his eyes closed. When he'd been sealed in the cryopod for the last time, Cammie had watched him through the viewing pane. He didn't look much changed now, although his expression seemed different, maybe from the poking and prodding in the cursory autopsy.

Then Tendari opened his eyes.

Cammie jumped back, sure it was caused by the dead muscles contracting. When the eyelids pulled back, Tendari's eyes were not just dead but black, empty, and full of stars.

Then he lifted his head from the operating table and turned it from side to side, as if wondering where he was.

Cammie backed away, unable to find words. Finally, she whispered his name, as if it could banish him like a child's superstitious fear.

The sound attracted his attention, and he turned, then sat up on the table. His skin was grayish, his body lean and well muscled despite his age. Cammie could see the cuts and rough sutures from where Stelland had taken samples and sewn him back up. She stumbled away.

Tendari adjusted his balance, planted his palms on the sides of the operating table, then swiveled his hips and swung his legs down. The cloth draped over his waist fell aside as he stood up. He was naked, threatening.

"How can you be alive?" she finally asked. "What are you

doing?" Her throat was dry. She prayed that she wouldn't hear his dark and haunting voice whisper in her head. She tried not to think of how she had obliviously rebuffed his clumsy romantic advances, but rather made herself remember their friendship.

"I want to help you, Dr. Tendari," she said. "Let me call the rest of the crew. We need to understand what's happening to you . . ."

Tendari spoke in a hollow, awful voice. "*They* are sleeping. *They* are locked inside the folds of the universe." He lurched a step forward. "Do not wake them!"

His mouth hung open and empty like a passageway into hell. His eyes were black and hideous.

"I must stop you."

He lurched toward her.

CHAPTER 45

Under the armored Osskkn dome, power levels rose as the automated defenses continued to activate. The temperature inside the base grew warmer, and the air was thicker with a furry scent of old rot.

Unable to intervene, Karla Arkourian had watched the rogue asteroid hurtle toward Nether Station before plunging like a cannonball down the wormhole. But the watchtower network was just getting started, now that it had spotted the presence of the intruders. The main base rumbled from the subterranean generators, and she knew the awesome power this alien technology contained.

Pedro Ashe frantically worked at his chosen substation, trying to use his new knowledge. "Still no comms, Captain. The jamming is at full strength, and I can't get through. No way to warn our people." He ran to a secondary control bank, pushing a withered Osskkn body aside to make room.

Arkourian turned in a slow circle as she studied the large control center, trying to force the information details to line up like soldiers in her mind. Feeling desperate, she wiped perspiration from her forehead. "By now Warren and Cammie must have gotten back to the station, so everyone knows about the danger of the wormhole, the threat of the Agoc." She let out a grunt of frustration. "But considering Benedict's pigheaded determination, Cammie's story might just push him to send the *Neil Armstrong* through anyway. He'll never be talked out of doing exactly what he came here to do." She sighed. "Let's hope Warren knows better."

Ashe swiveled his head on his scrawny neck, staring at her in concern. "Would Mr. Noor do that without us?"

"It's a communications blackout. He might think we're dead already."

"Well, I'm not dead yet." The young engineer pulled up another screen and concentrated on the alien symbols. "This base is the main hub of the Osskkn defensive network. Maybe from here I can shut down the automated weapons on the other asteroids—at least for now. Buy us some time."

After what she had learned and seen, Arkourian had no doubt that their bumbling experiments might pose a cosmic threat. Yes, Nether Station had an ambitious mission plan, but everything had to change now. *Everything.*

Once the Osskkn defenses targeted the station, the automated systems would make every effort to remove the threat. Arkourian knew their only chance was to remove the threat themselves, to take Nether Station out of the equation.

Instead of hanging in place to conduct research for six months, Arkourian would jettison the external modules, batten down the *Lethe* core, and begin the return voyage in emergency mode. It would be not a retreat but an evacuation. By removing Nether Station from the alien targeting cross, she could save them. She hardened her resolve. Even if Noor resisted, she made up her mind to countermand him, although it went against every fiber of her life's training. She knew what was at stake.

In the corporate world, it was called not a mutiny but a hostile takeover.

Arkourian slammed her palm down on the useless alien

communications console. "I have to get word to them!" Making up her mind, she strode back to her discarded exosuit lying against the wall. "Maybe from the *Lewis* I can send a tight beam direct to Nether Station, line-of-sight laser comm. That'll get through any jamming, and they've got to know what's going on. Unless they prepare the *Lethe* for immediate departure, they're all in great danger."

Ashe studied the projected chart on the dome overhead, the marks of the watchtower ring and the trajectory the single rogue base had taken. "The defensive systems could have smashed Nether Station to smithereens—maybe that asteroid was a shot across the bow."

Arkourian felt a chill as she thought of another possibility. "Or it could have been a messenger with a warning about what we're doing here. Just because all the Osskkn on this side of the wormhole are dead doesn't mean that nobody's home at Alpha Centauri . . ."

"I don't want to go through to find out," Ashe snorted. "I'm trying to shut these systems down. The base network was specifically designed to destroy any threat to the wormhole. They aren't going to mess around."

Arkourian donned her exosuit. "Neither am I. Let's hope the *Lewis*'s tight-beam transmitter works. You can't jam a straight-line laser."

Once inside the *Lewis*'s cockpit, she flipped toggles and powered up the console. A great deal of static and feedback spilled from her helmet speakers, even though the comms showed functional. First, she flicked the standard transmitter and hailed Nether Station.

"Do you read me? Benedict? Warren? By now I hope Cammie delivered the message about what these stations are for and what the Nether wormhole really is. We don't dare do any more tests, or Nether Station is going to be a target! These watchtower asteroids are designed to stop anyone from interfering. We need to terminate the mission—now. Prepare the *Lethe* for departure. Engineer Ashe and I are working to put the alien weaponry systems in standby mode so we will have time to get away."

She waited for a response, heard only a burst of static. When regular transmissions didn't work, she collimated the *Lewis*'s direct tight-beam laser comm. It was a last-ditch effort, but it would hammer her message through, even with the signal jamming. She repeated the first message and added, "I'm pulling the plug on the Nether mission. If we don't depart, the watchtower network will destroy the station."

No response.

She considered flying directly back to the station, but she couldn't abandon Ashe here, and they didn't dare leave until the weapons were neutralized. Leaving the *Lewis* powered down but ready for takeoff, she rushed back into the base.

Under the dome, she found the young engineer still frantically working. With his skinny, bent legs, he bounced from one station to another. "Captain, I found the nexus for the automated defenses—it's not far from where those sphincter tentacles glommed onto our heads. I'll need your help. Maybe we can send a widespread stand-down signal."

After Arkourian stripped out of her exosuit, she followed him. "Let's go."

Ashe was already heading into the deep asteroid tunnels. "Some of the ideas were rattling around in my head, but now the pieces are falling together. I know how this all works." He rubbed his forehead. "I guess I'm starting to think like an alien."

Far underground, they passed the hive-like communal chambers, agricultural grottoes, and eerie quicksilver portholes, until they reached the central chamber with coiled, bulbous machinery. Organic-looking generators pulsed like the internal organs of a being composed of energy and thought.

"These machines power the defenses." Ashe hurried to the wall. "When the main weapon fires, the concentrated energy from these generators is released through the parabolic emitters in the crater."

"Like a Death Star laser," Arkourian said.

Ashe cocked an eyebrow. "Yes. Exactly like that."

His fingers skittered over the alien controls as he hunched forward to watch readings on the translucent screens. Holographic loops and whirls appeared in front of his eyes. "The watchtower defenses are a set of instinctive systems. They automatically react if they sense an intrusion or provocation at the wormhole."

"Why didn't they blast us as soon as the *Lethe* arrived?" Arkourian asked.

"The Osskkn have been dead for thousands of years, and the dormant network was slow to wake up." His brows drew together. "Or maybe the star beings decided the Agoc were neutralized, and there was nothing to worry about anymore."

"I doubt that."

Arkourian went to a second bank of controls in the generator chamber, ransacking her brain for the same information that Ashe had assimilated, but though she had a solid engineering background of her own, the young man was the expert. She said, "If we can just keep the bases from blasting Nether Station, we'll have time to figure out how to respond, to get our people out of harm's way."

Ashe tried a new routine and grinned as more control lights brightened. The holographic maze glowing in front of his face whirled around, becoming thicker and brighter. He stepped back, elated. "I have access to the self-defense circuits now! They're linked across the watchtower network, and the weapon generators are waiting for instructions. I'm posing as an Osskkn."

"Good luck with that," Arkourian said.

Animated now as he took control, the young man swept his hand across the panel, swiveled to look at Arkourian. "Ha, I'm canceling them with a flourish—across the board, putting the defense network into standby mode. Nothing to worry about now."

Instead, the bulbous organic generators flashed and sparkled, building to a surge. Arkourian could feel the crackle of static electricity in the air, and her hair stood on end.

"I thought you were shutting them down!" she shouted into the rising din.

Jitters of static sprayed like fireworks from the spiked coils of the generator, and the glow grew so blinding that Arkourian had to shield her eyes.

Ashe frantically worked the panel, looking over his shoulder. "Almost got it." Sparks nipped at his fingertips. "Still trying to figure out—"

The energy from the generator spikes reached its peak and twisted into a snakelike beam, jumping, ricocheting. He tried to leap away from the console, but the incandescent whip slammed into him, engulfed his entire body. He jittered, caught in a lightning strike, and the pulse vaporized him in a blinding discharge.

The charred remnants of his body crumpled to the floor before Arkourian could even move toward him. "Pedro!" His afterimage was burned onto her retinas.

A second burst of power lashed out to smash the control panels into a smoking mass. It was malicious, intentional—destroying any possible access.

More energy crackled out of secondary stations, building to a new crescendo.

CHAPTER 46

As Dr. Tendari pushed himself away from the autopsy table, Cammie felt paralyzed. At first it was more confusion than fear. What sort of strangeness had the wormhole passage caused? She had been so shocked by his death that now she felt an irrational flicker of hope. "Is it really you?"

Tendari kept coming toward her. "I must stop you." His frigid voice came from the dead hollow of his chest.

By the third step, his body had recovered some balance and agility. Several of the rough black sutures in the Y autopsy incision split open from the strain. Tendari touched the wound with the flat of his hand, puzzled, then kept moving.

As she stepped back, Cammie made a last attempt to communicate with him. "Are you in there, Dr. Tendari? I don't understand."

"You cannot understand. You must not." His eyes were empty and black, like gravitational wells that tried to suck her in. "It would burn your mind to a crisp if you understood."

She stumbled back toward the wall intercom. "I have to call the others!"

"I will find the others. One by one."

"This isn't you! You've got to remember me. I'm Cammie—Cammie Skoura. We were friends."

He swayed, then swung his face back to her. He stood tall, powerful, completely naked. "Cammie . . . ah, beautiful Cammie."

He looked hungry, predatory. Cammie had been oblivious to his romantic thoughts—sexual thoughts? Now he seemed obsessed. He came at her, thrust out a grasping hand.

Refusing to scream, Cammie ran out of the medical center, past Dr. Stelland's bloody body on the floor, and into the corridor. Tendari paused to stare at the doctor's mangled corpse as if assessing, taking score.

Cammie kept retreating, knowing she had to tell somebody, get them down here. She stopped at the wall intercom in the corridor and activated it with a sweaty palm. "Hello? Hello? I need help!"

Inside the med center, Tendari stumbled around as if disoriented, then turned back to the sealed morgue freezer, fumbling with it as if he wanted to climb inside.

She used the delay, pressed her mouth close to the intercom, and shouted in a hoarse whisper, as if she didn't want Tendari to hear her. "Warren! Glinda! Mr. Noor—please, somebody!"

She heard only a click of static, then silence. The rats must have damaged the internal comms too.

Cammie looked up, finding resolve. She would have to do this herself. He was her mentor, her friend, no matter what else. Maybe she could seal Tendari in the med lab until she could get help.

Then he staggered out of the facility, took his bearings, and sprinted after her with a doddering, spiderlike gait—much swifter than she had expected. His dead black eyes locked on hers.

Cammie ran up a level to the next section of the station, the greenhouse module, using the same path the rampaging rhesus monkey must have taken. Before she entered the large, well-lit dome, she spun to glance behind her.

Tendari loped along, mechanically pumping his arms and legs like a powerful athlete. He didn't say anything.

Glinda had left the bulkhead entrance open when she'd hunted down the monkey, but after Cammie ducked inside, she activated the controls to slide the door shut.

Tendari advanced toward her, his dead face blank. The door closed on him.

Cammie backed into the once-peaceful garden. Irrigation sprinklers sprayed a moist fog into the air, mingling with the smell of rotted vegetation. She remembered how Dr. Stelland had found peaceful contemplation time here.

She jumped when Tendari began pounding on the door, trying to break in. Nether Station wasn't designed with armored locks and heavy security, certainly not in the agricultural dome.

She knew he could probably get in.

She rushed through the rows of sagging plants toward the exit in back. The greenhouse was sad and rotting, all the plants discolored with blight, drooping with decay.

Suddenly, Cammie was startled by a rustling in the leaves next to her, then a hissing, grunting noise. The savage monkey lay among the zucchini vines, impaled with Glinda's long screwdriver, its face matted with Stelland's blood. It had to be dead, but now it struggled and gnashed its fangs, pinned in place. It grasped at the screwdriver shaft, dead but not dead.

Just like Tendari.

Outside, the resurrected man continued to pound against the sealed doorway, and then the noise fell silent. Cammie paused, breathing hard, wondering if he had given up, gone somewhere else.

Then the wall controls lit up, and the bulkhead door slid aside.

He still remembered how to operate the systems! Perhaps some glimmer of Zachary Tendari was still in there—but that made him far more dangerous. Spreading his arms to hold himself upright on either side of the doorframe, he glared into the greenhouse, then came for her. She ran.

At the far end of the dome, Cammie worked the exit door, which led to the connecting corridor. On Nether Station, though, everything was a dead end—every module, every corridor, every compartment connected back around. She had nowhere to run.

She could circle the axis of the original *Lethe*, make her way to the observation bridge where Warren, Glinda, and Noor could help her fight the Tendari thing. Deep down, she still didn't want to hurt him, but she had to stop him.

Hoping that something still worked, she hit the comm unit on the greenhouse wall. "Dr. Tendari's alive! He's chasing me." She received no response, saw that the panel remained deactivated.

The big man came after her through the greenhouse, determined and unwavering.

Cammie ran out of the dome, barely keeping her balance in the station gravity. Even though she had spent so long here, her Earthbound reflexes still made her overcompensate. She struck her shoulder hard against the corridor wall, then careened onward.

Tendari kept coming.

"Don't you remember me?" she called back. "We came to study the wormhole together. You and I were going to test our theories—our life's work!" He didn't slow, and she kept backing away. "We wanted to understand the wormhole!"

"Never," he rasped. "Must stop you."

Cammie shot down the corridor, still trying to convince

him. "We know what's inside the Nether wormhole now. We know about the Agoc and the war. We don't have to—"

"Too late."

Ahead she saw the entrance to her astronomy module, where the two of them should have been working the telescopes and sensors, marveling at the wormhole. But the connected cylinder was a trap, with no exit.

Instead, reaching a corridor intersection, she came upon the ladder that dropped down to the lower deck. It was her best option. Maybe she could double back, find someplace safe.

Grabbing the rungs, she swung herself down and scrambled into the bed-and-breakfast deck, the long chamber filled with cold and silent cryopods.

Dr. Tendari's malfunctioning pod was propped open from when his body had been removed. The other containers still hummed, sealed and frosty, with life-support systems struggling to keep the occupants alive.

Panting hard, she rushed down the hibernation bay toward the lift on the far end. She hit the comm panel on the wall again, yelling, "Dr. Tendari's alive! He's trying to kill me—and all of us!"

Then, in the echoing empty chamber, she heard a loud thump followed by a succession of banging noises. She tried to make out what had made the noise, but nothing moved. Up above, Tendari seemed to be having trouble with the ladder that led down here. She had a little time to get away.

Another thump, very close.

From above, she saw Tendari's long naked leg extend down to the next rung, his bare foot probing. More of his autopsy stitches had burst open, and a curl of intestines looped down, getting in his way.

Another loud thud startled her, like a large bird slamming

into a window. Cammie looked from side to side as the heavy pounding increased into desperate hammering from multiple sources.

Glinda's unexpected voice in the comm speaker made her jump. "Whoa, Tendari's alive? What the hell are you talking about, Cammie?"

She didn't know how to explain it. "He got up from the autopsy table, and he's moving! Says he has to stop us from going into the wormhole."

Tendari dropped to the floor on the other end of the deck, and even in the low gravity he struck with a heavy thump. He crouched like an animal, looking around, and then his hollow-void gaze locked on her.

Cammie retreated along the line of cryopods—and a thunderous, wet boom made her gasp. She looked down at the pod and saw a long red smear on the viewing pane. Behind it, a hand moved; then a bruised fist smashed against the canopy again. Splayed fingers clawed the glass, trying to get out.

In the adjacent cryopod, she saw the same thing—desperate pummeling as a formerly frozen crewmember tried to escape. They'd awakened, and they were still alive! She had to let them out.

Even as Tendari lurched closer, grabbing a loop of intestines to hold them out of the way, she bent over the cryopod, trying to work the release controls. Maybe these other crewmembers could help her.

Then, behind the viewing pane, she saw the drawn, cadaverous face of Peter Hamada, Benedict Noor's primary assistant. His eyes were milky, his mouth bloody, and his teeth broken as he slammed his face with full force against the clear window. Hamada thumped again and again, cracking his forehead, clawing with bloody fingers. He left a red smear.

Cammie staggered back, bumped the next pod, which evoked a flurry of grasping fingers inside the chamber. Hands smashed into the canopy as the occupant tried to break out. All nine of the locked pods resounded with the unearthly struggles.

Tendari paused among them, as if fascinated. He gazed into the first cryopod, apparently feeling some connection to the re-animated bodies inside.

With a surge of adrenaline, Cammie shook off her confusion and bolted to the open lift doors at the far end of the deck. She ducked inside and sealed the doors, then slapped the button to take her back up to the engineering bay.

She saw Tendari stalking toward her, but then the lift doors slid shut and the elevator rose up out of his view. She knew he would keep following her, but at least she had gained a few minutes.

She emerged into the engineering bay, the equipment and suit-up room used by Glinda Roybal and Pedro Ashe. The large chamber held multiple tool lockers, equipment closets, and hanging exosuits. Cammie was small enough to hide inside one of the lockers, but Tendari would find her. At the far end of the bay, the inner door of the main airlock was open, ready for the engineers' next exterior operation.

She could climb into one of the exosuits, escape the station, make her way around to the hangar bay. He would not be able to follow her.

But she wouldn't have time. Cammie knew how long it would take her to don the suit, connect and seal all the components. And he was coming.

A desperate last-ditch plan occurred to her, and she immediately made up her mind. Cammie grabbed one of the spare exosuits and helmets from a locker and bounded to the open airlock. The empty suit flopped like a boneless corpse as she dragged it into the airlock chamber. Once locked onto its collar, the helmet lolled and bumped against the side wall.

Inside the airlock chamber, she arranged the suit to look lifelike, at least momentarily—as if someone had slumped there on the floor—and then she opened the helmet's faceplate. Working frantically, she propped the suit and faced the helmet away from the inner door. It would have to do; there wasn't time to do any more.

She grabbed a second helmet from the rack and backed away to one of the equipment lockers. She was shaking so much she could barely stand, but she could not hesitate. As she backed into the cramped locker, she tried to control her breathing. She pulled the door partly closed, hoping Tendari wouldn't notice her in there. She huddled in the shadows, hugged the helmet against her chest, and reached inside to flip the comm switch with her finger.

The lift doors opened, and the Tendari thing emerged into the bay, jittering, naked, displaying the awful wounds from his autopsy. Through the crack in the locker door, Cammie could see the horror of his face, the rigid, inhuman expression. She held her breath.

Tendari looked around to survey the changing room and equipment bay, hunting for her. He stared at the suits hanging on the rack, looked at the wall cabinets. He seemed to sense her nearby. Cammie knew he would find her.

She had to act.

Cradling the helmet close to her chest, she leaned forward to speak into the comm pickup. "Dr. Tendari, please don't hurt me. I have nowhere else to go!"

Her voice came out of the speaker inside the helmet propped inside the airlock. She had turned the volume to maximum, and now it drowned out her own muffled sounds in the locker.

Tendari snapped to attention, turned.

"Dr. Tendari, please!" she said.

He strode forward, his hands splayed like murderous weapons. His eyes locked on the silvery humanoid form in the airlock. Her ruse fooled him, and he shambled toward the airlock, thinking he had her cornered.

But as he neared the opening, he hesitated, wary. He turned, as if sensing something wrong.

Cammie pulled out her last weapon, whispered into the voice pickup. "Please, Dr. Tendari . . . *Zach*!"

Call me Zach.

He was startled as if he remembered the name, too, remembered her in a different way. He turned back to the airlock, took a closer look at the form lying there.

Cammie burst out of her hiding place and shot forward like a battering ram, kicking off the equipment stand. He heard the locker door slam open with a bang and began to turn, but Cammie plowed into him and knocked him forward.

The big, clumsy corpse stumbled into the airlock chamber where she had left the empty suit.

Letting out a hoarse scream, Cammie flung herself out and slapped the airlock controls, closing the inner door. Giving herself no time for second thoughts, she hit the decompression cycle and watched the progress bar as the air was sucked out.

The Tendari thing pounded on the observation window. He grabbed the empty exosuit, picked up the hollow helmet, and realized he had been betrayed. He pressed his mournful face against the windowport, and Cammie stared at him one last time.

But there was no Zachary Tendari—only the infinite emptiness of cold space. He was gone, long before today.

The outer airlock door opened and ejected him, sending his body tumbling out into space with the flopping silvery exosuit. He spun away, twitching and jerking as he froze solid to drift along in the vacuum.

"Burial in space," Cammie whispered to herself. She began sobbing.

CHAPTER 47

Nether Station was a mess. On the bridge, Glinda kept up her frantic efforts to bypass one fratzing system faster than another one failed. The vicious rats had mangled multiple circuit modules, but she was most concerned about life support, the station power systems—and the comms. What she would give to have Ashe back here helping her!

The alien asteroid bases continued to jam outgoing transmissions, but Glinda was finally able to jerry-rig part of the station's internal comm network. Over half of the intercoms were operable again.

Then, just as she turned her focus to the next emergency, Cammie's panicked voice burst through the speaker. "Dr. Tendari's alive! He's trying to kill me—and all of us!"

Glinda's head snapped up in surprise. "Whoa, Tendari's alive? What the hell are you talking about, Cammie?"

Warren hurried over to join Glinda at her station. "Where is she?"

"She went to the med center to take care of Doc Stelland's body." Glinda glanced at the module screens, toggling from room to room, corridor to corridor, but they remained dark and blank. "I don't have eyes on most of the station. Our internal cameras are down."

Noor clucked his tongue against his teeth. "That girl was devastated by the loss of her mentor. Maybe she found some hallucinogenic substance and is imagining that he's back?"

Glinda huffed. "If we have those kinds of drugs aboard the station, I wish somebody had let me know."

"Cammie doesn't imagine ghosts," Warren said, turning toward the lift. "I better see what's going on."

On their external display screen—which was one of the few functioning bridge systems—Glinda saw the nearest watchtower asteroid flare brighter in a clear energy buildup. "Whoa, another one's activating! If they keep throwing asteroids in our direction, one of them is going to hit us."

On the star chart, two more watchtowers brightened, and Noor squirmed in his captain's chair. "We need a Plan B. Perhaps we should escape the station? We could use the *Neil Armstrong*."

"I'll fly wherever you want, boss," Warren said. "But where will we go?"

Glinda felt cold. "I'd call that a Plan Z." Alerts flashed on her engineering screen, distracting her. "What the hell? The airlock just cycled in the engineering bay!"

Warren headed for the door. "I better make sure Cammie is okay."

Another bright flare caught Glinda's eye, and she zoomed in on the main asteroid base. What were Arkourian and Jack Ashe doing over there? She was afraid the rock would accelerate toward them like the previous one had.

Instead, it attacked.

A surge of light gushed from the alien base, an intense beam that struck Nether Station, hitting the spare habitation module where she had killed the first rat.

She let out a loud yelp. "Those bastards *shot* at us!"

The entire station rocked on its axis. The monitoring panels lit up like a Christmas tree decorated with only red lights, and the deck tilted at an extreme angle. Warren stumbled at the lift door and slid across the bridge deck to slam into Noor's chair.

"How much damage?" Noor demanded. "Did that blast hit our vital systems?"

"Hold on—I've only got a few external cameras." Glinda ran through her options in the controls, finding one burned-out camera after another until she finally got a partial view of the uninhabited module. A black scorch mark looked like a burn wound along its hull, and atmosphere spewed out like white blood.

Nether Station began wobbling, and Glinda grabbed the anchored chair to hold herself. "Could've been worse—that was just our spare habitation cylinder. It acted as a shield."

Then, to her horror, she saw the next two asteroid stations glowing with power buildup. They were going to fire again! "What the hell did we ever do to them?"

"Cammie explained the whole story to us," Warren said. "We should've believed her. The aliens are protecting the wormhole—they think we're a threat."

"I didn't believe or disbelieve her," Noor said in a sour voice. "We didn't have time to assess her story."

"But we aren't doing anything!" Glinda said.

A secondary explosion occurred in the damaged hab module as a compartment ruptured and spilled frozen gases into space. The observation bridge tilted so much it made Glinda want to puke. "That venting air in the damaged module is throwing us off-balance, causing a bad resonance."

"You mean it's going to get worse," Noor said.

"Trying to handle it." Glinda studied the controls, isolated the habitation module, then used bursts of the station-keeping jets to dampen the oscillation. "Jack and I spent all day connecting that damn cylinder. But it's always easier to break things than to put them together."

"Look out!" Warren shouted.

The second asteroid base spat out an energy bolt like a burst electrical bubble that slammed into the damaged module and then skirled in an afterwash that also harmed the astronomy cylinder.

The station lurched like a tree toppling over. Sparks showered up from one of the control panels at Arkourian's station.

The third glowing watchtower unleashed an energy blast, but because the station had been knocked out of position, the bolt flared past, barely missing them.

"That used up our luck for the day." Glinda furiously worked her systems in an attempt to close the loop before all the power failed. "Cutting the hab module's umbilical now so we can get rid of that deadweight. Explosive bolts activated—ready to jettison."

Her signal triggered the emergency disconnect, blowing the spare module away from the station core. After the extreme blasts they had just suffered, the *whump* sounded insignificant, like the bark of a little lapdog.

She let out a sigh. "Habitation module disengaged. It's no longer an anchor flopping us around."

Warren made his way to a second set of controls at the engineering station. "Half of Nether's attitude thrusters aren't functioning, and I don't think I can stabilize us."

As the deck continued to lurch like a ship on heavy seas, Glinda groaned. "It's going to take all the duct tape in the universe to hold the station together."

Benedict Noor looked grim and shaken. "I trust you to save us, Glinda. You're a miracle worker."

"Shit, I've already proved that." This was a minute-by-minute thing. Even if she fixed the sabotaged power systems and the failing life support, how long could the station last? And where would they go?

On the display screen, she saw yet another one of the watchtower asteroids building up energy as it prepared to fire.

CHAPTER 48

All the Osskkn creatures in the asteroid complex were long dead, but the base itself was awake and alive.

And angry.

After the blast that killed Ashe, Karla Arkourian staggered away from the pulsing organic generators. She was horrified by what had happened to her partner, but acutely aware that she might be the next target. She touched no controls, made no overt moves. Would the automated defenses work to purge her from inside the base?

Though incredibly tense, she forced herself to move in a slow and nonthreatening manner. The twitchy Osskkn sensors remained alert for intruders and sabotage.

Even outside the crackling chamber, she could smell vaporized circuits and burned flesh. She felt dizzy, nauseated, and furious.

She had been in multiple situations where she never thought she'd survive, but she was still here. Fate had had plenty of chances to take her. Arkourian did not give in to panic—she found a way.

With all the alien information crowded in her mind, she was aware of the energy weapons, and she comprehended what Ashe had tried to do. But the systems had annihilated him.

The automated watchtower network was aware that the Nether team had come to investigate the wormhole. Arkourian could think of no way to convince the systems that they were not enemies, not allied with the Agoc. If she could return to Nether Station, she would round up the team and depart from the wormhole forever. But she couldn't communicate that to the automated systems—the alien defenses would simply destroy the potential threat.

Unless she could shut them down.

Running to the adjacent chamber, she paused at the ominous quicksilver portholes, the data conduits that had force-fed them with information. As the generators thrummed and the asteroid shook with seismic events, she felt the network build to another imminent blast.

She had to shut down the mindless destructive systems until she could get back to Nether Station and force an immediate descent from the Kuiper Belt. The seven crew cryopods had been reset, supposedly clearing the deadly glitch, and the survivors could survive the long return flight . . .

But in the meantime, Nether Station was defenseless.

It was all up to her.

When Pedro Ashe had attempted to interfere with the systems, he had triggered his own death. He'd been too overconfident that he understood the alien technology, but a little bit of knowledge was dangerous. He had tried to do too much, all at once, causing the deadly backlash.

Arkourian needed to learn more before she made her next move, but she had little time.

As the base's defensive generators built to a greater intensity, the consoles glowed as sensors scanned and targeted Nether Station. Breathing hard, Arkourian convinced herself she could do this. She recalled the times she had flown over enemy lines into great peril. The mission had required it, and she'd done it. She had survived.

She knew all three of her lost husbands would have encouraged her now. *Fate be damned*, she thought. Karla Arkourian was no stranger to risks.

She knew how to get the information she needed.

Though her stomach churned with revulsion, she stepped closer to the largest quicksilver porthole. Back straight, she said aloud, "I need to understand the watchtower defense systems. Show me."

From the previous gorging of data, she could still hear alien-language thoughts inside her mind. Now she could communicate in an Osskkn way, as well as in the psychic and universal language of the star beings, the Yggroths, and other bizarre races from the ancient war.

She pressed her demand. "I have to know more!"

The vertical quicksilver hole swirled and shifted color, and the liquid-metal sleeve shot out like a striking viper. It engulfed her head, closed around her like a tight sphincter, and she found herself drowning in data, smothered in exotic mathematics, engineering, and technology.

The second experience was worse, because this time she remained half awake, unable to breathe, clutching at the silver tentacle that regurgitated information into her. She tried to send a message in the other direction as well, pushing her insistence. *We are not the enemy! We pose no threat! We will leave!*

She didn't know if the mindless systems understood her. Or believed her.

When the slimy metallic grip finally retracted into the porthole frame, Arkourian collapsed to the deck, gasping. She wiped at her face and hair, trying to get rid of the disgusting sensation.

Now that she had more information, though, she understood how Ashe had attempted to shut down the defensive network. All of it. His idea had been too extreme, attempting to neutralize the Osskkn defenses with a bludgeon, not a scalpel—and the automated guardians had reacted. Now Arkourian saw the fail-safes built into the network.

With this new flood of information, she learned more about the nightmarish Agoc. She could see this facility swarming with cricket aliens, each station monitored by Osskkn who had been liberated from enslavement and torture. These defenses were designed to prevent any trespass, and they did not care about human explorers.

But she also had to keep Nether Station from being destroyed. She might have to be ruthless with Benedict Noor, but she would bring him around. They would leave the wormhole far behind, without further provocation.

Armed with her greater understanding, she returned to the organic generator chamber where Ashe had been disintegrated. Though the main console had been wrecked, Arkourian understood how to reprogram the other systems now.

As she began to work with the systems, she felt the building energy around her, but she knew the defenses wouldn't blast her directly, as they had killed her companion. The Osskkn tech made so much more sense to her now!

The watchtowers were arranged at strategic points around the mouth of the wormhole, with powerful weaponry to defend against evil forces in league with the Agoc. Three asteroid bases had already fired energy beams at the station, surely causing significant damage. One of the blasts had miraculously missed, but now the weapons on a fourth base were reaching the tipping point.

Hoping she knew enough, she stepped up to the primary weapons controls. This would require a sensitive touch, but she needed to act quickly, before the next blast erupted.

Arkourian thrust her hands into fleshy, metallic sleeves, like holes in the intestines of the Osskkn controls. Her face twisted in disgust, but she gritted her teeth and located the connections she needed.

As she concentrated, her mind blurred, then snapped into sharp focus. Her own thoughts became part of the network's greater control system, and she experienced the buildup of power, the main base's weapon at her fingertips.

The fourth watchtower asteroid was ready to fire—now.

Arkourian tried to communicate with the network, to beg for a delay, to explain who they were, but the automated systems were dumb and relentless. She twisted her hands, finding an imaginary dial, and she guided the parabolic projectors, saw the lines in space, imagined a targeting cross.

The system allowed her to do that.

Suddenly, she had a better idea than deactivating the entire system, one that would fool the ancient alien defenses. Instead of shutting it all down and provoking a backlash, she could simply *retarget the beam.*

Arkourian thrust with her mind, pushing her command with sheer force of will.

With a release of power like an erupting geyser, she let the energy go. The intense bolt tore across space—and blasted the next watchtower instead of Nether Station, ruining the automated base before it could fire its own beam.

The blast shattered the hollowed-out rock, collapsing the tunnels, wrecking the embedded engines. In her mind and inside the network, that watchtower winked out, breaking into a cloud of incandescent rubble.

Arkourian slumped to her knees with relief. She had saved Nether Station for now, although the rest of the alien network remained a threat.

Through her connection with the Osskkn automated systems, she sensed a flare of anger in the residual star-being memories. She doubted the mindless systems would let her try that trick again.

CHAPTER 49

Cammie stumbled away from the airlock, desperate to get out of the engineering bay. She pushed aside an irrational fear that Tendari would somehow find a way to get back into the station.

He was gone now, and she was free of him . . . but he'd been gone before. He had been gone since she said goodbye to him when he went to sleep for the last time in the defective cryopod.

Tendari was already dead. Would the vacuum kill him again?

A violent shock tore through the station, and Cammie tumbled to the deck, sliding into the bulkhead as the floor tilted at an extreme angle. Alarms blared. Something major had happened to the station. She pulled herself to her feet and worked her way to the comm panel by the exit door. She shouted, but got no answer.

Another impact struck, and she heard a rumble of damage. The overhead lights flickered. Were they under attack? How was that possible?

She heard the grinding and tearing of metal, and she raced to the engineering bay's windowport. Outside, she saw the mangled habitation module drifting away, disconnected from the station core.

Had an asteroid struck them? That smoking wound looked deliberate.

Struggling to keep her footing, she grabbed the wall

handholds and worked her way out of the engineering bay. At the ladder, she climbed up past the bed-and-breakfast deck to the greenhouse level.

She almost screamed when Warren Drake suddenly appeared in front of her. "Cammie! I came to rescue you."

"I could have used you a few minutes ago." She forced her breathing to slow. "I rescued myself."

"Glad you took care of it." He grabbed her arm as the station shook again. "But now we've got bigger concerns. The asteroid bases started taking shots at us."

Cammie suddenly understood. "It's the Osskkn defenses! Even if the aliens are dead, the automated systems are always watching. They must have identified us as a threat."

Warren rushed her along. "The station is severely damaged, and we're out of equilibrium. I doubt Glinda can stabilize it—certainly not if we're under fire. Come to the bridge. The boss is talking about evacuation."

Cammie sprinted along beside him as he led the way. "Evacuation? Where would we go? And what about Captain Arkourian and Pedro?"

"They're cut off from communication, and we don't know what's happening over there." Warren paused to look at her. "But those asteroid bases are shooting at us."

Taking the straight-line path that would lead them to the bridge, they cut through the greenhouse. Cammie kept her head down, haunted by the memory of Tendari's gray, naked figure lunging after her.

Warren yanked her to one side. "Watch out."

The squash vines writhed like a nest of needle-covered serpents. Stems curled up, lashing out, and a vine looped around her arm. She felt it tighten, digging in, and she ripped herself free, tearing the fabric of her station jumpsuit.

In the bed of the huge plant, tumescent squashes rolled and pulsed like warty, cancerous logs. They seemed to be breathing. One zucchini swelled and strained, oozing slimy juices through the hard rind. Cammie dodged just as the squash exploded like a bomb full of rotten pulp and razor-edged seeds.

Warren hurried her to the door. "That's damned creepy."

As they reached the opposite bulkhead, the impaled rhesus monkey limped forward, grasping at the screwdriver through its chest. Its eyes were black and empty, its fangs like blood-smeared tusks. It blocked their way.

Suddenly, another explosion rippled across space with a blinding surge seen through the greenhouse dome. The intense burst strafed the transparent ceiling, damaging the windowports. Air spewed out in a rush.

The shambling monkey screamed and fell backward as sudden decompression sucked away the atmosphere.

Warren grabbed Cammie's wrist and pulled her like a rag doll to the connecting door, clutching the bulkhead. Together they stumbled into the adjacent corridor, and Cammie sealed the connecting door, trying to catch her breath. "Thanks."

"Anytime."

Finally, they reached the observation bridge, where Glinda worked the engineering consoles, her face grim. She shook her head as she tried one stopgap measure after another.

Benedict Noor turned in circles, as if wanting to shout orders, but he didn't know what to say. "Now what do we do?" He spotted Cammie and Warren as they emerged from the lift. "There you are! We need your help."

"No time for a debrief, boss," Warren panted. "We lost the greenhouse deck and the connecting levels. All hell is breaking loose."

Glinda barely looked up from her work. "No shit."

"We have no choice but to evacuate," Noor announced. "This station is irreparably damaged, and we're still under fire."

"I'll just call a cab," Glinda said. "Where the hell will we go?"

"The *Neil.* It's fully stocked and designed to carry an exploration crew. We can all fit inside." Noor's eyes had a dark, intense glint. "We have a choice between certain death and not-so-certain death. And you know how to fly the ship, Warren. I'm counting on you."

The pilot's face was determined. "Easy-peasy."

"The asteroid bases," Cammie said. "They have air, life support. We could survive there for a little while."

"No food, unless you like to eat dead crickets," Warren said.

"But those bases are trying to destroy us. You think they're going to kiss and make up?" Glinda cried.

"There are other possible destinations." Noor actually managed a smile. "We'll be pioneers and pilgrims, the greatest explorers of the human race . . . even if it is by accident."

The bridge continued to shake as explosions rippled through the station.

Glinda gave up in exasperation, raising her hands. "Okay. I have no control of anything, we're losing air, and it damn well can't be fixed. We're sitting ducks here."

"If I'm a duck, I'd rather not just sit." Noor strode toward the door. "To the hangar bay. Warren, crack your knuckles and prepare to fly us to safety."

"Yes, boss." He glanced at Cammie. "Let's go."

As the station rumbled and shook, the four of them worked their way down the ladder shaft, not trusting the lift. Cammie let out a sigh of relief to see that the hangar bay doors had not been breached. Alarms and flaring lights increased the chaos around them.

The *Neil Armstrong* waited in the bay, connected to power

and fuel umbilicals, ready to go, though the station's violent movement had shoved it partway across the deck.

Noor admired the vessel. "That's our only hope of survival—a lifeboat, courtesy of NOOR technologies."

As they ran toward the expedition ship, instinctively ducking low in case some ceiling girder might fall or hull plate rip off, Cammie heard a clatter, spotted an unexpected jerky movement.

Warren paused, looked around. "What the hell is that?"

One of the cricket aliens popped up from behind the *Neil*. Its black eyes were dull, and one of them was cracked. Parts of its exoskeleton had been cut open.

Ignoring them, the Osskkn reached up with clawed hands and tore at the cowling over the craft's engines. A metal plate had already been pried up over the exhaust cone, and wires and power trains had been pulled out.

When the creature saw them, it made an abrasive clicking noise from its damaged throat.

"It's Jiminy!" Noor said.

Cammie realized it was the specimen that Dr. Stelland had partially dissected. She suddenly remembered seeing Tendari turn back to the morgue freezer and fumble with the latch before he pursued her. He had intentionally released this Osskkn cadaver!

Warren was already moving as the deck lurched due to another gas explosion. He showed no intimidation or fear, just indignation as he strode forward.

Glinda ran beside him. "That bugger is sabotaging our escape ship!"

The Osskkn's movements were sluggish and deliberate, not nimble. It dug a claw into the engine cowling and rummaged around, ripping wires, damaging components without finesse.

Cammie knew this thing must be driven by the same force

that had resurrected Tendari's body. "They don't understand why we're here, but they're doing anything they can to stop us and Nether Station."

Warren seized the cricket alien by one of the beetle-like wings and yanked the reanimated creature away from the expedition vessel and tossed it aside.

Glinda was more vindictive. "We need that ship!"

As the Osskkn skittered across the tilted deck, flailing its segmented limbs, the engineer kicked it like a football player attempting a field goal. The alien was ancient, desiccated, and damaged, and its head flew off to bounce and clatter amid the debris in the hangar bay.

Noor started laughing.

As Nether Station shuddered and groaned, Warren let out a groan of his own as he looked at the *Neil*'s damaged engine. "That bastard! Now how are we going to fix this?"

"I need to emphasize that we have to go, Warren," Noor said. "Right now."

"We'll fix it." Glinda strode over to the wall and grabbed a tool kit. "That bug didn't know what it was doing, and the *Neil Armstrong* is robust, with a lot of redundancies. Maybe it's not so bad."

Cammie joined the other two. "Tell me how I can help."

Glinda and Warren bent together next to the engine casing, working in instinctive synchronization. "You can hand us the tools we need, and it'll go faster."

"The damned bug pulled the fuel line and disconnected the power train, but it's not ruined," Glinda said with a grim sigh. "Could have been a lot worse."

Cammie crouched and studied the various tools, handing implements to the two mechanics as they worked like a frantic pit crew in a championship car race.

With morbid curiosity, Noor bent over the decapitated body of "Jiminy" while the others worked.

Warren reattached two cables and triggered a diagnostic routine. The lights winked green. Glinda chuckled. "We're miracle workers."

Warren held the metal plate in place while Cammie and Glinda used a magnetizing pistol to reattach it; then Glinda fused the seam with a line of welding gel. The exterior of the ship still showed the marks of the alien claws, but the pilot was satisfied. "Good as new, boss—or at least good enough to fly."

Noor stepped up to the hatch as if it were his private limousine. "Then let's get out of here."

Glinda wiped sweat from her brow. "I'll be happy to get away from Nether Station before it falls apart, Benedict, but we're still shit out of luck. The *Neil Armstrong* has life support and supplies for a couple of weeks—but there's no way it'll keep us alive all the way back down to the inner solar system."

Another discharge rumbled through the station, sending them all reeling. The expedition ship scraped to one side and ripped an energy umbilical from the wall.

"No matter where we go," Noor said, "we can't stay here."

Warren ran to the expedition vessel. "Everyone aboard."

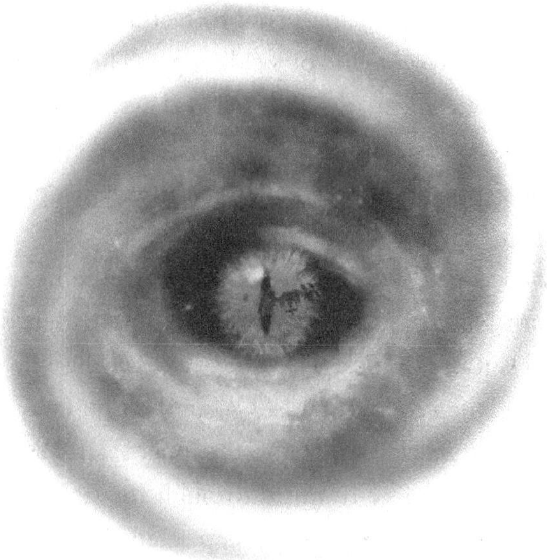

CHAPTER 50

After destroying another watchtower station with a diverted blast, Arkourian knew she couldn't fool the alien tech again. The data dump in her head let her understand the Osskkn defensive systems—but the systems also understood her.

This base now realized she was not an ally.

The network shifted its priority target—and Arkourian couldn't stop it. On the dull, polished screen of a console, the next watchtower base was ready to fire.

Nether Station was already battered, hanging in space like a sacrifice. It couldn't survive another blast.

She pounded on the substation and shouted, but the automated systems were not listening. "You caused enough damage! Our station is no threat to you—certainly not anymore. We are not your enemies! We'll leave!"

The asteroid fired its energy blast.

Since that watchtower was the most distant from Nether Station, the beam dissipated somewhat by the time it struck its target. Under high magnification, Arkourian saw that the station's greenhouse module had been damaged.

She squeezed her eyes shut and tried to form her thoughts into a command, and she shifted her mindset in an effort to communicate in the Osskkn language. Maybe the automated systems would respond to the alien thought patterns and symbols.

Instead, Arkourian felt the defensive network strengthening, ready to unleash one final combined blast. "Damn you, we are not the enemy!"

She had to convince these nonhuman systems that the ancient war was long over, that she was not a puppet of the dark elder gods. "Please!" she whispered, but she sensed no acknowledgment at all.

Even with all the background noise, Arkourian heard a rustle and clatter in the control room. She tried to locate the noise, but it was drowned out by the throbbing of the control stations.

Then, out of the corner of her eye, she saw movement, twitching insectile limbs. The mummified Osskkn husks scattered around the chamber began to move.

Several alien bodies turned their rounded heads and peered at her with soulless black eyes. They rolled, twitched, and crawled, climbing to their feet. Arkourian did not expect that these reanimated corpses would serve as mere spokesmen to explain ancient history.

The first Osskkn zombie staggered toward her, weaving on fragile legs and flailing its clawed hands. Two others came behind it.

The control panel on the console in front of her showed that the power levels inside the organic generators had reached their peak. The remaining watchtower stations had prepared for a simultaneous blast—a final combined outpouring would annihilate everyone on board Nether Station.

Arkourian tried one more subroutine, but the automated defenses were aware of her now and worked to block her efforts.

An alien claw grabbed at her leg, and she kicked it away. The husk tumbled unceremoniously to the floor, and two of its limbs snapped. It reminded her of a dried-up dead spider on a windowsill.

"I don't have time for this!" she hissed.

Three more reanimated Osskkn closed in on her. She pushed the first one with a mighty heave that sent it like a bowling ball into two others, knocking them down.

At the wall where Ashe had piled the corpses out of the way, it looked like an army of resurrected bugs rising up.

The combined energy weapon was ready to fire, but on the screens and diagrams, Arkourian watched in astonishment as the target shifted on its own. She sucked in a quick breath as she saw the new objective.

An incandescent discharge poured out of the parabolic emitters, eight separate blasts from eight asteroids multiplied into a column of concentrated power.

The combined surge struck its new target—the nearby comet with its cyclopean temple and frozen Agoc throne. The icy body was riddled with fissures and voids, and the energy beam split the comet like a hammer smashing a block of glass. With a titanic explosion, the fragments dispersed in a widening cloud of ice, rocks, and vapor, like a bloodstain from the elder gods.

She gripped the console to keep her balance. The target had shifted from Nether Station! Had she done that?

As the mummified cricket aliens closed in, Arkourian ran to a different console, trying to call up results, and she saw that Nether Station was still intact—barely.

Ten resurrected Osskkn clattered toward her, but she avoided them. "Thank god you buggers are slow." She snatched one, smashed it over her knee, and tossed the broken pieces aside. Then she grabbed the next Osskkn and wielded it like a club, batting away two others. They emitted a hollow, hissing rattle, no longer attempting to form words—or maybe the automated alien systems simply had no desire to communicate.

Arkourian crashed into the shambling, desiccated bugs, knocking them, breaking them. But they kept coming. She panted hard now, but she had cleared herself some space.

The lights inside the domed chamber dimmed. Many of the monitor screens suddenly went dark as the base systems began to shut down. On a monitor view of the lower generator grotto, she saw that the pulsing, bulbous machinery had expended its energy and faded into power-conservation mode.

She tapped into the controls, trying to understand what was happening, and she learned the grim results. "It's just one damn thing after another."

That climactic blast had depleted the watchtower's power reserves, and now she realized that the defensive network was designed to go dormant in order to recharge and regenerate. It would be a swift process on a cosmic scale, taking a year or two until the defensive network was back to full capacity.

But the base's life-support systems were shutting down, deemed unnecessary.

Was this what had happened before, millennia ago? With the network offline and regenerating, all the drones—the expendable Osskkn—had died.

Right now she wished they would stay dead.

Two of the broken alien husks tried to crawl toward her. She stomped on the back of one, crushing its carapace. She knew they would keep coming unless she spent days smashing every single one of them. But with the energy and life-support systems now powered down, would she even have days left inside here?

Karla Arkourian did not intend to die like that.

More cricket aliens shambled in from adjacent tunnels in a relentless horde. Arkourian spotted her exosuit near the airlock and knew what she had to do.

Getting back to Nether Station, even if it was damaged, was her only hope. Maybe someone was still alive over there.

She kicked and cleared away the zombie aliens and grabbed the suit, then climbed inside the airlock chamber. She sealed the inner door, hoping the mindless bugs didn't remember how to operate the controls. She wasted no time.

In the cramped airlock, she donned her exosuit and checked her reserves. After so many excursions, the air supply was getting low, but once aboard the *Lewis*—and away from the zombie aliens—she would be all right . . . for a little while.

She cycled through the airlock and emerged onto the asteroid's surface, looking around. Against the crater wall, she saw the huge parabolic dishes slumped in place, as if they'd been ruined by that final great blast.

Fortunately, the *Lewis* appeared to be intact.

In the minuscule gravity, she loped over to the landing area. Once she sealed and pressurized the pilot compartment, she could keep her reserve of air in the exosuit tank.

Calm, focused on the mission as always, she powered up the engines and flipped on the comm unit. "Nether Station, this is Captain Arkourian. Does anybody read me?" She hoped that the jamming had stopped once the bases had depleted their energy reserves.

If anyone was still alive on the station.

Only a burst of static came back in response.

"Nether Station?"

The powerful weapon strikes might have killed everyone aboard. The facility had never been designed as a battle station.

Discouraged, she switched off the comm and concentrated on her own vessel. The *Lewis* lifted from the crater landing pad and up into empty space.

She was the sole survivor, and she was out of options.

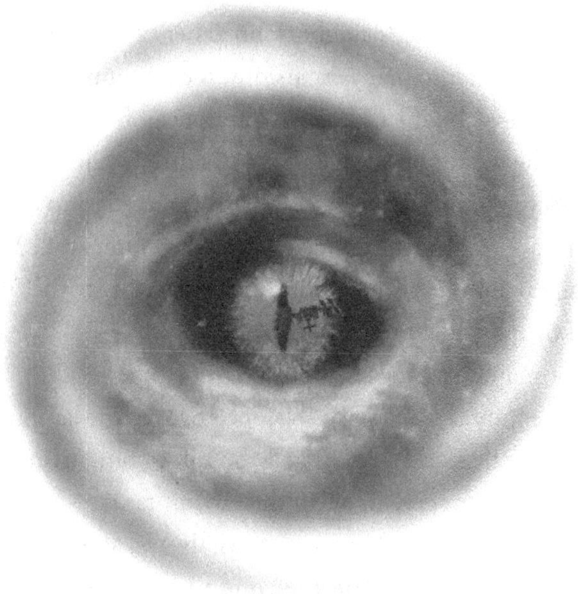

CHAPTER 51

Cammie watched Nether Station recede through the windowport of the expedition ship. Behind them, she saw the battered wreck of the *Lethe*'s core, the detached habitation module, the ruptured greenhouse dome blanketed with a thin miasma of frozen atmosphere. Some of the decks remained lit, but the power would soon fade. The station would no longer support life as more systems failed.

After a final spectacular surge, the Osskkn defensive bases had stopped firing and gone dark. But the damage was done. She feared that Karla Arkourian and Pedro Ashe were already dead.

She turned to her three companions, sure that they were the only ones left up here in the dark emptiness. Truly, the *Neil Armstrong* was their last hope, but they had no place to go.

Warren leaned back at the controls and made a strained attempt to lighten the mood. "Please remain seated with your crash belts fastened until we have reached our stable cruising altitude. Our time to destination is"—he turned back to look at the three distraught passengers—"I have no idea where we're going."

"How about away from the station before we all get blasted?" Glinda said.

"The Osskkn bases were lit up like beacons not long ago," Cammie said. "Now they're all dark."

As Warren swung the ship around, the wormhole came into view against the field of stars, both a void and a tantalizing gateway.

A human figure slammed into the front windowport.

Warren lurched back from the controls. "What the fuck?" Glinda shouted.

But Cammie couldn't tear her eyes away. Sprawled across the window was Zachary Tendari, his arms and legs spread, his naked body hard and gray. His eyes were open, frozen solid. His face pressed against the expedition ship's main window.

"I ejected him from the airlock," Cammie said. "He was trying to kill me!"

It was not possible, but he lifted his hand and smashed it down against the windshield.

Warren hit the ship's controls, fired the thrusters, and spun the *Neil* into a high-g barrel roll. Tendari's body tried to claw onto the hull, but the force threw him off and hurled him out into the gulf of space.

Cammie huddled in her seat, sucking in great breaths. "Leave me alone!" she whispered. "Forever."

"He's gone now," Warren said. "We're safe."

Glinda laughed. "That's a hell of an exaggeration!"

Warren ran his fingers over the expansive control deck after he accelerated away from the station, putting more distance between the *Neil* and the frozen body. "This ship has all the bells and whistles, boss."

Noor said, "The *Neil Armstrong* holds enough food and air for an extended survey of the Alpha Centauri system, if all had gone according to plan."

Glinda snorted. "Missed that target by a mile."

"At least we're still alive," Cammie said, still on edge from what they had just encountered. "Thank you, Warren, for getting us out of there."

"My pleasure, though it's only delaying the inevitable."

Behind them, Nether Station was a flickering light, the wreckage of Benedict Noor's grandiose dreams. "The inevitable always comes," Noor said in a heavy voice. "We all die. The important thing is what we accomplish and the legacy we leave. That we make an impact . . . and are not forgotten."

"No one will know about anything we did up here, all the science," Cammie said. "You shouldn't have kept all our logs and discoveries confidential, sir."

In his own seat, Noor leaned forward, his expression a distasteful frown. "My central NOOR teams have summary reports, but not all the details. They should have received my first transmissions by now. They'll have the information."

"But not everybody," Warren said. "Shouldn't this be some kind of major press release? Take a victory lap, boss."

Cammie could see the stubborn look on the entrepreneur's face. He said, "It would be naïve to give all of humanity this mind-bending information without any kind of filter—especially all that craziness about elder gods and ancient cosmic wars."

Offended, Cammie sat up in her seat. She actually ignored Noor and turned to her other companions. "That's one thing we can do while our air and supplies last. One vital thing—you all know how important it is, after what's happened here. We can transmit the complete story about the Agoc and the Osskkn bases, the comet temple." She lowered her voice. "It'll be our farewell message."

"Like a message in a bottle," Glinda said.

"Our signal would reach Earth, no problem." Warren ran his palms across the complex console. "This expedition vessel has a powerful comm system, the best in the business."

Noor sniffed. "I always include the best in the business."

"Then let's tell them what we know," Cammie said. "We can take turns, report the broad strokes."

"Let Cammie do the talking, since she has that alien encyclopedia in her head," Glinda said. "And no embellishing."

Warren groaned. "As if we need to embellish what we saw!"

"And who would believe such nonsense?" Noor said. "Even after the wonders we saw, there's no proof about those evil entities." He sulked back in his seat. "Besides, all that information belongs to NOOR. You can't just blurt it out to the whole human race."

"You're outvoted there, boss." Warren had an edge in his voice that Cammie had not heard before.

"This isn't a vote. We are not a democracy."

Glinda's face tightened. "We've got a three-to-one vote that this *is* a democracy, Benedict. It's got to be done."

Warren toggled two switches. "No need to rehearse, Cammie—just be yourself. Whenever you're ready to start . . ."

She drew a breath and told their story in a jumbled fashion, dizzy with the weight of responsibility. She did not like to be the center of attention, but this might be the most important transmission anyone had ever made. Whenever she faltered, Warren and Glinda added their own commentary. Even Noor reluctantly offered some insights.

The signal would take two weeks to reach any listeners on Earth, but this was a one-way conversation—nevertheless, Cammie felt relieved and drained but satisfied when they wrapped up the story.

And then they had nothing to do but drift, and wait to die.

"Just something to think about, if it gets to that point," Warren said, his voice serious. "The *Neil* has a full medical kit along with a pharma synthesizer with all the emergency drugs an expedition crew might need. We have, uh, some options."

"Drugs?" Glinda asked. "I call dibs."

Warren continued, "Those asteroid miners I rescued . . . I talked with them, saw their faces. They were completely convinced they were going to die, that their air would run out, and they had no hope of a rescue. I saw what it did to them."

"But you did rescue them," Cammie said.

"And who is going to rescue us out here?" Noor asked. "We are on our own."

Warren's expression fell. "I checked the pharma dispenser. There are painkillers and sedatives. If the choice is actually just drifting here until life support fails, and we watch each other slowly die . . ."

Defeated but still determined, Noor crossed his arms over his chest. He exerted command again. "Or we can die as explorers—or maybe even live. We've done it your way. Now we do the next obvious thing." His gaze turned flinty and hard. "You know what our destination has to be, Mr. Drake, and we know the trip is possible. We've got no place else to go."

Glinda groaned. "Shit, I knew somebody was going to suggest that."

Cammie's stomach tightened. "No, we can't do it."

Noor said, "We'll never be rescued up here. You know that, and unless you want to wait to freeze or suffocate . . ."

"Or die of boredom," Glinda said.

"No!" Cammie said. "The Agoc are in there."

Noor's voice rose as his passion increased. "We have to do what we came out here for. Cammie, you of all people should think of the science."

Instead, she was thinking of the ordeals they had already been through, and she feared it would only get worse.

He continued, "The probes showed it's physically possible

to make the passage. The rats survived. The monkey survived. That means we can survive."

Glinda let out an uneasy groan. "Yeah, I remember what happened to the rats and Fluffers. They were terrified out of their minds—oh, and afterward they turned into monsters!"

Noor scoffed. "Those were unintelligent creatures that had no idea what was happening to them. We're smarter than that. And you have seen the complex here, the asteroid bases—we know those ancient aliens used the wormhole for interstellar travel, and that means we can do it too!"

Warren shifted in his seat at the cockpit controls. "You're not wrong, boss. And I was supposed to fly this ship right through—I already signed up."

Cammie could feel their gazes upon her, as if somehow she had been delegated the decision-maker. She thought of the jumbled information in her head, the dire warnings, the Agoc and the guardians. "But going through the wormhole . . . the risk."

"I'd say we're beyond risks, kid," Glinda said with a dry chuckle. "If the choice is between a slow, cold death while playing card games with Benedict—or seeing what's on the other side of that wormhole, then I'll take door number two. It *is* what we came out here for."

Noor spoke up, issuing a firm command. "Change course, Warren. It's time to demonstrate some real flying."

Cammie knew she couldn't convince them otherwise. They didn't *know* the truth the same way she did.

The expedition ship flew toward the blurry, dark void in space.

CHAPTER 52

As the *Neil Armstrong* approached the wormhole—now even more tempting and more terrifying—Benedict Noor could not tear his eyes away. This anomaly had called to him for years with its enigmas and possibilities. Despite the fact that his ambitious mission had crumbled to pieces, he still reveled in the flood of new discoveries.

No single expedition, no single person, had ever unlocked so many cosmic mysteries, not even the greatest explorers he had admired all his life. Noor had pulled back the curtain on the universe, faced dangers that no human had ever imagined. His team had explored alien bases on asteroids, gazed upon a frozen temple for elder gods.

Benedict the First.

"We'll cross the event horizon in fifteen minutes," Warren said. "Flying steady." With a troubled look on his face, he turned back to face Noor. "So, boss, about that woman who went over Niagara Falls in a barrel . . . the first one?"

"Annie Taylor," Noor said.

"She survived, right? She was okay?"

"Not a scratch, according to the historical record."

"Wow." Warren let out a long sigh, obviously relieved. "And did it make her rich and famous?"

"Unfortunately, no. She died destitute and penniless."

"Whoa, that's encouraging," Glinda said. She was nervous

and jittery, and Noor could see beads of perspiration on her forehead. "I really don't want to see what's in there."

"We're intelligent beings," Noor said. "We'll be prepared. Just brace yourselves."

Cammie remained pale, her expression drawn. He could tell she really believed the incredible stories she had told. Then her green eyes flared with a sudden idea. "But we don't have to! Maybe it's better if we just—"

Noor needed to cut her off right away. They didn't have time for this. "The decision's been made. We're going to go through the wormhole and be the first humans to see Alpha Centauri. That was the ultimate objective of this mission from the very beginning."

Glinda mumbled, "If we're all going to die, we may as well die in another star system, just for kicks."

Cammie insisted, "No, I meant we don't need to *experience* whatever horrors changed the rats and the monkey! Remember: The sedated group of rats came through just fine. On the first trial with the . . . with Fluffers, when he was asleep, he seemed unaffected when he came back. What if it's only the conscious mind that gets driven mad inside the wormhole? What if it's our thoughts, our . . . souls that draw the attention of the Agoc?"

"The Agoc . . ." Noor muttered. The young woman's stories seemed so grandiose and extreme. Still, he had no cause to contradict her, given that he had seen the giant sculpture on the comet, and that dark mirror . . .

Cammie's voice grew more insistent. "The pharma dispenser in the medical kit has fast-acting sedatives. If we knock ourselves out, even for a few minutes, we'll be unconscious during the passage. That might keep us safe."

"What, and miss the experience?" Noor said. The idea offended him.

"And survive it!" Cammie said.

"But how am I going to fly the *Neil* if I'm unconscious?" Warren asked.

"The passage takes less than five minutes to Alpha Centauri. Autopilot can handle that—the previous probes didn't have a pilot, and they came home without a scratch."

Glinda's shoulders slumped. "I'm usually up for fun new things, but the operative word is *fun*. I wouldn't mind taking a nap through the trip."

Though uneasy, Warren grasped at the idea. "I suppose I'll have plenty to do once we get to the other side."

Cammie was already rummaging in the med kit, sifting through the catalog of vials in the pharma dispenser. She pulled out a handful of autoinjectors, pulled up the menu in the chemical database, and chose a concentrated sedative from the available synthesizer catalog. "Medazolam-K: fast acting, very quickly metabolized, and for use in an emergency." She looked up at Noor. "I'd say this qualifies as an emergency."

Warren held out his hand, as if the decision had been made for all of them. "Course is set. I'll take one of those." Cammie loaded the vial into the autoinjector.

Noor felt testy and defeated. "I haven't agreed to this plan yet."

Glinda took one of the autoinjectors. "Not much of a plan, but it sounds good to me. There's nothing to lose, Benedict."

As she filled an autoinjector for herself, Cammie said, "I looked into Dr. Tendari's eyes even after he was dead. I'm not going to let that happen to me—or us."

She passed the last autoinjector to Noor, and he grudgingly accepted it, but he sulked. They were almost to the wormhole now. "This wasn't how I imagined our first expedition."

Glinda's laugh was much too loud for the enclosed ship.

"Which part of this mission *has* gone according to plan, Benedict? Now it's all or nothing."

As Noor stared at the mouth of the wormhole, he felt his heart stretch, his thoughts bend. "If this is the only way we can get to Alpha Centauri, we'll be the first . . . no matter what happens."

He shook his head, but he couldn't drive away the eerie images from that obsidian mirror in the comet temple. The memories and doubts were like the cold breath of a ghost on his neck. But he was going to prove all those doubts wrong. He would get through and accomplish his greatest goal.

"Ready to go." Warren held up the vial. "These sedatives aren't going to knock me out all day, are they? I might have to do some fancy flying when we arrive at Alpha Centauri."

"According to the database, Medazolam-K has rapid recovery at small doses," Cammie said. "We should be out no more than fifteen minutes."

"I've had enough of this shit." Glinda pressed the autodispenser against the equation tattoo on her muscular right arm. The device hissed, and within seconds she slumped back. "Oh, that's nice . . ."

Warren looked at Cammie, who nodded. He eased the *Neil* closer to the event horizon. "And here we go, over the waterfall. Pleasant dreams. See you on the other side."

Noor said nothing. He picked up his autoinjector as Cammie dosed herself; then Warren did the same. Glinda was already quietly snoring.

On autopilot, the expedition ship glided toward the Nether wormhole.

As he watched Cammie's eyelids grow heavy, Noor felt as if he were about to fall down an infinite well. Maybe he was.

The other three slumped into sleep, but after a long pause,

Noor set aside the autoinjector. "I am not going to miss this." His eyes were shining as he leaned forward. The First.

The ship crossed the boundary and fell into a cyclone of hell. Though the *Neil* had barely moved, without accelerating, Noor was slammed back into his seat.

All around him, the lights were both blindingly bright and darker than open space. The ship spun around, whirling, stretching, tearing itself apart and then snapping back into a reassembled configuration.

Noor's muscles elongated; his intestines knotted. He lurched forward in the seat, and his mouth cracked open. He retched and vomited, but the only things that came out of him were colors and sparks.

Outside the windowports, he saw funnels of nightmares, strings of cotton candy and deadly poison. The lights scratched his eyeballs. The sounds were silent, yet thunderously loud, cracking the bones of his skull.

He found himself drowning in a universe made out of the same material as that awful black mirror.

Then he heard laughing, hungry sounds, cruel curses and threats. His own scream was a hollow roar that filled the vacuum of space and poured into the bottomless pit of the wormhole.

"No!" The terror came from his mind rather than his lungs. Every nerve was on fire, every heartless nanosecond pounded into infinity, and he was lost, moaning throughout the journey.

He saw eyes and faces, specters composed entirely of shadows and hate that pressed against the windowport. They tried to batter through the *Neil*'s reinforced hull and then extended psychic tendrils into the craft, into *him*.

Psychedelic lights and sounds roared around his head, encircled his neck. He suffocated in the echoes of unknowable truths.

And that was only the first second.

Outside, the gibbering monsters grew even more powerful. More and more of them were attracted to the passing ship, and Noor saw their baleful eyes; their sharp, enigmatic wings; their appalling faces covered with tangled tentacles.

These were the true incarnations of the gigantic ice statue on the cometary throne. Cammie's terrible stories about them were laughably inadequate. The things had been exiled, imprisoned . . . but now that Noor had come here with his screaming mind, he had disturbed those slumbering brains.

The Agoc were so mammoth, magnificent, and powerful that when they noticed *him* and locked their attention on *him*, his mind shattered. He no longer heard even his imagined screams.

As Benedict Noor went mad, the last thing he realized was that his journey had only just begun.

CHAPTER 53

Nether Station was her last chance, and it was a total wreck.

By the time the *Lewis* arrived, the facility was only a mangled landmark in empty space. The blasts had knocked the main core off its equilibrium, and now it tumbled like a carnival ride in the cold, dark vacuum.

Arkourian could see that the greenhouse dome had been gutted like a fish, and air vented into space. Another blast had struck the water reservoir, but the secondary habitation module had suffered the brunt of the damage, and it now drifted free, detached from the *Lethe* core.

She decelerated the recon ship on approach and used attitude thrusters to align herself. The hangar bay doors loomed just ahead, rocking back and forth as the facility swung out of balance.

"Landing this thing is going to be a challenge," she muttered. Good thing she had beaten Warren Drake in those flight simulations.

Arkourian activated the comm and hailed again, though by now she didn't expect an answer. "Nether Station, this is Captain Arkourian on the *Lewis*. Is anybody there? I'm going to try to land in the hangar bay, but this damage . . ."

She heard no response, not even Glinda Roybal making a wisecrack about how everything had gone to hell once Arkourian left. They didn't know Pedro Ashe was dead. They didn't know a lot of things.

Nudging the piloting controls with delicate motions, she matched the pitch and spin until the hangar bay doors looked almost stable in front of her, and then she initiated her approach. She sent the command string to open the hangar bay door controls, but only errors came back. Too much damage.

Frustrated, she input her overrides to force the bay to decompress, though it was not her preferred way of getting aboard. She needed to find any surviving crewmembers, but she felt heartsick, sure she was just going through the motions. Nether Station didn't look like it could last much longer. How could anyone still be alive there?

The hangar bay decompression was not complete, but the doors opened anyway, coughing out visible remnants of air. A minor inconvenience. Arkourian ignored it as she guided the *Lewis* into the large bay. This was going to be like landing on a moving roller coaster.

Debris lay scattered across the landing area, which shifted as the station wobbled on its axis. Broken loose from their anchors, crates and equipment racks scraped about. She was relieved to see the *Clark* there, which meant that Warren and Cammie had made it back—but to what? Surely they had delivered their message, so the others would be aware of the nightmarish Agoc and the true reason for the defensive watchtowers.

But was anyone left alive aboard Nether Station?

She landed the *Lewis* in a relatively clear area next to the other recon ship, then sent the command to close the hangar and repressurize the bay, but the large doors didn't seal properly. Arkourian fastened her helmet, just in case, before she climbed out of the ship.

Amber lights flared on the walls, then transitioned to magenta warning beacons. Air kept shrieking through a small gap in the hangar seal, and more debris started to slide toward the gap.

Arkourian fought her way to the connecting door that led into the main station, taking no time to look around. She had to get out of the bay before the pressure dropped enough, which would automatically engage the breach locks—then she would never get inside. She made it through and slid the bulkhead door shut. Moments later, red lights around the frame indicated that the bay itself was now off-limits. "Well, I guess I'm not leaving again."

Checking her oxygen reservoir, she saw that her exosuit had very little air, so she opened her faceplate to breathe the station's thin, cold atmosphere. Considering the damage she had seen from outside, there must be other breaches letting the air leak out.

She found a wall intercom. "This is Arkourian. Anyone home?"

Static. The comm system lights flickered.

"Any Nether Station survivors, please respond." After another burst of static, the intercom's power lights winked out. "Doesn't anything work?"

At least she could breathe, for now, and if she made her way to the engineering bay, she could refill her suit tanks.

First, she headed toward the observation bridge. The corridor lights flickered like the jittering reflexes of a dying man, and the shifting deck tilted as Nether Station continued to yaw and roll.

An explosion occurred somewhere behind her, and she fell to her knees as the station trembled, as if shaken by an angry hand. As she got up, she saw a long red smear along the white walls.

With a shudder, she ran up to the next deck. She tried other intercoms, still hoping to get a response, but heard only silence.

When she reached the bridge, she found it empty. Benedict Noor had left his showy captain's chair, and she saw no sign of

Glinda, Warren, Cammie, or Dr. Stelland. Most of the console screens were inactive, while others flashed emergency warnings.

Standing at her primary station, she called up the log to learn what had happened here. After having been immersed in the Osskkn systems and controls, she experienced a momentary disorientation to use a human interface, but she shook her head and focused.

The station log was garbled with incomprehensible reports about loose lab rats damaging the systems, of the rhesus monkey . . . murdering Dr. Stelland? She blinked in shock.

At the end of the log, Warren Drake and Glinda Roybal had recorded a summary, both of them looking shaken. The four surviving crewmembers had decided to abandon Nether Station. But the *Clark* was still there—

She managed to activate one of the hangar bay cameras, and now she realized what she had missed earlier. The *Neil Armstrong* was gone.

Arkourian's heart sank. With Nether Station rapidly becoming uninhabitable, the crewmembers had taken desperate measures. Even if the watchtower weaponry was neutralized, Nether Station was doomed regardless. The survivors had flown away, but where could they go? They also didn't know that the Osskkn bases were shut down to recycle and recharge for years, and they would be uninhabitable. They couldn't seek refuge there.

Arkourian stiffened. She knew Benedict Noor, and she knew damn well where he would have sent them.

She slumped into the chair at her bridge station. "I've got the house all to myself, and no one to invite to a party." She felt nauseated as vibrations shook the facility.

As she ran a full diagnostic of the station's systems, she grew more and more discouraged. She managed to reroute most of the remaining energy circuits and got the comm systems functioning again.

Without the alien signal jamming, maybe her message could get through to Earth. Somebody had to know.

Arkourian composed herself, took a quick breath in the cold, thin air, and activated the transmitter. She should have composed a concise report ahead of time, as she'd been taught in the military, but there was no time for that. Her story would be candid and raw—and true.

"This is Captain Karla Arkourian from Nether Station with a report, and a warning." She drew another breath, which only made her lungs feel cold. "This is our final message."

She spilled out her side of the story—everything she knew about the wormhole and the ancient races, the watchtower defenses, the malevolent elder gods, and the cosmic war from eons ago.

The story sounded ridiculous, but she prayed somebody would believe her.

Finished, she sat back and closed her eyes. That was it. She had nothing left to do.

Hull integrity had been damaged in many places, and air was leaking out. Power levels were dropping. Even if she made all possible emergency patches, the station wouldn't last long. She could never detach the modules and send the *Lethe* down on a five-year journey to the inner solar system, as she had hoped to do.

But Karla Arkourian always laughed in the face of Fate. So many times in her life, she had taken wild risks and then watched her loved ones die instead. She'd been confident, aloof, not even really caring about the risks.

But Fate had really fucked her over this time.

Other than giving up, going outside, and opening her

faceplate to the vacuum, Arkourian didn't see any options. She had burned all her luck.

Except, perhaps . . .

As the idea came to her, she realized it was a desperate chance—the slimmest one—but she wasn't going to surrender, no matter what. Fate would have to kill her itself; she wasn't going to take any shortcuts. If the ghosts of her husbands—Alan, Wen, and Afo—could talk to her now, they would tell her not to give up.

Maybe she'd get out of this. One more time.

Leaving the empty observation bridge, Arkourian scrambled down two levels, activating her suit light when she entered sections where the overhead lights had failed.

She entered the bed-and-breakfast deck, quietly laughing at her absurd desperation. The temperature had plunged, and she could see her icy breath, but that only added to the ambience.

She moved down the line of sealed cryopods and paused in horror to see bloody smears on the viewing plates. The interior chambers were fogged and stained with a red mist. One clawed and broken hand was still splayed against the glass.

Her heart pounding, she went from one pod to the next. The sleeping Schrödinger's cat crewmembers had all tried to batter their way out of the hibernation chambers. But were they really alive?

That was certainly a disincentive to her idea now. Arkourian shook herself, focused on the finish line. If she had any other option, she would take it.

She went to the seven empty pods that stood ready for the waking crewmembers and their next hibernation cycle. The cryopods were designed to keep a person alive and protected for years at a time, but something had gone wrong with the last crew shift. Dr. Stelland had supposedly fixed the glitches, overwritten the life-support operating system.

It should be fine now. Perfectly fine.

Nether Station shook again as Arkourian made her way to the empty pods. One of them had been reserved for her.

She set the helmet aside and stripped out of her exosuit, standing in her duty uniform. No sense keeping warm when your whole body was going into the deep freeze. She climbed inside.

After her desperate message to Earth, after all the questions that remained about the wormhole, maybe someday a research team would return, now that they were forewarned about the dangers.

Maybe they would find her.

Maybe the cryopod would last that long.

She lay back and activated the pod systems. Needles plunged into her arms, and she felt the fluids circulating, drugs that would maintain her tissues and send her into deep sleep.

Arkourian shivered as the chamber temperature dropped. The canopy slid into place, and the pod seals engaged. She imagined an undertaker hammering the nails into the lid of a coffin as she sank into the smothering blackness of encroaching sleep.

She hoped she wouldn't have endless years of nightmares.

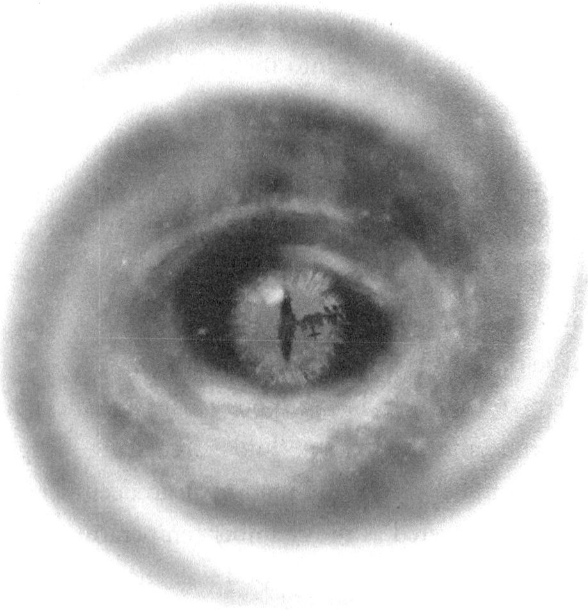

CHAPTER 54

When Cammie fought her way back to consciousness, she felt groggy and didn't know which universe she was in. She struggled to wake up completely, but she couldn't shake a deep and indefinable dread that tried to drag her back into the safe oblivion. Her skin was crawling.

When she opened her eyes, she couldn't comprehend the whips of intense colors, the whirlpool of neon blues, yellows, and scars of deep black in the last instants of the wormhole.

Realizing where she was, she gripped the arms of her rattling seat. The *Neil Armstrong* seemed to be corkscrewing, accelerating. She had no idea which direction was up or down, except that she plunged forward and then was sucked away, still caught in the tattered fabric of the cosmos. Her eyes flared with starbursts from within. Her bones shook, as if every cell were breaking apart.

And then it stopped, as if a bubble of reality had burst around her. The membrane of the wormhole passageway abruptly ended, and the expedition ship drifted along in normal reality again—a calm, black emptiness as they left the jagged, empty hole behind them.

At the pilot controls, Warren groaned and then slapped himself hard on the cheek. He hunched over the console and looked up to stare out the main windowport, trying to orient himself. He muttered to himself, "All right, I've got this." Falling back on his pilot training, he called up one screen after another and worked to stabilize the *Neil*, wherever it was. "I've got this."

Glinda leaned over the side of her seat and vomited, then coughed. "Whoa, I've had some bad trips before, but that was one for the record books." She heaved again, but nothing more came out. "Ugh, and I was asleep!"

Warren called back in a hoarse voice, "Cammie, does that thing have any caffeine? Or something stronger?"

She rubbed her eyes to clear the dark fuzz that clogged her mind. She fumbled with the med kit in her lap but couldn't focus on the vials and settings in the synthesizer. The pharma dispenser had a long and confusing menu of options. "Checking."

Glinda unclipped her restraining belt and pulled herself over to Cammie's seat. "In engineering school, I pulled more than my share of all-nighters. I know the very best designer stimulants." She pawed the screen to scroll up the options. "There, that's a good one—and that one too." She inserted her autoinjector and reloaded it from the synthesizer, hitting herself with the mind-clearing stimulant. She flexed her thick fingers. "Ah, that's better! Stone-cold awake and ready for anything."

Cammie loaded her autoinjector with the same compound and felt a surge of energy. She passed another one up to Warren. "Here, this'll help."

The pilot jammed it into his arm and sighed. "Better than a swift kick. Now, let's see where we are." Scanning the star field and the bright ember of a nearby red dwarf, he said, "Looks like we made it. Welcome to the Alpha Centauri system."

Cammie prepared one last dose of the stimulant and turned around. "Mr. Noor?"

She bit back a scream.

The entrepreneur gripped the arms of his seat with clawlike hands. His shoulders were hunched, and his back spasmed as he slammed himself into the rear padding again and again. His lips were drawn in a hideously extended grin, exposing teeth that were red from blood leaking out of his gums.

Crimson trails oozed out of his ears and down his neck, and a set of red teardrops dribbled from his tear ducts. But his eyes were blank and black, as empty as abandoned caves. His mouth hung open, letting out a guttural moan—the sound of despair wrung from a damned soul.

"What happened to you?" Cammie cried.

His chest shuddered, and he began to make choking, stuttering noises that might have been demented laughter.

Filled with energy now from the stimulant, Glinda pulled herself past Cammie's seat. "Benedict, what the hell did you do?" She snatched up the autoinjector beside his seat and saw that the sedative cartridge remained full. "Asshole." She glared at him. "He didn't take it! He stayed awake."

Noor's trembling grew more severe, like a seizure, and his laughter grew louder.

Cammie sucked in a deep breath. "He stayed awake through the entire wormhole passage! He stayed awake . . ."

"Help me with this, kid!" Glinda started pulling out the emergency crash webbing. "Click these buckles in place. Restrain his arms so we can keep him from hurting himself."

As Noor continued to cackle, his sightless, blank eyes skewered into Cammie. "Or hurting *us*," she said.

She remembered how the reanimated Zach Tendari had come relentlessly after her, insisting that he had to stop all of them, that he would destroy Nether Station to prevent them from awakening the Agoc.

It was too late now.

At the piloting controls, Warren's voice quavered a little, as if the stimulants had made him shaky. "Guys, you need to have a look out here. Not sure about the neighborhood we find ourselves in."

Leaving the now-restrained Noor lost in his insanity, Cammie and Glinda went to the front of the *Neil*. Prominent in nearby space, Cammie could see the white pair of Alpha Centauri A and B, but the nearest star was the dim red dwarf, Proxima, like the roiling red eye of a demon.

Their automated probes had been quick missions, not designed for a full survey of the star system. Now Warren projected a heads-up display, and Cammie saw bright points highlighted with guidelines to attract her attention. There were other celestial bodies around the exit of the Nether wormhole—a lot of them.

Still familiarizing himself with the expedition ship's controls, Warren flicked switches. "This vessel is top of the line, with the best sensors, spectral imagers, and optical telescopes. Let's see what it can do."

Cammie saw multiple asteroids in the vicinity of the wormhole exit, rocky bodies large enough to be planetoids or moons. "That's a more extensive network than the ring of watchtower bases around our side."

"That arrangement is definitely not natural," Warren said. "I've flown a hundred trips in our real asteroid belt. These moons and planetoids would never just drift here by themselves. These asteroids were *moved* here."

"Somebody must have too much time on their hands," Glinda said. "No one just arranges asteroids like chesspieces."

"The aliens do—the star beings, the Osskkn, the Yggroths," Cammie replied. "And now you can see the sheer power of the forces we're dealing with."

When Warren increased magnification, they could see huge impact scars on the nearest celestial bodies, like rays across the barren surfaces. As the largest planetoids rotated, Cammie spotted the glinting reflection of metal and crystalline surfaces—huge artificial complexes that were all dark. These ancient cyclopean bases must have been fortresses from the eternal war.

But it was obvious the bases were dead now, ruined. Huge fissures scarred the once-inhabited asteroids, cracks caused by titanic detonations or collisions. One planetoid turned on its axis, revealing that it had been fractured by an unimaginable blast.

Hiding in the shadows of the barren fragments were the hulks of defeated battleships: monstrous structures bristling with sharp ribs and protrusions—all of which had been bent, melted, burned out.

"Whoa, this is apocalyptic," Glinda said.

Warren added, "I hope those watchtowers don't wake up and start shooting at us. I had enough of that back at Nether Station."

Cammie tried to understand what she was seeing. "It's the wreckage of a battlefield." She ransacked the huge library of information crammed into her mind, trying to identify the design of the ships. This place had been the site of one of the ultimate conflicts. The star beings and their allies had driven back the Agoc here, but was it only a triumphant skirmish or the complete end of the war?

Cammie leaned closer to Warren. "Can you expand the field of view for a wider look around?" She was fully awake and alert now, thanks to the designer stimulants.

The sensors mapped the large asteroid stations and damaged planetoids. The *Neil* cruised past the geometric wreckage of what must have been an alien shipyard. Beyond the celestial rubble, the expedition ship detected another set of objects.

"We have company," Warren said.

Enormous, fully illuminated battleships were approaching

them like glowing deep-sea predators. The alien vessels were rounded and swollen, with sharp protrusions like dragon scales. Along their expansive hulls, bright ovoid windows shone like numerous blazing eyes, and hot blue ion trails poured out of their rear thrusters.

"Our probes didn't see any of this!" Glinda squawked. "I think I would have noticed a huge alien fleet!"

"Maybe the big ships weren't here when we took the first images," Cammie said. "Our automated probes came through transmitting a loud signal, shouting to get the attention of anyone at Alpha Centauri. And the rogue asteroid that swept past us and plunged down the wormhole—it was an Osskkn base, and it could have carried a full report. It could have called the cavalry."

Glinda groaned. "So, they'll know what we're up to."

"We're not up to anything," Warren said. "We're just trying to save our asses because *they* blasted Nether Station. We didn't have anywhere else to go!"

"Lie low," Glinda whispered. "Maybe they won't notice us."

Warren's fingers ran over the pilot controls, shutting down the *Neil*'s external lights and dampening their engines. The expedition ship hung dark and quiet, trying to hide in the rubble of ancient wars. "I'm pretty sure we know why the signal from the old ISA probe cut off so abruptly."

From the reservoir in her mind, Cammie finally recognized the configuration of the alien battleships. These were the most destructive warships from the primeval war, constructed by the Osskkn and the fungoid Yggroths, guided by the powers of the star beings. She translated what she knew so that the others could understand. "*Omega ships.* Those battle cruisers are called Omega ships."

The sensor panels lit up, and alarms thrummed inside the

Neil. "They've spotted us! We're being bombarded with signal queries." Warren looked at her. "You speak their alien language, right?" He activated the comm system, urged her closer. "Talk to them. Say that we come in peace, or take us to your leader—whatever works."

"I barely know what I understand," Cammie said, shaking her head. "And my mouth or vocal cords won't make sounds like that." She rubbed her throat.

"You better try, kid," Glinda said. "I don't care if you speak with an accent."

Though Cammie felt a wave of doubt, she knew she had to use the comm, had to try. "I hope these are the good guys," she whispered to herself.

Before she could open a channel, though, the colors and dimensions shifted in the wormhole behind them. Instinctive revulsion pushed through her as if she'd been given a deep-throated kiss by a nightmare.

Something large, dark, and terrifying began to emerge from the roiling void-mouth of the wormhole.

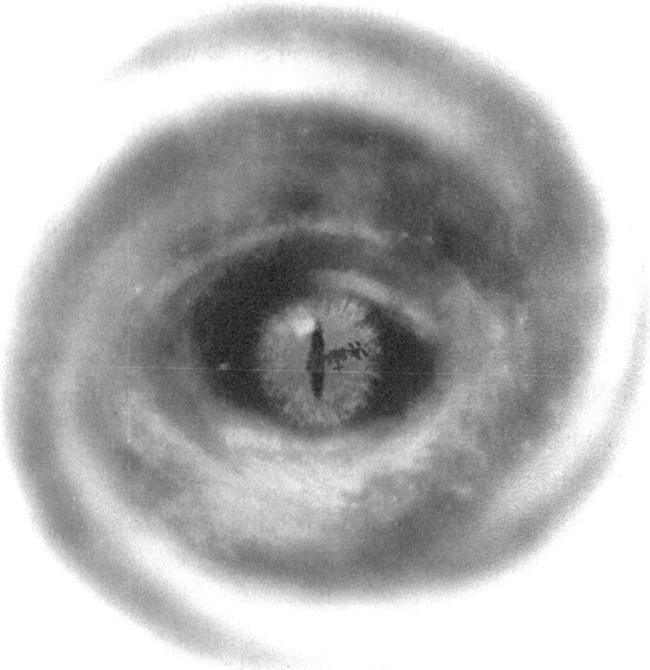

CHAPTER 55

Ripples rolled across the dimensional mouth: snarling whips of black poison made of night terrors. Suddenly, the *Neil Armstrong* became an insignificant distraction in the cosmic war.

Cammie's chest tightened, and she couldn't breathe as the pulsing evil rippled through space, like a malevolent carrier wave. "Can you see the Agoc? Can you *feel* them?" She cringed away from the front windowport as the eldritch roaring increased in her head.

Warren lifted his hands from the piloting controls. "Did we cause this?"

Cammie didn't know how to answer. Had their intrusive probes jarred awake the neutralized Agoc? Or was it because Benedict Noor stayed awake during the wormhole passage?

Glinda squeezed her eyes shut. "Oh shit, oh shit!"

The twenty Omega ships accelerated forward, each one the size of a city and armed with inconceivable weapons. Cammie knew that every giant alien vessel carried a small sun in its core, a power source that could wreak havoc on a planetary scale.

As the black elder gods clawed out of their dimensional prison, the Omega ships converged on the torn hole in space like a pack of wolves. The nuclear furnaces of their engines burned an incandescent swath across space.

As the *Neil* tried to hide, the alien fleet shot past the

wreckage of asteroids. Alien weapons powered up, igniting a vision-searing line along their hulls.

"They're not after us," Cammie muttered. "We're just a speck of dust to them."

It gave her little consolation, however, because they were still not safe. If the horrific Agoc broke out into the universe again, the war would flare up from star system to star system.

As the Omega ships converged on the wormhole, the intense lights on their hulls pulsed faster and faster.

At the event horizon, the Agoc manifestations looked like deadly tentacles and spider claws, each the size of a nebula.

Ultraviolet pulses from the enemy throbbed out in concentric circles, and an eldritch blast struck the nearest perimeter stations, the shattered asteroids and alien shipyard structures. Arcs of fabricated metal shimmered from the energy discharge, then lost integrity as they melted. One of the derelict orbiting stations sparked and flared in an explosion.

The Agoc reached out farther, prying open their dimensional prison.

As their embedded weapons reached peak capacity, the Omega ships closed in. Cammie knew that each one was capable of cracking a world open.

Warren shielded his eyes from the intense flashes across the spectrum. "They're like junkyard dogs going in for the kill. They were ready for this."

"They've been preparing for this moment for thousands of years," Cammie said. Though she had a vague idea of what was happening, she didn't grasp the tactics of the alien military commanders. "Our own probes must have put them on alert, and then that rogue asteroid came through like a crashing alarm gong."

"And now we're here," Glinda said.

Clustering close to the wormhole, the Omega ships split

open along meridian lines, and their hulls unfolded like the arms of horrific starfish. The glow inside their gullets flared as each alien battleship spat out a roiling compact star. Dense stellar material hurtled out like a cannonball, hovering on the edge of gravitational collapse.

Cammie said in an awed whisper, "Those Omega ships were designed and built by the star beings, and they carry amazing doomsday weapons."

Warren said, "I don't like the sound of *doomsday*."

Cammie pointed at the horrific nightmares crawling out of space and time. "Yes, but look what they're fighting against!"

At the wormhole's mouth, the Agoc extended ebony claws and tentacles, ripping the gateway wider in their desperation to surge into real space. With their hard-fought freedom, they seemed exuberant and vengeful.

But the Omega fleet stood against them, hurling suns at the cosmic trapdoor. The fusillade of compact stars slammed into the emerging Agoc, pummeling the evil blackness. The star weapons went nova in a flash of fire and radiation that drove back the horrific shadows.

Pressing their advantage, ten Omega ships pursued the wounded Agoc to the event horizon, even though they had already launched their core weapons. A flash of realization entered Cammie's mind, like a book flying open to the answers she needed. "They're full of antimatter. They're not coming back."

The alien battleships drove into the mouth of the wormhole, pushing the Agoc back. Then, just inside the dimensional gate, the Omega vessels collapsed their antimatter cores like bursting bubbles of negative energy. The massive implosion-explosion had enough force to fuse and meld the fabric of spacetime.

The wormhole exit twisted, distorted, then collapsed, shutting the passageway forever behind them.

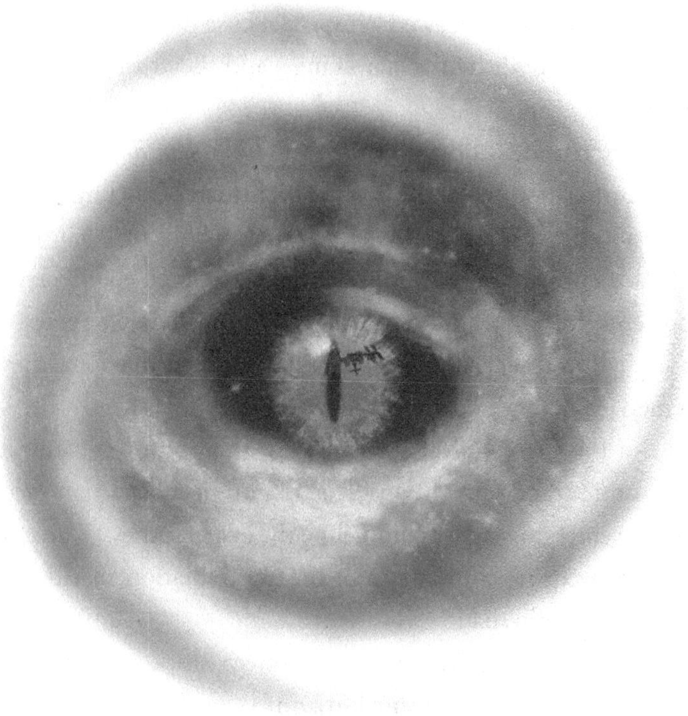

CHAPTER 56

In the aftermath, Cammie knew that the expedition ship couldn't hide any longer. She just hoped she and her companions could survive what happened next.

"Did they just slam shut the wormhole?" Warren asked. "I hope they locked those things in there. Tight."

"So much for ever going home again." Glinda slumped. She was shaking. "I guess I gave up on that a while ago."

Through the *Neil*'s windowports, they saw the glowing consequences of the weapons just unleashed. Space itself shuddered and pulsed, and radiation and planetary debris spread everywhere. Ten enormous Omega ships had annihilated themselves, sacrificed in the last stand against the Agor, but they had pushed the horrific entities back into their prison.

But ten of the battleships remained. And they were here.

Cammie feared that the consequences of her actions—*their* actions—could reverberate back to Earth and across the Galaxy. The Nether research team had been curious and ambitious, and it wasn't just Benedict Noor. He might have been foolishly stubborn, but he wasn't the only one to blame. Cammie herself had wanted to see and understand the Nether wormhole. She had wanted to unlock the mysteries of the universe, collecting answers like little baubles that she could share with Dr. Tendari.

Three Omega ships stationed themselves like guard dogs at the now-dissipated opening, but the rest of the battleships cruised throughout the wreckage of watchtower asteroids and shattered planetoid citadels. The intimidating vessels played sensor beams across the rubble and moved in a survey pattern. Hunting.

"I think they just remembered us," Warren said.

Two of the monstrous ships lit up, as if alerted. An intense burst of static sputtered out of the *Neil*'s speakers.

"So much for our hiding place." Glinda looked around, desperate. "Does this ship have any weapons? I don't want to go down without a fight!"

Warren let out a sarcastic laugh. "Yeah, I'll start provoking those juggernauts right now. You saw what they just did!"

Strapped in his seat and bound by restraints, Benedict Noor let out a hollow, chattering laugh of despair. Blood drooled from the side of his mouth.

As the Omega ships closed in, the static from the comm speakers became as loud as thunder. Blinding waves of light washed over the *Neil* as they were scanned.

Cammie pushed her way forward to the control deck. "Let me try to communicate with them. Maybe I can make myself understood after all."

"Be my guest." Warren toggled on their comms, selected broad transmission bands. "This better be as good as the Gettysburg Address."

"And let's hope the live Osskkn are more pleasant than the zombie ones," Glinda added.

But as Cammie tried to summon words in the alien language, her mind went blank. How could she talk to them? She blurted out in English, "We come from the other side of the wormhole. We are no threat to you." She was panting harder now, almost hyperventilating. "We have some important information that you need."

She felt a strange trance coming on as she connected with her subconscious. Her eyes dropped closed and rolled back into her head. She didn't know what she was saying—couldn't consciously form words that the Osskkn or the star beings would understand—but she managed to utter a desperate plea. The alien sounds hurt her throat and made her head pound.

One of the enormous Omega ships loomed up in front of them, the size of a small moon. Cammie could barely even make out the curvature of its hull.

Warren gripped the piloting controls, trying to keep the *Neil* stable, but he slumped back in surrender. A dark section opened up in the Omega ship, a huge doorway—then they were tugged forward, as if their vessel had been grasped by an invisible hand.

"Whatever you said, kid, I hope you didn't insult them," Glinda said.

Visions of history played in Cammie's mind, so many enslaved and wounded races from across the Galaxy, but neither Warren nor Glinda had any idea what they were about to see and experience.

Warren didn't bother to fire the ship's engines or attempt to pull away in an obviously pointless effort. "They could have just blasted us to atoms. I'd call that a little victory."

Benedict Noor continued to laugh.

The enormous alien ship was endlessly intricate and complex, dizzying and terrifying as they grew closer. Cammie saw more protrusions, external towers and outer conduits that looked like blood vessels and incomprehensible bloated organs. Glowing ovoid domes appeared to be blisters from some kind of cosmic rash across the hull plates, connected by lines of light, a circulatory system of energy.

"Things are about to get exciting," Glinda said.

As they drew closer and closer and *closer*, and the ship grew beyond Cammie's ability to grasp its sheer size, she thought of a fractal, with more and more patterns unfolding as they approached. Countless spaceships flitted about the Omega ship, like remoras around a giant shark. None of them paid attention to the *Neil.*

Transmitting towers, or maybe they were defensive-ray generators, looked like thistle spines. Numerous small bays pockmarked the outer expanse of the hull, many of them filled with ranks of smaller ships. Angular craft of yet another design were attached to the outer hull itself, clinging there like sleeping bats.

Warren sat restless at the piloting controls, unable to do anything. They were drawn toward one specific bay, like a great yawning mouth. It had appeared to be a tiny opening in the vast hull, but it turned out to be a huge hangar bay. Lights flashed around the opening as the *Neil* was pulled in.

"I hope they don't dissect us as laboratory subjects," Glinda said.

"They won't." Cammie sounded more confident than she felt. "We have to convince them that they need us, that we have special knowledge they can't get anywhere else."

The expedition ship was guided into a cavernous bay bathed in bright lights, a fleet of landed vessels, and numerous moving figures. The tractor beam delivered their ship to a cleared platform, like a quarantined area, and when the *Neil* settled down onto the deck, all of Warren's systems went dark. He slumped in the pilot seat. "Well, that's it."

Cammie steeled her nerves. "We should go greet them."

"Better wear exosuits," Glinda said. "Who knows what kind of atmosphere they breathe?"

Cammie swallowed hard, then shook her head. "We'll be fine. It's the same atmosphere as the asteroid base. If they meant to kill us, they would have done it already."

"I'm just the limo driver, remember." Warren disengaged the hatch and opened the *Neil*'s side door. When he extended the ramp, bright lights from the alien hangar flooded in. "You go first, Cammie—ambassador for the human race."

She lowered her voice. "Back on Earth, I never liked to meet new people—at all." Her throat went dry. "I'm not ready for this."

"Welcome to the club," Glinda said.

On shaky legs, Cammie stepped up to the hatch and blinked in the bright light of the vast hangar. With Warren and Glinda behind her, she emerged and walked down the ramp.

Gathered in front of the expedition ship were hundreds of the cricket-like aliens. The Osskkn swiveled their heads to show dark domed eyes, but these were different from the dead husks that had littered the asteroid base. These creatures were vibrant, healthy, alive, with their carapaces showing ripples of iridescent colors like a colorful Amazon beetle. Their rounded black eyes gleamed in the bright light. Moving articulated limbs in frenetic motions, they clicked and whistled in a musical cacophony, and somehow Cammie vaguely understood what the creatures were saying.

Behind the Osskkn stood rows of bulbous, soft forms—swollen humanoids made of white growths with fiber-like feelers that extended from hollow eye sockets. They made moist sounds as they moved, squishing and coming forward. She knew these were the Yggroths.

Behind her, Warren muttered to Glinda, "By comparison, even you don't look so ugly."

After a long moment of staring at them in awe, Cammie nervously raised a hand and spoke, trying to form words in the alien language. "We mean no harm to you. We are explorers."

The Osskkn clicked and whistled. The Yggroths slurped and sighed. Though completely overwhelmed, Cammie forced herself to stand firm. She and her companions needed to learn what was going on with this massive alliance. She could draw some knowledge from the information reservoir in her head, but she was far too inexperienced to communicate with them clearly. And she had a lot of explaining to do.

The alien horde stared at her, none of them approaching closer. Cammie tried again. Her throat was hoarse, and tears stung her eyes. She whispered to her companions, "I have to make them give us a chance."

The Osskkn and the Yggroths shifted aside, and a new voice spoke behind them. "Wonder of wonders, it's a good thing someone here can understand English. Your Osskkn has a terrible accent, young lady."

Cammie was so startled by the male human voice that she couldn't respond. She gazed across the sea of crowded aliens and saw a tall, thin man push his way forward. He had light brown hair and a large mustache. His voice carried an odd New England twang. Boston? Maine?

The stranger smiled at her. "I confess, it'll be good to talk to someone again. A lot must have changed back on Earth." His brows furrowed. "I don't even know how much time has passed."

Struggling to find words, Cammie finally said, "Who are you? How did you get here?"

The man let out a calm, warm laugh. "Now then, I was part of an Antarctic expedition—ages ago, it seems. Sponsored by Miskatonic University. Have you heard of it? My name is Archibald Benton. We found things in the frozen mountains of that unexplored continent . . . incredible things." When he looked away, his gaze was hooded. "That expedition didn't turn out well. The Mountains of Madness are aptly named, to be sure! But there was a dimensional opening, and I stumbled through . . ."

He snapped to attention as the sounds from the Osskkn and the Yggroths grew louder and more intense. The stranger gave a welcoming smile and gestured. "Come with me for a full debrief. We all have a lot to explain to each other." His expression was grim, and his pale skin flushed. "After so much time, the great war is starting up again."

Mystified, Cammie and her companions followed the man. She felt numb from all the alien sights, sounds, and smells. It was all too much for her to comprehend.

The great war is starting up again.

With a chill, Cammie realized that even though the Omega ships and their antimatter cores had closed the wormhole and trapped the monstrous elder gods within . . . the doorway was only sealed on *this* side.

She hurried after Archibald Benton, desperate for answers.

What might have come out the other end, in Earth's solar system?

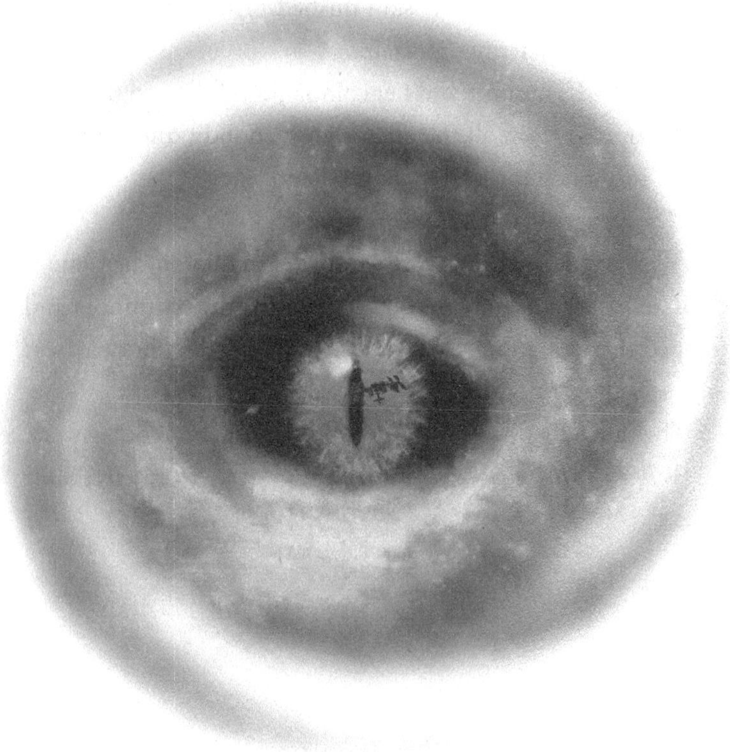

AFTERWORD

NETHER STATION: LOST IN THE EMPTINESS, AT THE DARKEST PART OF SPACE

Imagine a haunted house, but not on a hill in a ramshackle part of town.

Imagine being cold and isolated, far from help, far from human contact, except for the handful of misfits who are trapped there with you.

Imagine a doorway between dimensions, a possible shortcut to wondrous star systems and new planets—or is it a cosmic prison that holds terrors and powers unimaginable?

I've read science fiction ever since I learned how to read. I looked up at the stars in the night sky and dreamed of alien worlds and advanced civilizations. I watched *Lost in Space*, then graduated to *Star Trek*. I saw *Star Wars* in 1977 in its first run in the movie theaters. To my burgeoning imagination, the universe was a fabulous place.

But I also saw *Alien* when it first came out, and *Event Horizon*—which reminded me that space is dark, space is vast, and space is scary.

I had read the works of H. P. Lovecraft, many of which were originally published in *Weird Tales* magazine. His Cthulhu Mythos and his unique brand of cosmic horror were an enormous and profound influence on me as a writer. "At the Mountains of Madness," "The Colour Out of Space," "The Shadow Out of Time," and "Dagon" are, I think, some of the finest works of horror fiction ever published. They still make my skin crawl when I reread them.

When I was invited to do a novel for the Weird Tales Presents series from Blackstone Publishing, how could I not jump at the chance?

I wanted to do a science fiction haunted house story, a novel of cosmic horror, an action-packed, suspenseful story that would keep readers on the edge of their seats. I loved writing *Nether Station*, and I pulled out all the stops. I used the masterful techniques I learned from my one-time writing mentor, Dean Koontz. I polished the manuscript until every sentence was tight and tense—no slow parts, no wasted words, just adrenaline and tension. And Lovecraft fans will surely see dozens of Easter eggs sprinkled throughout the story.

And as you've just seen, since you're reading this afterword—unless you cheated and are reading this beforehand, in which case, shame on you! Stop right here and go back to page one—*Nether Station* ends on a hell of a cliffhanger. In fact, I think it's one of my two most jaw-dropping endings ever.

(The other one was the finale of the middle book in my Terra Incognita epic fantasy trilogy, *The Map of All Things*. At the end, every one of the characters was facing insurmountable monsters, incredible obstacles, horrific magic, and the imminent end of the world. After I delivered that manuscript, the editor wrote to say, "How the hell are you going to get them out of that?" I replied, "Don't worry. I'll figure something out." And I did.)

My philosophy as a writer is that you don't hold anything back. You put in the biggest, most bombastic perils, the most dramatic scenes, the most unexpected plot twists every time. Don't save anything for a rainy day, because if you're a real writer, your imagination will come up with something even better when you need it.

That's the end of *Nether Station*—cracking open a whole

new part of the galaxy, a host of alien races, and titanic battles in a cosmic war that can rip stars apart. The End.

How the hell am I going to get them out of that?

Don't worry, Dear Reader (or Dear Editor, if you're reading). Believe me—my muse is ruthless. My imagination muscles have been exercised enough that I knew I would find a way.

As a writer, I am a pretty diligent plotter. I like to outline everything well ahead of time, like an architect drawing a detailed blueprint before he starts digging holes and putting up walls, not knowing how they will ever connect.

That was how I wrote *Nether Station*. Each chapter was carefully choreographed before I wrote the actual words (although I did a lot of tweaking, fine-tuning, and rearranging before it was all done).

When I ended *Nether Station* with that cliffhanger, I had no guarantee there would ever be a sequel. *Weird Tales* and Blackstone had only bought the one book, and we would see how it turned out.

Well, I thought it turned out great, and I planted some seeds, set up foreshadowing and plot points so I knew where I would get started if I did get the chance to tell the second half of the story. But I didn't know most of the main points. In fact, I had only a few major ideas, without any inkling of how to connect them. I just knew the story had to be big. Really big. Cosmic, in fact.

Fortunately, it didn't take long before I got the green light to write *Nether Vortex*, the second half of the story. If *Nether Station* was an enclosed, claustrophobic, haunted house in space, like *Alien*, then *Nether Vortex* was more sprawling and action-packed, like *Aliens*.

It was time to get the brain in gear, to let the ideas flow and explode, and see where they went as anything goes. After

I brainstormed incredible scenes and developed plots and subplots, then I would organize them into bullet points until I had the blueprint sketched out. Then I would expand those bullet points into actual chapters and fill in the details, tie up loose ends, and rearrange events.

As an aside, I should let you know my writing method. For almost all my career—and that's getting close to two hundred books published now—I write by dictation. I go out hiking with a digital recorder as I let my creative juices flow. I dictate finished prose, just the way storytellers have told tales since the dawn of fiction.

I live in Colorado, and I adore the wilderness. I will spend miles and miles on the trail to waterfalls or isolated peaks or down into canyons, and I'll tell myself—and you—the story. Then my transcription app turns it into a Word document.

My writing brain is connected to the process of walking, exercising, and receiving external stimuli. (I've written a whole book on the technique, *On Being a Dictator*, if you want more information. I won't go into more detail here.)

So, when I was in the formative stages of *Nether Vortex*, after I had the bullet points sketched out but none of the full details of the story, I went hiking. A lot. *Nether Vortex* was really getting exciting, and I couldn't wait to start the real writing. But I had to flesh out all the chapters first.

On a camping trip in August 2024, six months before I was supposed to deliver the finished novel, I went on some very aggressive hikes into the Elk Mountains near Crested Butte, Colorado. I hiked up to a spectacular mountain pass with views worthy of the gods of Olympus. My brainstorm apparently triggered a thunderstorm.

The clouds came in, and I headed back down, picking up speed. The rain started to fall, then the hail. Thunder boomed in the sky. The steep trail got muddy and slick, like snot and Vaseline. I reached a particularly rough section with boulders, tree roots, and mud. I'd been fleshing out the outline to chapter 41—think of that when you read the book—when my left boot slipped out from under me, just like a cartoon figure stepping on a banana peel. I flew up, twisted my leg, and came down hard on it. I heard the bone crack. Then I slid off the trail, down into a rushing creek bed. I was entirely drenched and coated with mud, just like Arnold Schwarzenegger in *Predator.*

I had to crawl back up onto the trail, then got to my feet. I could barely put any weight on my left foot. Using my walking stick as a crutch, I painstakingly made my way down the rocky, muddy trail, in the pouring rain, for the last mile to get to my car. I knew something was wrong with my ankle.

Back at the campsite, I hobbled around on one foot to throw all my gear into the car because I didn't know just how swollen the foot would be the following day. I drove four hours home in muddy clothes with a throbbing ankle, through the mountains in the dark. I got home after midnight, and boy, did that warm bath feel good.

I later learned that I had broken my fibula, the narrow bone in the leg, which resulted in me having to wear a Darth Vader ankle boot for months, and then a tight ankle brace for another six weeks. It could have been much worse.

But creatively it posed a real problem. I had a five-hundred-page book to write in the next six months, and not only was I precluded from hiking; I was barely allowed to *walk.* I had trained myself for years and years to do all my creative work by walking and dictating. Walking/hiking/movement was a vital part of the inspiration process.

This was going to be hard!

But "a writer writes," as Billy Crystal says in *Throw Momma from the Train*. So, I sat on the back porch with my armored ankle boot propped up on a chair. I looked out at my view of the Rocky Mountain foothills, closed my eyes, and dictated chapters about unspeakable cosmic horror.

It worked. I think *Nether Vortex* turned out incredibly well, maybe even better than *Nether Station*. The first two teaser chapters follow. I hope I've intrigued you enough that you'll give the novel a read.

After all, the fate of the galaxy is at stake.

—Kevin J. Anderson
Monument, Colorado

Excerpt from

NETHER VORTEX

CHAPTER 1

Wide awake in the middle of the dark—the endless dark.

Space around Margo Noor echoed with emptiness, but she found it peaceful, a chance to escape the constant clamor and demands of her corporate life. It was also terrifying.

With the lights dimmed in her expansive stateroom on the *Obscura*, Margo gazed out into the emptiness and just tried to absorb it all. Her quarters had the best view on the entire ship, except for the command bridge. That was only appropriate, since she had financed this boondoggle expedition up to the hind end of space.

The large vessel had been built by NOOR Industries for an entirely different purpose; her brother, Benedict, had begun construction years ago, before he'd gotten himself lost, along with Nether Station. Margo deserved the spectacular view, although there hadn't been much to look at for the four years of this journey.

Now the *Obscura* was on its final approach, and if she looked just right, she could discern the stain of the mysterious wormhole.

Alone in the stateroom, she set aside her plate, leaving a few bites of her perfectly prepared filet mignon. She had finished the asparagus and the small baked potato. Bringing Lily Ono, her personal chef, on the expedition had been one of her best investments in this entire debacle.

Her short dark brown hair was straight and glossy, cut with razor-sharp bangs. Margo was sixty-two, but she looked forty, thanks to a good health regimen, good genetics, and antiaging treatments that cost more than a middle-income salary.

She refilled her glass of Beaujolais and stared out the window. Against the blackness of space, on the far edge of the solar system, the Nether wormhole was a distorted, discolored blur of void, like a badly healed blister.

Benedict had envisioned a shortcut, a tunnel through space and time right to the Alpha Centauri system. Her brother had big dreams, bold ambitions, and all the money he needed. Nether Station, humanity's first interstellar transportation hub, was Benedict's dream. Or it might be Benedict's folly.

Emphasis on the "dick."

The wormhole looked like a blinded eye, closed permanently, but distorted and bulging, as if something horrible pounded against it, trying to break out.

"This is our final message," Captain Karla Arkourian had transmitted just before the entire station fell silent for years. What the hell happened out here?

Once the Nether wormhole was discovered on the edge of the Kuiper Belt, an Earth Space Agency probe had vanished down that gullet in space. Afterward, the cumbersome governments had lost interest in funding further exploration, but Benedict financed his own damn expedition so he could establish a beachhead and plant his own flag—the NOOR flag, although publicly he called it humanity's flag. Aboard his large ship, the *Lethe*, Benedict and his crew had traveled five years to reach the wormhole.

But the expedition had gone disastrously wrong.

"This is our final message."

In Arkourian's transmission, the experienced military commander told an outrageous story of an ancient temple carved into a comet, a ring of watchtower asteroids filled with alien weaponry to guard against a cosmic evil.

A second, independent transmission had arrived from other members of the crew—Cammie Skoura, Warren Drake, and Glinda Roybal—who had evacuated the failing station to . . . where? Benedict had been with them on the expedition ship, the *Neil Armstrong*. They told a similar wild story about a devastating galactic war that had destroyed planets and exterminated alien races, an ancient evil called the Agoc that would devour souls. It was absurd.

Despite the passion of the other *Neil* crewmembers in their warning, Benedict had sat sourly on the edge of the image. It made Margo imagine a mutiny.

Then all contact was lost with Nether Station and the *Neil Armstrong*. Margo didn't know what had happened out here, but she wasn't going to judge without further information. She loved her brother, but it was a complicated relationship. Benedict was often an asshole.

Planning ahead even before the end of his long voyage, Benedict had ordered construction on his second wave of large vessels down in the asteroid field, eight modules that would comprise a NOOR fortress around the wormhole. *His* wormhole. Her brother was optimistic, or just foolish, but Margo had always given him the benefit of the doubt. Initially, his team had sent incredible files of their discoveries of alien technology about the watchtower asteroids—proprietary information for NOOR—and the company scientists had been delving into the data for years, making their own amazing tech breakthroughs. So, Margo knew it was all *real*, at least in that sense.

Now that Benedict had vanished, however, she was in charge of the entire company, and she had commandeered one of the second-wave ships, the *Obscura*, so she could find out what had happened up here. She wouldn't abandon her brother.

Recent NOOR advances in cryopod technology had eliminated the troublesome symptoms of hibernation hangover. Margo herself had gone down to sleep and come back awake every month during the long voyage so she could keep tabs on her corporate business, read summary reports, and dispatch detailed messages and decisions. She also took advantage of the waking days to enjoy a good meal or two. Then she would go back into the pod, sleep a few more weeks, and wake up to start all over again.

It had seemed unusual that someone as important as Margo Noor would accompany the long and dangerous expedition herself, but it was her brother at stake. Besides, NOOR spanned the solar system, and she could run her business wherever she was. She worked remotely, and there was nothing more remote than this.

The original *Lethe* had used old technology and slower propulsion systems, but since then, NOOR engineers had made significant advances, partly due to the secret data from the alien asteroid. Margo had funded huge teams of researchers, the best the human race had to offer, to keep improving the proprietary tech, leaving other Earth corporations in the dust. By now, interplanetary travel in the inner solar system was practically a commute, and the *Obscura* had shaved an entire year off the five-year voyage up to Nether. If NOOR sent further expeditions up to the wormhole, it might even become a practical operation.

Depending on what they found here.

She swirled the wine in her glass and took another sip as the door chime sounded. "This is Major O'Connor, ma'am."

Of course it was. Only a skeleton crew remained awake from the cryopods, and few others would call on her without an appointment. She let him in.

Shelby O'Connor stood straight-backed and formal, wearing his NOOR shipsuit, though it might as well have been a military uniform. His face was rugged, handsome, clean-shaven. At forty-five years old, O'Connor was the formal captain of this mission. Margo had worked closely with the man for a decade, and she trusted him, which she considered the most important qualification.

"Receiving our first images of Nether Station now. I thought you might like to come to the bridge."

Margo finished her wine in a single swallow. "We've waited four years for this, Mr. O'Connor. I am filled with both excitement and dread over what we'll find."

"At least it'll be an answer," O'Connor said as she followed him into the ship's corridor. "Captain Arkourian was never prone to exaggeration."

He had been a protégé of Karla Arkourian's, worked with her in the military, even joined her on some combat missions in Eastern Europe. But once Arkourian transitioned to corporate work for NOOR, she'd encouraged the younger officer to come over to the dark side with her.

Benedict had relied heavily on Arkourian as his exec—and she definitely kept him in line, never afraid to voice a frank opinion. Margo knew that Arkourian had been skeptical about the Nether wormhole expedition from the outset, but Benedict didn't always listen.

"Any response to signals yet?" Margo asked as she kept pace with him on the way to the bridge. After so many years of silence, though, she did not expect any reply.

O'Connor gave her a sidelong look, and she could see the concern on his face. "You would have been the first to know, ma'am." He was a no-nonsense, nuts-and-bolts man, and he did not like the unknown. "Since we arrive in twelve hours, I've begun reviving the remainder of the crew from the cryopods so they'll be ready."

"Agreed. They've had enough of a rest, and it's time to get to work."

The bridge was a full-fledged command center on top of

the *Obscura*. With the main crew still in the process of waking up, only one of her engineers sat at her station like a lighthouse caretaker. Yvette Grendel was a thin, dark-skinned woman with short hair dyed scarlet. She gave Margo a quick acknowledgment, then returned her attention to the screens.

Margo stepped up to the broad viewing wall. The *Obscura* raced toward its destination, but she still couldn't see Nether Station with her naked eye.

O'Connor enlarged the view on the main screen. "Here's our first look."

On the magnified image, she recognized the station from the original designs: the central core of the *Lethe*, with cylindrical modules arrayed around it. But now Nether Station was dark, cold, and damaged. The greenhouse dome was shattered, and the hull showed dramatic burn marks.

Looking up from her screens, Yvette's eyes widened. "We know there are asteroids and debris out here. Do you think it got caught in a meteor storm?"

O'Connor's expression hardened. "Captain Arkourian's message said that the alien asteroid bases fired on the station. We have to assume that's true."

Margo turned back to the black, starry field. "Let's hope we don't trigger any intruder alerts as we get closer."

Yvette commenced scanning the silent station as they closed in. "No energy readings—only a few hot spots above ambient temperature. All systems are shut down."

"It's been almost five years," Margo whispered. "Not a word from them."

"We have to assume everyone's dead," O'Connor pointed out. "Sorry, ma'am."

"We don't assume anything." Margo held out a finger. "Otherwise, there's no point in sending this whole expedition."

CHAPTER 2

No signal. No response. No energy signatures. Nether Station hung dark and cold, like a haunted house in space.

"You are not going to talk me out of it, Mr. O'Connor." Margo crossed her arms over her chest. Her expression was implacable, her eyebrows raised. "You know I could just fire you if you don't accept my answer."

O'Connor faced her, built like a brick wall and just as immovable. "You could fire me, ma'am, but you couldn't run the mission without me." He looked away, and his shoulders slumped. "Nevertheless, you're the boss. But I still think it's unwise for you to join the expedition to Nether Station. We don't know what went wrong over there."

"Exactly—we don't know." She extended her finger like a schoolteacher. It was one of her habitual gestures, but she thought of it as a trademark. "And I want to be one of the first people to see it. I am as qualified as anyone else."

O'Connor wasn't convinced, but she could see his acceptance—not defeat but resignation. "You're competent, ma'am, but you are not *expendable.* The rest of us are cannon fodder, to varying degrees."

Now Margo smiled. She did like the man a lot. "If I wanted to watch from a distance, I would have stayed home years ago and made everyone's life easier."

"You do have a point, ma'am." He turned to go. "Meet me

in the hangar bay. Three of us will fit aboard the *Alpha*. You can take the copilot seat."

The *Obscura*'s entire thirty-person crew was awake and functioning now. O'Connor chose Yvette Grendel to ride in the third seat behind him and Margo, because they wanted an engineer's perspective on what had happened at Nether Station.

The unimaginatively named *Alpha* was one of three short-range recon ships. Each vessel carried scientific and excavation equipment, even rudimentary weaponry and hull armor, though Margo could not imagine being caught in a shootout at the edge of the solar system.

Within the hour, the *Alpha* headed over to the dark structure that loomed in front of them, and Margo leaned forward, intent. In her exosuit, she could hear herself breathing; her throat and nostrils were dry from the compressed air, but also from tension. She sipped from the water tube and swallowed, but her voice was still raspy when she muttered, "Benedict, what the hell did you do out here?"

In the dim light, she could make out the curves of the original *Lethe*, which had become the core of Nether Station. Her brother had been so proud of the large ship before it launched, and Margo had wished him well, though her corporate duties kept her too busy to fly all the way out to the asteroid belt and see him off. The *Lethe* had flown out of the ecliptic, heading toward the barely understood wormhole in the middle of nowhere . . .

Now the station was a wreck, the cylindrical modules battered. O'Connor hailed repeatedly, though no one was going to respond. Nether Station was a big tombstone for Benedict Noor.

O'Connor guided the *Alpha* in a slow circle around the hulk, searching for the best place to dock. "The hangar-bay doors aren't active."

"Aww, that's just an engineering problem," said Yvette. "The three of us are suited up. Let me go over there and see if I can hack our way in."

While the other two remained strapped in, Yvette worked her way out of the *Alpha*'s back hatch to exit the spacecraft. With an expert hand, the engineer used compressed-air jets to scoot over to the large hangar bay. Reaching the hull, she crawled hand over hand to the control panel that operated the big hangar doors. She opened the access plate and poked around with her probe instruments.

Her words came over the suit comm. "The system doesn't appear damaged—just out of juice. I'm going to hook up my battery pack. That should be enough to goose it."

"Don't drain your own suit," O'Connor warned.

"Don't teach me engineering," Yvette countered. She connected leads from her life-support pack into the door controls, then jump-started the mechanism. "Open sesame!"

Tense in the *Alpha*'s copilot seat, Margo watched Nether Station's bay doors creak open. A few last gasps of atmosphere vented out like poisonous fog, dissipating into space. The hangar opened most of the way, then the doors ground to a halt.

"You can fit the ship through that, Shelby," Yvette said. "That took half of my suit power, and I'm not risking more."

"No," O'Connor said. "You're not."

The engineer drifted out of the way as the *Alpha* eased into the cavernous bay. Margo was breathing hard as she stared ahead into the large dark space. O'Connor activated the scout ship's front beams to light up the empty vault. The station's original two recon ships were landed in their appropriate zones, but the large expedition ship, the *Neil Armstrong*, was gone. But Margo already knew that, since they had received the lengthy transmission from Cammie Skoura and her companions after abandoning the station. They'd been lost in the wormhole vicinity for the past five years, so they had to be dead. Maybe there was another ghost ship drifting around in the uncharted emptiness.

Yvette jetted behind them in her exosuit as O'Connor set the *Alpha* down in a clear zone. Once he magnetically locked them to the deck, he prepared to open the craft's main hatch. He turned to Margo. "Let's go see what we can find, ma'am."

Soon the three suited figures stood together, shining their suit lights into the bay's murky shadows. At the two old recon craft, Margo spotted something under one of the landing struts—bent legs, part of a body. Her heart skipped a beat. "Look over there."

She strode closer to investigate, and O'Connor protectively caught up with her. Against the landing strut, they found a body, but it was definitely not human. The figure was small, frozen, and desiccated, with an insect shape—a body carapace, segmented legs . . . and no head.

Yvette joined them. "Aww, what the hell is that?"

Margo remembered the impossible descriptions of reanimated insect corpses from Arkourian's last transmission, as well as the *Neil Armstrong*'s report. "It must be one of those cricket aliens, the ones they found drifting in space."

"And why doesn't it have a head?" O'Connor asked.

Margo's urgency increased. "Come on, we'll find more answers in the main station."

Yvette forced open the hatch from the hangar bay, releasing more faint breaths of atmosphere, but Nether Station had mostly emptied itself to vacuum.

Shining bright handlights in front of them, they ventured into the claustrophobic corridors. O'Connor insisted that Margo stay behind him, and she complied. A faded, green phosphorescent glow emanated from intermittent wall plates, the last remnants of chemical emergency illumination. The light wasn't bright enough to cast shadows, but added an eerie, fungal glow to their surroundings.

"Hello? Anyone home?" Yvette transmitted.

"No one can hear you," O'Connor said.

"It's a common band. Somebody could pick it up if they're listening."

"There's nobody," Margo said under her breath.

A long, dark smear on one of the walls looked black in their harsh light. "Is that feces?" O'Connor asked.

Margo knew he was wrong. "It's blood."

Reaching the medical bay, they found more blood smeared on the walls and floor. According to Cammie Skoura's transmission, a lab monkey had gone on a rampage and killed the crew's doctor.

Margo made up her mind. "I want to see the bridge deck. Maybe we'll learn something from the logs."

They made their way to the *Lethe*'s control center. As soon as she saw the command chair in the center of the room, Margo imagined Benedict using it like a throne as he watched his crew perform their duties.

Yvette went from one computer station to the next, shaking her head after each test. Margo stared out the wide viewing wall into the ominous vastness, much closer to the wormhole. She finally felt she understood the fascination that her brother had experienced.

Nether was bone-chilling and unknowable—something that didn't belong in the universe. To her, it looked less like a cave opening and more like a barricaded gate. She'd seen the close-up images from the original space agency probes as well as the confidential data Benedict had transmitted back to NOOR.

Something had clearly changed in the meantime. It looked as if the wormhole had been sealed.

"We should split up and explore more of the station," Yvette said.

"Absolutely not," Margo replied. "We explore the remaining decks together."

"I concur," O'Connor said.

Leaving the bridge deck, they made their way to the crew quarters and found casual paraphernalia and personal keepsakes, but no clear answers. Next, the astronomy module was mostly intact, and the automated telescopes had continued to record years of observations. Margo would have her science team retrieve the records, since every scrap of data belonged to NOOR.

Down in the hibernation deck, they found a deeply disturbing sight. Seven of the units remained sealed like coffins—the crewmembers had never awakened from cryosleep because of the programming glitch that had killed Dr. Zachary Tendari.

Yvette bent close, shining her light through the viewing pane into the nearest sealed pod. "Aww, gross!" Heavy smears marked the inner surface of the glass. "Looks like somebody tried to claw their way out."

"That can't happen, even with the old, outdated cryopod tech they were using," Margo said.

Each of the pods held a similar bloody victim. It made no sense.

O'Connor was drawn to the last unit, one cryopod separate from the others. "This one's still functioning, just barely. Power levels are at rock bottom."

Margo marched over to him. "Still functional? Is someone still alive in there?"

When he turned his faceplate toward her, his normally stoic expression showed astonishment. "It's Karla Arkourian!"